# MARY CONNEALY

# COWBOY
# CHRISTMAS

BARBOUR
PUBLISHING

## OTHER BOOKS BY MARY CONNEALY

Lassoed in Texas series:
*Petticoat Ranch*
*Calico Canyon*
*Gingham Mountain*

Montana Marriages series:
*Montana Rose*

*Alaska Brides* (a romance collection)

*Nosy in Nebraska* (a cozy mystery collection)

All scripture quotations are taken from the King James Version of the Bible.

This book is a work of fiction. Names, characters, places, and incidents are either products of the author's imagination or used fictitiously. Any similarity to actual people, organizations, and/or events is purely coincidental.

Cover design: Lookout Design, Inc.

Published by Barbour Publishing, Inc., P.O. Box 719, Uhrichsville, Ohio 44683, www.barbourbooks.com

*Our mission is to publish and distribute inspirational products offering exceptional value and biblical encouragement to the masses.*

ecpa Member of the
Evangelical Christian
Publishers Association

Printed in the United States of America.

# DEDICATION:

To Elle, the precious new baby in our midst.

# ONE

*A mining camp in Missouri, November, 1879*

Y ou'll wear that dress, Songbird." Claude Leveque grabbed Annette Talbot's arm, lifted her to her toes, and shoved her backward.

Annie tripped over a chair and cried out as it toppled. The chair scraped her legs and back. Her head hit the wall of the tiny, windowless shack, and stars exploded in her eyes.

Stunned by the pain, she hit the floor, and an animal instinct sent her scrambling away from Claude. But there was nowhere to go in the twelve-by-twelve-foot cabin.

Her head cleared enough to tell her there was no escape, so she fought with will and faith. "Never." Propping herself up on her elbows, she faced him and shouted her defiance. "I will *never* go out in public in that dress."

"You'll sing what I tell you to sing." Claude, in his polished suit and tidily trimmed hair, looked every inch civilized—or he had, until tonight. Now he strode toward her, eyes shooting furious fire, his face twisted into soul-deep rot and sin.

"I sing as a *mission*." Annie tried to press her back through the unyielding log wall. "I sing *hymns*. That's the only thing—"

A huge fist closed over the front of her blouse, and Claude lifted her like a rag doll to eye level, but he didn't strike.

He would. He'd proved that several times over since he'd come here

5

with his disgusting demands.

She braced herself. She'd die first. Claude might not believe that, but he'd know before long.

"So, you're willing to die for your beliefs, heh?" Claude's fist tightened on her blouse, cutting off Annie's air.

"Yes!" She could barely speak, but he heard. He knew.

"Are you willing to watch someone else die, Songbird? Maybe your precious friend, Elva?" He shook her and her head snapped back. "I can always find another piano player."

"No!" Annie had to save Elva. Somehow. Of course Elva would be threatened. Annie hadn't had time to think that far.

Elva would never stand for this. Elva would die for her beliefs, too.

A wicked laugh escaped from Claude's twisted mouth. "She's easily replaced. But I'll *never*"—he shook her viciously—"find another singer like you."

*How had it come to this? God help me. Protect Elva and me.*

"My answer is *no*! Elva wouldn't play the piano for me if I wore that." Her eyes went to the slattern's dress hanging, vivid red, near the door. "She would refuse to play the piano for those vulgar songs."

"We'll see, Songbird." Claude laughed again.

Annie saw the evil in him, the hunger to hurt. He wasn't just hurting Annie to get his way. He was enjoying it. Her vision dimmed and blurred as she clawed at his strangling fist.

"I'll go have a talk with your frail old friend and then we'll see." He shoved Annie backward, slamming her against the wall.

She hit so hard her knees buckled. What little air she still had was knocked away.

Claude charged out, shutting the door behind him.

Annie heard the sound of a padlock snicking shut as she slumped sideways.

She became aware of her surroundings with no idea how much time had passed. In the falling darkness, she could barely make out blood dripping down the front of her dress. Tears diluted the blood and she wept.

"Do something, idiot! You can't just sit here crying."

Annie proved beyond a shadow of a doubt that she was indeed an idiot by burying her face in her hands and sobbing her heart out. The tears burned. She swiped at them and flinched from the pain in her blackened eye.

Shuddering, she lifted her battered face from her hands and looked at the dress. It seemed to glow in the dim light, as if the very fires of the devil gave it light. Indecent, vivid red silk with black fringe. No bodice worth mentioning, the front hem cut up nearly to the knees. The garment was horrible and disgusting, and Annie's shudders deepened. She shouted at the walls of the tiny, solidly locked cabin, "I won't do it!"

Claude had known before he'd asked that Annie would never wear that sinful dress and sing those bawdy songs. Touching gingerly her throbbing, swollen cheek, Annie pulled her hand away and saw blood. Her lip was split, her nose bleeding. She knew Claude's fists had been more for his own cruel pleasure than any attempt at coercion.

"Beat me to death if you want," she yelled at the door. "I will *never* again perform onstage for you!" She felt strong, righteous. Ready to die for her faith.

Then she thought of Elva. Annie's elderly accompanist was maybe, right now, being punished because Annie hadn't fallen in line.

Claude's cruel threats rang in her ears even with him gone.

For all her utter commitment to refusing the Leveques and singing only her beloved hymns, how could Annie watch Elva be hurt? Could Annie stand on principle while Elva was beaten?

The welts on Annie's arm, in the perfect shape of Claude Leveque's viselike hand, along with Annie's swollen eye and bleeding lip, proved the hateful man knew how to inflict pain. He'd proved he had no compunction in hurting a helpless woman.

Noise outside her prison brought Annie to her feet. He was coming back! Annie was sick to think what the couple would do to the elderly woman who had spent her older years worshipping God with music.

Sick with fear that they'd force Annie to watch Elva being battered,

Annie clenched her fists and prayed. God would never agree that Annie should wear that tart's dress, sing vile, suggestive songs, and flash her legs for drunken men.

But Elva!

*Please, Lord, guide me though this dark valley.*

A key rattled in the doorway.

Annie braced herself. If she could get past Claude, she would run, find Elva, and get away. Go somewhere, somehow. Throw herself on the mercy of the men in this logging camp—the very ones Claude said would pay to see that dreadful harlot's gown.

The wooden door of the secluded, one-room shack swung hard and crashed against the wall. Elva fell onto her knees, clutching her chest. "You have to run!" Elva, eyes wild with terror, lifted her head. Annie saw Elva's face was battered; a cut on her cheek bled freely.

Expecting Claude and Blanche to be right behind the gray-haired woman, Annie rushed forward and dropped to Elva's side. "Elva, what did they do to you?"

"I heard. . .I heard Claude making plans, awful plans for you. He caught me eavesdropping. He thought he'd knocked me cold, but I lay still and waited until he left. He'd hung the key on a nail, and I stole it and slipped away to set you free." Elva staggered to her feet, every breath echoed with pain. She stretched out a shaking hand, and Annie saw Elva's black velvet reticule. The one the sweet pianist, who made Annie's voice sound as pretty as a meadowlark, carried always. "There's money. All I've saved." Elva coughed, cutting off her words. She breathed as if it hurt. "T–Take it and go. There's a wagon. It's already left, but run, catch it. Ride to town. Enough." Coughing broke her voice again and Elva's knees wobbled. She clung tight to Annie. "Enough for one train ticket."

Annie realized what Elva was saying. "No, I won't leave you."

"It's my heart." Elva sagged sideways, clutching her chest. Annie couldn't hold her dead weight, slight though Elva was. They both lowered to the floor. "When Claude landed his first blow, I felt my heart give out. Oh, Annie, the things he threatened for you. The evil, ugly

words from a serpent's mouth. My precious girl. Run. You must run."

"I won't leave you. They'll kill you, Elva."

"No. My heart. I've felt it coming for months and tonight's the end. They can't harm me anymore."

"Elva, don't talk like that." Tears wanted to fall, but Annie had no time for such weakness. "You're all I have!"

"Your father. Go home."

"He doesn't want me. You know that."

Elva's hand closed over the already bruised place on Annie's wrist. Elva clearly saw what Annie had already suffered at Claude's hands. "Go. There's no time. What they want from you is a fate worse than death."

Annie gasped. Those words could mean only one thing. She glanced at the indecent dress. A harlot's dress.

"God is calling me home, my beautiful girl. He's taking me b–because He knows you'd never leave me. God in heaven is rescuing us both. I'll go home and so will you. I believe that."

Annie looked into Elva's eyes, and even now they clouded over.

"Go. Please. It's my fault you're in this place. I thought we'd bring the Lord to these people with your beautiful singing. I convinced you to stay when the Leveques took over. If you stay I will have died for nothing, sw–sweet Annie."

Elva's grip tightened until Annie nearly cried out in pain. Then as quickly as the spasm had come, it was gone.

And so was Elva. She sank, lifeless, to the floor.

Annie saw the very moment Elva's spirit left her body—a heartbreaking, beautiful moment, because now Elva was beyond pain.

But Annie wasn't.

*"If you stay I will have died for nothing."*

A loud *snap* of a twig jerked Annie's head around. She gazed into the nearby woods surrounding the sequestered shack she'd been locked in. The Leveques were coming.

*"What they want from you is a fate worse than death."*

As if God Himself sent lightning to jolt her, Annie clutched Elva's reticule, leaped to her feet, and ran.

*"There's a wagon. It's already left, but run, catch it. Ride to town."*

Annie gained the cover of the woods and, without looking back, began moving with painstaking silence.

She heard Claude's shout of rage when he discovered the cabin door ajar.

Poor Elva. No one to bury her. No one to make her funeral a testimony to her life of faith.

Annie hated herself for running away. It was cowardly. There had to be some way to stay and pay proper respect, see to a decent Christian burial. Every decent part of herself said, *"Go back. Face this."*

She kept moving. Elva had insisted on it. Common sense confirmed it. God whispered it in her heart to move, hurry, be silent.

Silence was her only weapon and Annie used it. She'd learned silence in the mountains growing up, slipping up on a deer or an elk. Slipping away from a bear or a cougar.

As much as Annie had loved her mountain home, she'd never learned to hunt. Pa fed the family. But she loved the woods and was skilled in their use.

Heading for the trail to town, she was careful to get close enough to not lose her way but stay off to the side.

Not long after she'd started out, she saw Claude storming down the trail toward town. He'd catch the wagon Elva spoke of long before she did. And, she hoped, insist on searching it. Once Claude assured himself that Annie wasn't there, she'd have her chance.

Annie felt the bite of the cool night air. She heard an owl hoot in the darkness. The rustle of the leaves covered tiny sounds she might make as she eased along. She knew the trail. She knew the night. She knew the woods.

All of it was filled with treachery.

## Two

*Ranger Bluff, Wyoming Territory*

Elijah Walker skylined himself on the cold mountaintop, itchy from the fight he'd had this morning with Pa.

His black stallion pranced and backed up a step. Walker knew his tight grip on the reins and pure irritation were affecting the animal. Then the horse snorted and Walker realized it wasn't just his grip that had bothered the thoroughbred.

Priscilla was far down the narrow trail, facing Walker's father. Well over a mile away, Walker said a quick prayer that two of the people he loved more than life would find common ground.

The bridle jingled and a rattle of thunder sounded in the distance. It was late in the year for a thunderstorm, but nothing about weather in the Rockies surprised him.

He was too far away to hear them, but he knew there was trouble between sweet, fragile Priscilla and his gruff, no-nonsense father. They were water and oil. And since Walker had told his parents he wanted to leave the ranch for her sake, things had gotten much worse. But he loved Priscilla, and the Rocky Mountain winters were too harsh.

They just needed to talk, spend time together. Once his pa came to love Priscilla as much as Walker did, things would be better. Pa wasn't well. The whole family needed to move out of here. They needed milder winters and an easier life.

Walker planned to find work in Denver—drive a stage or maybe open a store. Walker had no idea how to run a store, but Priscilla promised to help and she'd promised to make the learning fun.

Grinning, Walker thought of how much fun everything was with Priscilla; her generous kisses and innocent allure made him feel like the strongest, smartest man on earth. He was chomping at the bit to marry her.

Walker pulled the black to a halt and swung to the ground. He led the horse closer to the edge of the rugged trail, mostly sheltered from view so he wouldn't intrude on whatever passed between Priscilla and Pa. If either Pa or Priscilla looked up, his huge stallion couldn't be missed.

He kept hoping one of these days Pa would soften in his attitude toward Priscilla. To do that, they needed to spend time together.

The trail cut through some rugged land leading from the Walker ranch to the Medicine Bow River. The part Pa and Prissy met on was narrow and treacherous. Why'd they stop there to talk?

Probably just a chance meeting, though Prissy rarely sat a horse.

A high-pitched noise carried up the trail. The wind must have caught Priscilla's voice.

Walker leaned out, snickering at himself for hiding like a peeking child. His vision cleared the ledge just as Priscilla made a harsh, slashing motion with her hands.

His spirit sagged. They were fighting. Again. Pa just wouldn't give Prissy a chance.

*God, please help Pa to see in Prissy what I do. Please, Lord, I want to honor Pa and Ma in this, but I can't let this woman go. I love her. I know giving up the ranch is hard for Pa, but it's for the best. He needs to slow down. He's killing himself with work.*

The truth was, Pa wanted to die in the saddle. Walker could relate. He felt the same way. But making sacrifices was what marriage was about. He'd do this gladly to make his soon-to-be wife happy.

Knowing he needed to get down there and break things up, Walker

looked again just in time to see Prissy make one more wild gesture with that fussy riding crop she loved so much. The short whip hit Pa across the face and swiped his gelding's flank.

Pa brought his hands up to his face just as the horse reared, its shrill neigh carrying clearly to Walker.

Shouting, Walker headed down the trail fast.

Walker saw Pa's hands grab at his reins to control the horse just as Prissy slashed her arm again, this time on the horse's rump. The horse gave a terrible twist and kicked out, all four legs leaving the ground. Then it landed with a stunning jolt, and Pa lost his grip on the reins. He tumbled backward and slammed onto the ground, then slid toward the steep drop-off that edged the narrow trail.

Walker pushed his black hard, leaning low over the horse's neck. The trail wound so, Walker lost sight of Pa for long seconds. He goaded his horse, needing to get down there. The black's hooves slid on the loose rocky trail as Walker came around the curve.

Pa went over the cliff. His hands scrabbled at the ledge and caught hold. His head was barely visible.

Prissy had dismounted. No doubt to help Pa, pull him to safety.

"Use the horse!" Walker shouted. The horse had the strength to pull Pa up.

The wind must have blocked the noise or Priscilla would have never done what she did next. She stomped her heel onto Pa's fingers. She'd have never done it if she knew there was a witness.

Walker shouted in horror as he closed the distance at a breakneck pace, but the wind was in his face and the sound must not have reached Priscilla.

A low shout reached Walker's ears as Pa vanished.

"No!" Walker knew that drop-off. His pa had fallen for hundreds of yards. The rocks below that ledge were brutally jagged.

Walker jerked his rifle from the boot on his saddle and fired a shot in the air.

Prissy looked up.

The trail twisted again. Walker lost sight of his fiancée. The black sensed the urgency, because it barreled down that trail, sliding and fighting for footing, but game, as if the stallion rushed to save Pa, too.

When Walker could again see the trail, Prissy was gone. He scanned the area and finally caught a glimpse of her rushing away, riding her horse with surprising skill. She'd always acted slightly scared of horses. Now she clung to her gelding, running like a coward.

Running like someone who had been caught committing cold-blooded murder.

Walker's mind couldn't grasp it. Pa had loathed her. Ma had quietly but urgently warned Walker that Priscilla wasn't what she seemed. Walker had ignored them both.

He finally reached the ledge and threw himself off the black. Dropping to his knees, he leaned out and saw. . .

Pa—alive—dangling from a scrub pine nearly twenty feet down.

Walker's stomach swooped with terror and hope. "I'll get you, Pa. I'll pull you up."

His pa looked up, revealing a vivid red slash on his chalk white face. Priscilla's riding crop.

Walker snagged the lariat off the black's pommel. Lightning quick he lashed it to the saddle, spread out a loop, and lowered it.

Pa grabbed at it and caught it with his wrist just as the scrub pine gave way. Pa dropped nearly twenty feet farther—only the noose tightening on his wrist kept him from falling all the way to the bottom of the cliff.

"Hang on, Pa! I'll pull you up."

"Priscilla!" Pa gasped. "Priscilla did this!"

"I saw it all, Pa." Hand over hand, Walker pulled his pa up.

Pa's gloved hand began slipping through the noose.

"Hang on, Pa. The loop's slipping."

Pa had been pulled nearly level with the pine again, and he found a precarious handhold in the hole left by the roots. The noose was still on his wrist, but it needed to be around Pa's shoulders.

"Black!" Walker yelled at his horse. "Back up. Take up the rope."

The horse was the most intelligent animal Walker had ever owned. He quickly, carefully picked his way down the trail, stretching the rope just as he'd been trained when he helped bust steers.

Walker focused on Pa, breathing hard, bleeding from scrapes on his face and neck, besides the vicious welt on his face.

The rope came off Pa's hand, but he clung to the cliff side.

With slack no longer important to support Pa, Walker swung over the cliff and worked his way down hand over hand. His feet were dangling near to Pa's head when the clump of dirt and rock Pa clung to gave way, and with a shout of terror, Pa fell.

"No!" Walker roared.

Pa hit the rocks below with a spine-crushing *thud*.

The shock nearly knocked Walker off the rope. Only an impossible hope kept him going. "Black! Here, boy!" His shouts were instantly obeyed. The rope lowered him quickly until the horse above stopped. He was obviously at the edge of the trail. With twenty more feet to go, Walker found a handhold, and—mostly sliding and falling—he reached the bottom and rushed to his father's side. "Dear God, please help him. Save him."

His father's eyes blinked open. Blood trickled from his lips. But he was alive. Pa had survived the fall.

"Pa!" Walker kept praying as he dropped to his knees. Jagged rocks tore through his pants and scraped his skin, but he ignored it. Scared to death, he reached for his broken, bleeding father.

"Son," his father uttered, grabbing at Walker, hand shaking. His other arm didn't move. It hung at a terrible angle, broken for sure.

"Pa, just lie still. I'll bandage you up. We'll get you home."

"No!" Pa shouted then coughed, shaking his head, gasping from the pain. "No." He spoke more calmly. "Don't move me. I'm done, boy. I'm not going to get back up to that trail alive."

"Yes, you are." A rivulet of blood ran down a stone that pillowed Pa's head. "Don't talk like that."

"Listen to me, Elijah." Pa released Walker to clutch one hand to his chest. His face contorted in agony. "There's not time for foolishness. Priscilla did this."

"I saw. I'm so sorry."

"No, not your fault. Don't blame yourself. She's never shown this side of herself to you."

"But she had to you?" Walker listened while he unbuttoned his shirt. He'd rip it apart, bind his father's wounds, splint his arm, and get him home somehow.

"Nothing like this, but yes, we—Ma and me—saw the meanness in her from the first. We've tried to warn you."

"I'll have her arrested for this. I promise you. I won't stop until she goes to jail."

"Don't be making deathbed promises about revenge."

"This isn't your deathbed, Pa." Walker tore his shirt and didn't know what to do with the rags. Pa bled from his scrapes, but they were minor. No bandage could fix this. "Don't say that!"

*God, God, God, God, God.* Walker couldn't begin to know how to pray.

"Hate isn't what I want to leave. I love you, son. You're the best son a man could have. I'm so proud of you. J–Just don't m–marry Priscilla—" Coughing broke off Pa's speech, and the trickle of blood at the corner of Pa's mouth was heavier, choking.

"I won't. I won't marry her." *God, please save my pa. God, God, God.* "I saw everything. I've been a fool."

The coughing subsided. Pa went on. "Just. . .just take care of your ma, son. Ruby seems like a tough old bird, but inside she's a softie. We've had a good marriage. She'll hurt because of this."

*God, please, please help me. Tell me.*

"We both love you so much. You're the greatest blessing ever given by a loving God. Don't blame yourself for this. No one could have known she was capable of this." His pa's hand trembled.

Suddenly a trail of blood ran down the rock behind Pa's head.

Thick, dark blood. Too much, too fast.

"God, God, please, God."

"God is with you, Elijah."

Only then did Walker realize he was praying aloud.

"God loves you. Don't—don't hate. Don't. . ." Pa's eyes widened. His body went rigid, and a long, sharp inhale of air sounded then cut off. Pa's eyes fell shut as his whole body went slack.

"Pa?" Walker leaned close, suddenly feeling like a lost child. Three years old, alone on a cold mountain. . .the sun setting. . .setting in his father's eyes. "Pa, don't die. Please don't let my foolishness be the death of you."

But Pa was gone.

"God, God, no, no, no!"

But no prayer would bring Pa back. Walker knew it as surely as he knew that the woman he loved was a killer.

Walker's prayer ended as suddenly as his father's breathing. Walker clenched his fists and raised them, turning to God. But Walker could think of nothing to say.

Guilt closed his throat against prayer. Hate crushed any thought of his father's dying words. The guilt, the hate, branded Walker as surely as if Satan himself had stabbed him with a red-hot branding iron of a pitchfork.

Walker looked back at his father. "I'll care for Ma. I promise you that, Pa. I'll do it with a full heart. I'll care for her as surely as you did."

Pa was gone, beyond hearing Walker's pledge. Why hadn't he said those words before his father died? Why hadn't he returned Pa's words of love? Walker realized the rag was still clenched in his hand, and he heard another roll of thunder, as if God shouted His judgment on Walker.

He had to make it right. "I'll see her hanged, Pa." Giving voice to his fury was like letting the pressure off a boiling pot. It felt good to hate. "You said no revenge, Pa, no hate, but seeing her hanged isn't vengeance. It's justice."

Walker tasted the hate, savored it. He found the strength to look back at his father, dead because of Walker's foolish love for a woman.

With no words for prayer, Walker knew nothing else than to put one foot in front of the other. The first step was to take his father home.

The second step was to find Priscilla.

## THREE

*November, 1880*

Annette had never thought much about food until she didn't have any.

Her hands had begun shaking about a day out of Denver. She'd nearly blacked out twice. She'd slept, but her stomach growled and ached, and no sleep lasted long.

"Let's get rolling," the driver shouted.

Slowly, carefully, she stood from the bench at the stagecoach station. A cold wind blew her bedraggled hair across her face, and the dark blond tresses blinded her until she forced her hand to obey and unsteadily pushed the hair aside.

The driver heaved her bag onto the top of the stage, and she winced at the rough handling. "Please be careful with those." Her voice was as weak as her courage.

The driver either ignored her or didn't hear, and he threw more bags aboard.

It wasn't that her things were valuable. They weren't. But what was packed in that valise was all she had in the world.

She remembered the West as a place of little respect for finery—as if she owned anything that could be described as finery—so she didn't ask again. She forced her exhausted legs to work. She was almost there. This one last stretch of the trail on a stagecoach, then Thanksgiving and Christmas at the J Bar T.

She'd written her father, using a few precious pennies for paper and a stamp, stating her arrival time, then she'd left before he had time to write and order her to stay away. He wouldn't like it, but he'd be there to pick her up. Her father was a hard man, but Annie knew he loved her.

A father had to love his child.

*He does love me, Lord. I know he does. Just give me the strength to get there and he'll prove it. I know I'm bringing trouble with me, Lord. Please soften my father's heart when he finds out.*

Because Annie knew all too well that she was being pursued. She'd been running for a year.

First she'd raced after the wagons just as Elva had ordered, careful to wait and stow away after Claude had searched. Once she'd reached town, she'd hopped on the first train without regard to its direction, knowing the Leveques would be right behind her. The ticket had used up most of Elva's money, and the train had gone east instead of west toward Pa's ranch.

When she'd reached the first stop, she'd hidden on a freight wagon for the next leg of her journey. Then she'd hired on with a wagon train. She'd worked a short while at a diner until she'd managed to hire on with a cattle drive. That had been pure godly providence, because it was unthinkable that a single woman would be allowed to cook for men in such a situation. But God had arranged it all only moments after Annie had seen the Leveques coming down the street in a little cow town.

During the drive, Annie had been fed, and she was earning money and going the right direction.

She hoarded her pay, pinching every penny, working her way home. Once she reached Denver, she'd been able to earn a few dollars, washing storefront windows and doing odd jobs. The money hoarding had her living on short food rations and sleeping in livery stable straw. Doing those things, she'd earned enough money for passage, and when she'd known her arrival time in Ranger Bluff, she'd written Pa.

Now she was almost there. One more leg to this centipede of a journey.

She climbed the steps of the stage. The familiar blackness that plagued her circled in. Her vision tunneled and she waited for it to pass. It always did. But until then, the world swam around. She groped for the doorframe, but it wasn't where it should be. Just when the darkness was deepest, the paper-thin soles of her worn-out, toe-pinching boots slipped. She fell backward with a little squeal of alarm. She made a soft landing in someone's strong arms. "Excuse me. I'm so. . ."

Her effort at good manners was ignored as she felt herself set upright. Then she was more or less tossed into the stagecoach.

Whoever was manhandling her climbed in behind her, steadying her at the same time. He urged her forward. "Move across, miss. There're four of us riding."

Annie's head cleared and she found herself sprawled along one side of the stage. Weakly, she said, "I'm sorry." She wrestled with her skirts and heard something rip. Her last good dress. "Oh, no." She made herself small in the corner of the seat and scrambled to inspect the damage. She tried not to let it upset her. She would repair it. This was nothing to get upset about.

She fingered the rend with shaking hands. It crossed the entire front of her skirt at knee level and drooped open to show her muslin petticoat. Fumbling to cover herself, it all caught up with her. She broke down and cried.

"Oh, please," an exasperated voice rumbled in her ear.

The voice tugged on something deep inside her. She used the strength of that voice to get ahold of herself. She knew it was the man who had caught her, because he'd never stopped touching her since she fell.

"Miss, don't cry now. It's not that bad."

Another voice. Annie glanced across from her. A young man in an ill-fitting business suit, wearing thick round spectacles, smiled as he settled himself into his seat. He offered her a handkerchief.

Brokenly she whispered, "Thank you." She didn't take his hankie. She pulled her own out of her sleeve.

Dabbing her eyes, she noticed another man sitting beside the businessman. He was a cowboy with a heavy brown mustache that covered his mouth and hung down on the corners to his chin. His eyes were shaded by the brim of his white, trail-stained Stetson. He had the hard look of the West on him, which the businessman didn't.

The cowboy touched the brim of his Stetson. "Miss." He didn't smile. Something flickered in his eyes, something intense, almost fixating.

She had to force herself to look away from him. When she did, she accidentally looked at the man beside her. This time she couldn't look away.

"So you tore your skirt. Better head back East where folks care about such things." His voice was deep and smooth with a trace of roughness, like water rippling over stones.

The businessman gasped and she glanced at him. She could tell he wanted to speak in her defense, but he looked fearfully at the man beside her and held his tongue. A wise man perhaps, but a coward nonetheless.

Annie might well be coming from the East. . .if Missouri counted as the East, but she'd grown up in the West and she knew a coward when she saw one.

She looked back at the man beside her, and, for just a second, she was the untamed girl she'd been when she'd run wild on her father's ranch. "What I remember about the West," she said, "is that men spoke politely to women or they didn't speak at all."

The businessman clasped his hands together in front of him. It might have been panic, but Annie got the impression the poor, yellow-bellied man was praying—probably to be miraculously transported somewhere far away before the shooting started.

But oddly, Annie wasn't afraid. She'd taken the measure of the man beside her and knew she was safe, except maybe from his rude mouth. She caught herself holding back a smile, and that's the first time she realized she wasn't crying anymore.

"Better now?" Sparks of humor flashed in eyes as blue as the Wyoming sky.

"You did it on purpose."

"Can't stand tears, miss. Had to step in."

And this time Annie couldn't stop herself from smiling.

He wasn't dressed like a cowboy, but everything *except* for the clothes told her he was one. His skin was weathered from sunburn in the summer and windburn in the winter. His crisp, flat-topped black hat and vested suit seemed like a costume, although he looked comfortable in them. He'd removed his hat, and his hair was too long, as if finding time to cut it was just one thing too many. It was brown, and the ends were burned nearly blond from hours in the sun.

"Wise of you." She folded her hands in her lap and did her best to behave like the prim maiden the St. Louis boarding school had tried to create. "I'm afraid I'm exhausted. I've been traveling a long time, and between facing this last, long stagecoach ride, falling on the step, and tearing a gaping hole in the last good skirt I own, I lost my composure. If you hadn't been handy to insult me, who knows how long I'd have spent embarrassing you?"

The man studied her with narrowed eyes.

She couldn't imagine what a mess she must be, stained from travel. And she feared her cheeks were hollow from hunger, and her gray-blue eyes—so light Annie thought they were spooky—were even more startling with dark circles under them from lack of sleep. Altogether, she was sure she made a very unfortunate picture.

"A woman who'd cry over a skirt doesn't belong in Ranger Bluff." His expression relaxed. With a quirk of amusement, Annie wondered if the man would go so far as to challenge her to a shoot-out—as a technique for keeping her tears under control. "I doubt you'll survive a week."

"Really, sir,"—Annie folded her hands in her lap and sassed him right back—"although it was most kind of you to insult me out of my tears, I give you permission to stop now. I'm drowning in your charity."

The man smiled.

She had the impression his face wanted to crack from being bent in an unfamiliar direction. She found herself eagerly awaiting his next insult.

"The first time was for the crying. Now I'm just bein' nasty 'cuz you're a prissy city woman."

Annie arched one eyebrow at him. "I was born and raised near Ranger Bluff. I survived here for fourteen years. I imagine I'll still be here when you're long dead and deeply buried. When do you think that might be?"

The man's smile widened.

Annie braced herself and kept her mouth prim by sheer force.

The businessman broke in. "I'm Carlyle Sikes. I'm opening a law practice in Ranger Bluff."

Annie heard the expectant silence from all three men. She knew now she was expected to say her name. She also knew her father had a knack for alienating people and she had three chances of finding an enemy on this stagecoach. She'd probably find three.

Mentally she braced herself. "I'm Annette Talbot, Mr. Sikes. My father owns the J Bar T."

The cowboy who'd been sitting silently up until now didn't speak, but his gaze sharpened. Annie noticed it with the barest glance, and she felt more than saw the man beside her notice the cowboy, too. His weight shifted ever so slightly closer to her.

The man beside her touched the brim of his hat. "I'm Elijah Walker, Miss Talbot."

Annie's heart lifted at the familiar name. "The Walkers were our neighbors. I remember they had a son. I don't know if we ever met, though. We didn't get to town very often."

"Your father's still not one to come into Ranger Bluff. He's gotten to be a hermit over the years. Is he meeting the stage?" He asked not as if he was curious but as if he would grudgingly step in and care for her if need be.

24

This was something Annie remembered about the West—this neighborly kindness, given with gruffness but always given, especially to women.

Annie could think of nothing worse. "Yes, Father—Pa is planning to collect me. I've grown used to calling him Father back East. I'll have to remember Western ways." She made sure her voice was firm and prayed she spoke the truth.

The news that her father had become reclusive over the years didn't surprise her overly. He'd never been a friendly man and he'd withdrawn even more when her mother had died. From the infrequency of his letters and the odd contents when those letters did arrive with no talk of town or visitors, she could easily believe he'd cut himself off.

"Your father's range borders mine," Mr. Walker said. "It's short as the crow flies, but there's a mighty big mountain in the way."

Annie remembered that sheer, rugged mountain. And she remembered her father knew a way over it that cut hours out of the journey. He'd taken Annie on rides up a treacherous trail no one else knew of. Pa liked to spy on the Walker spread and covet it. He'd said often enough that he'd planned to buy it but the Walkers had stolen it out from under his nose.

"So, you're saying that except for a trail that winds through town and takes about three hours, we're next-door neighbors?" Annie asked sweetly.

"I reckon you could call us neighbors, Miss Talbot."

"And you've stayed on the ranch you grew up on?" She honestly wasn't one bit interested in Elijah Walker. She was just questioning him to pass the time.

"Yep, I'm in charge since my pa died."

Elijah's eyes turned so bleak that Annie knew the death had been a terrible blow. It made her think of her mother. "I'm sorry for your loss."

With a swift acknowledging nod of his head, Elijah turned the topic. "The Walker ranch runs along the west edge of the J Bar T. The border region between us is a mean, impassable stretch. We'll never cross paths." A sigh that could only be relief followed that statement.

Annie looked at Elijah. "How fortunate for us both."

Sparring with Elijah was so entertaining, Annie only distantly realized that the cowboy at an angle across from her didn't offer his name. He remained silent and she was glad. She already had her hands full with the coward and the insult king.

"Well, maybe now that I'm home, my father will forget his reclusive ways, Mr. Walker. Maybe I'll see all of you around Ranger Bluff from time to time."

"I'd be honored if you felt you could come to me should you need anything while you're in Wyoming." Sikes doffed his bowler hat. "I'll hang out a shingle in Ranger Bluff and be very easy to find."

Annie wasn't sure if he was offering her friendship or soliciting legal business. It didn't matter. She had no expectation of turning to him for either. "Thank you." She made no commitment beyond that.

"So, what brings you home after all these years, Miss Talbot?" Sikes asked.

The man was too inquisitive for Annie's taste. "I came home. No reason beyond that." A thousand reasons beyond that and none of them anyone's business. Annie didn't think she could bear to spend the next five hours on this stage being questioned about her life. Then she remembered lawyers liked to talk. "So, where do you hail from, Mr. Sikes?"

The man talked for at least an hour.

Eventually, despite years of training in good manners, Annie fell asleep. She awoke every time the stage hit a particularly deep rut or when her stomach would send a shaft of pain through her. But she saw Mr. Sikes sleeping, so her rude conduct hadn't sent him into a frenzy, thank heavens. Rather it was possible the man had bored *himself* to sleep.

And that's when she realized she'd been using Elijah Walker as a pillow. She lifted her head off of Mr. Walker's shoulder, dismayed. "Excuse me, Mr. Walker."

He lifted his head and seemed to be instantly awake. Or maybe he

was awake and just resting. "It's okay," he whispered.

Annie tried to shake the grogginess out of her head. "I'm sure it was uncomfortable—"

"Shh!" Elijah tipped his head at Sikes and continued whispering. "Please, Annette, if you have any pity for me, don't wake up that windbag."

Annie stifled a giggle. She thought she heard a muffled snort of laughter from the cowboy, too, although a quick glance told her he appeared to be sleeping, his arms crossed tightly across his chest, his head hanging forward so the brim of his Stetson shaded his entire face.

Elijah studied her in that deep, probing way he had. Then he leaned down and dragged his saddlebag from between his feet. With no comment, he settled the leather on his lap, pulled a strip of beef jerky out of the bag, and offered it to her.

Annie had eaten jerky many times as a little girl. It was dry, overly salty, and tough. Her mouth watered. She started to shake her head no, unwilling to take his food.

He simply laid it in her lap and turned back to his saddlebag. He pulled out a piece of the leathery meat for himself, and two hard little biscuits. Then he came up with a couple of withered apples. He put her share of the bounty in her lap.

She had to grab the apple to keep it from rolling onto the floor. She was simply too hungry to resist. The food he provided equaled a feast to Annie. Chewing slowly, her stomach threatened to rebel.

He took a drink from his canteen then offered it to her.

It was ice cold thanks to the November weather, and it soothed her parched throat and bathed her wounded stomach. Taking one slow bite at a time, her stomach finally settled. And when it did, her appetite roared to life. She thought she might wrestle the saddlebag out of his hands if he didn't offer her more food. Without making her fight for it, he gave her more jerky and a second apple.

As quickly as she'd been starving, she was stuffed. Juice from the second apple dribbled past her lips as she relaxed back against the seat.

Elijah leaned close to her and dabbed at her chin with his handkerchief. He murmured, "You'll never go hungry as long as I'm around, Annette. That's a promise."

"Most folks call me Annie, Elijah."

"Annette's a fancy name for a fancy city lady. It fits you. Most folks call me Walker."

"Well, I'll stick to Elijah, I believe. A prophet of God."

"I reckon I'm no prophet. Not much good at seeing what's coming." His expression turned bleak again, as it had when he'd mentioned his father.

She wished she could cheer him up. Remembering his technique of insults, she said, "Still, I like saying the name. I believe I'll ignore your wishes and call you Elijah, seeing as how I'll most likely never be calling you much of anything."

The sadness in his eyes receded as he smiled at her starchy tone. "If you're done eating, why don't you get some sleep? You look as tired as a grizzly bear heading for his winter cave. And you sound about as growly."

His eyes had no venom, despite his words. In fact, his eyes were the closest thing she'd seen to kindness since Elva died. Although in fairness, she'd been so busy looking over her shoulder, she might have missed some kindness along her journey.

Elijah had nearly saved her life with his simple meal. He'd given her water and lent his shoulder and the warmth of his body.

Now he was ordering her to sleep, and she decided this was a good chance for another insult or two. He needed to give up his bossy ways. She wanted to tell him she wasn't tired. And she would.

Just as soon as she woke up from her nap.

Annie very carefully leaned away from Elijah. It really was too improper for her to sleep sprawled all over the man. Her eyes heavy, she made a point of ending this strange business of letting him care for her.

She hated the idea of being a burden.

## FOUR

Her head weighed forty pounds if it weighed an ounce.

Walker's shoulder ached. The only food he'd had so far today had mostly gone down her gullet. And he'd had a dozen occasions to want to come to blows with her father.

And her father felt the same about him.

Every bit of that was the plain, bald truth. For all that, this was easily the best stagecoach ride of Walker's life.

He had a vague memory of a little sprite of a girl. He'd done no more than caught a glimpse of her in town a few times. He'd hated girls. She'd clung to her mother's skirt. They'd never spoken a word to each other—well, almost two words, once.

There weren't many children around, and he'd been intrigued by another small person. He'd watched her closely the few times they'd crossed paths and he'd been very aware of her watching back.

He had a flash of memory of Annette's bonnet flying off once. They'd both been in the general store, Annette hiding behind her mother's skirts, Walker standing as close as possible to the peppermint sticks, waiting for his ma to finish shopping so he could beg properly for some candy.

A calico cat had free run of the store and it had run across Walker's toes and then skittered the length of the room to wind itself around

Annette's ankles. She'd bent down to pet it, and her bonnet strings had dangled in front of the cat. The cat swung a playful paw at the string and snagged it with his claws, pulling the hat off her head.

Little Annette had squealed and reached for her hat, and the cat had grabbed it with his teeth and run. Annette had white hair back then. With her bonnet gone, he'd seen curls going in a hundred directions and crackling with static electricity until it looked like the fuzz on a dandelion.

There'd been a small commotion while everyone chased after the cat. Walker had ended up catching the good-natured critter, and he'd gotten the privilege of handing Annette back her silly hat.

She'd clutched her ma's skirt and smiled at him. Her ma had prodded her to say thank you, and the words had formed on her lips, but no sound came out.

But Walker was watching close. He'd read her lips.

*Thank you.*

And he'd read *thank you* in her eyes, too.

Once the bonnet had been restored and properly tied into place, her wild white hair had been corralled. But not soon enough that Walker didn't remember. Even a girl-hating little boy had known those curls were pretty—for a girl. He'd never been near her again that he hadn't wished for a glimpse of her hair.

Walker caught himself smiling over the sweet memory of those two not-even-quite whispered words.

Then he thought about Priscilla and it helped him remember Annette's fat head and forget the enjoyment. He forgot all about the warm, trusting bit of womanhood anchoring his left arm and thought about the only decent woman he knew—his ma.

She was going to enjoy the piece of yard goods and the length of lace he'd gotten her for Christmas. After a year, Ma had finally learned to smile again. Lines of grief had cut into Ma's face and Walker blamed himself for every one of them.

*"Take care of your ma, son."* Pa's dying words. *"Ruby seems like a tough old bird, but inside she's a softie."*

But there was too much strength in Ruby Walker's spine and joy in her heart to get stranded in her grief. Add to that, Walker's ma was a spiritual woman. And she spent her life nagging him to be likewise. He respected his mother more than any woman he'd ever met, and he trusted her, even if he figured the choices he'd made in life were unforgivable.

Oh, not unforgivable to God. God was sure to forgive His children—Walker believed that fully. What Walker didn't believe was that there was any reason to forgive himself. He wouldn't even ask God to help him find the way back to peace. Walker didn't deserve it. If that meant he spent eternity in flames, it seemed like a fair price to pay for bringing death home to his family.

The stage rattled. The fat-headed girl stirred in her sleep and drew Walker's eyes. Nope, nothing fat about any of her. It helped to think unkind thoughts. They took his mind off her pretty, straight nose and the riotous curls of her out-of-control hair—it had darkened over the years but it was still a pretty yellow color—and the fullness of her pink lower lip. The only plump thing on the pathetic slip of a girl. She was too thin, in fact. Hungry as a motherless wolf pup, too. But she hadn't asked, and that meant she had pride. A sin—or so Walker had been taught—but he respected a person who didn't mooch and didn't whine.

The more he thought about it, Priscilla had always done plenty of both. *Wonder if she'll have any luck with that in the territorial prison?*

Thoughts of Priscilla cleared his mind of studying Annette Talbot. Priscilla had covered up monstrous flaws with her fluttering eyelashes and overly generous kisses. He could see clearly now that she'd used womanly temptations to lure him in. And it had worked.

Thinking about it made Walker sick. The times he'd kissed her and she'd responded as if she were swept away with her love for him. Walker had been the one to call a halt to their heated embraces. He'd thought he was protecting an innocent who loved him madly.

He was a fool.

But he didn't have to stay a fool.

Scowling at the sleeping woman beside him, Walker knew innocent young ladies didn't travel across the country alone—which meant sweet, hungry Annette Talbot was a liar and a fraud just like Priscilla. Well, Walker wouldn't let a woman starve. He wouldn't let one come to harm. . .unless it included sending her to prison as he'd done with Priscilla. So, caring for her and letting himself be used as a pillow were only what any decent man would do.

He was just now returning, wearing these fool city duds, from attending Priscilla's trial. She'd managed to fool around and get the trial put off with her woman's charms, but finally he'd brought her to justice. And he'd been the key witness. He'd told everything he'd seen: the welt on his father's face, the way she had a chance to save him and had, instead, stomped on Pa's fingers, and the way she'd run and kept running.

It had taken Walker a month to track her down and bring her back to the sheriff. Then, because he'd caught her out of Wyoming, there'd been some trouble over the trial, and they'd ended up trying her in Laramie.

Priscilla had sat on that witness stand and wept pretty tears and told pretty lies until Walker was afraid they'd let her go free. Except this wasn't the first trouble Priscilla had been in, and that had also come out.

Walker had done the hard work of searching WANTED posters and wiring and writing to witnesses. He'd even paid with his own money for witnesses to three other crimes to travel to Laramie and testify against the foul woman he'd nearly married. All of it added up to revealing Priscilla as a woman who made her life with evil.

Shaking ugly, guilt-laden memories away, Walker turned his thoughts back to Ma's Christmas present. That was safe.

His mother was the finest woman he'd ever known, but Walker just didn't have it in him to spend a lot of time mulling over calico and lace, no matter how much his ma would like it. The distraction wasn't enough to keep his attention off the lady beside him.

She was little more than a girl. He doubted she was more than a teenager. He'd noticed her sleeping on the bench inside the stage

station. The last stage had come in the night before, and this one left in the morning. The station agent had confirmed that she'd slept there all night.

Walker took in her worn shoes and threadbare dress and the skimpy shawl around her shoulders instead of a warm coat. He'd noticed her sunken cheeks. It all said she was broke. She was obviously traveling alone with no money, and she must be near to starving. Of course maybe her funds had just lately run out. Maybe her old coot of a father had sent her plenty of money and she'd frittered it away at the beginning of the trip. Maybe she'd been robbed and was too proud to throw herself on the mercy of strangers for food and a night's lodging.

He didn't think so. He saw worry, even desperation, in her blue eyes. The color was so light it reminded Walker of fog. He'd been lost in fog before, and he thought if he weren't careful, he could get lost in her eyes. Of course, he'd have helped any woman in need. Any *person* in need, come to that. But he didn't have to enjoy it so much.

She shifted beside him and her honey blond hair slipped free, here and there, from the bun she had under her wilted bonnet. He wanted to brush it back off her forehead just to see if it was as soft as it looked.

Then he wanted to push her away from him before he could do such a stupid thing.

He did neither. He sat without moving and let her sleep and wondered where that weird old hermit, Joshua Talbot, had come up with such a pretty little daughter.

He ought to catch some sleep himself, and he did close his eyes, but he wasn't a man to relax completely. He didn't like the looks of either man who rode with them. Ranger Bluff had one lawyer, Nevill Pruett, and he couldn't keep busy. Walker doubted Sikes was telling the truth. As for the other man, he couldn't keep his eyes off Annette. Walker didn't see evil intent in the cowboy's eyes, but he was a man and Annette was as pretty as a Wyoming wildflower. Walker wasn't about to let down his guard around either of them.

## FIVE

Annie awoke feeling nearly human. She'd slept most of the five hours of the stage ride and she wasn't hungry for the first time in weeks. A smile quirked her lips. *"For I was an hungred, and ye gave me meat: I was thirsty, and ye gave me drink: I was a stranger, and ye took me in."*

Elijah Walker had done all of that for her. He treated her as if he thought she was an angel, visiting him, and God was watching to see how he'd behave. Annie wondered if Elijah was a Christian who really was motivated by whether God was watching or just a decent, generous man. Or both.

She shifted her weight and realized, sometime during the long ride, she'd been covered with a heavy buffalo robe, which had helped make the cold bearable. It wasn't exactly "naked, and ye clothed me," but it was close.

Annie knew the rest of that verse. She sincerely hoped she didn't end up sick or in prison just so God could test whether or not Elijah would visit.

The sharp voice of the stage driver preceded the horses' beginning to slow. The jingle of the traces and the rattling stage pulled her further from her groggy state. She lifted her head to look out of the window and realized she was wrapped in Elijah's strong arms. Startled, she pushed away from him, and he immediately helped her sit upright.

"Elijah. . .I mean, Mr. Walker"—when had she started thinking it was all right to call him by his first name?—"I'm sorry. That must have been. . ."

"I'll remind you that folks around here call me Walker." He pulled the buffalo robe higher on her chest and moved away from her. "I was glad to be of service."

He smiled at her, but the humor didn't reach his eyes. His politeness now wasn't as kind as his insults had been previously. "We're coming into Ranger Bluff now. The trip is finally over."

She stared into those eyes of his. They were a blue that could only exist in the purest things of nature: water and the sky. "I've never slept so peacefully. Thank you."

His eyes changed into something just as blue, just as natural: marble and ice, hard and cold. He nodded and looked away, overly interested in the scenery of the little town of Ranger Bluff outside of his window.

The stage jerked suddenly to a stop. Annie flew forward across the seat. Three sets of hands caught her. She was firmly returned to her seat. Mr. Sikes's hands were slowest to leave her body but not slow enough to raise a fuss.

She looked around the stagecoach. Both Elijah and the cowboy had noticed and were studying the lawyer through narrow eyes.

The stage shifted as the driver climbed down off of his perch and the door opened. With stiff movements, the passengers began to alight. The cowboy went first.

"I have to ask you to hurry along, folks. I'm runnin' real late." The driver talked to them as he climbed up the back of the stage and started tossing baggage down. Annie's went sailing past the door before anyone got out. The bags hit the ground and a puff of dust kicked up in the air.

Then Elijah was there, too late to protect Annie's bags from abuse but in plenty of time for his own.

Annie moved woodenly down the steps to the ground. A mean wind was blowing and she pulled her shawl tight around her shoulders.

Walker lifted her valise off the street and set it up the one step onto the station platform.

"Elijah, over here."

Elijah turned, and the voice was so joyful Annie couldn't help turning, too. An elderly woman, rail thin, her face weathered, swung, spry as a child, from the seat of a wagon and ran to welcome him.

He dropped the trunk and swung the lady up in his arms. "We're mighty late, Ma. I s'pose you've been sitting here all afternoon."

"I figured the stage'd come late. I laid up supplies and rustled up a cup of coffee with the parson's wife. The two of us are plotting how to get you to come to church, so beware. A rider came in half an hour ago saying he'd seen the stage a-comin', so I got down here right on time."

Elijah took her arm and turned toward his wagon. Annie felt a pang of fear as he headed away from her without a word.

"Whose satchel were you hauling?" His wizened mother resisted his hand and turned to look straight at Annie.

Annie saw Elijah jump as if he'd been jabbed by a hatpin. "Oh, Annette." He turned back to her. "I meant to make sure there was someone here to meet you."

He'd meant to but obviously forgotten she even existed. The pang in Annie's chest was ridiculously painful.

"Your name's Annette?" The lady pulled away from Elijah and approached Annie. "What a beautiful name. Well, pleased to meet you, Annette. I'm Elijah's mother, Ruby Walker." Ruby extended her hand.

Elijah put his arm around his mother and gave Annie such a hard look that she might as well have threatened the woman instead of shaken her hand.

Annie marveled at the elderly lady's firm grip. It was the kind of grip that could hold a lot of people up. Annie hadn't had anyone hold her so solidly in years.

Except maybe Elijah had held her nearly this well on the stage, but he'd been asleep so it didn't count.

"Elijah was very kind to me on the stage," Annette said. "He fed me

and let me use his buffalo robe. You've raised yourself a fine gentleman. And please call me Annie."

Ruby laughed, and there was a rueful tone to her voice when she said, "You've seen a side of my boy few have, Annie."

Elijah jiggled his mother a bit where he still held her. "Now, don't go giving her a bad impression of me when I've worked so hard to trick her into thinking I'm nice."

Elijah's teasing reminded her of his good-natured insults when the trip had begun. Where had this gentleman been when the stage pulled into Ranger Bluff? Annie felt safe near him now. "Elijah treated me as if God Himself were watching. I was hungry and he broke out beef jerky and apples. I was thirsty and he shared his canteen. I was a stranger. . ." Annie let the rest of the verse fade with a grin and a small shrug of her shoulders. It was obvious from the light in Ruby's eyes that she knew how the rest of it went.

Ruby said, " 'I was a stranger, and ye took me in.' "

"Well, he didn't exactly take me in, but I fell climbing onto the stage and he saved me from the fall then *hoisted* me in." Annie smiled broadly. "You're a believer then?"

Ruby left the shelter of Elijah's arm and rested her hands warmly on Annie's shoulders. "I most surely am. I hope you can join us for services on Sunday morning."

"I intend to if at all possible. The J Bar T is a far piece out of town. If the weather is fierce, it won't be easy."

"This is Wyoming," Elijah said dryly. "The weather's always fierce."

"You've come to Ranger Bluff to stay at the J Bar T?" Ruby's bright smile faded.

Annie's heart had lifted when she found another Christian woman in this remote corner of the world. The last thing she wanted to do was upset Ruby. She wondered if Elijah's mother could be counted among the multitude who'd been offended by her father.

"You don't sound happy about that. What has my father done to you?" She spoke lightly, hoping Elijah's mother wouldn't transfer any bad feelings from her father onto her.

"Annie Talbot." Ruby nearly breathed the words, and her eyes took on a distant look as if she were looking through Annie and into the past. "I remember you, child."

Ruby's hands tightened on Annie's shoulders. "My, you've grown into a lovely young woman. It's not that I've had cause for trouble with your pa, Annie girl. It's just that the J Bar T has fallen onto bad times of late." Ruby talked as if she were picturing those hard times in her mind and was very worried about what came next for Annie. "The land is still there, but the word is your pa isn't working it anymore. He's sold off his stock and let the place decay."

Ruby's hand rubbed up and down on one of Annie's shoulders. The hand was rough with calluses but gentle, too. "No one's seen him in months. Some say he's abandoned the place. Others believe he's become a complete hermit. I don't know if you'll find the J Bar T a welcoming place."

Annie glanced at Elijah and knew he was thinking the same thing. Annie thought of how often her father had seemed to care for nothing except his land and his herds. She doubted he had changed so much as to abandon them, despite gossip to the contrary. It wasn't his love for the land that had Annie worried. It was his love for her.

She squared her shoulders and defended her father. "My father— Pa will welcome me home. I'm hoping I can get him to rejoin society somewhat." She also hoped desperately that he'd stand in the gap between her and the Leveques.

"Society," Elijah muttered, "in Ranger Bluff."

It reminded Annie of how long she'd been back East and how she'd picked up their way of talking. *Father* instead of *Pa. Society.* She smiled. It would all come back.

Elijah shook his head. Then his brow furrowed. "It's a long way from help if you run into trouble, Annette."

Annie didn't have a response to that. The whole world was a long way from help in her experience. Except Elijah, with the acts of a

Christian and the eyes of ice, had helped her. "My father should be here any time to pick me up."

Elijah looked around the quiet streets of Ranger Bluff. There were no wagons in sight waiting for the stage. Ruby looked worried and reached back to tug her son's arm. She must have tugged hard, or maybe even pinched. Elijah flinched, gave his mother a narrow-eyed look, and then opened his mouth to speak.

"Walker, you're back." A shout turned them all around. "I've got a line on some Herefords coming west that might be for sale." A long-limbed cowboy who looked about Annie's age came striding up onto the sidewalk and grasped Elijah's hand.

Elijah shook back vigorously. "Tell me what you heard."

"Eli, what about the trial?" Ruby asked as Elijah began walking away.

To Annie it looked like Elijah deliberately didn't hear his mother. And he most certainly forgot Annie existed. Before, when he'd turned away from her, it had hurt. Now she was relieved.

She suddenly wished they'd all leave before they found out her father was *not* going to come. Annie expected to sleep in the stage station tonight and rent a horse tomorrow with her one carefully hoarded coin. As hungry as she'd been, and with hope still in her heart, Annie had pragmatically saved back the price of a rented horse to take her home. She'd made it halfway across the country on Elva's bit of money and her own hard work. Finally, here she stood, with trouble on her trail, but home only a shout away. . . . A long shout, admittedly, but still. . .

It wasn't Elijah's job to take care of her. That was her father's job. And somehow it was important to her that Elijah and Ruby Walker didn't see her father fail.

Ruby grimaced at her son, which reminded Annie of the question about some trial. None of Annie's business.

Ruby came to Annie's side. "The ride out to the J Bar T is a rough one. Let's go sit in the diner. Nell Denton runs it, and she'll give us a cup of coffee while we wait for your pa."

Annie couldn't spare the money for a cup of coffee, but Ruby had a firm grasp of her arm and she found herself being propelled across the street to Nell's. Annie and Ruby sat at a long, roughly constructed table, one of two in the diner.

A sturdy, gray-haired woman in a brown gingham apron came over to them wielding a pot of coffee like a broadsword.

"None for me, thank you," Annie quickly said, fearful the woman would pour without asking then discover Annie couldn't pay. "I'm not a coffee drinker." The coffee smelled wonderful, but Annie didn't consider her words a lie. Today, and every day until she earned some money somehow, she definitely wasn't a coffee drinker.

Nell's deeply wrinkled face fell into downward creases, as if she was being thwarted, as if pouring coffee was a mission from God rather than a way to make a living. But she didn't wield her pot in Annie's direction. Ruby had a cup. Nell poured a cup for herself and sat down with a tired sigh. She was round from too much of her own good cooking, and her hair was pinned back severely. "Feels good to get off my feet for a minute. Any time now a crowd of half-starved men will come stampedin' in here demandin' supper. I've got the stew bubbling and a square mile of apple cobbler ready, so I can sit for a spell."

Ruby laughed. "I've seen 'em. A herd of runaway cattle is exactly what they're like." Ruby tipped her head in Annie's direction. "Nell, I'd like you to meet Joshua Talbot's daughter, Annie."

Annie dusted off her best school manners. "How do you do."

Nell turned a curious eye on her. "Never heard tell-a no daughter for that man. Where'd you come from?"

A nosy question for a certainty, but Annie answered. "I was sent East to school when Mother died. That was six years ago."

Nell nodded. "Before my time here."

"I understand my father doesn't have much to do with the town these days."

Nell snorted. "Never did that I recall, and I've been here...four, five years now."

"I came into the country before that," Ruby said. "Eli was a half-growed boy, taggin' his pa and me and fifty head of cattle in sixty-nine, the year after they declared Wyoming a territory. We settled west of Ranger Bluff. My husband died a year ago and Eli took over the ranch."

"And you remember my mother and me?" Annie despaired of her father's reclusive ways. Even back then they'd stayed mostly to themselves.

"A bit. Just to say hello on the street."

"I was born out here twenty years ago last month. You and my mother had to be among the very few women. It seems like you'd have been friends."

Ruby shrugged. "We had our hands full, digging a living out of these mountains. Didn't have time for much else."

"Mother died. Father—Pa shipped me out to St. Louis to boarding school. I've been there ever since." Annie left out the last two years—the first one joyful with her mission group, the last one a growing horror with the Leveques.

"You said you were a Christian?" Ruby leaned forward as if she were eager to hear any word from a fellow believer.

"Yes, Mother raised me in the faith, and the school I went to was a good one, with a fine course of Bible study. I planned to stay on and teach, but I changed my mind and came home instead."

"Why'd you change your mind?" Nell's questions were as blunt as her attitude about her stampeding customers.

Annie froze, unwilling to admit that her father had abruptly discontinued her support, leaving her unable to pay even a pittance for her schooling. She was also not going to lie. In the end she said, "It was for several reasons. Among them I missed these rugged mountains and the wide Wyoming sky. And I wanted to see my father again. He's getting older, and I didn't want to settle so far from him."

Then a sweet dream of her heart made her add, "I am so happy to be able to spend Christmas with him this year. The journey out here seemed to take forever. I was afraid I'd never get to spend Christmas with my father, surrounded by these beautiful mountains again. We had snow in St. Louis, but not a lot and it didn't last long. I remember how white and crisp Christmas was and the bittersweet and evergreen Pa would bring in the house. I'm looking forward to that again."

"It's a cold place, Wyoming, but there's snow enough to coat the land and give the look of purity to Christmas. And you've had a Bible education." Ruby sounded awestruck. "I didn't know there were schools, outside of seminaries, that taught such things. I'll bet you could teach us all a thing or two, Annie."

Annie smiled at Ruby's deeply wrinkled face and saw the kindness and wisdom in her eyes. "I think I could learn more from you, Ruby. I have book learning, but I don't have much experience with living. God was good to me in St. Louis, but we were all very sheltered, and well. . . it's not such a great accomplishment to live a Christian life when there are no temptations. We got rewards for prayer time and Bible reading." She didn't mention her years of loneliness. And her penniless state all through school and her weakness, when she finally had a chance to be strong and face down the Leveques. She'd thought many times after she'd run that the only reason she'd have ever bent to their horrid demands was to protect Elva. With Elva dead, Annie should have stayed and stood fast against evil.

This had come to her one dark night along the trail home. She shouldn't have run. She should have fought the Leveques. Denounced Claude to his face when he told her he'd put her up in front of a room of evil, drinking men wearing a slattern's dress.

No one could make her sing a crude song. Claude couldn't force her to flaunt herself. She could have used that barroom to ask for help, to speak for her faith. Even if she suffered for it, she should have done it courageously and paid whatever price her defiance of sin cost. But she'd been too afraid.

Her courage had grown as she'd neared home and her father's protection. It wasn't lost on Annie that finding a backbone, once she was near to having her father's protection, was another kind of cowardice.

She'd always been a polite girl, overly obedient. It had led her into trouble and she deserved whatever happened to her. But those days were past.

"Now, I hear my father is a recluse, and I'm going to live far out in the wilderness. I imagine I'll find out what I'm made of soon enough. But I accept that. I'll bear it as a cross and use every experience Wyoming holds for me to strengthen my faith."

"Bear it as a cross? What do you mean by that?" Nell asked.

Annie quoted, " 'If any man will come after me, let him deny himself, and take up his cross, and follow me.' Helping my father and serving God in a place where it's not, maybe, so easy is the cross I'll take up. I willingly do this. I even prayed that God would give me this cross and give me grace as I deny myself and follow Him."

"Oh, honey." Ruby reached across the table and took Annie's hand. "I don't think you need to pray for crosses. This life is hard enough without praying God will make it more difficult."

Annie smiled at Ruby. "Whatever burden God gives me, I'm prepared to take."

"Don't we pray that we can lay down our burdens when we become believers?" Nell asked, glancing at the street.

Annie thought she saw movement outside and expected customers to come flooding in. "We lay down the burden of sin but not the burden of service and courage. I plan to stand fast before God with whatever load my shoulders must bear. And if the load ever gets too light, I'll pray for more."

Ruby's grip tightened on Annie. "If you ever need to talk, send a message. If your pa still has cowhands out to the place, one of them can tell Nell. She'll get word to me, and I'll find a way to come and see you."

"I heard there aren't any hired men left out there." Nell cradled her coffee, absorbing the warmth.

Annie faltered in the face of Ruby's terribly sincere offer and Nell's unsettling certainty. Ruby seemed sure Annie was going to be in need.

In the end she turned her hand over and grasped Ruby's. "Thank you." Annie looked at Nell. "And if I need help and there are no hands to send, I'll just ride in myself."

Ruby's hand clutched Annie's almost as if a spasm had run through the gray-haired woman. "If you don't have a chance to come for help. . . well. . .have you got a gun?"

With a gasp, Annie shook her head. "No, of course not."

"A woman can defend herself. You're going into rough country. Even if your pa is there, it wouldn't hurt for you to carry some kind of protection."

Unable to imagine shooting anyone, even Claude, Annie shook her head. "No, my faith is in God and secondarily my father. I'll turn to them for protection."

Ruby's eyes narrowed as she unbuttoned the sleeve of her dress and reached up her arm. She pulled out a metal pipe. "It's as fine as it can be to put your faith in God and your menfolk, but why don't you take this with you, just in case."

Moving too quickly for Annie to prevent it, Ruby opened the wrist of Annie's dress and tucked the foot-long length of pipe against Annie's arm. "You'll probably never need this, but keep it by you."

"Wh–What about. . .you?"

"I've got a spare."

"You want this?" Nell produced a knife out of the waistband of her apron. "I've got a gun in my dress pocket."

Annie's head was spinning from the bloodthirsty suggestions of these two sweet ladies. "No, thank you. Th–The. . .the pipe is enough. I don't need more."

"I wish we had more time." Ruby patted Annie. Her arm settled on the table with the dull *thunk* of lead on wood. "I could teach you a few tricks that would give you a lot better chance of managing should someone wish to do you harm."

"I'm sure my father"—who wasn't here—"and his hired hands"—who might not exist—"will be all the protection I need." Annie thought

of Claude's fists and was suddenly quite happy to have the length of pipe.

*God, is that all right? Is it a sin to want to whack Claude?*

Annie felt sure if the dreadful occurrence ever came that put her within Claude's reach again, the horrid man would give her ample reasons to use the pipe. God might even help her perfect her aim.

"Like I said, last I heard there aren't hands out to the J Bar T anymore," Nell said. "Your pa is runnin' the place by hisself."

Impossible. The J Bar T was too big for a one-man operation. It made no sense, and Annie suspected both Ruby and Nell knew it. She didn't want to answer any more questions. It was too discouraging.

"I left my valise at the station." She rose from the table. "I'm going to see to it then check the hotel for accommodations in case my father doesn't come until morning. Thank you so much for keeping me company."

Both ladies insisted on a hug good-bye.

Annie almost cried from the pleasure of their motherly embraces. She hurried out of the diner before the supper crowd came in. She didn't want to be there if Ruby decided to eat. Not drinking coffee was a reasonable state of affairs, but neither Ruby nor Nell was going to believe she didn't eat.

## SIX

Annie marched through the bitter, whipping winds to the station, made sure her valise was tucked behind the counter, and, not wanting to answer the station agent's questions about where she planned to sleep, went for a walk around the town in the cruel cold.

As she stepped outside, she saw Elijah leaving the livery stable with the young man who had greeted him. They were talking as they walked along.

Before they caught sight of her, she quickly ducked back inside. She didn't want Elijah feeling obliged to care for her anymore. She glanced back and saw the station agent looking at her. And why not? This was a quiet little town. There wasn't that much else to look at.

She stepped back from the small window in the stage station's door and saw Elijah stride down the board sidewalk. He and his friend entered the diner. Then another man followed him in and another. Nell's stampede had begun.

Once Elijah was inside, Annie went outside and hurried down the street to the general store. She had no needs, and no money if she did have needs, but she didn't want to be in the stage station if Elijah came looking for her. It might bring shame on her father.

She kept an eye open through the general-store window for the father that she hadn't seen in six years. It frightened her to think it was

possible she wouldn't recognize him. Nor might he recognize her. That thought brought a burn of tears to her eyes as she touched the pretty fabric and inspected a barrel of nails.

After a time she left the store and wandered into any other place of business she could find, to avoid the station. She browsed and borrowed each building's warmth as she avoided Elijah and every other person she'd met in Ranger Bluff.

Near the time the station would lock up for the night, Annie went back in and sat calmly on the bench. She gradually warmed up enough that her cheeks were burning and her head felt thick from the comfort of the fire. She rested her head on the wall behind the bench and let her eyes fall shut.

Annie jerked awake when someone gave her shoulder a gentle shake. Her eyes flickered open. The cowboy who had ridden on the stage with her was crouched down in front of her. Startled, she realized she'd slumped sideways and was sleeping on the wooden bench, her feet still on the floor.

The cowboy supported her, helping her to sit upright. Her legs were buzzing from lack of circulation. Her head was dull. As she straightened, she felt the weight of the pipe in her sleeve and was disoriented for a moment until she realized what it was.

"If'n your pa doesn't get here, I'll escort you out to the ranch."

He had a Texas drawl so thick it reminded her of Elva. Before her husband died and she'd turned to traveling with the mission group, Elva had lived in Texas and raised a passel of sons.

Annie tried to clear the fog from her head. It was very dark.

The station agent stood by the door, jingling a set of keys in his hand.

*Elijah left me.*

She felt betrayed.

"What time is it?"

"Time to close up, miss," the agent said, his polite voice at odds with his impatient body movements.

She said to the cowboy, "I'm sure my father will be in by morning, sir. It's too late to set out for the ranch tonight."

"It's Michaels, miss." The cowboy rose to his feet. "Gabe Michaels. Chances are your pa never got your letter, or he's laid up for one reason or another. I'll make sure you reach the ranch safely."

Annie looked at Gabe Michaels. His hand still rested on her shoulder, and she thought it was too familiar of him. She felt instinctively that she could trust this man, but she didn't believe it was proper for any man to touch her, and she inched away from him.

The image of sleeping on Elijah's shoulder flickered through her mind. That had been entirely different.

She looked past Michaels to the station agent. "Would it be all right if I just slept here tonight? You can go ahead and lock me in."

The agent looked from her to Michaels. "It's only three days till Thanksgiving, Miss Talbot. A nice young woman like you shouldn't be stranded here. Come on to my house. My wife will have supper on. We're full to the rafters with young'uns, but you can sleep by our fire."

Annie smiled at the kind man but shook her head firmly. "I won't impose on your wife or you, but thank you kindly, sir. I don't need supper. I went to the diner with Ruby Walker." Absolutely true. She hadn't eaten while she was there, but these men didn't need to know that. "If I could just be allowed to sleep here?" She let the question dangle.

"I don't see any harm in it." With a warning tone he added, "You don't want to be on the trail this late. Morning will be soon enough."

Michaels said coaxingly, in a tone that didn't match the intense light of his eyes, "Don't you go out on that trail alone tomorrow, Miss Talbot. If your pa doesn't make it, I'll get you out there safely."

She and Elijah had struck up a friendship on the stage. Annie realized that if it were Elijah offering to escort her, she'd agree. But she couldn't say the same for this cowboy. The strange part of that was she was right not to accept Michaels's offer and she'd have been wrong to accept Elijah's. Thank heavens he'd abandoned her before she could forget he was little more than a stranger.

"I'm sure my father will come," she said politely. "I'll just plan on waiting for him, thank you."

A silence hung between them. Michaels's eyes were as dark as hers were light, and they seemed bottomless, like she could look forever and not see everything in the man.

The station agent jingled his keys impatiently and broke the spell that wrapped itself around Annie. She glanced away from Michaels.

As if it were an order, Michaels said, "If your pa doesn't show tomorrow, don't let anyone else ride with you. You'll be safe with me—and Elijah Walker looked to be a man you could trust. But no one else." His droopy mustache nearly covered his mouth when he spoke.

Thinking of the cowardly Carlyle Sikes, Annie decided Mr. Michaels showed signs of being a good judge of character. She had no intention of going anywhere with this man or any other, including that deserting rat, Elijah. She'd take care of herself.

Michaels's gaze caught hers again and she had the odd sense that he knew what she was thinking. Well, mind reader or not, she wasn't going with him. But tomorrow morning would be soon enough for that fight.

"Good night then, gentlemen."

Michaels frowned and ran his hand over his mustache several times in an agitated motion. He was clearly displeased with her, but he didn't push. "Good night, Annette." He walked out.

Mr. Michaels shouldn't have called her by her first name. The man was far too familiar for comfort. Impudent even. She sniffed at his retreating form. What a bossy man.

"Before I go, miss...um...well, Elijah Walker left this for you." The agent went back to his desk and lifted a small cloth bag off the counter. "I didn't think I'd mention it in front of that other man." The station manager handed her the bag.

"What's this?" Annie couldn't imagine.

The agent shrugged then came across the room to hand her the bag. "Weren't my place to look, miss. I've banked the stove for the night.

There's plenty of kindling. Go ahead and stoke it all you want. No need to get cold."

"Thank you."

"And there's an outhouse around back." The agent flipped a lock on the door. "You can let yourself out then lock up once you're inside." The agent demonstrated the twisting lock on the door. "Lock up after me now, miss."

Annie carefully moved on her numb legs to the door and did as she was asked.

The man walked away briskly as if a good meal awaited him at home. His footsteps faded as he left the station platform.

As soon as he was gone, she began walking the length of the small building, clutching the bag in her hands. Once the circulation returned to her legs and feet, she stopped, rested Elijah's sack on the counter where the agent had first picked it up, and found. . .food.

Fighting down the urge to cry, Annie pulled a tin pie plate out of the bag. There was cold chicken and biscuits. She also found another apple in there and several pieces of jerked beef. Had he told his mother that Annie had no food? He had to have brought this from the diner. No one could have missed it. But even the agent hadn't known. Maybe he'd been discreet.

Ashamed, Annie couldn't resist. She took the meal to the potbellied stove, with its glowing red teeth, and warmed the meal, barely able to stop herself from wolfing it down cold. Nothing had ever tasted as delicious as that heavy gravy filled with slabs of tender chicken and thick with carrots and potatoes. Elijah had even remembered a fork— although Annie was quite sure she was hungry enough to have eaten it with her bare hands if there'd been no utensils.

With a full belly, Annie pulled her valise out from under the bench and used it as a pillow when she lay down on the hard wooden bench.

*God, please send my father to me. Send him before I have to deal with Gabe Michaels in the morning.*

Elijah had seen to her food, but he'd left town without saying

good-bye. Of course she'd carefully avoided him, but she hadn't run into the woods and ducked behind a boulder to hide, now, had she? If he'd wanted to, he could have found her.

Sniffing in disdain, she was surprised by an urge to cry. Loneliness welled up in her. Homesickness. She was lonely for her father, not that rude Elijah Walker with his ice blue eyes. She didn't miss him one speck. She'd wanted to thank him for the food is all, simple courtesy. Otherwise, he was just another stranger she'd met on a stagecoach. She didn't want to see him any more than she wanted to see Michaels or Sikes. She did hope she'd see Ruby again sometime, though.

Her stomach no longer aching, she eased herself around, hunting a more comfortable position on the bench. There wasn't one to be found. She tried to ignore the growing excitement as she realized that tomorrow she'd see her father for the first time in nearly six years. And mere days after that, they'd be together sharing Thanksgiving. She took such joy from the idea that it kept her awake and restless as surely as the hard bench. To pass the time, she recited memorized Bible verses and prayed for her old teachers.

She wondered if she'd eluded Blanche and Claude Leveque at last. She prayed for God's protection until she could get to her father and finally be brave. The prayer took a selfish turn with all her fears. So she included Elijah and Ruby, even if it did sting a little to think of them.

At last she began to doze. Her last thought as she fell asleep was, *"Dear Lord Jesus, please give me crosses to bear."*

She was so full of her own plans, she decided to ignore a still, small voice saying, *"More of them?"*

## SEVEN

Gabe Michaels appeared bright and early the next morning. Unfortunately, Annie's father didn't.

"It's almost Thanksgiving, the beginning of a holy season, Annette." The cowboy pulled off his gloves then slipped them on again. For someone so calm and cool eyed, he seemed overly nervous. "Let me see you home. It would be a double tragedy if you came to harm this time of year."

Tempted to take him up on his offer, Annie's good sense prompted her to decline. "There'll be no tragedy to mar this season of thanks, Mr. Michaels. My father will come. I know he will." By now, she was fairly sure he wouldn't.

"Annette, you have to listen to reason," Michaels persisted.

"I haven't given you permission to call me by my first name." Annie thought she sounded as stiff as an old ironing board, but the man was behaving improperly, and she had to insist he mind his manners.

He crouched down in front of her where she sat on that same hard bench she'd slept on. Thankfully the station agent had arrived and she'd awakened and been alert when Mr. Michaels came. She didn't feel at so much of a disadvantage with him this morning.

"I'm sorry, Miss Talbot. Of course you're right. I forgot myself." He rose, turned away, and then removed his gloves again. "I'm just concerned for your safety. It's not—I. . .I—" He broke off his awkward

speech and worry furrowed his brow beneath his shaggy hair. "I have a strong feeling that you'd be in danger on the trail."

Annie's gratitude faded as the man's insistence grew. He seemed upset with her to the point she was grateful for the watchful presence of the station agent, and she decided to put an end to the pressure. "I neither want nor need your help. Please quit pestering me, Mr. Michaels, and move along. I don't appreciate your behavior, and I can promise you my father will take exception to it as well."

His kind eyes faded to an annoyed glare. "Fine. Wait for your father." He jerked his gloves on again then jabbed a finger at her nose. "But don't you dare be so foolish as to ride out to the J Bar T alone!"

Michaels stalked out before Annie could castigate him for his high-handedness.

Carlyle Sikes appeared just after Michaels left. His offer of assistance was a near-perfect echo of Gabe Michaels's. Not cranky, however. Wheedling. But still overbearing. Annie sighed with exasperation from all the protection at her disposal. Surely if every man in Wyoming was prepared to protect her, then there could be none left to harm her. Therefore, she didn't need any of them.

She would most likely be in good hands with the mild-natured young lawyer, but everything in her recoiled from being indebted to him. Add in his cowardly streak and surely he wouldn't be of much use as an escort. She'd momentarily considered letting Mr. Michaels ride out with her, but never would she agree to Lawyer Sikes's solo company. She didn't want Sikes—or anyone else—to think she was the kind of woman who accepted favors from strange men. She thought of the way Elijah had fed her and couldn't regret accepting his generosity.

When her father still hadn't appeared midmorning, Annie decided it was time to take matters into her own hands. She waited until Sikes and Michaels were nowhere to be seen and headed out to rent a horse from Gibby's Livery Stable and Smithy.

She walked past the diner, and savory aromas wafted out, reminding her she hadn't had breakfast. It was a severe temptation to buy a meal with the money, but she resisted the urge. All she had to do was get to her father's ranch and she'd have all the food she needed. She'd been on her own since she'd run from the Leveques in Missouri, and she knew how improper that situation was, a young woman traveling unescorted. But there had simply been no other choice. So, she'd go these last miles alone as well.

While her horse, a mouse-colored mare, was being saddled, she went back to the stage station and carried her carpetbag out to the privy. After some consideration, she began putting on her clothes. She didn't have much, but with no coat, the clothing would protect her from the cold, and the extra bulk of carrying her valise was more than she wanted to deal with. She put on everything she owned and could hardly move when she was done.

Gibby, the hostler, gave her a comically confused look.

Annie politely ignored the raised eyebrows. "Is my horse ready?" Annie fervently hoped she could leave immediately so as few people as possible saw her in such an embarrassing light. Gibby had already given her considerable trouble about renting the horse. She'd had to resort to—well, not lies really—but she'd allowed the man to think her father awaited her elsewhere in town.

The man tipped his hat. "Ready and waitin', miss."

He boosted her onto the mare, because, though she'd been a good rider in her day, bundled up as she was, it was doubtful if she'd have made it without assistance. Then she rode out, using the rear door of the livery to avoid prying eyes on Main Street.

After she cleared the shelter of town, she was glad she'd done such a silly thing as wear all her clothes, because they were the only reason she could stand the cold. The wind wasn't whipping today as much as it had yesterday. But the cold had a sharp, skin-burning quality to it. She loosened her shawl, wrapped it around her head, and pulled it over her face until only her eyes were uncovered. Her feet soon began to feel the cold, but the rest of her was reasonably comfortable.

She'd been gone a long time, but she still remembered well the

trail to the J Bar T. It had changed some. It was no longer the well-worn road it had been when the thirty hands her father employed had traveled frequently between the ranch and Ranger Bluff. But it was still the same. Mountains loomed in front of her. A gap opened into a canyon that led to the ranch house.

She made the horse move along swiftly, afraid of the encroaching chill in her feet. The canyon she rode through was deep with snow, and Annie remembered times when this gap had been so filled in that the Talbots were shut off from town all winter. But it didn't happen often. The winds usually whistled through the canyon and swept a path clear.

When she came out the other end of the canyon, she had a momentary wave of doubt. The land opened up wide and there was no trail to be seen, not so much as the ruts from old wagon wheels.

As she pulled her gray horse to a stop, the world closed in. Everywhere she looked was nothing but mountains and arroyos, cutting one another to pieces. The valley in front of her sprayed out through several passes, all snow covered. . .all unfamiliar. She had no idea which one led home.

She focused her memory. She'd come this way a hundred times as a child. Suddenly, she was the Israelites leaving Egypt and wandering into the wilderness. *"But made his own people go forth like sheep, and guided them in the wilderness like a flock."* She took comfort in that verse. "I am one of Your people, Lord. Guide my feet. Guide me through this wilderness."

Like a flame, a memory lit up in her mind. She saw the cleft in the rocks to her left and knew it was the way as surely as if God had sent a pillar of fire. Smiling, she chirruped to her horse, and the mare seemed to be guided by a divine hand, too, because she headed out willingly.

Annie traveled confidently along the narrow switchback trail that climbed before her. She remembered it well now. All she had to do was get over just this one last pass to find the plateau that was her home.

She wound in and out of ever-thicker groves of trees. Once she saw a long swag of bittersweet, with its bright orangey red berries glowing among the green of the pine branches that supported it.

Bittersweet. How well she remembered her mother's love of the colorful fall berries. She'd fuss at Annie's father until, with grudging good humor, he'd bring long branches of it in. Mother would decorate the house, line the fireplace mantel, make wreaths, and drape it on windowsills. Then she'd gather up any small twigs and runaway berries and fill a bowl to put in the center of their table. And while she worked, with Annie alongside, Mother would talk of Christmas and the tiny baby born in a place more humble than even the cabin where the Talbots lived.

Annie thought of those precious memories of her mother, and on a whim, she picked a generous length of the bittersweet and mused on where she'd hang it in the ranch house. Her father would come to the door, and there she'd stand. The bittersweet would remind him of her mother. It would remind him of a loving time in their family. The memories, more than the berries, would be her Christmas gift to him.

Finally, just as the sun was at its peak, even riding low in the southern sky as it did in winter, she emerged into the mountain valley that was her home. She'd be in time to share a noon meal with her father. She hugged the prickly bittersweet to her breast and smiled at the sweeping mountains, covered with trees and brush. She gloried in the lush winter grass that showed here and there between the drifts of snow. The gushing, ice-lined stream of water that cut through one corner of the plateau poured out of a rock behind the house and curled down out of sight until, far below, it joined with the rushing waters of the Medicine Bow River.

Her eyes fell eagerly on her home. She gasped.

A travesty.

Her home was desolate. The wood, once whitewashed, was weathered to a dismal gray. Many spindles of the porch railing were broken and missing. The porch roof hung drunkenly, collapsed all the way to the porch floor on one side. Shutters were missing. Refuse peeked through the snow and covered what once had been a pretty, well-tended yard. The

corrals were falling to pieces. The barn doors sagged open, obviously not in use for keeping the milk cow and chickens inside.

Annie's meager hope that her father would welcome her evaporated. Her stomach clenched and she was glad it was so completely empty or she'd have been sick right where she sat.

❧

"I'm telling you that little girl looked sick."

Ma had said hello to Walker as he came in to find the noonday meal steaming on the table. She'd thanked him again for the new piece of goods. And then she'd gone straight to nagging.

She'd nagged before they'd left Ranger Bluff, nagged nonstop during the ride out to the ranch, nagged through supper and all evening until bedtime, then started in again at breakfast. Walker had worked hard all morning then come in for his dinner to be greeted with. . .surprise. . . nagging.

Walker smiled. It was great to be home.

"I offered to take her home, Ma." How many times had he said that? "I'm telling you she wouldn't have any part of it. And I went back to the stage station and left a plate of dinner. Then I walked all over town looking for her. You oughta know. You pestered me into it then followed me around."

"You gave up too easy, Eli. You need to ride into town and make sure she's okay. What kind of decent man just up and abandons a sweet, little, defenseless girl?"

"Abandons?" That pinched a mite. "You heard her say I was like God's hands and feet right here on earth. I fed her. I gave her a blanket. I was a regular guardian angel to that little woman, and then she ups and disappears. It was deliberate, too. She didn't want any help. You admitted that yourself."

"Just 'cuz she didn't *want* any help, doesn't mean she doesn't *need* it. A man's gotta do what's right even if it ain't easy, and you know it, young man."

"Young man?" Walker couldn't hold back a grin. "You haven't called me that since I split the seat on my Sunday-best trousers two weeks after you made 'em for me, almost twelve years ago. They were my sixteenth birthday present, and you threw a fit that near to tore up the rest of my clothes. I wasn't much of a young man then, and I'm sure-as-you're-born not one now."

Ma liked a certain amount of wrangling, and that was a fact. Walker decided he might as well accommodate the poor woman. It would never do for Ma to realize how much joy her complaining gave him. This was the first real fussing she'd done since Pa had died.

Walker had been gone seeing to Priscilla more than he'd been home for the last year. After Pa died, she'd just become so all-fired sweet and thoughtful it had near to broken Walker's heart. She wasn't his feisty ma at all.

Even if she had shown a spark of her old crankiness when he'd ridden in and stayed a week or two, Walker could tell her heart wasn't in her nagging. But yesterday, Walker had told her Priscilla was locked up tight and would stay locked up until all her pretty-girl looks had faded into the evil old hag she was bound to become. It wasn't enough. Walker would have liked to see her hang. But the judge ruled that Priscilla hadn't planned the killing ahead, and no woman should be hanged for a moment of anger.

If the witch hadn't stomped on Pa's toes, Walker might have agreed. That looked planned to Walker every time he relived it—which he did about five times an hour.

The judge at least locked her up tight and for a long time.

Now, since Walker had come home with the news that Prissy would spend the next ten years in the territorial prison, the old gleam of spirit was back in Ma's eyes. She had reverted to her old, cranky self. That alone had been worth the last year of Walker's life, pitting himself against Prissy's sweet lies and innocent denials.

"Elijah Walker"—Ma slapped a platter of fried chicken on the table so hard Walker was afraid she'd cracked the plate, but no matter how cranky Ma was, if she was feeding him, she wasn't seriously upset—"you get on your horse and ride back into town and make sure she's all right."

"Ma, I'm sure her pa came for her." He did his best not to groan aloud at the thought of that long, cold ride into Ranger Bluff. He was thoroughly sick of towns and being away from home.

"If you don't find her in town, ride out to the J Bar T and be sure she made it. And make sure her pa welcomed her, too." Ruby shook her head in disgust as she slid a heaping plate of fried potatoes and a bowl of milky chicken gravy onto the table. "Why anyone would want to go out to that wreck of a ranch and live with that old coot Joshua Talbot is beyond me."

"If I go out there, I'll be lucky not to come home with my backside full of buckshot." Walker started scooping the delicious-smelling food onto his plate. Ma could just scold all she wanted. He'd get started eating and consider the nagging as his entertainment. "He's so quick with that shotgun'a his, no one in the whole Wyoming Territory will go within a mile of that place."

"All the more reason to make sure she's okay." Ma plopped a plate of her flaky biscuits down beside Walker's right hand and put a bowl of stewed tomatoes nearby.

He helped himself between bites of tender chicken with a crispy coating. "He won't shoot his own daughter, for heaven's sake."

"Joshua is crazy as a loon and you know it." Ma added a crock of butter and a small dish of shining red jelly. "He might see his daughter, think he's shooting a two-headed buck, and have the poor girl for dinner."

Ma had an answer to everything.

Walker needed to follow up on the news of those Herefords anyway. "I'll go. I want to make sure she's all right myself." And that was the truth, but a sorry truth to Walker's way of thinking. He didn't want to care what happened to that fragile woman, but he did. It felt too much like his concern for his delicate Priscilla. It had all been lies then, and no doubt Annette Talbot's neediness was lies now.

Ruby's face curled into a frown. The wrinkles on her face were deeper, as if grief had carved itself into her skin. Walker wished he'd have arranged a noose for Priscilla just to pay for those deep lines of sadness.

"If you were going anyway, why didn't you just say so?"

Walker had managed to eat four pieces of fried chicken, a couple of potatoes' worth of fried potatoes, three biscuits, a mound of stewed tomatoes, and a slab of pie while his ma worked her mouth. Now he wiped his lips, stood, and hauled his ma out of her chair and hugged her until she squeaked. "I didn't say so because I love the sound of your naggin', Ma. Guess that makes me as crazy as that old lunatic, Joshua Talbot."

"I do *not* nag." Ma pulled away, narrowed her eyes, and then grabbed for her towel. She got two good snaps in before Walker managed to run out of the house, laughing. He heard his ma laughing, her old booming laugh, as he made tracks for the barn.

And more than nagging, her laughter came very close to healing the aching gash left in his heart. He'd been responsible for his father's death. Not through any direct action but through foolishness. Through stubborn, arrogant selfishness.

Ma had never said a word to fault him for it. She was a saint and that was that. But she knew and Walker knew.

Priscilla was locked up and Walker had his foolishness under control. If he could just keep his life exactly how it was, maybe someday, when he proved to God he wasn't such a fool, Walker would feel like he'd been punished enough and could dare to ask God to give him a chance at eternity in heaven.

But for now, Walker's guilt burned him like a sea of fire.

Eternity with the same thing was what he deserved.

# EIGHT

Claude slipped into the room where Blanche had taken refuge.

He shoved a chair under the doorknob and looked through the gaps in the walls.

"Were you followed?" Blanche sat on the floor of the derelict shack. She looked exhausted, used up. His pretty wife was long gone these days. She didn't have the touch anymore. It was her fault things had fallen apart on this scam.

"Shut up." Claude already was sure he hadn't been followed, but he wasn't ready to listen to Blanche's nagging yet. He kept staring out, letting the cold wind cut through him rather than turn and face his wife and the disaster her failing singing voice had brought upon them.

This was the fifth town they'd needed to leave in the dark of night. In this one, the townsfolk got onto them in time to retrieve their money, too, so Claude was leaving empty-handed.

Minutes passed until the cold drove Claude away from the wall. "Without Annette we're ruined." Claude slapped his flat-crowned hat against his leg. He looked around the wretched building. Long abandoned, no windows, leaking roof. And of course there'd been a cold, driving rain all day. It reminded him of the room where he'd imprisoned his songbird. He'd had her in his hands and she'd flown away.

Blanche drew her knees up to her chest and didn't speak. Her very silence echoed like an accusation. He was the one who'd made the move on Annette. Brought out the dress. Put the pressure on. He'd been so sure she was ready.

There was no furniture in this hovel. It wasn't their home. They'd just studied the town before they'd set up their theater and picked this as a fallback position.

Then when someone noticed the cards were marked and the whiskey was watered down, Claude led them on a merry chase while Blanche scooped up whatever money she could and ran for their prearranged meeting place. Except along with her voice, Blanche had lost her nimble fingers. Claude had seen most of the money flying up in the air as he'd run.

"I got away with only twenty dollars this time." Blanche glared at him.

The sun setting barely lit up the windowless shanty because of the holes in the walls and ceiling. There were stripes of light coming in. . . like the bars on a jail cell.

Claude could still see her scorn. As if this was his fault. "I told you to keep that door locked. You let that pious church lady walk right into my gambling hall."

"The door was locked when I left." Blanche surged to her feet. "You went through it later. You're the one who forgot. How'd you let that old hag past you? I suppose you were looking for a bottle somewhere." Blanche stalked toward him, her fists clenched, her jaw taut.

Dispassionately Claude studied her as she advanced. His wife was still slender. She fit into the dress he'd tried to force on Annette well enough. But lines of bitterness were taking their toll on her looks as she neared forty. No reason he needed to keep that from her. "It wasn't that long ago we wouldn't have needed the pretty Miss Talbot. *You* could hold a crowd with your voice and your looks while I handled the gambling and whiskey."

"And *you* could fleece a table of gamblers and leave them none the wiser." Blanche grabbed the lapel of his best black suit—also his

last. He'd managed to leave something behind in nearly every town. Running forced a man's hand. "Your hands aren't as steady as they once were because you like that rotgut you sell."

Rotgut whiskey was what he'd been reduced to. But life looked a lot better to him with some of the edges eased through a brown bottle. He needed a drink right now. Since he didn't have that to relieve his tension, Claude grabbed Blanche's wrists and pulled her hands away before she tore his coat. It was worn now, and he had neither the time nor the money to replace it until he got Annette back under his thumb. People were more generous with their money if the man skimming it from their pockets looked like he didn't need it.

Claude stared down at his wife, increasing the pressure on her wrists until pain was visible on her face. Life had been cruel to her and it showed. She liked the whiskey every bit as much as he did. He'd been planning to get rid of Blanche and run off with the fair Annette Talbot, but of course the songbird wasn't interested. The tidbits of attention he'd shown to test her made the little snob recoil.

Claude had managed to cover up his misbehavior well enough to keep Annette in the troupe. Soon enough, with his heavy hand doing the training, she would lose her hoity-toity airs and agree to anything Claude proposed, including running off with a married man.

That was pretty much how he'd gotten Blanche. She needed a home and food. Of course Blanche was street-hardened and knew what game she was playing from the first.

Annette still clung to that stubborn religious claptrap. But Claude had a knack for humiliating people, women especially, until he dragged them down to his level. He had just turned sixty, and Blanche was by no means the first. He used them up and tossed them aside. It was time for Blanche to go. He needed a replacement, and Annette would be perfect. With her looks and voice he could line his nest for old age.

Thinking about her made him furious. She was less than nothing. No family except a father who'd abandoned her. No money. No prospects. Nothing but her ignorant faith. She should have been grateful for

Claude's interest. He'd find the little bird with her meadowlark voice who had flown away from him. Then he'd clip her wings forever.

He hungered to land that lesson on Annette with his fists.

"Are we going to stop fooling around and go after her?" Blanche's grating voice scraped into his vicious daydream. "There should be a letter waiting in Denver if any of the men picked up her trail. But if they haven't, we'll just go to her pa's ranch and wait for her there."

"Yes, we're going. No more stopping to pick up change along the trail in these one-horse towns." Claude shoved his hand into the breast pocket of his threadbare suit and pulled out cash.

Blanche's eyes lit up. Her greed was the thing he liked best about her.

"I doubled back through town and cleaned out the till in the general store. They've closed down for the night and I slipped in and out without trouble. We can afford to make the trip in style now. I'll even wire some of the gang once we're down the trail a ways."

"She always talked about home, so we know that's where she'll head eventually. She only headed east on that train because it was the first one leaving town."

Nodding, Claude added, "We'll study the layout around her pa's ranch. If we can't take her easy, we'll set up shop. Start a little theater just like always, above board, all respectable. And we'll start up the rumors, make sure no one in town will believe a word Miss High-and-Mighty Talbot says. Then, when it's time to take her, no one will take her part, and she'll come along with us willingly."

Snorting like an old hog, Blanche said, "I doubt willingly."

"Unwillingly then." Claude laughed. "Let's get out of this town and find a train heading west. I'm tired of waiting. It's time to play out this hand."

Blanche laughed along. The crone had no idea her days were numbered.

It quenched Claude's thirst for liquor to imagine subduing the songbird. Once he'd gotten her back, he'd make sure she forgot what it meant to be free. Or safe.

Annette had expected safety. Instead she found ruin.

"Pa, what happened?" The bittersweet she hugged now seemed prickly, like it enjoyed adding to her hurt. Pa would never have let the place fall to pieces like this.

Annie shook off the fear that had stopped her in her tracks. She gathered her courage and nudged her horse onward to the collapsing house. Once near the porch, with its sagging roof and broken steps, she awkwardly swung down from the rented horse. Her knees were so swathed in the fabric of all her clothes, they didn't bend easily. That was just as well, because they were quaking from fear.

There'd been a time when the J Bar T had thirty top hands. There was always a sentry watching the mountain path. She doubted Wyoming was safer now than it had been, but it was obvious there were no cowhands about to keep watch.

She stood, clinging to her horse until her knees stiffened. A prayer for courage helped her cooked-noodle muscles work again. God had told her to come home, hadn't He? This entire long journey, when she'd run from the Leveques, worked her fingers nearly to nubs, gone without food and warmth and sleep—it had been so clear. This was where she needed to be.

And back in the small towns around St. Louis where her troupe had performed, even before the Leveques had become involved, home had cried out to her, called her. She'd always known she'd return here to her pa, but the time hadn't seemed right. . .until the awful night when she'd been forced to run. But whatever reason had driven her to come home, she had never doubted it was a message from God.

Now she doubted.

She shook off her fear, clutching the bittersweet close as if she could somehow wring out of it those long-ago pleasant memories from childhood. Remembering her courageous words to Ruby Walker, she shouldered her cross, tied the horse to the rickety hitching post, and then marched up to the door.

She had to bend her head to get under the sagging porch roof. Then she knocked politely on a door that looked apt to collapse. The pipe in her sleeve slid down to her wrist, reminding her of Ruby's weapon. Ignoring it, she stood warily on the once-proud porch.

With her head ducked low to avoid the slouching roof, she began to get angry. "How have you let the ranch come to this, Pa?" Hearing her own voice strengthened her spine a bit. "You were always a difficult man, stiff-necked and prone to criticism. But another weakness you were heavily endowed with was pride."

The door remained stubbornly closed.

"That pride should have kept the J Bar T in better condition. How have you let things fall into such poor repair?"

No one answered.

Her angry muttering ignited her usually mild temper, and she let her anger loose on the door. If her father was truly a recluse to the extent he wouldn't come to the door, then she was going to beat the door down and go in uninvited.

At her first landed blow, her horse snorted. Annie turned to calm the animal only to see it rip the wood free of the hitching post.

"No! Stop!" She dashed forward and whacked her head on the derelict roof. Staggering backward, she clutched her head and managed to crack her skull with the stupid pipe.

The horse galloped away without a backward glance—heading back to town for its own stable.

Abandoning her just like everyone else.

It was all just too much. She dropped the bittersweet and turned back to the door. "*Father*, open this door!"

Her demand was greeted with silence.

"Pa, it's me, Annette." She hammered on the door. It took about ten blows before she realized she wasn't really knocking. She was furious and terrified and taking all of that out on the remnants of her once-beautiful home, now a derelict wreck.

Father wasn't here.

Like getting punched in the face with a closed fist—something she knew about thanks to Claude Leveque—it hit her that she should have always known.

Father quit sending money. He quit writing.

He was dead.

Possibly he'd just up and moved on, abandoning her, but dead or moved away was the same from where she stood right now. It left her alone—in the winter—at an abandoned house in Wyoming.

Her wish that father would welcome her, protect her, agree to reenter society a bit with her, was all a stupid, stupid, stupid dream.

Her arm dropped to her side, and the pipe scratched her wrist. She wrenched open the sleeve of her dress and tossed the pipe aside. It clanked on the porch floor and rolled up against the wall. What ailed her life couldn't be solved with a length of iron.

With trembling fingers, she turned the pretty white porcelain knob. Annie could remember Mother polishing this piece of rounded white glass. Mother had laughed about the vanity of it and had been proud of this bit of fanciness. Father had acted put upon about the flashy knob, but he'd smiled back then and allowed an occasional indulgence.

He'd loved Mother. Annie knew that in his own brusque way, he'd loved her, too. Until Mother died. Father's ability to love had simply died with his wife. And all the years since hadn't brought his heart back to life.

The door dragged as she lifted and pushed to get it to move. Rusty hinges squawked in protest. But Annie threw her weight into it and saw. . .filth.

Dust and cobwebs covered the house. There was one main room that had, to the right, a fireplace, dry sink and hooks, and shelves; and, to the left, a sitting area. This semblance of furniture remaining lay under dust and rags and unrecognizable garbage strewn everywhere.

Past the sitting area was a short hallway. Her parents had a bedroom on the left. Annie's was on the right. The doors to those rooms stood open. At the end of the hall was a lean-to on the back, which Annie could see from where she stood. Pa had kicked off his boots and hung his heavy coat in that room when he'd come in from chores. What she could see of that little room looked jumbled with trash.

"Well, Annette Talbot, you've been brave long enough." Her voice startled some small creature, and Annie heard scratching and rustling and a small *squeak* in a pile of refuse beside the fireplace.

Annie neatly closed the door like any civilized woman entering a house. She went to the rocking chair that her mother had adored. The seat was stacked high with paper and rags and old clothes. She knocked it all to the floor then settled herself in.

She'd held the tears when Elva had died. She'd been too busy running for her life.

She'd held them when she hid on that wagon heading down from the logging camp. She'd been too careful not to make a sound and get thrown off.

She'd held them when she'd stowed away on that train. Keeping away from the train crew had kept her so busy that she'd not spared a second for the foolishness of tears.

She'd kept a stiff upper lip to assist in looking competent when she found work on a wagon train heading west. Then she'd remained in control as she rode on stagecoaches with strangers, usually men.

She'd almost given in to despair when she'd torn her dress, of all silly things to cry over, but Walker's insults had saved her from breaking down completely.

Now she was cold, hungry, alone, penniless, horseless, and terrified. She had nowhere to go and no one around to witness her weakness, and she had all the time in the world.

Annie cried.

She wept out all the grief and stress and fear and hunger and abandonment and despair she'd stored in her heart all this time.

She might have stayed there crying all day and maybe for the rest of her life. Why not? It wasn't like she had anything else to do.

But after she'd been at it a good long time, she mopped at her eyes with her wilted hankie, and while she was doing that, she saw a dirt-covered case of cans. It looked like food.

Father was beyond a doubt gone and gone for good. Whether he'd died or run off didn't matter. . .except for an ache in her heart she recognized as grief that didn't know where to go. In fact, as much of a hermit as he seemed to be, her father could have fallen off a cliff or been eaten by a bear months ago and no one would have noticed.

Annie made a mental note that if she figured out how to survive this she'd never let herself get so cut off from other people that no one would notice if she were dead or alive. . .an appalling way to live. As she made that decision, she stiffened her knees and her backbone and prayed aloud.

"I asked for a cross to bear, Lord." Annie liked the sound of her own voice. It helped remind her that she wasn't truly alone, because God was with her. Also, there was very obviously no one here to tell her she'd lost her mind. "So. . .uh. . .I suppose I owe You thanks for this answered prayer—and forgiveness for being an idiot to ask in the first place. And God, please let there be something to eat in those cans."

Sitting a bit longer, she wiped the tears from her eyes and remembered she was a child of the West. "I was raised out here, Lord. If there's no food in those cans, then there's food in the Medicine Bow and there's food in the mountains. Father taught me how to set a trap and spear a fish. I can find roots under the ground and berries cured on the bush."

She knew how to shoot a gun, too, but she didn't own one. Then a new light flared in her brain. She could make a bow and arrow. It was a game she'd played with Father when she was growing up, and she'd been a fair hand at it. Yes, she'd be fine.

Lonely, but fine.

She noticed the bittersweet vine lying neglected on the floor. Rising, she went to the vine and lifted it, inhaling its sweet, cold smell. Squaring her shoulders, she turned to the wreckage of the cabin and carried the vine to the mantel coated with dust but still sturdy.

"I'll dust later, but for now. . ." Annie lifted several rags and cans and assorted debris off the mantel and rested the vine along the length of it. Stepping back, the memories of childhood rushed in. Yes, her dreams of a loving Christmas reunion were shattered, but that didn't mean the old traditions held no joy. This had been a happy home and it could be again.

But first things first. She turned to the cans across the room and prayed with every step she took.

# NINE

"Annette Talbot's horse came in alone? When? How long after she rode out?" Walker was plumb short of patience, and listening to Gibby's excuses was wearing him down to a nub. The old coot had rented Annette a swaybacked nag that now stood placidly in the corral just outside the back door of the livery.

"The critter came moseying in about an hour ago."

*Mosey* was about right. The horse was easily fifteen years old, and Walker had seen livelier rocks. "And you didn't go out and check on her? She might've been thrown. She could be lying on the cold ground with a busted leg." Walker kept snarling as he swung up onto his black stallion. Now he was going to have to ride all the way out to the Talbot place, which, he admitted, he was going to have to do anyway, but it seemed to help to yell at someone.

"I had people backed up asking for help, Walker." Gibby was an easygoing guy and didn't have a mean bone in his body. He didn't deserve the sharp side of anyone's tongue and Walker knew it. "It ain't my job to go chasing after every foolish little woman who rents a horse."

"And you shouldn't have rented it to her in the first place. Letting her ride out of town alone—"

"She wasn't alone. That's the main reason I didn't check on her."

Walker stopped, his anger cut off at the pass. "Who was with her?

71

Not that slick city lawyer?" The thought caused Walker a pang that felt strangely like jealousy. Priscilla had given him a few causes for that. Walker, like a fool, always blamed the man and overlooked Priscilla's come-hither ways.

"No, her pa."

Startled, Walker leaned forward, surprised away from the ridiculous irritation at Sikes's attentions toward Annette. "You saw him? No one's seen Talbot in town for months."

"Uh, no, I didn't see him. She said—" Gibby lowered his brow.

"What did she say exactly? She told you her pa was waiting on her? Are you sure she wasn't lying?" Walker knew city women lied. It was a plain fact of life. In fact, all women lied. . .except his ma.

"Well, come to think of it, I asked her about riding out alone. She said something about her pa, something like, 'I know better than that. My father. . .'" Gibby scratched his head absently. "Whatever she said, I took it to mean her pa was somewhere in town and he sent her over to rent a horse."

Gibby Newton was a pure genius with shoeing horses, but the man didn't have the brainpower of the average fly, no offense to flies for the insult.

"Why wouldn't Talbot have brought a horse with him if he came in to fetch his daughter home? Or bring a buckboard?"

Shrugging, Gibby turned to the gray nag, standing calmly on three feet in his corral. It was by far the most pathetic of the several horses there. Each of them Gibby either needed to shoe or kept to hire out. "I never saw her pa, and. . .and now that I think of it. . .she asked to go out the back door. Made a point of stopping me when I led the horse toward Main Street—almost like she was slipping away. At the time, I figured her pa was out that direction."

"So she lied."

"Well. . .let's say she led me to believe a lie. I don't think a flat-out lie came from her lips."

"And why'd you rent her that nag?" Walker had a need to punch

someone, and Gibby letting Annette have the most worthless beast in his remuda might be reason enough.

"She asked for it. Said something about wanting a gentle mare. I refused to let her have the old nag at first. But I mentioned that I rented horses for fifty cents then let her have her pick. She. . .she asked if the old horse cost as much. I told her no, I'd let her have that one for two bits." Gibby, wearing a heavy coat and fur-lined boots, gave Walker a worried frown. "I think you've got the right of it, Walker. She did go out alone."

And she probably didn't have fifty cents to her name, but Walker didn't mention that. Gibby was a good man. He wasn't one to take advantage of a half-witted woman or turn his back on someone in need. Which meant Walker was taking out his crankiness on an innocent bystander. He calmed down. Gathering up his reins, he resigned himself to a long ride out to the Talbot place in the cold.

"Walker, I'd have refused to let her take the horse if I'd known."

"I know, Gibby."

Walker's eyes went to the door as that black-eyed cowboy who'd ridden in with them on the stage strode into the stable. Walker remembered very well that the man had never offered his name, but he'd had watchful eyes that told of a man who'd lived a long time in a hard land.

"Have you seen Annette Talbot?" The cowboy looked at Gibby then turned to Walker. "Either of you?"

Walker didn't like the man's tone or his overly sharp concern. "What's your business with her?" From horseback, Walker watched the man give his full attention to the question.

The cowboy scowled. "I've got no business with her, nor any business with you."

"You're the one who came in here asking questions."

A stubborn-mule look took over the man's face for a long stretch of seconds as he held Walker's eyes. Finally he shook his head, not as if he'd lost the staring match, but as if he'd made a decision about whether he could trust Walker or not. "I'm just worried. Her pa never came for her last night, and I thought. . .well. . .she wouldn't exactly look me in the eye when I told her not to go riding out alone. I don't know where her pa lives, but it's a dangerous land for a woman alone."

"I know where her pa lives. I'm riding out there now to make sure she made it all right."

The man hesitated. Walker expected the newcomer to insist on coming along. At last, through narrow, dark eyes, the man nodded. "Name's Gabe Michaels. I'd appreciate knowing if she's all right."

"Is she something to you?" Walker didn't know why he'd asked that. He was positive Annette hadn't met Michaels before they'd shared a stage yesterday. Then Walker remembered what a skillful liar a woman could be.

"Nope." The man looked down at his hands as he adjusted his gloves.

The motion was casual, but Walker didn't like it that Michaels didn't look him in the eye when he answered. "I'll make sure the word gets back to Gibby about the woman, so you'll hear if you check back."

"Obliged." Michaels looked up then turned and left without saying more.

Usually Walker thought he could read a man well. Honest, shifty, cowardly, steady, lying, honorable. . . Women not so much, but with men he had no problem. But as he watched Michaels stride off, his boots thudding on the packed dirt of Gibby's livery stable, Walker couldn't quite pin the man down. He came across as decent, but there was something more here. Lies, Walker was almost sure. But lies about what?

"It never occurred to me that a woman would ride out like that, hardly any clothes on." Gibby drew Walker's attention from Gabe Michaels.

"What?" Walker's horse skittered sideways at his shout.

"Well, bundled some but no good heavy coat. No gloves. Her boots were worn down, too, full of holes. Bound to be freezing if she took a fall and had a long walk."

"No coat?" But of course she didn't have a coat. She hadn't had one

on the stage, just that shawl, and she'd only carried one valise, not large enough to contain a coat. "That little idiot." Walker wheeled his horse toward the back of the stable.

Gibby hustled to get the door before Walker crashed a horse-and-rider-shaped hole right through the solid wall.

His stallion was at a full gallop before he cleared the building.

Claude laughed with satisfaction as he nailed the WANTED poster up to the train station door.

He hurried in the sharp wind down the main street of the little Wyoming town to meet Blanche. "If little Annette comes this way, they'll put her in shackles and toss her in jail until we come back."

"Good." Blanche smiled, her satisfaction as cold as the Rockies in November. "I checked the train schedule, and this is the last stop heading north. We'll need to take the stage or go on horseback from here on."

"Worthless, savage place, Wyoming. The whole West—full of barbarians. Let's ride the horses. The stage will be slower and shake us to pieces." Claude didn't add that his money was running out. He'd lost one too many hands at the last stop in Nebraska. Time was, he'd have cleaned up with his cardsharp skills. But he wasn't as nimble as he'd been once, and the men he played had cool eyes. He'd been too afraid to cheat. He needed that pretty songbird to feather his nest.

"It's too cold. Let's take the stage."

"Quit whining!" With no desire to admit he was short on funds, Claude took out his frustration on Blanche. "It's just as cold on the stage, and we'll be on it twice as long. I should have left you behind in St. Louis and handled this alone."

Blanche got that look on her face, the one Claude loved. Fear. She needed him a lot more than he needed her. She knew, without his brains, she'd still be back in that bawdy house where he'd found her. Probably sunk a lot lower than dancing by now. "A horse is fine. I was just asking."

And Claude made a subtle point of letting her know things weren't safe for her. She was jealous of the songbird, but she wanted that nice shiny coin that came along with the girl's extraordinary talent. "Let's saddle up. I'm glad we paid to have the horses ride the train along with us rather than sell them like you wanted." He was especially glad, because if he'd converted the horses to cash, he'd have lost all of it last night.

"We can make a lot of miles by nightfall if we leave now." Blanche was all of a sudden eager to fall in with his plans.

Satisfied, Claude headed for the livery stable, hating the thought of sleeping outside in this nasty weather. He'd find a way to deny Blanche a hotel's lodging later. And he'd make it seem like she was a weakling for asking. "Annette the Songbird has cost me a lot of money and inconvenience." Claude looked down at Blanche and saw her anger matched his own and was aimed at the right place, the prim-and-proper missionary, Miss Talbot. "I'm going to see to it she pays for that."

Blanche nodded and strode along beside him, heading for the horses.

❧

"Canned beans." She'd loathed them as a child. Now they made her mouth water, and she had to resist the urge to hug the can.

She had about a two-week supply if she lived on only canned beans. But she'd find food long before that. In fact, she remembered the Medicine Bow flowed year-round, even if it was sometimes flowing under solid ice. There were always plenty of fish to catch.

Her mouth watering, she dug around, wondering if she'd have to smash the cans open against a rock, but found a can opener. It wasn't unusual for an abandoned cabin to be used by those passing by. And usually, if they took something, they left something behind, thinking of the next man who might need shelter and supplies.

With that, Annie whirled to look closer at the fireplace. A wooden trunk, so covered with dust she hadn't noticed it, stood within a few feet of the hearth. Annie hurried to check on it and found it full of kindling.

And she also found a small tin inside the trunk that held matches.

Picking from the abundant trash, she piled paper in the hearth and added kindling, then larger sticks, and finally a log. She had a fire going within minutes then turned her attention to opening the beans. She slid the can close to the fire, huddled up to the crackling, flickering flames, asked God to bless the food, then ate a warm, hearty meal of beans and daydreamed about fried trout.

The bitter cold was pushed back by the fire.

Her hunger was brought under control by the beans. She felt pretty good, all things considered. At last she found the energy to consider the mess she was in.

She looked around the room and decided to use some of her newly discovered strength cleaning. She had to make it at least habitable in time for bed. The fried fish could wait until supper. . .or breakfast.

The cabin was in an open clearing surrounded by rugged woodlands. Directly to the west of her cabin was a high overlook above the Medicine Bow River. The river didn't freeze over solid in the winter—usually— and if it did, Annette's pa had taught her ice fishing. The path down was difficult to traverse, especially when it was snow packed. She could do it if she was careful.

There was a second path—an uphill trail that split off from the down-hill side. She'd traipsed along behind her pa on that treacherous trail many times. It cut miles off the trip to the Walker spread, though things had always been so hostile between Father and the Walkers that they'd never gone that way to see the nearest neighbor. Instead, she'd gone with him to an overlook. Her pa had coveted the land Elijah's father had homesteaded, and he had developed the bad habit of hiking that rugged trail to look down on that neighboring ranch and seethe.

Turning from the unpleasant memory of her father, Annie turned to God, and a natural extension of that was music. The words of an old hymn came to her lips as easy as breath. It was like prayer to her. . . and praise and worship. It was the gift God had given her out of His graciousness.

"All Hail the Power of Jesus' Name" came to her, and she let that great hymn lift her spirits as she searched around the house and found a straw tick in one corner. "All hail the power of Jesus' name! Let angels prostrate fall; bring forth the royal diadem, and crown Him Lord of all. . . ."

She dragged the battered mattress outside and pounded dust out of it to make it bearable for bedtime. While she whacked away, she sang "A Rest Remaineth for the Weary." It was a song of mourning but also of exhaustion. She was experiencing both today. "A rest remaineth for the weary; arise, sad heart, and grieve no more; tho' long the way and dark and dreary, it endeth on the golden shore."

With the mattress dragged back in and laid on the floor, she decided to wash the layer of dust off everything she could reach. She discovered to her relief that the well out back worked, and she discovered a basin to use to collect wash water. This brought "Shall We Gather at the River" to her lips: "Shall we gather at the river, where bright angel feet have trod, with its crystal tide forever flowing by the throne of God? Yes, we'll gather at the river, the beautiful, the beautiful river; gather with the saints at the river that flows by the throne of God."

She even found an old buffalo robe so she had greater protection outside, which reminded her of how God kept His promise to protect her always. She pledged to herself and to God once again to live more boldly for Him, to trust God to protect her and stand on His promises, to willingly take up her cross and follow Him.

The afternoon was well upon her, and she was making real inroads on the worst of the mess in the main room. She hadn't gotten a single lick in on the bedroom yet, but she'd drag the straw tick close to the fire for tonight and stay warm more easily. She ate another can of warmed beans in her still-decrepit home then turned back to her cleaning. The place would sparkle before she slept for the night.

With a smile, she admitted *sparkle* might be aiming a bit high, but at least she'd have a clean spot to sleep. She sang as she drove out the dirt and vermin.

A horse whinnied from just outside the door.

"Annette? Are you here?"

Elijah. He'd come.

She fought a short battle against tears and won. With a stiff upper lip, she got to the door just as he began pounding. She swung it open.

He was so tall, dark, and kind. He'd worried about her. He'd really ridden all this way to make sure she was all right.

*God, bless this man.*

His eyes lit up. "Annette? You're all right? I heard you singing. Was that you?" He looked so relieved. Suddenly, as if he couldn't hold back, he pulled her into his arms and hugged her, lifting her off the floor so her toes dangled.

It had been so long since she'd had any human contact. Well, she'd slept on him in the stage, but that hardly counted. His mother and Nell had hugged her. That had lasted just long enough to make her crave more.

She'd never had a man's arms around her before. The strength was amazing. When he jerked her close, he was so solid and strong it was like being slammed into a warm, living wall.

"Yes, I'm fine." She couldn't resist putting her arms around his neck. They held each other tight.

Those blasted tears that Annie would have thought she'd used up threatened again. She squeezed tight. It was so nice to be held.

"Annette, your horse came back without a rider," Elijah spoke into her ear. "I thought—that is, I was afraid you'd—you'd. . ." Elijah didn't go on.

A shiver of pure pleasure leeched into Annie that was about more than a hug from another human. She felt restless and warm, despite the wide-open door and all her heat escaping from the cabin. "You rode all the way out here to check on me?" Annette felt a bit light-headed with pleasure to think he cared enough to come all this way.

"Yeah, of course." Elijah held on still, but he lifted his head and stared down into her eyes. "I don't want you to be hurt, Annette."

His eyes seemed to reach inside her and touch something tender.

Then those same sky blue eyes flickered from her eyes to her lips, and the look made them feel dry, so she licked them.

"I'm sorry." He let go, pulled her arms loose, and took two quick steps back, almost falling off the porch. He probably would have if the sagging porch roof hadn't cracked him in the head. The roof knocked his Stetson off. He caught it in his hands and looked at it as if it held the meaning of life. "It's just...the...the place looked deserted. I was worried."

He twisted his hat around in a circle, his hands sliding along the brim. "I mean, there was smoke coming out of the chimney, but everything—the cabin—is so badly damaged, I was afraid you might..." He didn't seem to be able to string another word onto the ones he'd already said.

"It's so sweet of you to worry about me." Her heart felt like it was melting under the concern and kindness.

"And then I heard your voice." He stopped talking and looked at her strangely as if he had been charmed into a trance.

She had learned to expect that. But her singing was to glorify God, not herself. And certainly not to enrich those dreadful Leveques.

"So, you're good then. Your father...he...he always took such pride in this place. What happened? Is he sick? I haven't even checked on him. He wasn't one to welcome company, but still, he hasn't been in Ranger Bluff for a long time. I've been a terrible neighbor. I'm so sorry."

"Pa's not...able to visit with you right now."

"Why not?"

"It was nice of you to check on me. You can see I'm fine." She wasn't fine at all, but she'd promised God she'd be brave, and it was high time she started.

Annette had appreciated Elijah on the stage, but then he'd gotten surly in town.

Now she remembered her first impression.

Elijah Walker was a gallant, heroic white knight.

## TEN

Your pa isn't here, is he?" Elijah's brows slammed down. "You're out here alone." Walker shook his head. "No, that's impossible. Only an *idiot* would even consider staying out here alone."

Elijah Walker was a rude, cranky old goat.

"What are you doing out here?" Elijah stormed into the cabin, jammed his Stetson on his head, then jerked his gloves off, looking around as he tucked them behind his belt buckle.

A few minutes ago, Annette had been congratulating herself on how much better the cabin looked. And it did, but only compared to before. Now, seeing it through Elijah's eyes, Annette had to admit that after hours and hours of cleaning, the place was still a *mess*. She absolutely refused to apologize for that.

"I'm sorry about the—"

"This place is a *mess*." Elijah glared at every cobweb-filled corner.

How foolish to apologize, but Annie hated that he'd caught her with such an untidy house. "I did not invite you into my—"

"Why did your pa let this place go to ruin? If he's here then get him." Elijah crossed his arms, looking for all the world like he needed to restrain his hands to keep from strangling her.

She knew how that felt. "That is none of your busi—"

"Get him, Annette." Elijah talked over the top of her. "Or I'll go find him. Unless you want to admit you lied about him being here."

That was so rude. And she hadn't lied. She'd never actually said her pa was here. Implied perhaps, but not said.

"If he's too sick to care for himself, I'll help you get him to the doctor." Elijah turned to study the two side-by-side doors. It wouldn't take Elijah long to investigate all the possibilities as to where her father might be.

"I am asking you to leave." Annie rushed around Elijah before he could charge in and check the bedrooms. It was foolish to keep her father's absence a secret, but then it wasn't the first foolish thing she'd done in her life.

"Ask all you want. I'm staying." Elijah looked past her shoulder at the doors. "Joshua Talbot, you get out here." His shout shook dust loose from overhead, which sifted down on both of them.

"Go home, Elijah."

"It's *Walker*. No one calls me Elijah. Is your father even here?" He took a step toward the doors.

Annie blocked him, her arms wide as if she were herding a recalcitrant longhorn. Not a bad comparison, except of course Elijah was a bull, and they were famous for running right over people. "You heard me. Get out."

Elijah stopped.

Thank goodness. Annie had once read a book about a matador, and the poor man ended up trampled into the dirt.

Her own personal *el toro* shifted his gaze to her, his chin lowered. She waited for him to paw the ground and snort. "He isn't here, is he?"

"Now Elijah, there's no cause to—"

"That's a *no*. Get your things. You're coming home with me."

"I most certainly am not!" Annette plunked her fists on her hips, glad she had someone to yell at. This day had been full of stress and fear and tension. She had plenty of bad feeling to spread around.

"You'll walk out of this place under your own steam or facedown over my saddle." He took a threatening step forward.

Even though his words made her feel rescued and treacherously glad he'd come, still she couldn't go with him. "Elijah Walker, what I do is none of your concern. If you haul me out of here, we can stop by the sheriff's office and I'll have you arrested for kidnapping."

"There were no horses outside." Walker reached for her, checked the movement, then crossed his arms over his chest and tucked his fingers tight under his arms.

"Father is out riding." To be completely honest, Annie probably should say he *might* be out riding. It was possible. If he was alive, there was a fair chance he was riding, wherever he'd gone.

"Don't take that snooty city-girl voice with me." His hands came free and he jabbed an index finger straight at her nose. "He's *not* out riding. I've had enough of your lies. I can't abide a lying woman. This valley is covered with snow. Yours were the only tracks in, and it's pretty clear the horse tossed you, because it was a riderless horse that left meandering tracks back out of the valley. Your pa is gone."

"Don't you dare come in here and start taking over." She stepped up closer to him despite the jabbing finger. She found herself possessed of a tantalizing vision of choking someone—Elijah to be specific. It called for some serious restraint.

"The corral is so badly shot it wouldn't hold a horse." Elijah took a step of his own, unfortunately a step closer. The man wasn't backing down worth a hoot. "My first reaction on seeing it was that the whole place looked deserted. Then I saw smoke coming from your chimney."

"I'm an adult woman." Annie jabbed him in the second button of his blue cotton shirt. He wasn't the only one who could poke at a person. Then she realized her hands were free and that choking vision remained.

"I told you he'd fired all his hands." Elijah shoved her jabbing index finger aside. "A couple of them work for me now. And I told you there was a rumor that he'd deserted this place. Well, it's plain as day to me that the rumor is true. Get your things—if you have any things—and let's get going. It's getting late and we've got a long ride."

*Humph, the big bully could just stand there and take his poking like a man.*

"I'm not some child to be ordered around." She dodged his hands and jabbed again, only sorry she didn't have long fingernails, filed to a sharp point.

"Ow, stop that." He grabbed her hand and glowered down at her like a threatening winter storm cloud getting ready to blizzard all over her.

"He's getting older."

Elijah's grip hurt her wrist, not because he held her roughly but because his hands were unusually warm. Hot. Burning hot, really. Annie wondered what kind of lining he had in those gloves to have kept his hands so warm. She tugged to escape.

Elijah let her go and rubbed his hand on his dungarees, as if the very act of touching her was so repugnant he had to wipe the very memory of touching her off.

She rubbed her overheated wrist, which made her mad, so she jabbed again, immediately wondering what evil impulse had prompted that. It was as if she was asking him to put his hands on her again, and she'd never do that. "He wanted to cut back." *Probably.*

Elijah seemed more willing to let her poke away this time. He shoved his hands into the front pockets of his pants, lost some of the rage set into his expression, and seemed almost distracted. Good, maybe he had pressing chores to attend to at home and he'd go away.

*And leave me here alone, the big, dumb jerk.* The frightened little girl inside of Annie who'd been abandoned by her mother and father and everyone else she'd ever known wanted to beg Elijah to stay.

"You're guessing." He shook his head as if to forget whatever was distracting him. His fists were clenched in his pockets. "You haven't even seen him, have you? And he brought a big herd of cattle to town nearly six months ago, late spring it was, while he still had drovers, then more later—a little bunch after he was working the place alone. But I never dreamed he sold out completely. Figured the rumors for gossip and that he was just culling his herd."

Elijah was making too much sense and Annie couldn't stand it. It was one thing for her father to abandon her, ignore her, leave her completely alone in a dangerous world while she had evil people pursuing her. It was another thing to have everybody know the man who was supposed to love and protect her didn't care if she lived or died.

Tears burned her eyes. It was too much. She could not stand Elijah Walker knowing this. She forced her fear, humiliation, and heartbreak to flip over into rage—a much stronger emotion. And who better to rage at than—

"Get out of here right now, Elijah." Slashing her hand, she almost slapped him in the face. Too bad she missed. "You are not welcome here. You're trespassing and I'm telling the sheriff if you don't go. I'll have you arrested."

"Telling the sheriff? Fine. Come back to town with me and tell him. Sheriff MacBride is a good friend of me and my ma. He'll side with me."

"My father will be back soon. Get out."

"Where are your things?" Elijah stopped short and stared at her. "You're wearing them, aren't you? Everything you own in the world is on your back because you're freezing to death."

"It was a cold ride out but I'm fine now. There's food and kindling on hand, and I know how to get more. Father will be back for supper."

That was a lie. She hadn't meant to outright lie. It was a sin and Annie didn't sin to the very best of her ability. She'd run from the Leveques, risking her very life to avoid being forced into sin. And now she stood lying to a man who wanted to help. True, he was humiliating her. True, his words were breaking her heart. But his intentions—though delivered with the grace of a wounded bull moose—were honorable.

The tears threatened again. She needed her rage back. Annie turned and stalked to the single chair she'd uncovered. She plunked herself down and refused to look at him.

"Go away, Elijah. I don't want your help."

*Be honest.* It took courage to be honest.

She raised her chin and looked Elijah square in the eye. "I don't know where my father is."

Elijah's jaw tensed until Annie wondered if his teeth might break.

"But I am staying here." She lowered her eyes to her lap and grabbed the arms of her rocker to resist if he tried dragging her out. "It's *my* home and you have no right to take me from it."

Silence stretched in the room. Annie wondered what Elijah was thinking, but she didn't dare look at him to try and discern his mood. Her tears were too close.

Suddenly, Elijah's legs filled her vision. She refused to lift her gaze from her lap.

Elijah hunkered down then ducked his head sideways until she couldn't help seeing him.

She saw kindness.

Annie would rather have him yelling.

If he didn't go back to being a grouch, she was going to cry.

And probably leave with him.

And prove to the whole world she was worthless, so worthless her father didn't care what happened to her.

Well, it was the truth, so why fight it?

"You're right, you know." He spoke just above a whisper. "I have no right to drag you out of here."

She couldn't help raising her chin a bit to look directly at him.

He quit tilting his head but stayed crouched. "But I'm right, too. You can't stay here alone."

"I can." She would have started in fighting again, despite her still-burning wrist, but she knew her voice would break on the very next word she said. And a woman couldn't get her back up and fight for something she knew was pure stupid if she was crying like a baby.

Ignoring her protest, Elijah went on talking. "So, I'll ride home and fetch my ma to stay with you."

"I can't ask Ruby to do that."

"And I'll gather up a few hands to help me do some repairs, just

enough to make this place livable."

"You will not." His high-handed ways were enough to stop her tears from falling. She hoped.

"And we'll give your pa every chance in the world to show up."

"I'm sure he's just out hunting or trapping." She was *not* sure, but it was definitely a possibility.

"And when you're ready to admit he's not coming and decide you no longer want to be here alone, you'll let me take you somewhere."

Where, though? The question was *where*, because she had no where in the world where she belonged. Except, maybe, right here.

"If you don't want it to be my place, if you don't think my ma, the finest Christian lady in the whole Wyoming Territory, is a good enough companion—" Elijah's voice rose, as if taking offense at her insult to his mother, which was stupid because she'd never insult Ruby Walker.

"I love your mother, and I will not impose on her."

"Then we'll find a place you do like."

"You will not."

Elijah straightened and began pulling on his gloves as he headed for the door.

"You stop right there, Elijah!"

He looked back, a faint smile on his very harassed face. "It's Walker. I'd prefer you call me that, Annette."

"It's Annie. I'd prefer you call me that."

With a snort, Elijah said, "Annie's a friendly kind of name, and I'm not feeling all that friendly right now. And I was neither consulting you nor asking your permission. I was telling you how I'm spending the rest of the daylight I've got to burn. I suspect I'll see you later, Annette." He jerked on the last glove and tugged on the brim of his hat in a cordial act that didn't show on his face one bit. Then he left, dragging her droopy door closed behind him with too much force.

By the time Annette got to the door and wrestled it open, he was riding though the pass toward Ranger Bluff.

He'd left her.

She wanted to shout, *Stay away!* and beg him to come back with the same breath.

The first tear rolled down her cheek as he disappeared. He'd be back. She knew it even as she leaned against the doorframe and watched him go. She stood there sobbing her heart out for all the abandonment in her life.

Elva had even gone away. Of course God had called her home, same as her mother and possibly—probably—her father. But all Annie saw was a lifetime of loneliness. It hit her like one of Claude's fists as Elijah vanished.

What better reason to cry?

*God, dear Lord God in heaven, what is wrong with me? Why oh why do I so desperately wish he'd stayed just one more second?*

# ELEVEN

He'd have kissed the daylights out of her if he'd stayed one more second.

Walker wasn't much of a one to harass his horse, but he kicked the feisty black stallion into a ground-eating gallop. He was running away, pure and simple. But it didn't matter because he was coming back.

Fast.

With a chaperone.

In fact, there might be hands from the Walker ranch in town. He could send them out to watch over the stubborn little woman. She'd only be alone for a little over an hour.

In the Wyoming Rockies, full of mountain lions and grizzlies and wolves, as well as more than its share of two-legged varmints, an hour could be a real long time. He shouldn't have left her. She ought to be on this horse with him right now. He should have at least ordered her to stay inside. He was leaning low over his galloping horse, running away but racing to find safety for her at the same time.

He straightened and almost pulled his horse up to go back. Then they'd fight some more.

He'd have that one more second. He'd end up kissing her. And that terrified him.

Cam MacBride, the sheriff, would be inclined to overlook a bit of kidnapping for a cause this good, so Walker could just snatch her up and drag her along to town. But he didn't dare. It was a pure, hard fact that if he held her on his horse for an hour, he might well find himself doing something really foolish before that hour was up, like caring about another frail, whiny city girl.

*God, did You make me stupid on purpose? Or am I just not using the brain You gave me?*

With a start, Walker realized he was praying. Annette had pushed him to pray for the second time. . .or was it more? And that's when Walker remembered Annette's singing voice. He'd never heard anything so beautiful. The song was pure praise to God. It was more powerful than the finest sermon Walker had ever heard. Pa had loved music, and so had Walker, but he hadn't sung a note since Pa died.

The empty place left by his pa's death—the emptiness that he'd been left with when Walker had betrayed his earthly father—suddenly had a shape and a name. God.

That space had been revealed to Walker by the singing and by that little spitfire, Annette.

Walker didn't thank her for it.

He'd tried to fill a void in his life with a woman before. And though this was a God-shaped void, coming to him through Annette's singing, it reminded him too much of how badly he'd fallen for Prissy.

He leaned forward and kicked his long-legged stallion hard. He seemed to catch his urgency, because he opened up and sprinted toward town.

❦

The footsteps on the porch jerked Annie's head up. Her singing was sadder now, lonelier, but it still gave her peace. And now Elijah had come back!

She swiped at her tears as she rushed for the door.

God had answered her prayers and sent her help.

She threw it open.

"Miss me, little Songbird?" Claude Leveque grabbed the front of her dress in his fist and pulled her right up to his nose.

Annie screamed. She stumbled back and Claude lost his grip, but he kept his nasty smile.

Blanche cackled from behind Claude. Looking past Claude, Annie saw pure cruelty and hate in the woman's eyes.

How had Annie ever believed these two were Christians? How could she have been so naive? She'd obeyed them without question too many times. She'd accepted their little nudges, moving her an inch at a time away from her ministry into something more worldly. That obedience was a betrayal of God. Annie hated her compliant spirit, the weakness and the cowardice that had led her into being used as a front for sin.

*Be brave.* The Bible verse she'd embraced ran through her mind.

*"If any man will come after me, let him deny himself, and take up his cross, and follow me."*

Then Ruby's words followed like an echo. *"This life is hard enough without praying God will make it more difficult."*

Maybe denying herself and bearing any cross she was given was enough. As Annie backed away from the horrid Leveques, she decided to stop asking for more crosses to bear. She kept dropping them anyway. Just like she'd dropped her lead pipe.

But she had this one cross in front of her to deal with. Surely she hadn't prayed Claude into visiting.

She remembered her vow to be brave—while hiding behind her father. She really was a fool. True bravery demanded that one stand alone.

So, by way of standing, she straightened. "I'll never work for you."

Claude and Blanche both laughed.

"You'll eventually be willing," Claude said. "But you'll be working right away, willing or not."

"You can beat me into the ground, even kill me. I'll never sing for you now that I know about the vile gambling den running in your back room. I won't be part of the cards and dice and liquor. You can't make me sing. You can hit me for as long as you wish, but I'll never sing a note for you."

Blanche's eyes narrowed as if she were greedy for the hitting to begin.

"Don't you know, Songbird, that there are things I can do to you worse than death?" Claude's look was almost one of pity. "I might not be able to make you sing. But there *are* things I can make you do."

Claude began laughing.

A new idea came to Annie's very active mind. She didn't know if this one qualified as brave, but she sensed it came straight from God.

*Run.*

Whirling, she dashed out the back door.

"Stop her!" Blanche shouted.

Claude kept laughing. "She can't go far."

The back door led straight to the overhang above one of the countless tributaries of the Medicine Bow River. The treacherous trail up led to the Walkers'. The downward branch went to the Medicine Bow. She planned on going up, but by chance Claude dashed out of the house and positioned himself so he cut her off from the foot of that secret trail. She'd intended to follow the downhill slope slowly and carefully later, to fish. Now she was forced toward it at top speed.

Claude came after her, slowly, confident that he had her cornered.

She took the first few steps of the trail, and just before the path became nearly vertical, she glanced back.

The expression on Claude's face, though still confident, was now more determined, as if he realized she could slip away. "Now settle down, Songbird. You'll learn to like working for old Claude."

Claude resumed laughing and picked up his pace, his hands now nearly close enough to grab her. "You're straightlaced as they come now. But you'll calm down after I break that prudish spirit of yours. I predict the day'll come soon when you'll *beg* me to let you sing."

Annie turned to face the trail and stretched her foot down to the

familiar foothold. She'd scaled the trail daily as a child.

Claude made a grab for her just as she dropped out of his reach. He wasn't visible for a few seconds and Annie scrabbled for fingerholds. Then his head appeared. He'd gotten on his belly and was peering over the edge at her. "You won't get away from me. Why make this harder than it needs to be? You'd like to be with old Claude, wouldn't you? Better than this cold cabin. C'mon back up, Songbird."

Annie saw he enjoyed watching her risk her neck. She could barely move. Some of the footholds seemed to be gone. Or she didn't remember the trail correctly. It was sheerer than she remembered, as if maybe a landslide had swiped the cliff smooth.

She glanced up and saw Claude had turned and begun working his way down after her. He'd found the first foothold, and now he looked down and seemed to feed on her fear.

She continued edging away from him. Then the last foothold was gone. There was nowhere to go. She was trapped on the face of the cliff with Claude above and the Medicine Bow River below, foaming white around countless rock. The river was straight down fifty feet. There was no way down, not from here.

Claude moved a step closer and turned to assess her situation. A shout of triumph erupted from his grizzled mouth. Annie noticed how worn and dirty he was. The Leveques dressed in the finest of clothes. But they'd come a long, hard way to get her. She knew without a doubt they'd never let her get away, not once they put their hands on her.

"God, why did You lead me here?" She thought of the Israelites in the desert whining about how hard they'd had it. Time and time again, when they'd think all hope was lost, God loved them anyway. God cared for them even when they didn't believe, because they were His children.

Annie faced the river roaring below. She called to the sky, "I'm Your child, too, God. And if You want me to survive this day, I will."

Claude laughed. He was within a few feet now. "Saying your prayers is a good idea, Songbird."

Annie saw a ledge that was less than an inch wide. Shocked at the absolute fearlessness with which she decided her course of action, she shouted, "I won't go with you!"

"You don't have a choice."

"Oh, I have a choice all right." She raised her voice to be heard over the river and the winter wind and looked up to see Claude held a gun in his hand.

"Get ahold of her, Claude." Blanche now looked down from the cliff top and goaded Claude. "Let's get out of here."

"I'll never let you take me."

He didn't want her dead, she knew that. But the cruelty in his eyes said he was hungry to hurt her.

The tiny ledge held and Annie reached her foot down for the next one. Then she slipped. Rather than feel terror, she felt uplifted that she'd faced danger bravely. She shouted to her Father in heaven, " 'They shall bear thee up in their hands, lest thou dash thy foot against a stone.' "

Her handhold crumbled and she screamed as she hurled toward the icy, roiling waters that tumbled over and around rocks far below.

# TWELVE

"She'll be fine, Ma," Walker said for the tenth time even while he knew he was dragging his heels about going to check on her. "Will you quit your worrying?"

Walker couldn't quit worrying. Why should both of them be doing it? Of course Walker was mostly worrying about getting too close to Annette again. No telling what would happen if that pretty little thing snipped at him once more. The fact that he pictured himself grabbing her and kissing her was not helping him calm down.

It skipped across Walker's mind that he'd never pictured himself doing that with Prissy. He'd had the longing to be her husband and he liked kissing her plenty, but he hadn't had her on his mind, not in this way, ever.

"I can't believe you left her at her pa's ranch." Ruby jammed her hands on her hips. "I raised you better than that, Elijah Walker."

"Well, if you'd finish your packing, you could get going. I'm sending five men to ride along with you, and then you can stay over there and help set that cabin to rights for Annette. You're wasting time nagging me." Walker wasn't enjoying his ma's nagging now. She was slowing down the trip back to the Talbot place. As much as he wanted to avoid the pretty, snippy little Annette, he felt an almost desperate need to get back to her—which was exactly why he wasn't going.

That voice. He could still hear it, ringing like the finest bell, tugging on something deep in his soul. He'd felt like he was in the presence of an angel. It had charmed and calmed something inside him. He wanted to hear her sing again.

No, he did *not* want that. He was going to avoid her completely.

Surely Frank was out there by now. Walker had found him in Ranger Bluff and sent him. But Walker wouldn't rest until he'd seen to her safety. And Ma kept packing her satchel, more and more with the food and supplies she thought Annie might need. From the looks of things, Ma was moving to the Talbot place permanently.

Besides that, she'd been treating him like a four-year-old, and a poorly behaved one at that, ever since he'd come in the door. Now he was being served her scolding while she packed up his whole house. "Ma, I told you, Frank will see to her until we get there." Walker remembered how much he'd liked his ma's nagging earlier.

He'd been a naive fool.

He'd forgotten his ma was an expert nagger when she thought it was called for. The trouble was she always thought it was called for, and, even worse, she was usually right.

"Frank isn't good enough. He's a complete stranger to Annie. She is a respectable young lady, and she isn't going to want the company of a man she doesn't know!"

"She doesn't know me either, Ma!" That wasn't exactly the truth. He felt like he'd gotten to know Annette real well—a lick too well, come to that.

But admitting that wasn't going to get his mother to move faster. She'd probably start packing even more junk if she knew how interesting Walker found Annette.

"We just met yesterday. Frank met her when you came to the station. She knows he works for me, and I gave him a note telling her I'd sent him."

"You should never have left her in town after she came in on the stage. I told you to go find her."

"I searched. She'd dropped off the face of the earth. She was deliberately hiding and you know it. She said she didn't want me to bother, and she did everything she knew to see I didn't." Walker would have done some nagging of his own at his ma to hurry up except Ma was rushing and whirling, grabbing things, stowing them, then getting more. She was moving like a cyclone already.

He'd wanted to bother Annette all right—both after the stage had unloaded and today. He'd wanted to give her a warmer coat and make sure she had a good meal and see that she had somewhere safe to sleep. And most of all, he'd wanted to warn her against going out to the J Bar T, and now he wanted to get her out of there.

The more he thought about it, the worse leaving her out there alone bothered him.

But Frank would make sure she was taken care of. Walker had told Frank to go look out for her and not let anything run him off until Walker's ma got there. Frank was young, close to Annette's age. But he had good judgment. He'd handle it. "You know what I think, Ma?"

His ma paused from her frantic activity to smirk at him. "I'm surprised to hear you think at all. I reckon you're going to tell me what about."

Walker smiled at her and pulled her into a bear hug.

She slapped at his arms but then she hugged him back fiercely. He was glad he'd brought her a Christmas present.

"I think we'll give the independent Miss Talbot a chance to get a little lonely, then we'll bundle her back onto the stage and send her back to St. Louis. Her pa is gone. She ain't gonna want to admit that for a while, but she'll eventually have to. She'll face facts and go back East where she belongs."

Walker thought of the bleak Christmas ahead for Annette if she stayed in that house alone. . .or if by some chance her grouch of a pa came home. He wished he could have found a way to bring her here. Maybe she'd calm down and come. He'd let his ma work on the little snip.

"Invite her over here for Thanksgiving." What had made him say that? He didn't want Annette over here.

"I'm planning to."

Of course. Walker should have guessed. Still, it wasn't right to leave her there alone, and Ma wouldn't miss spending Thanksgiving here at home, with him. He was definitely going to see her again. Walker tried to feel unhappy about that. . .tried hard.

"Once we lure her away from the J Bar T, she'll realize how ridiculous it is for her to stay in that dump. She'll never want to go back." Which would mean she'd be here. Walker considered slamming his head into the wall just to clear it of the dangerous thrill of pleasure he got from thinking of Annette being here at his house.

His ma looked skeptical. "She has some odd notions, that one. She talked about taking up her cross and following Jesus, but she had a different idea about it than I've ever heard."

"If you're about done packing up the whole house, I'll lead ten pack mules up to the back door and we'll load up, then you and the men can head out." Walker ducked Ma's talk of God every chance he got.

"I won't start preaching, Eli. You know the truth of God. You know you need to forgive yourself for your pa's death and get back to your faith. The decision is up to you. But Annette said she's praying for God to give her crosses to bear. I'm afraid she could look right into the face of danger and not back down because she thinks she's a coward and she's so determined to live bravely for God."

"She seemed like city ways had taken all the sense out of her. That just sounds like more proof." Walker thought of how hungry she'd been and how cold in her few clothes, all on her back. Nope, there wasn't a scrap of sense in anything Annette had done. And if she'd ridden the stage all the way she'd traveled—from St. Louis to Ranger Bluff— unchaperoned, she might be an improper little thing, too, despite her talk of God. To look at her, she seemed an honorable young woman, but Walker was a bad judge of women, no one could deny that.

Walker grabbed his hat off the nail by the front door and said

stubbornly, "I'm going to get the horses hitched up and we'll go, whether you've finished packing up the all and sundry or not. Until we get there, Frank will take care of her." He practically ran out of the cabin before his kindhearted mother could make him think any more about the brave but foolish Miss Talbot.

Asking for crosses to bear.

The little songbird was a half-wit, and even God would have to agree with that.

He clapped his hat on his head as he strode toward the stable. As he walked, he felt sorry for Annette. The day after tomorrow was Thanksgiving, and it was going to be a bad one. Christmas even worse. Walker felt sure her father was gone for good. No one had been in that house in a long while. Or maybe the miserable grump would come back and Annette would realize she'd have a terrible life if she stayed on that ranch.

He hoped she'd already let Frank get her back to Ranger Bluff. She could make tomorrow's stage, and Walker would gladly pay for her passage. Walker felt a strange twinge as he thought of Annette and Frank taking that long ride in from the ranch together. Walker wasn't that much older than Annette, but he felt like he'd lived decades longer. Annette and Frank might suit.

The idea made Walker a little uncomfortable, but he couldn't put his finger on why. He decided he ought to see Annette one more time before she left the territory—Just to tell her good-bye and make sure she had food for the trip. That decision didn't completely satisfy whatever was eating him, but again, Walker, a man used to making hard decisions fast and often, didn't know why.

He finally decided it was because she wanted a joyful reunion with her father. Instead she might spend Thanksgiving in tears in a cold, lonely stagecoach headed for Missouri. There were some hurt feelings in store for Annette. But when that happened, she'd just have to handle it.

Walker was sorry for her disappointment, but once in a while a person met up with a few little bumps in the road.

Annie twisted and screamed in terror as she plummeted toward certain death. She tried to turn her mind to God and accept that she'd be with her heavenly Father this very day.

She felt a slice of pain cut across her shoulder and opened her eyes to see that foul Claude with a gun drawn. He drew a bead on her with his rifle. For a split second, she thought she saw someone standing beside him, but she tumbled head over heels and instead of the gunman, she saw the roiling water rushing toward her. She wished she'd kept her eyes closed.

She hit with stunning force. She slammed into something and her thoughts muddled. There was nothing for her but slashing cold and pummeling rocks. Icy water slit at her like a thousand razors. She was battered by one rock after another and swept tumbling along at a breakneck pace. No place on her body was spared the beating.

The thick layers of clothes protected her somewhat, but their weight dragged at her, pulling her underwater, bogging her down. Her lungs reached their limit, begging for air, then she surfaced, almost as if a mighty hand rested on her back, shoving up. She gasped and dragged brutally cold air in. Her lungs filled with frost. Then she pitched down again and gulped in a mouthful of water. The water sucked at her and hurled her along, playing with her, kicking and batting like a schoolboy frolic with a ball.

Suddenly she was airborne. With her jumbled grasp on consciousness, she wondered if she'd taken wing and flown away. She spun around as she fell and saw she'd gone over a low waterfall. She splashed back into the wintry water.

The torrent carried her on. The vicious cold tore at her skin. She struck out against the water, trying to swim, but what little instinctive struggling she did became too much trouble. She went flying again, this time observing with odd detachment that she'd fallen a long way. The mountains rose up around her on every side, and there wasn't a

handhold anywhere even if she could have made her arms obey her to reach for one. She always had air when she most needed it, but the frigid water gnashed her bones.

She became aware of herself as if she were someone else...someone who hovered overhead and watched with detached interest as the young woman, bound in layer after layer of cloth, dipped and twirled, flew and sank, in the brutally chilled water. There was a beauty to the benumbed body rushing along with the whitewater. Annie was humbled by the musical dance of death.

She heard a voice and turned from the unfortunate girl below to see a long, white tunnel. The light shining through that tunnel was beyond an earthly source. No sunlit day, no blazing fire, no flaming candle compared to the purity of that light.

"Come home, Annette." Her mother stood at the end of that tunnel of light. "It's time."

Though Annie stood on nothing solid, she found she could walk toward her mother. The tunnel was long, but the light was irresistible and warm. She was bathed in the heat of that loving light. She drew close enough to see her mother's face, and Annie remembered for the first time in a long time exactly what her mother had looked like.

Her mother reached out. Annie reached out. Their fingers nearly touched. Joy such as Annie had never known was within her grasp.

Pain blindsided her—a wrenching pain at the back of her neck. "No!" She reached for her mother. Someone, a holy Someone who Annie knew was Jesus, lingered behind her mother. He'd always been there, waiting to welcome His servant home. Only now He was waving.

Good-bye.

Annette didn't want it to be good-bye. She wanted to stay with her mother and Jesus. Her mother's love was the finest she'd known on earth. Jesus' made mother's love pale by comparison.

A fist pounded on her, worse than the rocks, because this was deliberate. She was flipped over on her stomach. The ground was sand and frozen, jagged rock. The blow to her back made her vomit water and cough it out of her heaving lungs. The agony of the fists added to the wrenching grief of losing her mother, and her lost chance to be with her Savior was unbearable.

But there was no escape. She was forced to bear it as the beating went on. Her body was dragged across brutal, cutting granite. Someone was trying to kill her, but why, when she'd already died? It must be Claude. He was the only one who had threatened her.

Her eyes blinked open and she saw Walker. All she managed was indignation. Such a rude man. She had half a mind to tattle to his mother.

Before she threatened to do just that, the weight of her near drowning dragged at her brain and gave weight to her eyelids that she couldn't hold open.

"Elijah. . ." He deserved a scolding for this indignity. She would see he got it, but a nap must come first.

Just a quick, quiet nap.

❧

"She's alive!" Walker swept Annette into his arms and vaulted onto his horse. He shouted over his shoulder, "I saw her eyes open for a minute, but now nothing. I've got to get her warm." He kicked his horse into a gallop up the rugged trail toward the cabin.

"I thought you said Frank was with her at the J Bar T." Jimmy Ray Pike leaped onto his own horse, and the two of them made tracks for the ranch house.

"I did. Ma and some hands were headed over there." Walker did his best to shelter this poor, wounded dove.

The two men didn't speak again, needing every ounce of concentration to take this narrow path, with the steep drop-off, at this speed. They crossed the worst stretch, and Walker spurred his horse, racing toward warmth for Annette. He reached the cabin and pulled his stallion to such a sudden halt, the animal threatened to rear.

Sprinting, clutching Annie, a cold, still weight in his arms, Walker

shouted, "Ma, get the fire built up in the downstairs bedroom."

Ma came out onto the porch. "What in the world?"

"It's Annette." Walker ran past his mother. "We just pulled her out of the river! Her eyes opened for a second. She spoke my name. I pounded the water out of her chest, but now she's passed out."

Ruby dashed after Walker, passed him, and threw open the bedroom door. Walker sometimes let his ma rile him, but he loved her and knew her grit. Right now there was no one on earth Walker would rather have fighting for Annette's life.

Ma tossed two thick quilts on the bed. "Lay her down. We've got to get her out of those clothes before she freezes to death."

Jimmy Ray rushed in, toting an armload of wood, and threw it into the bedroom hearth.

Walker and his mother fought the clinging wet fabric. They stripped off one dress, then a shirt and blouse. "What in the world is she doing wearing all this?" Ruby asked.

Walker knew she'd worn it to keep from freezing, but his ma didn't expect an answer. She was too busy. They continued undressing her until she was down to a single layer.

"Leave us now, Eli. I'll get her changed into something warm and call you back. Put the kettle on to heat while you're out there, then hold up a quilt in front of the kitchen fireplace to warm it. I don't want this fireplace blocked, not even for a minute. And have Jimmy Ray dig up every quilt in the house and keep warming them."

He could barely force himself to leave Annette's side. Her skin was pure, icy white, her lips a dreadful shade of blue. He *did* force himself to go, though, because lingering even a second could be the difference between life and death. It was too improper for Walker to even think about staying to help. Ma could handle this. She was thin but made of pure iron.

Walker rushed out, yelled orders at Jimmy Ray, and threw more kindling on the fire. He put on the tea kettle, took a second to strip out of his soaking wet shirt, and put on something dry, thinking Annette didn't need a soggy cowboy helping her warm up.

Ma called him back seconds after he'd finished changing. Walker grabbed the quilt Jimmy Ray had warmed and hurried in. The wet quilts they'd laid Annette on were tossed aside, and Annette was wearing one of Ma's voluminous nightgowns. Walker covered her with the heated quilt before he was asked, tucking it around her sheer white feet.

"She's breathing. The river didn't get her, but the cold might." His ma wrapped a towel around Annette's wet hair. "This towel should be warmed, too, and we need another one for her feet."

Walker ran out to see to it. They gently removed the first towel and replaced it with the second and wrapped her icy feet. By then a newly warmed quilt was ready, and they quickly lifted the one on her and put the new one underneath.

There wasn't so much as a movement from Annette as they lifted and wrapped. It was like tending a corpse. Walker knew because he'd tended his father's body before he was buried.

Walker was chilled to think the end result of this could be death for Annette. Her music, her courage, that sass, blanked out for all time.

As a team, with Jimmy Ray working steadily at the fire on quilts and towels, they surrounded Annette with heat. Through it all Annette lay motionless. Pure white and ice cold like a waxen doll. But a broken doll, Walker thought.

"Look at her eye." Walker could barely breathe at the sight of Annette's badly battered face.

His ma said, "It didn't look so bad at first. The cold water kept it from swelling. When I changed her into the dry nightgown, I saw bruises everywhere—" His mother's voice broke.

Walker had a vivid image of the ugly welt that was closing Annette's right eye repeated over her entire body. "The river gave her a beating, that's for sure." His heart clenched as he thought of the pounding she'd taken.

"Something worse, Eli."

"What else? How can there be anything worse?"

"I didn't tend to it because getting her warm had to come first."

"Didn't tend to what?" Walker didn't like the look on his mother's face.

"Didn't tend to the gunshot," Ma said flatly.

Walker froze. He felt as stunned and white and battered as Annette. "Someone shot her?" He could blame the river ride for the bruises, and he could blame an accident for the river ride. But a gunshot meant someone was after this sweet young woman.

Ma nodded, her face severe as she looked her son in the eye. "Who would do such a thing to this little girl?"

Walker didn't answer, because to voice the first name that came into his mind was unthinkable. At last it had to be spoken. "Her father?"

"Impossible," Ma breathed. "Nothing could make a father do such a thing to his child."

Everything in Walker rejected the thought. Joshua Talbot was a grouchy old hermit who was always looking for a fight, but he wasn't a monster. Unless. . . "Could he have lost his mind? He wasn't there when I went over, and there was no sign he'd been around for a long time. No tracks in the snow, no horses or cattle around the place. But could he have come back after I left?"

Silence stretched between them.

Annette remained as still as death.

Jimmy Ray came in with another quilt heated until it was warm as toast. They replaced the cover over Annette. Jimmy Ray added wood to the fire in the bedroom until it raged, bringing the room to a simmering temperature.

"I'll warm up some of that soup we had for dinner. If we can coax some down her throat, it might warm her from the inside out." Ma turned to leave.

Walker saw a ripple of movement beneath the covers. "Ma, wait!"

She whirled around.

Annette began to shiver.

# THIRTEEN

Frank Beacon opened his eyes, his body wracked by shivering. The whole world was pitch-black. . .as dark as the deepest night in winter. Which it might well be. He was lying flat out on the icy ground, his head so sore he couldn't think of moving.

He blinked, trying to make his peepers work, and he got nothing. He tried to rub his eyes and found his hands wouldn't obey him. It took a good tug and a sickening swoop of his stomach to realize he was bound hand and foot. His hands were tight behind his back, and as that thought took hold, he realized he was blindfolded, too. He dipped his head to scrape whatever was covering his eyes away and nearly cast up his dinner, the movement made him so sick. He gasped for a deep breath to stave off the twisting in his gut.

"Get tough, you no-account varmint." The sound of his own voice calmed him somewhat. He very slowly, jarring his head as little as possible, rolled sideways and was able to push against the frozen ground and shove the blindfold away. Once he could see again, the moonlight and stars helped him get his bearings. He was behind a boulder. How in the world had he ended up here? Someone must have dry-gulched him.

But why?

His head was too foggy to come up with any answers. And it was too cold to stay here pondering. He gritted his teeth, bracing himself to take the pain he knew was coming, and scooted toward the boulder. He turned around and used his elbows to sit up then used the boulder to prop his back against.

Fumbling with the ties at his back, he found he could lift up his backside and slide his hands under, pulling them down his legs and getting them in front of him. They weren't tied too tight. He pulled the blindfold away. The cold had numbed his hands enough that they didn't want to work, but Frank managed to untie his feet and stagger upright. He hunted for the knife he kept in his boot, but his fingers were just too numb to push up his pant leg and get to the knife.

Careful to look around for his attacker, Frank saw only the empty trail that he recognized as the one running north out of Ranger Bluff. He wasn't sure, but it looked like he was a long ways from town. His head was blank. He could think of no reason he'd come to be out here.

There was no solution to his troubles except putting one foot in front of the other. He set out for town, working at the ropes on his hands as he walked. He'd gone about a mile, near as he could judge, when he finally got his hands free. He had had plenty of spare time to start in worrying about freezing to death. Shortly after that, he rounded a curve in the trail and saw his buckskin standing there, three-legged. With a sigh of relief, Frank walked toward the horse with soothing talk. The long-legged mare stood and let him approach her. She'd gotten the reins wrapped around her ankle and was held in place. He caught her and freed her leg. She thanked him by butting him with her head and jiggling his head so badly he nearly wretched. Fighting the nausea, he mounted up and started toward Ranger Bluff at a slow, steady walk, afraid anything faster would knock him back into a dead sleep.

The cold seemed to eat at his arms and legs; his toes and fingers felt lifeless. Fear gave him the guts to goad the horse into a trot. When that hurt too badly, Frank set her into a smooth gallop. His head pounded as if someone were taking a stick to his skull, but he forced himself to keep going, knowing he'd be dangerously frozen soon, if he wasn't already. He'd seen plenty of cowpokes missing fingers and toes. He didn't want to join their lot if it could be prevented.

He saw lantern light in the first building on the edge of Ranger Bluff and headed for it. The livery stable. Gibby Newton was working late. Frank rode his horse straight into the open door and shouted.

Gibby almost jumped out of his skin. Gibby, who wrestled ornery horses into shoes and had a reputation for his hard fists and steady nerves, clutched his heart like it was giving out on him. "What happened, Frank?" Gibby came closer, his fright apparently over as quick as it began.

The horse lurched to a stop. The world twisted around and Frank fell off. He'd never made such a fool of himself before, but he just tipped sideways and couldn't stop.

Gibby moved fast and caught him before he hit the ground. Then Gibby tucked an arm under Frank's shoulders and held him upright as if Frank weighed ten pounds instead of two hundred.

"What happened to you?" Gibby stared at Frank's chest in a way that made Frank look down despite the pain of moving his head.

In the lantern light, he saw blood covering the front of his shirt. The sight of so much blood helped clear his thinking better than anything so far. He reached for his head and discovered a nasty gash just above his hairline in the back. Frank got his thoughts together enough to say, "I don't know."

"It looks like someone knocked you on the head." Gibby started walking, not requiring much assistance from Frank, which was good. He wasn't capable of giving much. "Were you knocked out? You're freezin', man. We gotta get you warmed up. How long have you been riding?"

Frank really wanted to tell Gibby to shut up. All the questions were making his headache worse. Finally Frank said, "What day is it?"

"Tuesday."

Things started clicking into place. He'd driven Miss Ruby into

town on Tuesday to pick up the boss. The next day—today—the boss had asked him to. . . "Where's the lady who got off the stagecoach with Walker?"

"Gone out to her pa's. She rented a horse and rode out. Strange woman, that'un. She made me think her pa was waitin' for her, but Walker said that weren't so."

Frank didn't take the time to try and track down Gibby's thoughts. He'd get lost for sure. "Have you heard from her? Did she bring the horse back?"

"Frank, this happened early this morning. The horse came in alone. Walker rode out and came back through town again. He didn't say much, but I saw you ride out of town toward the Talbot place."

Frank remembered more. "Walker sent me out there. I. . .I started out. . . I can't remember." Frank shook his head and it gave a sickening throb. He tried not to move it again.

"Someone must have knocked you cold. Let's get you over to the doc."

"I need to get to the Talbot place." Frank pulled away from Gibby and his knees gave out. He'd have hit the floor face first if Gibby hadn't caught him.

"You're not going anywhere for a while." Gibby started heading for the doctor.

Frank was too weak to resist. He didn't like to think of that pretty young girl out so far alone. He'd gotten a look at her when she'd climbed off the stage and he'd looked forward to having her company. It had pleased him that Walker had trusted him with the job. Whoever had whacked him was out there. And a dry-gulcher was pure coyote. The low-down skunk would be more dangerous to a woman alone than he was to a cowpoke like Frank, and he'd been plenty dangerous to Frank. "Can you find someone to send out to Walker's? I need to tell him what happened."

"First thing," Gibby assured him. "I'll go myself just as soon as we get you to Doc's place."

"Thanks." Then, as if he'd finished his task and could now rest, his knees turned to butter and he collapsed.

Her tremors started small and didn't last long before she lapsed back into the deadly stillness. But each time they returned more violently. Between Walker, Ma, and Jimmy Ray, they kept the blankets warm and a heated wrap on her head and feet.

They didn't have time to question the gunshot that creased the top of Annette's shoulder.

Walker hadn't even seen it. But he never forgot there was someone out there who'd gone after Annette with a gun. That had most likely either scared Annette into falling into the river or she'd been pushed.

His ma prayed as she worked, and Walker found solace in the words. He'd do all he could to care for Annette, and after that, what happened was up to God.

"You know, Eli," Ma said, "there's no telling when she fell into the river, but it looks to me as if she was there awhile by the number of cuts and bruises."

"There's an overhang up the mountain a ways from her pa's place. If she fell in there. . ." Eli couldn't finish the thought as he imagined that high cliff.

"You're thinking if she fell in there, she had to go over the North Side Falls and through both stretches of whitewater above and below it."

Walker shrugged. "That's not a ride many people live to talk about."

"I can't think of a single one," his ma said. She looked down at their battered patient.

It made Walker furious to see the blue bruises darkening her silken skin. That lovely head had rested on his shoulder nearly all through that stagecoach ride. And he'd turned his back on her and left her to this fate.

For the first time since they'd started fighting for Annette's life over an hour ago, Walker thought of Frank. Frank would *never* have let this

happen. He would have died trying to save her. And if he'd gotten to the Talbot place and found Annette missing, he'd have ridden like the wind to get back and sound an alarm. Walker should have sent men to the river immediately to look for his cowhand.

Or his body.

Jimmy Ray picked that moment to come in with another armload of wood.

The room was already so warm Walker's shirt was soaked with sweat, and he had to wipe his brow constantly to keep from being blinded by saltwater running off his forehead.

"J.R., has Frank come back?" Frank and Jimmy Ray were saddle partners. Jimmy Ray was a dozen years older and always treated Frank like a little brother.

"No. I've been wondering about that myself. If he rode her out there, he wouldn't have left her till you got back, and if she was gone, he'd have hunted awhile then come a-running." Jimmy Ray knelt by the fire and pitched the sticks of kindling in with a mite too much force.

Walker said, "Miss Talbot was shot."

Jimmy Ray dropped the wood and turned around, still kneeling on the floor. "Frank wouldn't have stood for it when he was with her."

The already-roaring flames crackled and jumped high, eating through the new fuel.

J.R.'s eyes narrowed and he looked from Walker to the woman they'd fished out of the Medicine Bow.

"Unless her pa came back and Frank left Miss Talbot with her pa," Ruby said through teeth clenched to control her temper.

"There was no sign of Talbot when I was there. And Frank wouldn't have left her with her pa if he'd'a thought the man was dangerous," Walker added.

"So where's Frank?" Jimmy Ray got to his feet. "I'll send some men to back trail him."

Walker nodded, afraid of what they'd find. "Make sure they ride primed for trouble. Anyone who would shoot a woman and throw her into that river wouldn't hesitate to do the same to a cowhand. I'll understand if you want to go, Jimmy. We're okay to handle things now."

Jimmy Ray nodded. "I'd like to see after the boy if'n I can. I'll send someone else in to mind the fire." He left the room at a fast clip, and the door to the outside opened and slammed shut seconds later.

Annette shivered again. For the first time, as she shivered and Ma prayed her sweet comforting prayers, Annette seemed to respond to the voice. She made an effort to open her eyes, but every time they flickered open they'd fall shut again as if the weight was too much.

The shivers went on and on, wracking Annette's body until Walker feared it would tear her apart inside. Walker found himself praying along. He'd been forced into prayer by this little woman a lot of times, and he'd barely known her a day. But he wanted Annette to be all right. He kept the words inside him so his ma wouldn't get her hopes up, but he prayed, all right. He prayed hard.

"Think of that wild river, son. I've been to that overhang. Think of the rocks under it. And she washed up here, miles and miles away. And you just happened to be down there watering your horse. You normally wouldn't have done that, except I was riding over to help her. It's a miracle. God wasn't ready for her soul yet. A miracle, plain and simple."

Walker looked away from Annette's trembling, battered face. Her teeth chattered together. It was hard to look at her so injured and think God had a hand in this. Then he looked away from Annette and saw the toughness and the wisdom in his mother. He smiled. It surprised him how easy it was to say, "It surely *is* a miracle."

"And for there to be a miracle, there has to be a God, Eli."

Walker could feel the force of his mother's faith. And he knew the prayers he'd been praying silently had been reaching Someone. He could feel it. With a sheepish grin he said, "I know you're right, Ma. I know there's a God. I just don't think He forgives me."

"No, Eli. It's forgiving *yourself* that's the stumbling block." A light of joy beamed from his mother's face. "But maybe you're getting there."

A weight seemed to lift off of her shoulders.

Walker felt the guilt of adding to his ma's suffering. This whole last year, guilt and anger and vengeance had driven him. And that added to Ma's grief. He did have to let it go. He had to find a way to forgive himself, just for Ma's sake. Then he thought of Prissy and how easily he'd been made a fool and didn't know how he could forget that. . .or trust or respect himself again.

"I think God isn't quite done with Annie Talbot." Walker picked up a quilt to hold it to the fire. The room was so warm now it probably wasn't necessary.

Ma nodded. "He's gone to considerable trouble to spare her, I'd say."

Walker leaned over Annette and felt her skin and ached for how badly hurt she was. "Seeing He went to so much trouble to save her and deliver her to our doorstep, I wonder what He's got in mind for her."

She finally quit this longest and most violent spell of shivering yet. Her skin had just a bit of warmth to it.

He looked close, studying her intently, and for the first time there was a wash of color on her icy white cheeks. He brushed those cheeks softly with his coarsely callused hands, regretting their roughness.

He barely heard his mother say, "I wonder."

She sounded smug, but when Walker glanced up, her face was pure innocence.

❧

Annette's eyes fluttered open and she looked into the face of the man who'd been saving her ever since she met him.

He jumped up from the chair, where he sat beside her bed, before her eyes had been open for more than a second. "Hi." Then he leaned over her.

"Elijah?" The room was lit by a lantern. It must be night.

He felt her forehead as if checking her for a fever. Then he brushed her hair gently back. "You're awake. Thank God."

He sounded as if he was truly thanking God. She remembered he'd spoken differently about God when he'd been talking to his mother. It was all foggy, though. She couldn't imagine how she got here.

"We pulled you out of the Medicine Bow." Elijah spoke as if he'd read her mind.

"Th–The river?"

"Yep. We're at the calm end of a mighty nasty stretch. You must have been swept along a fair piece. You were the next thing to frozen, and you're so bruised up you must have crashed into a hundred rocks. Ma's worried about your ribs, but nothing looks to be broken, and the bruises will heal."

"How did I get in the river?" Annette lifted her hand to inspect her condition and realized her whole body was buried under a foot of blankets. "You must have taken every blanket in Ranger Bluff to cover me."

"Nope, just every blanket in the house." Elijah smiled.

*I was sick, and ye visited me.*"

Annette was sorely tempted to cry with gratitude. "Thank you."

"It was the least we could do for someone tough enough to make it over those rapids."

One brief memory flickered through her slow-moving mind. "I didn't make it alone." Annette tried to shift her weight, but every move was pure agony. "I gave myself up to God's keeping and He—He lifted me up, Elijah,"—now tears threatened for sure—"each time I needed air, each time the cold almost overwhelmed me. Yes, I'm here because God willed it. It wasn't my time." She could remember that. "But how did I come to be in the river in the first place?"

"I don't know how you ended up in the river, but God held you in the palm of His hand, and He guided my footsteps to be there for you." Elijah pulled a blanket up closer to her chin.

A little gasp distracted Annette from Elijah. She looked over and saw Ruby standing in the doorway. Her face was alight with pleasure as she listened to her son. The full impact of what Elijah had said hit Annie. It was a profession of faith. Only yesterday at the depot,

he'd been unreceptive when his ma and Annie had talked of their faith. Annie looked back at Elijah. In awe she realized God had used the terror she'd gone through. He'd used her pain to reach Elijah's heart.

Elijah smiled and leaned closer.

Annie waited for the next sweet thing he would say.

"If you found Frank, then bring him in here so I can clobber him."

Annie pulled back, startled at Elijah's harsh tone. Then she realized he'd turned to look at someone coming in the door.

"Someone beat you to it, Walker. Frank's at the doc's in town. Someone knocked him out, tied him up, and left him stuck behind some boulders, unconscious. They went to a lot of trouble to make sure no one found him for a while."

Elijah pivoted away from Annie, and the closeness she'd sensed between Elijah and God faded as anger turned Elijah's expression hard.

Ruby faced the man who stood behind her and glared at him for interrupting.

"What?" the man asked Ruby in confusion.

Ruby shook her head and sighed deeply. She came over to Annie and brushed her work-roughened hand over Annie's hair. "We've been so worried about you!"

Elijah left Annie and went to talk to the man.

Ruby touched Annie's forehead and cheeks and fished for a hand under all those blankets. "Oh, Annie, I think you're going to be all right. Of course I never doubted it. God sent you here to me so I could take care of you."

Annie managed a feeble smile, and when she moved her lips her whole face hurt. She winced. Ruby knelt beside her with a concerned expression. "I reckon you're going to be almighty sore for a spell, Annie. But you'll heal. Would you like something to eat?"

An appetite she didn't know she had roared to life. "I. . .I'm hungry, but I don't know if I have the strength for much."

Ruby said briskly, "We'll give you whatever you can handle."

She dashed back out of the room, her spry movements at odds with her age.

Elijah had pulled Jimmy Ray out the doorway and the two of them seemed to be discussing something fervently. Elijah was very angry, and Annie could see that the man with him made it worse every time he opened his mouth.

Annie didn't think her first words to a man she didn't know should be, "Shut up." Still, she was tempted. She wanted Elijah to come and talk about his faith and say sweet words to her again.

Then Ruby was back. "Eli, quit jawing with J.R. and help me sit Annie up. If Frank's all right, you can get to the bottom of this later. Now we need to see to Annie."

Elijah exchanged another terse word or two with Jimmy Ray. Then he turned, grim faced, all that sweetness burned away by anger. His hands were gentle, though, as he eased Annie into a sitting position. Every inch of her body wailed in protest. With her teeth clenched to keep from crying out, Annie let them sit her up.

"You may have some broken ribs." Ruby sat beside Annie on the bed and lifted a bowl of something that smelled wonderful. A spoon clicked against the white pottery bowl. "None of them seem to be displaced so they may just be cracked. It'd be a wonder if they weren't. When they're wrapped tight they'll be okay, but I didn't want to do that until the chill left you." Ruby began spooning up a thick stew.

Annie hurt every time she opened her mouth, but nothing could have stopped her from eating that flavorful soup.

Elijah sat across from Ruby, bracing Annie's shoulders forward. He was so warm and strong.

Annie wanted to burrow up against him and steal all that wonderful heat for herself. She resisted as best she could. She finished the bowl at the same time she ran out of energy.

"I can get you some more," Ruby said solicitously.

"No, thank you. It was delicious. But I can't keep my eyes open to eat any more."

Elijah eased himself away from her and settled her back against the pillow. When he let loose of her, she wanted to cry out in protest. But that took even more energy than eating.

Her eyelids, each weighing about ten pounds apiece, drooped closed, and it felt so good, she left them that way.

# FOURTEEN

W e'll take it." Claude didn't have the money to pay the rent, but the building was empty and the gullible owner believed his promises.

Claude shared a firm handshake with the skinny city mayor who owned this abandoned heap on the far end of Ranger Bluff's main—and only—street. He did his best not to hustle the guy out, but it wasn't easy. He had a lot to do before they opened their little theater with a gambling hall and bar in the back room. Some towns wouldn't have cared one bit if Claude opened such a place. But towns like that already had their share of saloons. It was harder to make money there.

No, Claude much preferred a town that didn't allow drinking and cards. There were always plenty of people who were interested in such things and no competition. Claude would quietly spread the word and the money would start rolling in.

The look of the town told him it was settled. A school and a church stood at the end of town away from his building. Not a single bar was included on the line of businesses. Ranger Bluff was in serious need of some livening up.

And he and Blanche knew exactly how to do it.

"I've already wired the men to come. They'll be here in a week or two. We can start up tonight with you singing. We'll play it like we always do. We're putting on a wholesome show. And we'll work in a

word or two about being cheated and lied to by our former songbird."

"She didn't survive that fall, Claude. No sense wasting time telling that same old story."

Claude had stolen the money to send the wire. He didn't have enough left to leave town. "This is just in case. I could see a bit of that river. She had to go over those falls, and I'm sure she's dead. But blackening her name is just a precaution. Then even if she did survive, we can still stay here awhile, build up our cash reserves, fleece the folks in this town who aren't quite as good and decent as they let on, and then move on." Shaking his head, Claude said, "I sure did hate losing her. That voice of hers was as good as gold."

"I heard tell of a mining camp up in the hills." Blanche stood with her hands fisted on her hips, looking around the dusty building. "The mines are played out, they said, but there are still a few hard cases chiseling a trace of color out of the hills. Those folks are always gamblers and drinkers."

"And if we can get a few folks in the front door, even just to listen to you sing—"

Blanche cut him off. "My voice isn't what it used to be. But I can hold an audience long enough for you to put a whisper in an ear or two about the back room."

"Just barely long enough." Claude knew he couldn't alienate Blanche now. He'd lost his songbird. What a waste. That girl could have made him rich.

"And once they know about the back room, they won't care about the floor show."

Claude looked at Blanche and smiled. He really was fond of the old girl. An old girl, twenty-five years younger than he was. An old girl he planned to dump at the first opportunity. Money *was* money, after all.

But Blanche had a twisted soul, just like his. Their twists fit together well. He only knew one way to make women submit, and that was with degradation. He hurt them until he brought them so low they felt lucky to be with him. He'd had many partners and it had always taken that, and it would have taken that with the prissy Annette. But not Blanche. She was degraded when he found her and seemed to take sick pleasure in his treatment. He'd enjoyed that enough that he'd married her. He liked having her at his side, for now.

He looked around the building. They needed to spend the afternoon cleaning, and that was beneath Claude. Blanche didn't like it much either but she'd do it. For now, the only thing they had to go on was Blanche's voice and the marked cards in his vest pocket. With time, they could set things up nice. A roulette wheel, liquor, a few girls. . . There was money to be made if things went really well.

If things didn't go well, they'd make a fast score and get out of town and meet up with the other players somewhere else.

Winter in the Rockies didn't appeal to Claude. He'd cruised the Mississippi on a paddle wheeler and run wild in New Orleans as a youngster. But he'd found out fast not to bet against the house. The owner of those riverboats and Louisiana gambling dens made the big money. When he'd had enough of the solitary life, he teamed up with his first woman, and because he never had the funds to start his own place, he started his own road show.

That'd been twenty years ago, and he'd been living to suit himself ever since.

Now wasn't the time to make Blanche suspect she was on the way out. She was still slender. Her looks were fading but they weren't gone.

"Let's celebrate our new home, honey." Claude pulled her into his arms.

As always, Blanche did exactly as she was told. . .and a little more.

❧

"What did Frank say?" Walker pounded his leather gloves against his leg as he paced the length of the cabin.

The morning after Annette's ice-cold swim, she slept a natural sleep rather than a bitter-cold unconsciousness. Ruby was out fetching eggs. J.R. had just ridden in with news.

"Well, for one thing, he never got to the Talbot place." Jimmy Ray found Frank last night at the doctor's, but his saddle partner had been too woozy to talk. He'd gone in again this morning before dawn and was back before Walker got started with chores.

"So, where'd he get attacked?"

"I back trailed him to the place on the trail he woke up. There were a pair of riders who waylaid him, but wind scudding snow across the trail had blurred the prints to the point I wouldn't be able to identify the horses. And you know if anyone could, it'd be me."

That was no boast. J.R. was the best tracker in the area, if not in the whole territory. Walker trusted his hired hand completely.

"There was blood on the rocks where Frank fell, and I saw plenty of signs that told me they dragged him to hide his body." J.R.'s words were laced with rage. "I s'pect they thought he was dead, or would be soon. Frank got dry-gulched, sure enough. The kid didn't even know he had a bullet crease in his head until the doc told him. He lay there for hours before he woke up. Freezing cold and mighty lucky to find his horse or he'd'a never gotten back to town alive. His fingers are frostbit. The doc thinks he might lose a couple of 'em."

The man had a cool head and had survived a long time in the rugged West. A man didn't do that if he went looking for trouble. But J.R.'s expression told Walker he was looking for it now.

Walker held Jimmy Ray's gaze for a long time, thinking what to do, how to get to the bottom of this. "What do you make of it?"

Jimmy Ray said darkly, "It wasn't a robbery. They didn't take his horse."

"Feisty horse, not that easy to catch if you shoot from cover and knock the rider off."

Nodding, J.R. said, "True enough, the horse had run off a ways. Maybe whoever was shooting couldn't catch the cayuse. I might go back out and look a little farther down the trail toward the J Bar T. I only looked at the place Frank was shot. Maybe I can find a sheltered spot that will give me a better idea of who was out there."

"Annette is still too weak to talk, and she doesn't remember anyone shooting her. She's got flashes of memory of the river ride but nothing else after I left her place. I'm wondering if whoever knocked Frank out might've gotten him out of the way after he shot Annette—or maybe before."

"Sheriff MacBride was headed out early this morning to see what her place looked like and see if he can get a line on her pa."

Walker nodded grimly. "Yes, I'd like to get a line on a man who'd abandon his daughter, too."

"That will take some doing. My father is dead."

Both men turned toward the feminine voice.

Walker got his mouth working first. "You shouldn't be out of bed."

Annette smiled politely. "Nonsense. I'm warm, rested, and well fed. Completely recovered." She stood, fully dressed in the same worn dress she'd had on in the stagecoach. Ma had fixed up the gaping hole in the front and washed it. The dress, and Annette, looked as rough as ten miles of mountain road.

"What do you mean your pa is dead, Miss Talbot?" Jimmy Ray asked.

"I remember enough from last night that I know you helped save my life. I think you can call me Annie. And I'd like to go into town and talk to the man who got hurt trying to help me."

She gave Walker a look so snippy she might as well have just slapped him and yelled at him for abandoning her to her fate. She might as well have accused him of tossing her over a cliff. Walker did his very best to stop the low burn of temper.

"Obliged, miss. It's J.R." The cowpoke tipped his hat then clumsily removed it.

Walker looked at Annette's battered face and the careful way she moved. Giving her orders seemed like just the way to handle her. "You're not up to going anywhere for a long time."

Annette ran her hand carefully over the bump on her forehead. "I must look a sight. Your mother won't give me a looking glass so I can see myself."

"Your eye's swollen about halfway shut like you just came out of the

losing end of a boxing match. The whole left side of your face is scraped raw. I've seen men thrown from a bronc who had that red rashy look."

"I need to find out what happened to that man. I still need to get to town."

Walker's ma came in from collecting eggs.

Walker continued with his list of her visible injuries. He'd start on her arms and legs, her cracked ribs, and the gunshot wound after that. "You've got a bruise on your forehead so ugly it's—"

"Eli!" Ma cut off the list of Annette's injuries.

"What?" Walker arched his eyebrows, surprised at his ma's temper. "The woman wanted to know."

"Hush, Eli." Ma put the eggs aside and set right in like she was a mother hen herself, clucking at Annette. "Just because I let you get dressed doesn't mean you're ready to ride into town. Let the men handle this, and stay here to keep me company."

"No. The sheriff was going to ride out to my father's ranch. If the sheriff found him, I want to know right away."

"If he found your pa, the sheriff will send him out here to fetch you home." Walker crossed his arms, stubborn.

"We won't be gone that long, Ruby." Annette said it like the decision had already been made. More politely she added, "I'll be glad to help with the chores when I return."

Walker went back to his pacing and slapping his gloves as he got back to the most interesting thing she'd said. "What about your pa being dead?"

Annette said stoutly, "I don't want to tell this story more than once. If the sheriff went out to the J Bar T, then he'll know it's abandoned. Pa loved that ranch more than. . ." Her voice faltered. Walker saw her square her shoulders and steady herself. "More than anything."

More than his daughter. That's what Walker suspected she'd planned to say.

"He wouldn't leave it. That ranch was the only thing my father ever cared about. At least once my mother died." Annette's voice faded a bit as she walked to the fire and extended her hands to the warmth.

She didn't include herself in the list of things her pa loved either before or after her mother's death. Just two days ago, at the stage station, she'd said her father loved her. And she'd said it like she meant it.

Walker knew it had been a hard two days for Annette Talbot.

"I suspect he—he died out in the mountains." She glanced up from where she stood at the fire. Tears brimmed in her eyes.

Walker's throat tightened. Tears scared him to death. His ma wasn't much of a crier, but Priscilla, that scheming shrew, had cried all the time. He'd found himself willing to do anything to stop her. "Stop that crying. We don't have time for it." Walker didn't mean to bark at her, and he saw his ma plunk her fists on her hips.

"Sorry, sorry." Walker apologized fast before the scolding started. "Of course you're sad. Your pa is missing. . .or. . .or dead."

What had they been talking about? Oh yeah.

"You're not coming to town. Forget it. You shouldn't even be out of bed. You'll collapse before we get you on horseback and die after all our hard work to save you."

"Eli. . ." Ma sounded tired for some reason. And she'd just gotten out of bed.

"I will *not* collapse. And if yesterday didn't kill me, then a ride into town won't either. I had a terrible experience and now it's over." She sounded so reasonable when it was obvious she was completely insane.

"You'll catch your death of cold and die."

"I'll borrow a warm coat and be fine. I'll see if there's work to be found in town. I know I can't go back to the ranch. It's dangerous." Annette's brows knit together. "I still can't remember what happened. Who would have shot me?" Annette looked at Walker's ma. "Mrs. Walker, I'll need to borrow a coat if possible. I promise I'll return it. If I can find work I could send it back with someone right away and—"

"Now you're talking nonsense, Annie." Ma hurried over to pull Annette into a hug.

Annette hugged her back something fierce.

It occurred to Walker that Ma had never offered Priscilla a hug. No, Ma had never warmed up like this to Priscilla, though she'd tried to be polite. He thought maybe since he'd discovered himself to be a poor judge of women, that he should trust his ma's instincts and believe Annette was a decent sort.

He decided against it. "You're not coming. And you're not getting a job in town. It's not proper."

"I need to see if the sheriff knows anything. If he finds Pa, I'll be able to go home with him. If not, then I need to talk to the man who was injured last night and see what he knows."

"That's a whole different thing than hunting work." Ma pulled back and fussed at Annette, straightening her dress collar, smoothing her hair, in a way she only did with family. "I won't even consider letting you go unless you promise to come right back here. If your pa shows up, then of course you'll go with him, but otherwise you're staying with us and that's that. Tomorrow is Thanksgiving, and one of the hands brought in a turkey. They've got another couple to roast out in the bunkhouse. I'll be baking all day, and we'll have pumpkin and mincemeat pies. And we'll have potatoes, mashed and full of butter, and all the trimmings. We'll spend the day in thanks for God's many blessings and the richness of the harvest."

"And what about this man who shot Miss Talbot and threw her into the river?" Jimmy Ray asked with barely controlled rage.

Walker knew how the man felt. Now wasn't the time to give thanks, not with a gunslinger running the hills. He slapped his gloves in his hand and his steps lengthened. A man needed a bigger house to pace properly.

"We can be thankful she survived." Ma clutched her hands together, looking anxious.

Walker was put in mind of his father, who *didn't* survive. He felt a chill of his own that had nothing to do with the cold weather at the thought of his ma caring about this little city gal. Every protective instinct Walker possessed told him to take care of Annette Talbot. And every survival instinct of his own told him to get her on that stage and get her out of here before he found himself even more strongly drawn to her.

Before he could hear her sing again.

His boots fairly rang on the wooden floor as he tromped.

J.R. shook his head. "I won't be thankful while a back shooter is runnin' loose. Whoever shot Miss Annie's gotta be the same one who attacked Frank. He's shot two people, both from cover. That makes him as dangerous as a rabid wolf. Who knows who'll be hurt next."

"He shot me, or I guess he did." Annette rubbed her shoulder, her brow furrowed. "I didn't even know I'd been shot until someone told me. Are you sure it's a bullet wound?" She looked at Ma.

Walker scrubbed his face with one hand and groaned. "Of course we're *sure*." He paced and slapped his gloves. "Don't you think I recognize a bullet wound when I see one?"

"Hush, Eli. Then he threw you into the river?" Ruby asked.

Annette's eyes narrowed as if she were searching the depths of her brain for a memory. "No, nobody threw me in. I—I remember falling."

Walker stopped pacing, his hand frozen in midslap. "You fell?"

"Yes," Annette said tightly. "I—I remember being on the path down. I used to climb down that all the time when I was a child."

Ruby, standing beside her, hugged her shoulders and pulled her close to her side. "But even while you fell, God held you in His hands and kept you safe."

"He did." A smile bloomed on Annette's face. " 'For he shall give his angels charge over thee, to keep thee in all thy ways.' "

Walker knew the Bible when he heard it quoted at him.

Ruby smiled. " 'They shall bear thee up in their hands, lest thou dash thy foot against a stone.' "

"I was in God's hands all along." Annette sighed and looked just plain blissful. Especially for someone who'd been shot.

"And that's true every day, not just when you're facing danger." Ruby nodded and hugged her, mindful of her bruises and the wounded

shoulder. "I'm sure a ride to town won't hurt a thing."

Walker looked at the two of them, fast friends, grounded in the same faith. Courageous as a pair of mama grizzlies. All because of their trust in Jesus Christ. His heart warmed as he thought of the strength he saw in these two women. Then Annette looked over Ruby's shoulder, and her bruised face twisted the anger in his gut. He quit thinking about God and remembered what needed to be done. "J.R., when's the sheriff supposed to be back?"

"He should be there already. Last night I told him what had happened with Annette. He'd already gone to pick up Talbot when I checked on Frank this morning."

"He won't find him," Annette interjected.

"Maybe he'll find someone else, whoever did this, and bring him in." Walker walked to the door and pulled a heavy buckskin coat off its peg.

"I'm going with you!" Annette declared. "I'm rested, and although I hurt all over, it's mostly stiff muscles. Moving around will help loosen them up. From your horrified expressions I assume I look terrible. Good. If the sheriff brings someone in, I want to be there to face this man. I want to tell the sheriff what really happened, to the extent I remember. If I look this bad it will only add weight to what I say."

"I don't look horrified because of your looks." Walker shook his head in disgust. "You're battered and cut and shot and someone is trying to kill you. You're not riding into town. You need to rest." Walker felt his temper rising. "Stay here with Ma and give yourself a chance to heal. If you want to work your muscles, you can help her make pie."

"I'm going to talk to the sheriff and ask Frank a few questions. Maybe hearing him tell what happened will jar my memory."

"No, you're not going." Walker jerked the coat on. "That's ridiculous. You're barely on your feet. You almost died yesterday."

Annette crossed her arms. "If you leave me, I'll saddle a horse myself and be ten minutes behind you on the trail. So, unless you plan to lock me up, I'm coming!"

Walker scowled at the stubborn little filly. There was a lock on the door to the bedroom she'd been sleeping in. He could pen her up tight and he was sorely tempted. His eyes swung to Ma. "I don't suppose you can be trusted to sit on her while I'm gone."

"I'll help her saddle the horse." His ma stood side by side with Annette, her arms crossed in the exact same stubborn stance as Annette's. The two women faced him down.

It set off his temper to have them siding against him like that. Like a match might set off a stick of dynamite.

"Now you two listen to me." Walker jammed his Stetson on his head. "I am the head of this house. And that's a pure fact handed down straight from God."

Ma started her nagging. "You're not head over—"

Walker cut her off. "It does so include being head over my ma. The man's in charge, and I'm the man, so what I say goes." His voice got louder until he was shouting at both of the mulish women. "And I say it's pure foolishness for you to go to town, Annette Talbot. So that's the end of it. You're staying home." He jabbed his finger at the headstrong little woman then turned to point at his ma. "And you're going to mind me. I won't have her out on the trail one day after she almost died of the cold, and that's that."

## FIFTEEN

He let her sit beside him on the buckboard.

On her way to Ranger Bluff, Annie considered what a mystery men were.

Of course, in his own rude way, Elijah was just trying to take care of her. Still, all the frowning and one-syllable orders he gave made his *care* something to endure rather than enjoy. The instructors at her boarding school had been strict, but they'd mainly ruled with love, and Annie was inclined toward obedience anyway. Getting shouted at was new.

So was ignoring that shouting.

Ruby helped her learn the way of it.

J.R. had passed them, riding horseback, headed toward her father's place.

Annie wanted to call out for him to search for signs of her father, but even if Father had died near the ranch, the Rocky Mountains had a way of swallowing people up. Annie doubted she'd ever see her father again.

Annie trembled inside to think of how she was defying Elijah's orders. It was completely unlike her. She'd always been such a good girl. In fact, she prided herself on her obedience—in a humble way, of course.

She'd twisted herself into knots obeying her grouchy father's every request. She'd done all right when her mother was alive, but afterward, nothing she'd done was good enough. She'd failed, and he'd sent her away.

The whole first year at her school, she'd battered herself over what she could have done differently. If she'd made his life easier and been more dutiful, would he have let her stay? She'd thrown herself into being the best-behaved girl in school and had done very well there.

Then she'd gotten involved with the mission group, and there'd been nothing there to object to either. Until the Leveques. Now Annie could see the many hints of danger before things had come to a head with Claude. She was tempted several times to leave the group or tell someone that Claude's looks and touches made her uncomfortable. But instead she'd tried harder to serve God and control her unhappiness. And in the end, that quest for obedience had led to Elva's death.

The time had come at last for Annette to find a backbone, to be courageous for God. Even as she ran for home, she'd promised God she'd be obedient to Him alone and she'd bravely turn away from anything that wasn't of Him. She'd stop taking the easy way out and being so agreeable and compliant—as soon as she could hide behind her father.

The Leveques. Something nudged at Annie's memory but she couldn't say what. It had something to do with whatever had happened to her that led to her fall from the cliff. . .and being shot. Maybe she just lumped all danger into thoughts of Claude and Blanche. She shivered with fear.

Elijah looked over then drove with one hand while he adjusted her buffalo robe he'd wrapped around her. "You shouldn't be here."

Ah, too bad. It had been much better when he wasn't speaking to her. That appeared to have come to an end.

"I'm fine."

"It's too cold. You could have died yesterday."

"I didn't die. I'm fine, Elijah. Fine!" It was a sharply cold day, but even so, the robe, the coat, the wool-lined mittens, the hat, the scarf, the double

socks, the boots, the heated bricks by her feet, and the heat of Elijah's annoyed glare were keeping her warm. She shivered because of whatever lurked behind that blank wall in her memory. Who had shot her?

"You're shivering. And my name is Walker."

"Your name is Elijah, and I'm perfectly warm. I'm just. . . I—I can't remember what happened for an hour or so yesterday. Trying to remember scared me and that's the shiver you saw."

"I've heard of that after a hard whack to the head. You'll probably remember after a while."

Her whole body shook for one hard, cold second.

Elijah felt it and glowered at her.

"I don't think I want to remember." Her voice was faint.

Elijah's scowl smoothed, replaced by concern. "You need to. You might still be in danger if whoever attacked you is roaming free."

"I know. Are you sure that cut on top of my shoulder is a bullet wound? I could have hit a rock sticking out of the cliff. I could have just slit—"

"I'm sorry, Annette. But no amount of wishing is going to make that anything but what it is. Someone shot you."

"A drifter."

"I hope so." Elijah leaned close so his solid shoulder touched her. "Because then it's not personal, and he's got no reason to come after you again. But someone knocked Frank cold and left him. In Wyoming in November, leaving a man on the trail like that is risking his life. Whoever did that didn't care if Frank lived or died. And it's most likely the same person who shot you."

"I'm a coward. I've always taken the easy path rather than face up to bad things."

"What's that mean, easy?" Elijah gave her a look like she meant she'd done improper things.

A blush added to her general warmth. "Oh, I don't mean sinful things, like the way is broad and the road easy that leads to death. But I've lived an obedient life. I prefer peace to conflict. I'm trying to be stronger, braver, pick up my cross and bear it. I thought I was being brave when I headed for Father's ranch. Now I know it was stupid, not brave. I should have known better than to ride out there alone."

"I told you that."

That smug statement made Annie grit her teeth and quit confessing. "Yes, you told me that. Your ma told me that. Gabe Michaels told me that. Mr. Sikes told me—"

"When did you talk to all of them?"

"The night before I rode out to Father's."

"How'd they find you? I looked all over."

"You did?" It wasn't so hard to keep from snipping at Elijah all of a sudden.

Elijah shrugged and shook the reins as if hoping the horses would run.

Well, fine. He didn't want to admit he'd worried, so she wouldn't pressure him. In fact, he probably hadn't worried. No doubt his mother had nagged him into hunting for her. She knew now she could be brave without being foolish. It had to be possible. So no more delays. She'd start being brave right now, with no one to lean on.

She kept her shoulder leaned firmly against Elijah as she made that decision. He seemed to think it helped keep her warm, so she cooperated. It occurred to her that this might count as leaning on someone, but that wasn't how she saw it, so she kept close.

When they got to town they went to the jailhouse.

"Sheriff MacBride is back." Elijah nodded at the sleek gray roan tied in front of the lawman's office, then swung down, came around to help Annie, and strode to the door.

Annie couldn't make her feet move. He almost went in without her. In fact, she was considering going to Nell's for coffee, or rather, to watch other people drink coffee since she was without funds.

Elijah had finally noticed she wasn't at his side. He came back and caught her arm carefully but firmly. "You're not going to turn yellow now. Not after you insisted on coming all this way." Then despite his rough grip, his voice was soothing. "I'll be right beside you, Annette.

No harm will come to you."

Annie looked into his warm, kind eyes for a long time. Then she nodded and followed him, determined to be courageous and stand bravely for God.

And here was Elijah to practice on. She planned to defy him at every turn until she got really good at it. And if she forgot and started minding the grouchy man, Ruby would help her remember.

They found a cranky sheriff just back from a long, cold ride that yielded him no answers. They went to the doctor's office, and Frank was no help either. He didn't even remember being shot. He'd seen no one. By the time they gave up questioning poor, battered Frank and talking with the sheriff, Annie was exhausted.

"Ready to go home?" Elijah had a smug tone to his voice.

Annie knew she needed to pin his ears back.

A man rounded a corner at the far end of town and went in a doorway.

Annie only caught a glimpse of him out of the corner of her eye. She didn't even see his face. But she knew.

Claude Leveque.

And where Claude was, Blanche was close behind. The Leveques were in Ranger Bluff.

Like a floodgate opening, all her memories at her ranch rushed back. The cruel threats Claude had thrown at her. Blanche's evil laughter. Running, the treacherous path, slipping, Claude's gun.

The shock of the sudden and total recall of yesterday's events staggered her. Elijah caught her or she'd have sunk to the ground.

"Annie!" Walker steadied her.

Her stomach rebelled, and Annie had to fight not to lose her breakfast. Her gunshot shoulder burned like fire. Her blackened eye throbbed and her abraded face ached. All thoughts fled of defying Elijah or, even better, facing down the Leveques. She caught hold of Elijah's broad, strong shoulders and held on tight. She knew now that Claude had shot her, but would the sheriff believe her if Claude called her a liar and a thief? She knew Claude had probably already begun the whispers about her character.

"We need to get you home, Annette." Elijah's voice seemed to come from far away, and yet he had her in his arms. She felt his lips move against the top of her head as he spoke. "I should have never let you come to town with me."

As if he'd called her back from the brink, Annie steadied herself a bit and took a quick glance at the spot she'd seen Claude. She read a newly painted sign over the door Claude had entered, and that told her something else—Claude had gone into the law office of that rude, overly inquisitive Carlyle Sikes from the stage. A lawyer. If Claude hadn't publicly accused Annie of anything yet, he might be doing it soon. Maybe he wanted a lawyer at his side when he made his charges. "I—I think you're right, Elijah." And maybe she was really wrong. Guilty of what Claude might even now be charging.

Elva had said the money was saved, but Elva had made no more money with the mission show than Annie. Where would Elva have gotten that bit of money? It might well be that, in her desperation, Elva had stolen the money from the Leveques, honestly claiming it as due her and Annie.

"Of course I'm right, stubborn woman." His words were unkind but they were spoken softly, even affectionately. But earlier Elijah had spoken of Annie traveling alone. He'd be ready to believe the worst. Even Ruby would doubt her and demand she be removed from the company of decent Christians.

It was too much. Obeying Elijah was too easy.

"I'm ready to go home. You were right, Elijah, this trip was too much for me."

◎◟◞

Gabe Michaels dropped the curtain and ran. His boots thundered down the steps of the boardinghouse where he'd rented a room.

He should have watched Annette Talbot more closely and caught

her before she vanished from town. But right now he had his chance.

The papers he carried at all times crinkled as he rushed across the wood floor leading to the back door. A heavyset woman in the kitchen noticed him and called out a greeting, but Gabe didn't take time to reply. He didn't slam the door. Not wanting anyone to notice his coming, he ran in the dirt alley trying to circle around in front of Walker and Annette as they headed for the buckboard, parked in front of the general store, loaded with supplies.

Gabe caught a glimpse of the wagon and Walker, helping Annette across the street as if her knees were giving out. He bristled at the sight of Walker cozied up to Annette. But no reason he should. Walker probably needed more help than Annette, if only the man knew it.

Gabe wondered if Annette had already wormed her way into Walker's good graces. When Gabe had gone hunting for her, he'd found the trail of a woman with a knack for leaving behind adoring fans and disturbing rumors. It left Gabe with no idea what the woman was really like, and he intended to find out. And there was an easy way and a hard way.

He'd try the easy way first.

Walker liked being right. But right now he wished like crazy he'd been wrong.

Annette had gone pale as a ghost and looked to be near collapse. Head bowed, all the fire was gone from her voice.

Walker had craved obedience earlier. He'd been spittin' mad he couldn't manage to get it. But now he wanted her squabbling with him. At least that meant she was feeling chipper.

Kinda like his ma when she was nagging.

Walker should have known Prissy was no good just because she was so agreeable. Who wanted that in a woman? He kept his arm around Annie's waist and half carried her to the buckboard.

They'd nearly reached it when someone appeared on Annie's other side.

"What's wrong? Let me help." Gabe Michaels was still in town.

People minded their own business in the West and Walker hadn't thought much about the quiet cowpoke on the stage. But now it needled that he had no idea what Gabe Michaels's business was here in Ranger Bluff.

Michaels slid his arm around Annette's shoulders and looked prepared to lift the woman off of her feet.

Walker wanted to punch the guy in the face, which made no sense. He was worried about Annette. He wanted to help. That didn't make the low-down polecat a bad guy.

Walker stopped the rush to his wagon. His mind had been fixed on getting Annette home, but now he stopped. "We're fine. She's just tired."

Gabe looked at Annette without acknowledging that Walker had even said a word. "Are you sick? What happened? Gibby at the blacksmith shop said you'd gone out to your ranch alone. I told you not to do that, Annie." Then Gabe must have gotten a good look at Annette's face because he gasped and stumbled to a stop.

"What happened to you?" Michaels's eyes came up to meet Walker's, as if he were on the brink of accusing Walker of beating the woman. "What did you do to her?"

"I didn't do anything to her. I found her like this. Worse than this." There was no time for Michaels's foolishness. "Now's not the time—"

Annette cut Walker off. "Thank you for worrying. I'm safe with Walker, Mr. Michaels."

Walker chafed over her polite manners when she could be getting sick.

Michaels's eyes slid between Annette's bruised face and Walker. Then he eased his hand off Annette, which was good.

Walker was about to "ease" that arm right out of its socket if Michaels didn't turn loose.

The man looked closely at her as he smoothed his overgrown mustache down. "Were you hurt out at your pa's ranch? Is he here? Did he bring you in?"

"No, my father wasn't at his ranch. It appears he's gone. Or maybe... maybe d–dead." Annette's voice shook but she went on. "I—I fell into the river."

"What?" Michaels shouted.

The wind whipped on the cowboy's long, trail-stained duster and whipped it back far enough Walker could see a six-gun strapped on his hip. Standard equipment in the West, Walker was wearing one, too. Still, it gave the man a dangerous appearance, and Walker didn't want a dangerous man near Annette.

Walker thought the man looked ready to catch hold of Annette again. He braced himself to prevent that with a closed fist.

"I was swept downriver to the Walker ranch."

"How far is that? The water has to be freezing." Michaels studied Annette as if she were collapsing at his feet at this very moment. *Which she might well be,* Walker thought irritably. Couldn't the man see Annette needed to get home?

*Home?* Annette was home when she was at Walker's ranch? That caused Walker some discomfort that he'd like to take out on Michaels.

"We've got to go. Annette needs to get—" Cutting himself off before he could say *home* out loud, Walker thought a couple of seconds. "Annette needs to get some rest. Ma's looking out for her."

Michaels's concerned eyes left Annette and shifted to Walker. He tilted his hat back with one thumb, and Walker noticed the man's hair was too long, as if he didn't have the time or the sense to get a haircut once in a while. Walker ignored his own overgrown hair.

"Yes, I'm sorry." Michaels looked back at Annette as if his eyes were drawn to her against his will, the sidewinder. Then Michaels glared at Walker. "What were you thinking to bring her out in the cold so soon after she's had such an awful experience?"

Walker clenched his fist, though honestly he might as well punch himself in the face. He deserved it. Michaels was right. Not that Walker had been given much choice.

Michaels looked back at Annette. "You look so tired. I'm sorry I'm keeping you." He hesitated, obviously not ready to shut his yapping mouth and move along. "I didn't know how to say this before, until I'd met your father."

"Didn't know how to say what?" Walker glowered at the cowpoke. The hesitance didn't fit with the cool-eyed customer Michaels appeared to be. "Whatever it is, spit it out. We've got to get on home."

Flinching, Walker realized he'd said "home." He hadn't meant to.

"I wanted to ask your pa if I could call on you, Miss Talbot." Michaels's eyes switched to Walker, with a quick side trip past the arm Walker had slung around Annette's waist. "Now maybe it'd be right to ask you. You're Elijah Walker, right?"

As if what? Walker was her *father*? That burned Walker bad.

"She's not up to such a thing right now, for heaven's sake. Keep your fool questions to yourself." Walker didn't know much about courting, but he was pretty sure that asking a woman's parent or guardian if it was okay to call was absolutely proper. But, since Annette had neither, Elijah, though he was in no sense Annette's father or guardian, decided if Michaels was stupid enough to ask Walker's permission then the answer was no. Absolutely not. In fact, Walker decided then and there that no one ever could gain his permission to court Annette for as long as she lived. Tough luck for Michaels.

And every other man in Wyoming Territory.

And even if Walker did declare himself her guardian—the thought made his stomach dance around —he'd not do that now. Of all times and places. That'd be left for the future, the far distant future. Long after Michaels had wandered clear out of the Rockies.

"This isn't the time or place for me to ask." Michaels stepped back. "I'll ride out to the Walker ranch and ask proper." He tugged on his Stetson brim as if saying good-bye.

*Well, about time he moved on.* Michaels's eyes settled on Annette, and suddenly Walker felt as if he wasn't even there.

Walker stood in the middle of town, with his arm around a woman, a woman staying at his ranch, and some other man asked to call on her. That took a lot of nerve, and he would have pounded that nerve straight out of Michaels with bare knuckles if he hadn't needed to keep Annette on her feet. "Let's go, Annette. You need to get off your feet." Walker started dragging the woman along, almost carrying her. He lifted her to her tiptoes and made her come along to the buckboard.

He caught Annette looking back over her shoulder. She even lifted her hand and waved to that idiot cowpoke. "I'll see you another time, Mr. Michaels."

Michaels was at their side then, dogging along beside them like a hungry calf. "I'd be obliged if you'd call me Gabe, Miss Talbot."

"I'd like—"

"We've gotta get on the trail." Walker cut off the chitchat and swung Annette up onto the buckboard seat.

Annette looked back as if, given half a chance, she'd finish her courting right here and now. Then her eyes went past the cowpoke and focused on someone else.

Walker didn't go around like he might have. Instead he climbed up beside her, pushed her on over, grabbed the reins, threw off the brake, and slapped leather on his horses' broad backs.

He yelled to get the horses moving and left Michaels in a whirl of snow and dust. He glanced back in the direction Annette was staring and saw a stranger talking with that lawyer, Sikes, who'd been on the stagecoach.

With a snort, Walker wondered if Annette was sparking every man in town. Walker reached back and pulled the buffalo robe forward and wrapped it snugly around Annette, tempted to throw it over her head just so more men couldn't see her and take to chasin' after her.

As they drove out of town, Walker fumed about the men clustering around Annette when she was obviously not up to any courting. Then he remembered how she'd let him support her. She allowed him to hoist her up to the high seat of the buckboard. It was all wrong.

Annette didn't obey him worth a hoot. How sick was she really?

"Are you sure you can sit up? Would you rather lie down in the wagon bed?"

"No, thank you. I'm f–f–fine." Her voice broke. She kept her head down as if she'd lost all the muscles in her neck.

"You don't sound fine. You sound like you're about to faint."

A sniffle was her only response.

Tears. *No, no, please, anything but tears.*

Walker's throat threatened to swell shut in panic. He briefly considered tossing himself off the buckboard. If he did it just right, maybe the wheels would roll over his head. He could not *stand* tears.

Did Annette know that? Was this deliberate?

Priscilla had known. She'd gotten her way too many times with tears. In fact, she'd almost gotten a jump on their wedding vows more than once. She'd cry over some little nothing. Then she'd beg him to hold her.

He'd hold her gladly. And he'd soothe her and promise her anything in a desperate effort to stop the tears. They'd wind up in each other's arms in ways improper for an unmarried couple, even an engaged couple.

Walker looked back on those false tears and hated himself for being stupid. He'd believed *his* control had kept Priscilla untouched for their wedding night. He'd taken her willingness as proof Priscilla loved him and was swept away. It had made him feel manly and honorable and wise to be the one maintaining their purity.

It should have made him feel like a fool.

Now Annette's tears brought up that same wild urge to do anything to stop the crying. But he refused to be a fool again.

"You either get in the back of this wagon and rest or quit your cryin'." Walker turned to her, forcing himself to be strong when he wanted to beg. "I can't abide a woman's tears, and I'm not puttin' up with 'em."

Annette dug through the buffalo robe and produced a kerchief from somewhere. She wiped her eyes and blew her nose in a very unladylike way, then lifted her chin. "I apologize. I am not normally a crying woman."

Walker snorted. "All women are *crying* women." Honesty forced him to add, " 'Cept my ma. She's never been given to the waterworks the rest of your kind seem bent on showering men with."

"I do *not* shower men with tears." She sounded horrified.

Well, women could pretend up a storm when it suited them.

"Seems like you've been on the verge of cryin' most every time I've seen you."

"Well. . .I'll admit it's been a trying few days." She glanced at him. Her smoky blue eyes were drenched, her lashes wet and shining with tears, her nose shiny as a new penny. Her lips were pink, swollen, glistening, pouty, and pretty. So pretty.

She needed help. She needed a hero. She needed him.

"That's the only time it counts!" He slammed a fist on his knee and tore his eyes away from the heart-softening temptation of that vulnerable face and those trembling lips.

She jumped.

"You think you get credit for not cryin' when things are going good?" Walker pretty much shouted that last bit at her. Calming himself as befitted the head of a household—and before he set her off crying again—he continued, "When everything's hunky-dory, not crying is nothing to be proud of."

Her jaw tightened. Her eyes narrowed. The hand holding her kerchief clenched into a fist.

Good, she was mad. He'd take that any day over tears.

"*Excuse* me."

Yep, he'd made her mad all right.

She about peeled his skin with those two words. And she wasn't done.

"You're right of *course*, Elijah. My life up until now has been nothing but *leisure* and *wealth*, so I wouldn't know *how* I'd react in a crisis." Her voice got sharper with each word.

Walker was afraid she was honing her voice into a weapon with plans to gut him. Still. . .way better'n tears.

"Except for my *mother dying* when I was young, I've never spent a bad day in my life. Oh, there was my *father* sending me away, a thousand miles or more to *school*. That didn't bother me, so it's no test of whether I'm a crier or not. There were my years in a school surrounded by *strangers*. I was fine with that."

Walker couldn't imagine much that was lonelier.

"There was the fact that my father barely paid the tuition, leaving me not a cent of spending money in a school mostly populated by *rich* girls who turned up their noses at my worn dresses. In fact, they gave me their hand-me-downs, snickering and sneering at me all the while, but I took their teasing to mean they *liked me*. Since I had to wear those clothes or go about in nothing, I brushed off their *bits of high spirits*."

Walker figured he'd've driven a fist through the face of the first person who sneered and been tossed out of school. But that's not the same as crying.

"Being the only student who received no *letters*, no *visits*, no *birthday gifts*, no *Christmas presents* and was never allowed to go *home*, not even in the *summer*, wasn't the *least bit* upsetting."

Walker was halfway to crying himself from the sound of Annette's life. "Now, I didn't mean to—"

"You're *right*, Elijah." The bite in her voice told him he was wrong, wrong, wrong. "I wouldn't know if I'm given to tears because my life has been a twenty-year-long stroll through a field of sweet-scented petunias. I stand corrected." She sounded calm. Her voice dripped with sarcasm, but it was a low, steady voice. Not a word of it was shouted.

Until—*"No doubt I'm the biggest crybaby who ever lived!"*

"I'm sorry." Preparing to duck if she threw a punch, Walker kept an eye on her while he hurried the horses along. He needed to get something solid between him and Annette. A human shield.

His ma would do nicely.

"I'm sorry, okay." Honesty forced him to admit he didn't sound all that sorry. "I've just had all I can take of crying women, that's all. You

don't deserve what I said. I'm just real touchy around tears."

That diverted her from both tears and anger. "I thought you said your mother never cries."

Walker made a mental note to talk about his ma and nothing but his ma.

"She seems so steady and strong. I'm surprised, but I suppose—"

"Not Ma. I already said Ma don't cry."

"Well, I've never seen another woman anywhere near you. So how do you know anything about the topic?"

He roared, "Priscilla cried all the time!" Then he snapped his mouth shut. What in the world had possessed him to let her name cross his lips? And in front of the second-cryingest woman he'd ever known.

Maybe she'd let it pass. Maybe she had more yelling to do at him. Maybe she'd just settle in and cry the rest of the way home.

"Who's Priscilla?"

Maybe Walker would rope a Wyoming blizzard, break it to the saddle, and ride it in next spring's roundup. "No one."

"*Elijah Walker*, you're not going to compare me to some woman, with that sound of contempt in your voice, and then not tell me who she is. I won't *stand* for it."

Well, at least she wasn't crying anymore. "I prefer yelling to sobbing, but couldn't you find a medium and just talk normal?"

*Or better yet, shut up and look at the scenery.*

Walker was an idiot about women, but he knew better than to say that out loud.

"I believe I've just been reminded of something pitifully sad." Annette sniffled and dabbed at her nose. "Why, I believe I feel like weeping the whole ride home."

It was all as fake as it could be. She wasn't pretending not to pretend. But considering how Priscilla had conjured tears, he didn't trust Annette to not dig up salt and water to spare and set her eyes to leaking.

"I was engaged to her."

"*Was?*" Not a trace of crying in her voice.

*Thank You, God.*

Walker decided it wouldn't do Annette any harm to know he was onto the wiles of a woman. "Yes, *was.*" Walker couldn't hold back the anger. "She killed my *pa*! I had her thrown in prison."

Why had he said that?

Dead silence stretched between them, broken only by the horses' softly clopping hooves and the creaking wheels and the jingle of the traces.

Walker had only recently gone back to praying, and then not much for himself. But right now, he begged God with every ounce of his strength for the silence to last.

"Walker, what happened?" Annette let loose of her hankie and got her arm out of the buffalo robe far enough to grab his forearm. "Tell me."

It was only grudgingly that Walker didn't take back his earlier thanks to God, way back when he'd been grateful for silence. He sure wasn't giving any more. "No. I won't tell you. It's enough that you know my foolishness over a woman's wiles cost me my pa's—" His voice broke. Horror swarmed up his spine like he was being attacked by locusts. He was not about to cry. Even when they'd buried his pa he'd never shed a tear. He'd been too busy plotting revenge. He squared his shoulders and dug deep for that anger now.

He found it easily.

"I've learned my lesson and I won't soon forget it. Priscilla's in prison, and it doesn't come within a Rocky Mountain mile of making up for what she did to my family. I deserve to be in there with her just for being such a *gullible fool* as to believe a woman isn't up to something when she cries. Now, just sit quiet. If you have to cry, so be it. But it won't get you anything from me, so you can give up on that right now."

He'd been looking forward while he talked, but now he turned and glared at her.

She was opening and closing her mouth like a drowning fish.

Speechless.

A woman speechless.

He decided to enjoy it for whatever brief parcel of time it lasted and slapped the reins on the broad backs of his team.

He focused so completely on hurrying home he couldn't say later if she cried or not.

But he knew for dead certain he didn't.

# SIXTEEN

Annie made dead certain she didn't shed a single tear for the rest of the ride home.

And she vowed she would never cry again.

Not when poor Elijah carried around such pain without shedding a tear.

Just from his few words, Annie knew guilt was eating at him like a cancer. She felt sick for what he and Ruby had gone through. And then she remembered Claude Leveque and came within an eyelash of crying her heart out.

The fear whipped like a cyclone through her heart until her soul cried out to the Lord.

*Lord, lift me up.*

*"I did."*

Annie jumped. She looked sideways at Elijah, but his eyes were riveted on his well-behaved team as if they had tried to make a break for it—straight over a cliff—ten times since they'd begun this wretched ride home.

He certainly hadn't spoken those words—*"I did."*

The voice wasn't Elijah's. But it was so clear. . .as if someone sat on the seat beside her. Or even sat *inside* her somehow. Those two words, *"I did,"* were so at odds with the thoughts that were twisting around

146

inside her that they couldn't have come from her own mind.

She sat up straight when she realized the truth.

God.

*"I did."* He had already met her needs to a miraculous degree.

Here she sat, bouncing along on Elijah's buckboard, as alive as could be despite what she'd gone through.

Protected.

She glanced at Elijah. A cranky protector without a doubt, but she knew he'd keep her safe or die trying.

She had nearly left this earth yesterday, but God had—her heart soared—God had lifted her up.

She remembered at that moment the glorious glimpse she'd been given of heaven. She whispered to herself, " 'For to me to live is Christ, and to die is gain.' "

A new, deeper love for God washed through her soul like hot rain. Nothing could touch her inside—in her soul—where it really counted.

*"I did."* Such a simple message. A pure and simple reminder from God her Father.

The dread vanished, her riotous thoughts calmed.

Claude was here. Claude had terrible plans for her. It was all true and terrifying. But her heart lifted as surely as God's hand had lifted her up out of the raging waters.

Inwardly she prayed, *Thank You, Father in heaven. Help me to live as You would have me live and let go of my worry.*

She was so deeply moved by that sacred experience that she almost cried.

Then she remembered her prickly companion and regained her composure. No. No more tears. How dare she cry in the face of a miracle? God had lifted her up.

And just this moment He'd *reminded* her of that.

No longer would Elijah have to worry about her tears. That courage she seemed to always be scrambling for was in her grasp now. God had protected her. God had spoken to her.

She inhaled, knowing an almost perfect bliss that she had a concrete moment of communion with God.

Claude's face, cruel and ugly, floated before her. He wanted her back. She knew the value of her singing all too well. He would already be spreading his poison about her in town.

Well, fine. Ranger Bluff might well be closed to her now. It mattered not because she had no intention of going back. God had swept her to the Walker ranch. Ruby seemed inclined to let her stay forever. Perhaps she just would.

That wasn't the same thing as living boldly for God, but it seemed harmless enough. She could live boldly at the ranch.

Except she probably shouldn't stay. Ruby was there, so it was perfectly proper, but the basic truth was she was an interloper. A beggar.

She decided to work as hard as she knew how while she was at the Walker ranch. Surely that made her more of an employee than a beggar. And she'd try to find someplace else to go.

Perhaps a teaching position would come open. Not in Ranger Bluff, if Claude did his work poisoning her reputation. But if not here, then where? How would she find a job far away? What if the accusations from the Leveques followed her? She'd have to go somewhere no one knew her. California perhaps. She'd write a letter to inquire as soon as she found a way to earn money for paper and a stamp. . .and figured out where to write.

And she'd speak as little to Elijah as possible, since he was obviously off women forever, thanks to that horrid Priscilla.

And never, never, ever again would she cry.

Satisfied with her plan, she settled in to ride quietly the rest of the way home.

At least Elijah wouldn't have to worry about her wanting to go out and about. She'd go back to his ranch and stay there until she found a way to leave, then she'd go somewhere far away and live bravely for the Lord there.

Where she could be sure to never run into anyone who knew her.

"Are you sure she knew it was me?" Claude sat shuffling cards, keeping his hands limber. Except he felt the now-familiar ache in his joints and hated it. He couldn't deal off the bottom of the deck with half his former skill—couldn't slip a card out of his sleeve nearly as slick.

But the songbird was alive. Everything was looking up.

"I was watching close." Blanche polished the counter that ran along the back of their decrepit new shop. She stood up there to sing at night. "I can't believe she survived that fall. We've still got a chance of taking her."

Claude felt his mouth watering to know he could still get his hands on pretty Annette Talbot. He looked with distaste at the grubby building. "I wonder how long this dump has been sitting empty?" It didn't matter. It was theirs now. Until they earned enough to leave town. They never stayed anywhere long. But maybe, with Annette's talent, he could set up permanently in San Francisco. Buy a classy place, get some roulette wheels, and hire dealers and barmaids. He glanced at his wife, working so hard to clean up this dump. "We'll be open tonight, so be ready for the show. Nothing bawdy."

"I've already got it figured out." Blanche looked up from her scrubbing. Her hair dangling loose, dirt on her face, wrinkles around her eyes. . .she was becoming uglier every day. "Tonight I'll sing patriotic songs, old spirituals, tunes to offend no one."

With a low, cruel laugh, Claude dealt the cards, cutting in a card off the bottom of the deck, another tucked up his sleeve. He'd lost some of his deftness, but he was still pretty good. "The money's in something a bit naughtier, girl."

"I know." Blanche's eyes shone with greed. "But not the first night. Nor maybe the second. We'll see what the town standards are. See if they're easily offended."

"Some of 'em will be. And some of 'em'll *enjoy* being offended. I'll see if anyone's interested in stepping into the back room for a few hands of cards. Nothing big. I'll just win enough to afford a bottle or two of whiskey. Then as the bottles empty, I'll refill them with rotgut."

"I've already got a batch brewing. The general store gave me credit."

Claude laughed. "Trusting folks make our lives a lot easier. We'll find who has a thirst for liquor, a fixation for cards, an eye for a skirt kicked too high, and we'll make sure they know we can provide that. Then we'll be in business."

"Our little Annette looked scared enough at the sight of you. She won't be back to town anytime soon."

"Good. I've already let a few things slip. If I did it right—and I did—townsfolk ought to put it together to figure out the pretty angel has soiled wings."

"And when our chance comes to take her, no one will object."

"Object?" Claude sneered. "They'll hand her over to us. They'll be on our side. Good folks have no wish to consort with a thief and a liar like our pretty songbird."

Distracted by visions of making that foolish girl sorry she'd ever defied them, Claude's cards slewed sideways and sprayed across the table. He'd fumbled them like a schoolboy. He glanced up, glad to see Blanche hadn't noticed.

She began singing quietly, then louder, warming up her rusty pipes. She hit a sour note and Claude flinched. Blanche's day was done.

As he stacked the cards and began shuffling again, he hated having to admit it, but his day was done, too.

He had to get that songbird back in his cage.

# SEVENTEEN

Y ou're a wonderful cook, Annie." Ruby wiped her hands on her apron as she stood at Annie's left elbow and watched the top crust on the apple pie settle in place.

Annie's heart ached with a kind of love so old she couldn't identify it. But it reminded her of her mother. She'd done a lot of baking with her mother before she'd been sent away to St. Louis. And of course the boarding school had lessons in womanly skills. But there was no denying Annie was not a dab hand at piecrust. "Thank you." Once the crust was centered, she dared to look away from the delicate work and grin at Ruby. "But it's mainly your doing and you know it."

The two of them shared a smile.

"We worked together, how about that?" Ruby asked.

The scent of cinnamon and apples lifted Annie's heart, and the pretty pie almost ready for the oven gave her a wonderful sense of accomplishment. Annie had done the work, but Ruby had talked her through every step or it would never have gotten done so nicely. Nodding, Annie finished crimping the edges of the apple pie just the way Ruby had shown her.

Then Ruby swung open the door to the heavy stove. "The pumpkin looks done. Let's get it out to make room for the apple."

Annie picked up a towel to protect her hands, ducked under the blast of hot air from the baking chamber, and carefully pulled out the steaming pie. The top had risen and cracked. Only the slightest bit of brown touched the bright orange of the pie. The luscious aroma of rich nutmeg and cream blended with the generously sweetened pumpkin.

Annie rested the pie on the kitchen table then went to the apple. She paused as Ruby scooped a few tablespoons of sugar into her hand and sprinkled the top crust with glistening white sugar. When she stepped back, Annie lifted the pie and slid it with a scratch of metal on metal into the burning hot baking chamber.

"It'll need to bake for an hour or so." Ruby gave a little huff of satisfaction. "You're exhausted, girl. Go on to bed. We'll be up early tomorrow."

"Ruby, I shouldn't be putting you out of your room like I am." Annie had said this several times since she had returned from Ranger Bluff and found Ruby had moved all her things upstairs and declared the single downstairs bedroom to be Annie's.

"Now girl, you know it's the only proper place for you."

"With you here, it's fine for me to stay upstairs in the smaller room. I shouldn't be taking over such a grand place while you're crammed into that small bedroom."

"It's not the proper way of things to have you upstairs so close to Eli."

"Ruby, honestly, do you think I'd—we'd—that is—" Annie's cheeks heated up and she couldn't say more.

"I don't think a single improper thing would happen." Ruby rested one of her kind, work-callused hands on Annie's shoulder. "I know you're a good girl, and I trust my boy right down to the ground. But it's a bad appearance, and I won't have a single word said against you because you're staying here. I intend to be very careful to see your reputation isn't sullied. You'll take my room and that's that."

Wanting to protest, Annie knew on her best day she'd lose a battle of wills with Ruby. And today was nowhere near her best day. She was exhausted, aching in every joint, and she'd had enough shocks to send

her hiding under the covers for the rest of her days.

She'd used up more of her strength going to town than was wise. Elijah really had been right—and didn't that pinch to admit.

She should have stayed home. Then she wouldn't have seen Claude. She wouldn't have remembered what caused her fall. And she wouldn't be twisted up inside with this sick fear. But considering she now remembered Leveque's horrible threats at her father's cabin, it was for the best that she knew the danger that lay close at hand.

"Did you check the henhouse before you came in, Eli?" Ruby looked at her son.

Annie's eyes followed Ruby's, and she saw Elijah, fast asleep in the rocking chair in front of the fireplace. Annie thought he looked incredibly handsome in the firelight. The crackling flames cast a reddish glow to his brown hair. His eyelashes were so long she could see them lying on his cheeks from across the room. A soft snore told her he was deeply asleep. With a fond smile for the overworked man, Annie said, "I'll go, Ruby. Don't disturb him."

"And I suppose I'll send an exhausted young woman out on a cold, dark night to search for eggs, when she doesn't even know where the chicken coop is." Ruby turned and snatched her coat off a peg.

"If I go, you get to stay warm and my poor boy gets to sleep." Ruby looked back as she shrugged into her buffalo skin coat. "He was up with the sun today."

"Ruby, nonsense. You don't have to—"

"It will take only a few minutes." Ruby reached for the door, moving so briskly Annie knew it would take something big to stop the sweet woman.

But it struck Annie as utterly wrong for Ruby to go out while two much younger people stayed inside. "But I'd be glad to—"

"I gathered them this morning." Ruby talked over top of Annie. "But if there was a late layer, the egg will be frozen and ruined by morning. We'll need every egg for tomorrow's Thanksgiving dinner, so I'll go check on them quick."

"Ruby, for heaven's sake." Annie stepped up to where the coat Ruby had loaned her hung.

"Don't even ask." Ruby opened the door. "You'll have me thinking I'm an old woman if you say I'm not up to fetching a few eggs. It's not that cold and I'm not sending you outside again tonight. You need to rest even more than Eli." She went out, and considering she wanted Elijah to stay asleep, Annie thought the woman slammed the door extremely loud.

The blast of cold and the noise jerked him awake instantly. "What's going on?" He was on his feet, looking around as if they were under attack and he only needed to figure out which way to run to put himself between Annie and danger.

Yes, she knew he hadn't quite registered that his mother was gone and was no doubt thinking his protective thoughts about Ruby. He would protect Annie, too. It was a fact that settled on her heart with surprising sharpness and a sweetness that rivaled the finest apple pie.

"Your ma ran out to the chicken coop for a second. She'll be right back."

Elijah turned, wiped his hands across his face, and came more fully awake. "Oh, okay. Why didn't she send me if she had chores outside?"

Annie smiled. "Because you were asleep. Go on up to bed." She waved her hand at the cabin stairs that led to a second floor holding three bedrooms. "I'll watch over the pies until your mother comes back."

Elijah sniffed the air and was suddenly fully awake. Annie knew it by the way his eyes sharpened and focused on the pie that sat, still steaming, on the kitchen table. He turned to it as if the steam curling out of the pie was a lasso, tossed over his head and pulling him in. He strode across the good-sized main room of the house straight toward tomorrow's dessert, sniffing with exaggerated noise, his face stretching into a delighted smile.

Annie launched herself between Elijah and that pie. He reached around her, and she slapped his hand as if he were a naughty schoolboy.

He straightened and glared. "What?"

"The pie is for Thanksgiving."

"I'm feeling pretty thankful for it right now. I just want a taste of crust. Please." His voice was half coaxing, half whining like a child. But the glint in his eyes told Annie he was teasing her.

"Why, Elijah Walker, shame on you." She decided to play along, wondering when she'd last had fun teasing someone like this. Possibly never. Certainly never with a man. "You have the look of someone who might try and sneak a bite if I so much as turn my back." Annie rested her hands on her waist and gave him a scolding glare, fighting to control a smile with only limited success.

"Miss Talbot, you can trust me." He might as well have shouted that he was lying, from the insincere tone of his voice. The man was determined to have a bit of that pie.

"Go on with you." Annie shooed him away with waving fingertips. "In your mother's absence, I have become the guardian of this pie and I will not shirk my duty. I'm not afraid to smack your fingers. She'll thank me for it, I assure you."

Elijah shrugged and looked wounded. "Fine, then." He turned his back.

Annie smiled at his nonsense as she reached for the towel that had been left lying on the table. Out of the corner of her eye, she caught a quick movement and whirled around. She blocked Elijah just in time as he darted for the pie. He bumped into her hard enough to send her back against the table. She stumbled and for a moment thought she might well fall straight backward into the dessert.

Elijah caught her at the waist and kept her from disaster. He pulled her away from the table. "You almost ended up sitting in that pie. Then it would have been ruined with me not having so much as a sliver." Elijah's eyes took on a conspiratorial gleam. "C'mon, let's team up. You want a taste as badly as I do." Elijah looked over her shoulder to peak at the pie. "There's a broken spot on the crust. I'll share it with you."

Annie laughed, and Elijah's smile widened until he joined in with the merriment.

He leaned a bit closer, his hands still holding her. "I won't tell Ma." His voice was a ridiculously loud whisper. "If you promise not to either." Then their eyes caught, grinning at their nonsense, joined together in something fun and secret and silly. Then the joining turned into something else. Something warm. Something wonderful.

The smile faded from Elijah's face.

Annie felt her own die away.

"I heard you singing the other day," Elijah whispered. "When I came to your pa's ranch."

"I know."

"You have the most beautiful voice." His hands slid from her waist to her back, and his arms tightened. "It was like listening to an angel straight from heaven."

"Thank you, Elijah." His eyes pulled at her, drawing her more strongly than the delicious scent of a beautifully baked pie.

"Why don't you sing more, Annette?" He'd pulled her against him. "I love to hear you sing." He spoke so softly it was good that he was lowering his head so she could hear.

"I'd love to sing for you." Annie lifted her face.

His lips brushed hers.

The door swung open.

Elijah jumped away as if he'd grabbed a red-hot pie pan straight out of the oven, although his expression was one of horror more than pain. But the pain was there.

In the split second before he wiped it away, Annie remembered the way he'd spoken of Priscilla. She remembered his desire to protect his heart. More than embarrassment, more than her confusing reaction to Elijah, she was upset by knowing she'd become part of that pain. In fact, she'd made it worse.

Elijah looked at his mother.

Ruby slid a speculative glance between Annie and Elijah, and there was no way to deny the savvy woman had taken in the whole situation instantly.

"Uh. . .good night." Elijah turned and rushed up the stairs as if the door had swung open and admitted a pack of starving wolves rather than one elderly woman.

Only if it were wolves, he'd have stayed and put himself between Annie and danger. As it was, he'd left her completely alone with Ruby, who now had plenty of time to focus strictly on Annie.

The sweet woman had a very strange, slightly wolfish expression on her deeply lined face. Annie could only assume Ruby was annoyed that a woman, a charity case, brought into the Walker home on sufferance, had misbehaved nearly the first instant Ruby's back was turned.

Annie's cheeks were so hot with embarrassment they could have finished baking the pie on her head.

"Go on to bed, Annie." Ruby moved to the basket of eggs on the kitchen counter and added two more.

Ruby wasn't going to scold? Demand an explanation? Question Annie's honor?

Annie couldn't quite believe it, but she was too embarrassed to ask why she was given this reprieve. She set the towel down, and it stuck to her fingers. She looked and saw she'd twisted it until she'd practically tied herself up. She freed her finger and bolted, nearly as fast as Elijah.

Quickly and quietly changing into her nightgown, provided by the Walker family, she slipped into her bed, provided by the Walker family, pulled up the soft, heavy blankets, provided by the Walker family, and tried to go to sleep in the warm room, provided by the Walker family.

Once her head was on the pillow, she turned to prayer.

*God, I promised to live boldly for You once I got to the West.*

Annie knew she was a coward. Her obedience, combined with an unwillingness to confront trouble had led her to disaster.

*Now here I am, Lord. In the West. I know I was hoping to have Father stand by my side. . .or better yet in front of me. Instead I've made the Walkers take responsibility for me. I've betrayed my vow to be strong for You, heavenly Father. Forgive me. I know I need to leave.*

If her earthly father was dead, or even permanently gone, then

Annie had no place here in Ranger Bluff. Then she thought of her place in Elijah's arms. Her mind stirred with embarrassment at being caught. . .kissing? Kissing Elijah Walker? What had come over her? It was humiliating to be caught in such a situation.

And humiliation wasn't all she felt. Not even close.

She pulled the covers over her head as if that would block the mental image.

Elijah had the excuse that he was half asleep. She'd stumbled and he'd had to rescue her. God had bestowed in Elijah a heroic reflex he couldn't control.

But she had no excuses. She was certainly no hero, and she proved that on a daily basis.

*Dear God, when I asked for crosses to bear, I never dreamed I'd be dropping them left and right. Maybe You need to only give me unbreakable burdens for the next little while, until I get better at this.*

Elijah's warm eyes and gentle lips reminded Annie too clearly of the pain that had accompanied his embarrassment.

Suddenly she realized that if she wasn't careful, she could drop and break the most fragile cross of all. . .

Elijah's heart.

And she might drop hers and shatter it right along with his.

# EIGHTEEN

Annette Talbot was a pain in the neck.

Walker stormed through his morning chores. He growled at the hands when they wished him a happy Thanksgiving.

He'd grabbed half a loaf of bread on his way outdoors, rising long before dawn to dodge his ma. . .and Annie and didn't go in at all for breakfast. The loaf was gone and he was starving and he'd wandered too close to the house once, about an hour ago, and smelled the turkey roasting. His ma was an uncommonly fine cook.

Now the morning was gone and so were his excuses.

Thanksgiving.

*God, what am I supposed to be thankful for, huh?*

Good health. A prosperous ranch. Honest, hardworking cowhands. Enough snow to fill the mountain gaps and supply the springs in the summer. A healthy spring crop of calves that would winter well and bring a good price. Priscilla locked up tight and for a good long time.

His ma not yelling when she walked in on her son. . .

Kissing their guest. . .

When Ma left them alone for about five minutes.

Oh, he could think of things to be thankful for. Rather than go in, Walker dabbed a loop over one of the saddle horses in the corral nearest the barn.

None of the things on his "thankful list" overshadowed the thing he had to be *un*thankful for.

Stealing a kiss from Annette.

She wasn't a woman with many choices, and Walker had put her in a terrible position. She had nowhere else to go. Every time Walker thought of that, he wondered if she might put up with unwanted advances for fear she'd be cast out in the snow to starve and freeze and die.

Cross-tying the horse inside the barn, in a pen, Walker tried to remember how she'd acted, what she'd said. Had she been interested in him. . .or just well and truly trapped? It made him crazy to think of such a thing, which is exactly why he should never have kissed her.

The horse snorted and Walker realized he'd been standing there, staring into space, remembering details, every move and sound and scent. He shook his head and went to get the hoof-trimming tools.

It wasn't proper. He'd had no right to give in to the intense curiosity about how Annette would feel in his arms and how she'd taste.

Now he knew and he remembered how perfectly she fit in his arms. She'd tasted like a dream come true.

And that brought him to the thing he was most unthankful for in the whole world. He wanted to hold her again. And trying to remember how she'd acted was just his wanting to think, over and over, about that sweet moment when he'd held her in his arms.

Women got a man stirred up. They turned a perfectly normal man into a fool. . .which reminded him that Annette might not be such a fragile, beautiful, innocent girl. Priscilla had surely given that same impression.

Walker felt his spine growing back as he lifted the horse's front right hoof between his legs, faced toward the horse's hind end, and began running his rasp over it with a dull grating sound. He leaned his shoulder into the calm animal to keep him in place while he considered what he knew about Annie.

He knew for a fact she was a liar. Right this second he couldn't remember exactly what she'd lied about, but she had. All women did except his ma, and right now he didn't overly trust her. What that look

had been on his ma's face, he couldn't guess, but he was sorely afraid Ruby approved of Annette, when she'd barely tolerated Priscilla.

Now what had Annette done to deserve that?

Probably told a bunch of lies. Which meant she was probably an even better liar than Priscilla.

And even if he couldn't quite pin down Annette's lies, he knew for a fact she was a full-blown idiot. She'd pretty much only survived this long through direct, miraculous intervention from God. A woman shouldn't need a miracle a day to stay alive. Not even God had time for that nonsense. A person needed some survival skills, and Annette had none.

Walker finished with the horse's hoof and ducked under its neck to start on the other front foot.

The old beast whickered at him, shifted his feet, and jerked on the crosstie, jingling the metal in his halter.

Walker noticed the horse's impatience, but since Walker needed to stay out of the house, the horse was just going to have to put up with the attention. While he rasped away, he thought of Annette's soft lips, and eyes that spoke of loss and fear and need. Such pretty eyes. So soft and light blue and unusual. As if God had created her with an eye toward beauty.

But her physical beauty didn't begin to touch the sound of her singing voice. Where did a little sprite of a thing like Annette Talbot, with that old he-goat of a father, come up with that amazing voice?

Walker had to hear it again. He heard it in his sleep last night, what little sleep he got, and it had jerked him awake. He lay there listening, thinking maybe Annie was singing down in her room. Finally he had to admit he dreamed it.

He got lost in that dream right now, standing up, wide awake, and pondered on how he could coax another song out of Annette. *Just ask. Ask nicely. Ask real nicely.*

Walker finished the hoof and turned to grip a hind leg. The horse he was tending jerked Walker out of his daydream by kicking him in the backside. Probably a good thing, because from the way his mind was traveling, Walker knew Annette wasn't the only idiot on the ranch.

He was one, too.

He was proving it right now because he was driving himself halfway to death with work—a good trick because there wasn't much to be done—when suddenly his unruly thoughts began to speculate on just how stupid the children he and Annie would have might turn out to be.

He pondered that at length.

With undue interest in finding out for sure by getting married and having a few, he'd caught himself thinking those fool thoughts about five times already this morning. Or ten.

Or maybe ten an hour.

He straightened from the horse and considered tossing himself into the Medicine Bow. Maybe the raging current and chunks of ice would clear his head.

Ma stuck her head out the door and shouted, "Eli, for heaven's sake, where are you? Dinner's ready!"

He had to give up and go in there. He let the poor horse free, who snorted at him and trotted off on its perfectly fine hooves. Walker hung his file on a hook and admitted he had no excuses left.

On a normal day, he could have ridden up into the mountains and come home after bedtime, half dead from cold and exhaustion. Or maybe he'd have stayed a day. . .or two. Or a week.

Maybe get back in time for Christmas.

He'd have figured out some excuse, something he needed to check on. But it was Thanksgiving. No one was going to believe that today he needed to flush the high-up hills for a stray maverick and brand him with a running iron.

He couldn't even convince himself that was a chore that needed doing without delay.

Trudging toward the house, Walker wished he'd given that river dunking more serious consideration.

❧

Annie had hoped against hope Elijah would find some pressing chore

to do. . .high up in the mountains. . .that kept him busy all day. . .or for a week. . .or until Christmas. . .or spring.

Surely by then she could get her embarrassment under control. Maybe she could volunteer for such a chore in the mountains.

That would be better. Elijah could stay here and she could hunt for strays all the way to the Montana border.

It was his house after all. He shouldn't have to go away.

She heard him pounding up the back steps as if he couldn't wait to eat.

The idiot.

She could barely keep from running to her room as the door swung open. And here he came anxious for a meal. Well, all that proved to her was that kissing her had been some nasty manly whim that meant nothing to him. And that made her feel like she was an idiot, too.

Which she was.

The proof of that? She'd spent the morning with a recurring day-dream of his kissing her again. In fact she was wondering that right now, as he stepped inside and took up more than his share of the cabin.

Just how stupid would their children be, anyway? Six of them, stair steps—four big brothers with brown hair and two little sisters, blond like her, who loved to sing and bake pies with their grandma Ruby.

Annie had a wild impulse to bang her head against the wall to stop the images of their children.

And she would have been able to handle all of that, if it weren't for the pain she'd seen in Elijah's eyes and knowing she caused that pain.

Ruby had the table set and the turkey centered, beautifully brown, a sharp knife at the ready for Elijah to do the honors of carving.

"It smells great in here, Ma." Elijah headed for the washbasin.

Annie wondered if he'd looked at her, but she couldn't tell without looking at him and she forced herself not to. Well, maybe one peek, and he wasn't looking. The big, dumb jerk.

A plate of four bowl-shaped baked squash steamed beside the turkey. The dark green squash with their vibrant orange flesh swam with brown sugar and butter in the place left empty by the scooped-away seeds. There was a bowl of potatoes whipped smooth and dripping with butter.

Ruby had produced a carefully stored set of beautiful clear glass dishes. A large oval plate for soft dinner rolls took the place of Ruby's usual loaf of bread. There was a smaller round plate for a ball of butter and a tiny bowl no bigger than Annie's cupped hands which Ruby filled with quivering red currant jelly. The pies stood ready on one end of the table. Glasses of milk sat at each place, with a pitcher handy for refills. The table looked festive and bountiful. The smells were heavenly.

"Eli, take the head of the table. Annie, sit across from me. I'd like to be on the side nearest the counter and cupboards if I need to fetch anything."

Annie hadn't been here long, but she already had an assigned seat. Ruby was mainly talking to shoo Annie to the table. So Annie sat down, her back to the wall, nearly squirming with embarrassment.

He'd yet to speak to her, not so much as a hello. Fine with her. She prayed silently that the man would never speak to her again.

Ruby reached her hand across the table, sliding her arm between the turkey platter and the pies. Smiling, she wiggled her fingers to let Annie know she wanted to hold hands.

Annie caught Ruby's right hand. Then Elijah took Ruby's other hand. There was a moment of silence that began to stretch awkwardly. Finally, as if he were being prodded by spurs, Elijah raised his hand to Annie's and she grabbed hold, wishing the floor would swallow her up. Their hands entwined and rested on the corner of the table that separated them.

"Will you pray, Eli?" Ruby smiled as if she'd just gotten word that she'd inherited a gold mine.

"That was always Pa's place, to pray. I'd like for you to do it, Ma."

Shaking her head and squeezing Elijah's hand, Ruby said, "No, you're the head of the house, son. It's right and proper for you to lead us in prayer."

"Well, if you don't mind, I'd just as soon not do it." Elijah sounded mule stubborn. "I've got no liking for taking Pa's place. I don't feel right about it. And yesterday, when I told you to mind me because I was head of the house, you said—"

"Now, Eli, don't start on that—"

Annie would have let them squabble all day if she hadn't been holding Elijah's hand. . .strong fingers that were gripping her hand tighter as he argued with his ma. His hard calluses almost scratched Annie's skin—almost. Instead, holding Elijah's hands felt warm and wonderful and like the safest place she'd ever been. "How about we sing a prayer?" Annie blurted it out to cut off the argument and bring the issue to a resolution. Anything to get away from Elijah's touch.

Elijah had avoided eye contact but now he turned to her. "I heard you singing out at your place. I'd like to hear more."

The only reason she knew he looked was because she finally looked at him. He'd seemed so kind at the cabin, when he'd caught her singing. But he hadn't complimented her then. Instead he'd gone to growling about her being out in the middle of nowhere alone. But last night he'd mentioned her singing right before he'd—

"You would?" Her heart went softer and warmer than the butter melted in the core of those steaming hot squash.

"Annette's got an uncommon beautiful voice, Ma." He turned to Ruby. "Have you heard her sing?"

"Why no, I haven't." Ruby looked at Annie with a surprised and pleased expression. "You haven't mentioned it before, son. I'd love to hear a song, Annie."

Elijah's grip tightened yet again and he gave her an encouraging nod.

"All right. Yes, I'd be pleased to sing. We had a favorite at the school I attended. We sang it every Thanksgiving, and many other times, too."

Annie began quietly, letting the words be a true prayer. "Come, ye thankful people, come, raise the song of harvest home; all is safely gathered in, ere the winter storms begin; God, our Maker, doth provide for our wants to be supplied; come to God's own temple, come, raise the song of harvest home."

There were three more verses, and Annie continued on. There was so much to be thankful for. She closed her eyes, praying her thanks to God for her survival on her trip here and in the river.

"All the world is God's own field, fruit unto His praise to yield; wheat and tares together sown, unto joy or sorrow grown; first the blade, and then the ear, then the full corn shall appear; Lord of harvest, grant that we wholesome grain and pure may be."

With her song, she gave soul-deep thanks for the bountiful meal, Ruby's generosity, and the warm family home she was now sheltered in.

"For the Lord our God shall come, and shall take His harvest home; from His field shall in that day all offenses purge away, give His angels charge at last in the fire the tares to cast, but the fruitful ears to store in His garner evermore."

Even though it hurt her heart, she couldn't help thanking God for Elijah's strong hand in hers. This meal, this day, this moment was the nicest Thanksgiving of her life, or at least since her mother had died. Considering the week she'd just had, she found it a bit of a miracle that her heart could be so full of thanks.

"Even so, Lord, quickly come, bring Thy final harvest home; gather Thou Thy people in, free from sorrow, free from sin, there, forever purified, in Thy presence to abide; come, with all Thine angels come, raise the glorious harvest home."

A shiver of delight raced up her spine to think of that final harvest home. She'd seen a glimpse of that in the river. She knew what awaited her in heaven now, and she could never fear the end of this life.

She finished her song and opened her eyes to look at Elijah.

He was watching her with something close to wonder on his face.

"That was beautiful, Annie, just beautiful." Ruby spoke barely above a whisper.

Elijah said nothing, but his grip on her hand remained and his eyes seemed bent on invading her heart. " 'Free from sorrow, free from

sin.' That's Pa now, isn't it, Ma?" He kept his grip on both Annie's and Ruby's hands but looked to his mother.

"We miss him." Ruby nodded. "But he was a man of faith, Eli. He's part of that glorious harvest, and he lives in heaven now. Free from sorrow."

"I can't imagine it." Elijah frowned. "When I think of Pa, all I see is him clinging to that branch, the roots giving out. I see his hand slipping through the loop on my rope and falling and bleeding to death in front of me. I couldn't do anything to stop it." Elijah's eyes fell shut.

"I'm so sorry you've got that memory to plague you, son. When Annie sang her song, I could picture him as he was when we were first married. That's how he is in heaven, Eli. He's feeling fit and healthy now. He can swing a scythe again and ride for long hours on the range." Ruby looked at Elijah. "You're the very image of him, son. I'd forgotten that until just now. You know, his health had failed in the last couple of years. That's why he couldn't hang on."

Shaking his head, Elijah kept his eyes closed. "I can't see it. I can't see anything but him dying and I couldn't save him. I should have been able to save him. I shouldn't have brought death to this house to begin with. I'm so sorry, Ma. I was such a fool over that woman."

Turning to Annie, Ruby smiled. "That's a gift you've given to me. I'll always treasure it. Thank you. I'm so thankful you're here."

Annie added another prayer to God, including yet one more thanks. Ruby had been blessed by her song. If only Elijah would be. She'd just learned more than she'd ever hoped about Elijah's father's death. He'd fallen due to some actions of Priscilla. Annie ached for the horrible thing Elijah had gone through and the scars it had left on his heart.

"God forgives you, and you *know* your pa would never want you to suffer like this over his death. He had a bad heart, Eli. He lived a good long life, but he was nearing the end. You can blame Priscilla all you want, but she has no power over life and death. It was your pa's time."

Elijah's chin dropped and his shoulders slumped as if the weight of the world rested square on his shoulders.

"This is a day for thanksgiving, not for pain or blame. Your pa would want you to be happy."

Elijah's only response was silence.

This was why he wanted no part of a crying woman. And this was why she could never let him kiss her again. The silence stretched and Annie became aware that the three of them still held hands. It wasn't her right to be a part of their family circle.

She thought of the gossip that Blanche and Claude would spread. Soon enough it would reach Elijah's ears. It would remind him vividly of the untrustworthy Priscilla. Elijah, and probably Ruby, too, would believe the lies. Annie could feel the pain already, before it had started. She needed to break from this circle. "I—I—" Words failed her.

When Annie spoke, she broke whatever held them all still. Elijah dropped her hand. Annie pulled free from Ruby, too. Ruby and Elijah still held fast to each other, as they should.

Ruby settled a worried look on her son. Ruby was kind, a true Christian, but she had to be worried about her son, so newly grieved by the actions of Priscilla, now casting eyes on another woman. A stranger.

"Cut the turkey, please, son."

Annie saw the two Walkers' hands cling a bit tighter then let loose. The movement made Annie feel like an interloper. She busied herself selecting a roll then began passing the dishes.

Elijah laid a generous slice of white meat on her plate.

The bulk of the talking was done by Ruby. Annie answered any questions politely and briefly. Elijah did the same.

The whole Thanksgiving celebration went very well considering she and Elijah never spoke to each other or looked at each other again.

# NINETEEN

Elijah had done his best not to speak to or look at that pesky Annette Talbot for running on three days now.

He could do it. He could keep this up for the rest of his life. He just had to concentrate on anything and everything except that pretty little woman with her soft blue eyes and that angelic voice that seemed bent on sneaking into his heart and staking a claim.

He could do it without any problem at all.

"I gotta talk to you about Miss Talbot, boss." Frank spoke just above a whisper and jerked his head toward a quiet corner of the snow-covered ranch yard.

Walker gritted his teeth to keep from shouting that he didn't want to hear a word about Annette.

Still, Walker followed along.

Frank had a white bandage peeking out from his Stetson. His coloring wasn't quite back to normal, but Frank insisted he'd work rather than lie in bed. No one had been able to stop him, and he seemed to get stronger, rather than be set back, so Walker let him work.

Walker furrowed his brow at Frank's serious expression. "What is it?"

"There's talk in town." Frank dropped his voice to a whisper and his eyes darted around.

Walker leaned toward Frank to catch his low voice. "Talk about what?"

"About Miss Talbot."

Walker jerked his head upright. "What?"

"Shh. . ." Frank looked around and made Walker aware he'd next thing to yelled.

"What kind of talk?" Walker felt his neck heating up with embarrassment. Had rumors started about Annette and him? Had he looked at Annette in an improper way while they were in town?

"Word is she's been. . .out and about. . .the last few years." Frank tugged on his gloves like a nervous tic. "And done things that—that make her. . . uh. . .well. . .make her no—no better'n she oughta be, you might say."

"Who said that?" Walker was furious on Annette's behalf.

"Gibby."

Frank was young and Walker resisted grabbing him by the throat based on that alone. "You and Gibby were gossiping about Annette?"

"I wouldn't do that." Frank's face fell and Walker knew he'd hurt the boy's feelings. "And neither would Gib. He told me because it upset him. He knew she sorta lied to him about rentin' that horse, but other'n that he thought she was a fine, decent young woman. And he never told no one about that sorta lie because it weren't really a lie, only she let Gib believe something that weren't true without really saying a single untrue thing. So, that's *not* a lie. That's just Gibby being his own self. And he only told you about that sorta lie, and he didn't think you'd spread trash around."

"Of course I wouldn't." Walker's embarrassment had firmly shifted to rage at the thought of gossip going around about Annette. Was it because she'd ridden all the way west alone? It was an outrageously improper act. Or because she'd gone out to her pa's ranch alone? That was more foolishness than improper, but foolishness might be enough to set tongues wagging.

Walker paused in his listing of all the things Annette had done that might have spurred folks to blacken her name. What exactly had prompted her to ride out here all the way from St. Louis alone, penniless,

with no father waiting for her? And come to that, she seemed a might old to be coming straight home from her school days. She'd said she was twenty, so she hadn't come straight home. She'd been doing something for a couple of years at least. Had she spent those years being—being—Walker's stomach twisted. "Being no better'n she oughta be," as Frank put it?

When he'd met Priscilla on a buying trip to Denver, she'd had a hard-luck story, too. He'd made arrangements to protect her and bring her to Ranger Bluff. She'd insisted on—on— Walker fumbled for the word Priscilla had used.

*Propriety*. That was it.

She'd needed a female companion. Priscilla had found one and Walker had paid for two tickets. Priscilla and the elderly lady had lived in a house in Ranger Bluff. Walker paid the rent. Priscilla and her friend had accompanied the Walker family to church.

Walker didn't notice—or rather, didn't care—at the time, but Priscilla's companion would often step out of the house while Walker visited. Far too often for precious propriety.

Somehow, they'd end up alone, and when that happened, Priscilla had always ended up in tears. Walker had offered comfort. They'd end up locked in each other's arms, and it was Walker who'd always called a halt. He'd never seen the pattern until after Pa was dead. He felt tainted by that.

It also occurred to Walker that there'd never been gossip about Priscilla. Her so-called propriety had all been on the surface while her heart was full of rot. While he was seeing to having Priscilla locked up, he'd found out Priscilla's escort and chaperone had a lifelong history of cheating and lying. Priscilla had learned it at her knee.

"It weren't like Gib spread the gossip." Frank pulled Walker out of his dark memories. "He just told me 'cuz he knew she was out here and thought you oughta know. You haven't been to town since she came here from seeing the sheriff, and Gibby's not gonna speak of such to your ma."

Walker pulled his Stetson low over his eyes and studied the ground, not sure what to say, even less sure what to do. He finally looked up at Frank, wondering if Frank had any ideas.

Catching himself, Walker realized Frank wasn't much more than eighteen years old. The kid was barely old enough to dress himself, let alone offer words of wisdom.

Walker felt compelled to protest, to defend Annette. But what did he really know about her? Never again would he defend that little snip of a lying woman.

Then he thought of that song. That beautiful hymn. *"Even so, Lord, quickly come, bring Thy final harvest home; gather Thou Thy people in, free from sorrow, free from sin. . ."*

Annette had sung those words as if she delighted in the idea of the Lord coming. Only someone who felt fully confident that she'd be among the final harvest would sing those words in that way. No woman could lie when she sang those words so beautifully. Those words of thanksgiving, in Annette's song, were the most honest things Walker had ever heard.

Or else Annette was a liar.

"Thanks for telling me. I—I don't know how to put a stop to gossip once it's spreading." He knew a couple of ways. He could punch a few gossiping townsfolk in the face. And of course there was one sure way to restore the good name of a woman who'd been dishonored.

Marry her.

Walker's stomach took a dive and swooped around. Did the idea make him sick or thrilled? Strange that the two reactions felt the same in his belly.

"It's easier to fight a forest fire, and that's a plain fact." Frank shared a sympathetic look with Walker.

"Get back to work."

Nodding, Frank moved away, his breath white in the brutal cold of the northern Rockies in winter.

Walker felt his own heart chill until it seemed the white cloud that

came out every time he breathed had nothing to do with the bitter Wyoming winter and everything to do with the ice wrapped around his heart.

And then, across the corral and the yard, Walker saw Gabe Michaels ride up to the ranch house and swing down off his horse.

Walker's heart warmed to a boil.

The knock at the door startled Annie. No one had ever knocked before.

Annie glanced at Ruby, who shrugged. "Answer it."

Annie hurried to the door and swung it open.

Gabe Michaels.

The tall, lean cowboy pulled his Stetson off his head. "Howdy, Miss Talbot. I've come to call on you. Remember, we talked about it?"

"Hello, Mr. Michaels." Come to call? What did that mean exactly? Ruby came up behind Annie or she might have stood there staring, letting cold air in forever.

Ruby nudged Annie aside. "Howdy, stranger. I saw you getting off the stage with Eli. I don't believe we've met."

Ruby hadn't said come in or given the man a particularly friendly greeting. That wasn't like her. Ruby was usually the very soul of kindness. Annie had been a stranger on the same stage and Ruby had as good as swooped her up and taken her to the diner. Just this morning Ruby had claimed everyone in the area called her Ma and she'd nagged until Annie had agreed to call her that.

Still, Ma was capable of speech so she had Annie beat. Had this man said something the other day about asking if he could call on her? Maybe. She'd just seen Claude and she'd been busy panicking.

"My name's Gabe Michaels. I spoke to your son the day before Thanksgiving. I asked permission to call on Miss Talbot. He was worried about her being overly tired from her fall into the river so we didn't settle anything. Maybe you're who I should ask." Mr. Michaels looked between Ruby and Annie with his intense, too-black eyes. As

173

before, Annie got the sense of his watching her with more than the usual interest. What was he looking for?

"Eli, we've got company."

Ma's words made no sense. . .until Annie looked past the cowboy's broad shoulders to see Elijah striding toward the door.

"I see we do. I've met Mr. Michaels, Ma. You can let him in. For now." Elijah came up beside Gabe and made a gesture that seemed a bit grand for a rancher, sweeping his arm toward the house.

Ruby stepped back, catching Annie's arm to pull her along.

"Thanks. Call me Gabe." Mr. Michaels came in, looking from Ruby to Walker and back as if he were checking them for hideout guns.

Probably wise. Annie thought of the pipe Ruby had given her before she'd ridden out to Pa's ranch and wondered if Ruby kept an extra up her sleeve while she was at home.

"We'll call you Mr. Michaels for now. We don't know anything about you." Elijah stayed near Mr. Michaels. Annie was getting that protective vibe again from Elijah. But nothing about Mr. Michaels seemed dangerous, and, truth was, Annie had known Mr. Michaels as long as she'd known the Walkers.

Her eyes left Elijah to look at their guest. He'd come to call? On her? Like he wanted to be her. . .beau?

Annie's stomach sank as she realized Elijah seemed a bit too pleased with refusing Mr. Michaels's perfectly polite request that they call him Gabe. Oh, Elijah was definitely smiling, but the smile seemed a bit frozen.

Of course, it was cold out.

Ruby closed the door, still holding Annie's arm.

Mr. Michaels came in and Elijah made that same phony polite gesture toward the chair nearest the hearth. Mr. Michaels looked about awkwardly when no one offered to take his hat or his heavy duster coat. He kept the coat on and set the hat in his lap when he took the rocking chair Elijah offered.

Ruby didn't exactly *drag* Annie to the far side of the hearth, but

Annie didn't try to escape either. Dragging might have come into it if she had.

Ruby motioned for Annie to sit down in the rocker facing Mr. Michaels. There was a third rocker pushed back against the wall that Annie imagined had belonged to Elijah's father. Where had Priscilla sat? Maybe neither Ruby nor her husband could stomach being in the room with the horrid woman. For propriety's sake though, no doubt one of them had to stay, so rather than build a new chair, they'd spelled each other to give their nausea a chance to settle.

Annie had never met the dreadful Priscilla, true, but she knew without a doubt she'd have detested the woman on sight. What was Elijah thinking to get involved with her? The whole line of thinking annoyed Annie to the point she wanted to scold Elijah for being so foolish. Instead, she began rocking.

The two Walkers positioned themselves between Annie and Mr. Michaels. Ruby pulled up the unused rocker. Elijah grabbed a chair from the kitchen table, flipped it around, and straddled it, resting his arms on the chair back.

An awkward silence ensued.

When it had gone on far too long, Elijah smiled. "So, cold enough for you?" Elijah's effort at small talk rang with mockery.

The three rockers squeaked and again silence went on too long.

"Very cold." Mr. Michaels turned his hat in his hands, running his fingers along the brim. It was a nervous gesture that didn't match with the confidence she'd seen in those dark eyes on the stage.

Was he really interested in courting her? Annie had no interest in the man. For heaven's sake, she'd been too busy trying to keep her eyes off Elijah. But it was thrilling to be wanted by such a handsome cowboy.

"Where do you come from, Mr. Michaels? Tell us about yourself." Ruby spoke in a starchy voice that made Annie look at her and arch a brow.

"Well, umm. . .hmm. . ." The hat turned in Mr. Michaels's hands faster. "I—I'm from, well I've spent the last ten years in the cavalry. Just mustered out a mouth or so ago. I've got a stake and I came up here looking for ranch land."

Annie thought that sounded extremely normal, if a bit adventurous. "Well, that's—"

"Where'd you serve?" Elijah seemed determined to carry this out like a courtroom, complete with cross-examination.

Annie thought this might actually be the proper way for a guardian to decide if a young man could come calling, but a few manners included in the questioning wouldn't do a bit of harm.

"Mainly in Texas, some in Arizona and New Mexico. I went in at eighteen. Lately I'd begun to itch to quit roaming, put down some roots, start a family." Mr. Michaels's eyes flickered to Annie's and quickly away. "And I'd had enough of the heat, so I headed north. Miss Talbot here is a lovely young woman and I'd like to call on her."

Ruby and Elijah stared at their guest in a way that was quite rude. And it wasn't like Annie was all that sensitive. They weren't even pretending to cover their hostility.

Ruby shook her head. "No, I don't think that'll do at all. Once you've found land, started up a ranch, built a home, perhaps you can stop back. For now you've got nothing to offer a woman."

A mischievous impulse made Annie say, "You know, I've got a ranch and a home."

"Annie—" Elijah started in.

"Maybe Mr. Michaels could buy the J Bar T?" Annie talked right over the top of him. "With Father run off, I imagine it's mine. Mr. Michaels could have everything set up for himself in a single day." She smiled at her suitor. "You could come back tomorrow."

"It's not yours to sell, Annie," Ruby reproved her.

Annie felt a bit of the sting. She really had been impudent. Although she wasn't sure why she had to behave herself when the Walkers didn't.

"Thanks for the thought, Miss Talbot. That's right generous of you. And I'll take that to mean that once I've met the Walkers' conditions,

you'd at least consider my company." He rose from his chair. "I'll find a ranch on my own. I've already done some scouting and found a likely spot or two. I'll be stopping by the land office sooner than you'd think." Mr. Michaels headed for the door, settling his hat on his head firmly. "Then I'll be back."

He turned at the door and looked straight at Annie, who rose. "You seem like a truly fine young woman, Miss Talbot. I'd be honored if you'd agree to spend time with me."

Annie smiled.

Elijah rose from his chair and stepped between her and Mr. Michaels so she could no longer see the man.

Speaking through Elijah, Mr. Michaels added, "I'm a churchgoing man. Maybe I'll see you at services tomorrow morning."

As the door opened and closed, Annie at last remembered why she couldn't let any man call on her. Her initial reaction to Mr. Michaels's attentions were negative because of Elijah and that single kiss they'd shared while Ruby fetched the eggs the night before Thanksgiving. But Elijah had spent as much time fussing at her as being kind. Although when he'd been kind, he'd been very kind indeed.

But kissing Elijah wasn't why she couldn't step out with a man. Mr. Michaels might want to take her to town.

And she couldn't go to town because Claude was there.

## TWENTY

Church services begin at nine o'clock, Annie." Ruby set the plate of pancakes on the table with a smile.

Annie had dreaded this moment and now it was here.

"I'd like for you to sing in church today." Ruby turned back to the stove and poured out batter for the next batch of perfect pancakes she'd brown on her griddle. "The folks in town will love your voice. I declare, just listening makes a person feel closer to the Lord."

"I'm not going to accompany you today, Ruby. I'm—" Annie stopped. She absolutely refused to make an excuse that amounted to a lie to get out of going to town. Especially to get out of going to church. That was a sin Annie refused to have on her soul.

She knew if she claimed exhaustion, left over from her ride down the river, Ruby would let her stay home without a second thought. But Annie wasn't going to lie, ever. She still thought of the way she'd misled the man in the Ranger Bluff stable and knew it for a sin. Just because not a single dishonest word passed her lips didn't mean she wasn't guilty. She'd prayed for forgiveness and God had granted it. If she ever came face-to-face with the stableman, she'd ask his forgiveness, too.

She would not now add to her sins, not even to spare sweet Ruby's feelings. "I don't want to be in town. I feel—" Well, there was lying. . .and

then there was telling every single thing a body knew. That wasn't necessary. "I'm not going today." She lifted her chin, prepared to take Ruby's scolding like an adult woman.

Ruby wasn't even looking at her. Instead she flipped the last pancakes onto a plate, set it at the head of the table where Elijah would sit, pulled her griddle off the cast-iron stove, and tugged on her coat, all in a matter of seconds.

Annette heard the door open and turned.

"Eli, you goin'?" Ruby asked just as Elijah came in the cabin door.

"Nope. Maybe one of these days though, Ma."

Ruby walked toward him and stopped to rest a hand on his cheeks, flushed red with cold. "Well, that's fine, son. I hope you do. Maybe in time for Christmas."

Ruby swept past Elijah, tugging on her bonnet as she left. With the door open for a few seconds, Annie was able to see a buckboard standing outside and a crowd of riders alongside it. The Walker ranch must have a lot of hands who were believers.

Elijah's eyes landed square on Annie. He turned as the door snapped shut behind him. "Hey wait!" Elijah looked at the closed door.

The jingle of the harness rang out and the wagon could be heard rolling away.

Turning back, Elijah looked at Annie, scowling as if she'd pulled a gun on him. "Why aren't you going to church?"

Again she had the perfect chance for an easy out—lie.

*God, please make him quit staring at me like I'm a typhoid carrier.*

At a complete loss for words, Annie simply shrugged her shoulders and turned back to the last bites of her pancakes.

"No." Elijah was beside her in two long strides. He shook his head like a bad-tempered bull. "I'll catch them. You're a God-fearin' woman. You need to get to church."

Annie looked up, her mouth full. Not sure what to do about Elijah ordering her to go to church, she just chewed then washed her pancakes down with a big swallow of milk. Was it possible Elijah had changed his mind overnight and now wanted her to keep company with Gabe Michaels? Annie's head was spinning just trying to keep up with the ornery man. Finally she said, "I'm going to stay home and have a quiet worship time by myself."

Then an idea came to her like an inspiration straight from God. "You're welcome to join me." She'd seen Elijah's uncertain relationship with the Almighty. This would most likely scare Elijah into going back to work, even on the Sabbath.

"Okay. Sounds good." Elijah sat down and pulled his plate, stacked high with steaming hotcakes, closer. He buttered them and generously poured on warm syrup Ruby had boiled up fresh this morning, then began eating.

Not sure what to do short of walking out on the exasperating man, Annie poured him a glass of milk and pushed the plate of oversized sausage patties toward him.

Walker took all five, probably a half pound of meat.

It occurred to Annie that the man's mouth was full. He appeared to be starving and Ruby's food was irresistible. That left him defenseless. . . or more so than usual anyway. . .because his mouth would be too full to talk. Maybe she could use this time to scare him away. "I'm glad you want to worship with me, Elijah." There, that oughta do it.

Elijah swallowed. "I'd enjoy that." He spoke with absolutely no problem and he showed no sign of running.

Annie considered that Elijah might not be as enamored of his mother's pancakes as she was. Or maybe he was just used to the delicious breakfast and knew there would always be more where these came from. Annie envied that kind of confidence.

"Why don't you sing a hymn or two while I finish eating? Then we'll clean up the dishes and settle in to read from the Good Book and have a prayer."

She wanted the man to rediscover his faith. Ruby had made it clear that she was worried about her son. So what could Annie do but agree? She finished her milk.

"Would you mind getting me a cup of coffee before the singing starts?" Elijah asked.

"Of course not." The soothing aroma of the piping hot liquid she poured into Elijah's cup matched the wonder of his showing interest in a church service.

"Thank you, Annie. Now the song, if you're willing." Plowing through the tower of hotcakes and the mountain of sausages with impressive speed, Elijah looked at her expectantly.

The smallest mission field she'd ever seen. Well, it was a plain fact that large group or small, a hundred folks or only one man, people came to the Lord one heart at a time. So, she'd gladly sing and worship with Elijah.

She sang "Now Thank We All Our God," "For the Beauty of the Earth," and "Bringing in the Sheaves." She sang as Elijah finished his meal and enjoyed his coffee.

"That's beautiful, Annie. It really does make people feel like they're closer to the Almighty. Let me help you clear the table. Then we'll have a worship time."

As the plates and cups and silver clicked together, Annie had to force herself to speak the words she knew she must. "I thought you were feeling separated from God, Elijah. I'm so glad you want to worship with me."

Elijah shrugged as he shaved a bit of soap off a bar then poured hot water into a basin. He poured more into a second basin for rinsing.

Annie knew the system from working beside Ruby. Since it appeared the man wasn't going to talk to her, she kept up her tidying. "I'll do that. You've been out working hard for hours." Annie was uncomfortable allowing Elijah to do women's chores.

Rolling up his sleeves, Elijah grinned at her. "You think Ma didn't teach her only child how to help around the house? I've washed my share of dishes." He plunged his hands into the steaming, soapy water.

"Ma had no daughters to help her, so I got trained to help inside and out." Elijah grinned at her and kept washing. "Here." He thrust a plate at her and nodded at the water he'd poured into the rinse basin.

Uncertain how to reclaim the kitchen, Annie rinsed and wiped while Elijah washed.

"Uh. . .Annette?"

"Yes?" Annie dried a tin cup.

"How old are you?"

Annie thought she remembered being told never to ask someone's age. It was rude. Well, Elijah being rude was nothing new. "I'm twenty years old."

"So, tell me about yourself." Elijah handed her a plate.

Annie decided she could do this. She could work side by side with the man without wanting to yell at him. . .or kiss him. Maybe it was a sign of maturity. She'd had a very maturing few days. "What would you like to know?" She dried the plate and set it aside until Elijah finished the other one.

"Tell me about your school. Ma called it a Bible school."

"Well, not Bible school really, but we took classes on the Bible."

"Did you graduate?" Elijah focused on the silverware in his hands, running a washcloth over the tines of a fork.

"Yes."

"You're a real high-school graduate, huh? There aren't too many of those out here. The school in Ranger Bluff goes through twelve grades, but what few children there are. . .the boys go back to the ranch to work and the girls get married."

"I think that's common. But I had no interest in marrying anyone from St. Louis. I always wanted to come back to the mountains. And we were very sheltered. It was an all-girls school and no dating was allowed."

"So what did you do after you graduated?"

Annie paused. Something about the tone of Elijah's voice bothered her. It was almost too casual, too offhand. What did he want to know this for? "I traveled with a mission group. There were about ten of us at first. An elderly lady played the piano for me and I sang hymns, like

the ones I sang this morning."

Elijah dropped the last of the silverware in Annie's rinse water and turned to look at her, drying his hands on the dangling end of the towel she held. "I reckon those were about the prettiest songs I've ever heard."

"Thank you, Elijah. I'm so honored that you seem to like my singing. It's not skill on my part. It's simply something I've always done. A gift God gave me that I try to use to serve His kingdom." Annie's gaze dropped as she thought of how her gift had been abused.

"What is it? You seem really serious all of a sudden."

She didn't look up. His voice beckoned her to confide in him. But she dared not tell anyone what she'd been through. She was terrified of being connected to the Leveques. And once she was, she'd be thrown out. Cast into the world on her own.

And why not? The Walkers didn't owe her their support and shelter. She was already on her own. Why deny it? Why hide behind others? She wasn't the only woman to have no home. But being homeless and hungry was one thing. Being forced into the life Claude and Blanche had planned for her was something else. Being alone in the world wasn't her fear. Even death didn't scare her. But Claude's threats, she heard them ringing in her ears as he'd come for her at Father's house.

And he'd hurt Elva. Would he hurt someone else she cared about if she failed to do as he asked? She needed a good job and a safe place to live, paid for with her own income. Closing her eyes, she prayed to be strong, courageous, to live bravely for the Lord.

She should tell Elijah everything. If he chose to show her the door, it would be his right. If he took her side, would he go into town and confront Claude? Her cheek seemed to throb with the memory of Claude's fist on her face from that night so long ago when Elva died. Claude wouldn't fight fair. Elijah could end up hurt or in jail. Claude might even use threats against Elijah or Ruby to force Annie into going with him quietly. No matter what she chose to do, this would end badly. Only silence protected everyone. "Are we done here? I'd like to begin our worship service now."

Elijah stared at her.

She stared back.

At last he sighed and walked past her toward the rocking chairs that stood in front of the fireplace on the other side of the room. "Fine. Yes, let's worship."

Sitting down in front of the roaring fire with such fear in her heart wasn't a good way to worship. But the Bible verses Elijah read lifted her spirits. The music did its wondrous healing work on her soul. Elijah had a fine voice, and after some cajoling he sang along quietly with her. They ended their time together in prayer.

No hand-holding this time.

Some of the courage Annie so desperately sought came to her. As long as she was allowed to hide from the world, she could be brave.

## TWENTY-ONE

Remember what a coward that girl was?" Blanche hissed.

Claude hushed her as they met outside the church. "Wait'll we're well away. I don't want anyone associating us with her."

They moved away from the thinning crowd.

Blanche stopped to stare after a buckboard surrounded by cowhands.

Claude caught her arm to keep her moving.

"If we get our hands on her once, she'll come along. She'll do as she's told," Blanche added.

If she didn't, Claude had a good idea of how to break her spirit. He thought of the way she'd risked her life rushing down that treacherous path and felt a chill that seemed to have nothing to do with the bitter weather. It seemed to come at him like a blast from that church building they'd just left.

"I heard talk about the girl," Blanche added.

They had mingled after church, visiting and, more importantly, listening. Talking about their musical shows in a way to put the townsfolk at ease. Attending church was essential when they came to town. They needed the respectability to overcome community opposition to their shows, especially when they gradually turned it into a gambling den and dance hall.

"Some of our rumors circulating?" Claude had heard a word or two himself. He'd done his best to fan the flames of gossip without letting anyone know the evil talk had started with him.

"Some. But I got an idea where she might be hiding, too."

They were nearly to their building when Claude risked a look back. They'd left the congregation well behind. "Okay, tell me what you heard."

"It was a conversation going on behind me. I listened but I was careful to show no interest."

"Fine, fine, get on with it." Claude fought down his irritation with Blanche. He'd have strangled her if she'd admitted to showing interest, so of course she denied it. But Blanche knew how to play people. She probably had handled it well.

Lately, she sang like a scalded cat though. He had to get rid of her.

A few folks had come in last night. That fool, Sikes, among 'em. He should know to stay away. And that narrow-eyed cowboy who Sikes said came to town on the same stage as him and the songbird had come in. He'd even asked for a whiskey right out in the main room. Claude had played innocent. It was too soon to outrage the town.

Blanche's singing was nearly bad enough to drive them back out. But most had stayed. There wasn't much entertainment in this town.

They even left a dollar or two in the hat. It was far too early to suggest a gentleman's game of poker in the back room, but Claude had a good eye for avarice. He thought he'd seen that gleam of greed in more than one man's eyes as they watched Blanche sing her sedate hymns and anthems.

"I heard someone say something about beautiful singing."

"Did you see who?"

"Yes, I glanced back." Blanche reached for the doorknob and they let themselves into their building. They headed for the back room where a meager, cold lunch awaited them. "I saw her then later got her name. Ruby Walker. She said something about Thanksgiving dinner and the girl singing instead of saying grace."

"That sounds like our girl. She's one for praying while she sings, no

doubt about it." Claude shook his head in disgust at the waste of such talent.

"I asked just idlelike where the Walkers lived."

"No! I told you not to show any interest!" Claude clenched his fist, tempted to use it on this stupid woman.

"I was careful. I asked in passing. I was only told it's west of town and I didn't ask for more."

"Which one was Ruby Walker?"

"She was skinny and tall. She wore a dark green dress and had on a heavy black coat that had a green wool bonnet with a red flower on the side."

There weren't that many people there, even less women. "I know who you mean."

"I watched when she rode off. She musta had ten cowpokes riding beside her. All real alert, sat their horses well. They headed straight west on the main trail."

Claude had seen that group leave town, too. He grabbed the thread-bare coat he'd just slipped off. "I'm going out to catch their trail."

"You should'a never sold our horses. You'll look like a fool if you walk. People will notice."

Growling with frustration, Claude pulled on his coat. Blanche was right but he'd never give her the satisfaction of admitting it. "I'll be careful. I'll head into those thick woods to the north then swing around to the west. I'll just walk a short ways. I'm not good readin' a trail, but maybe if I hurry I can find some high ground and see them even yet."

"I'll get coffee going. You'll be freezing cold by the time you get back. Why can't we buy a bit of meat, Claude? We had a good supply of money when we headed west. What happened to it?"

Claude was leaving through the back door and Blanche was lucky. He'd have backhanded her for daring to question him if he hadn't been in such a hurry. "Just get the coffee on. Let me worry about spending the money. And maybe you should practice your singing. You sounded like a cat gettin' swung by its tail last night."

He looked back and saw the hurt on her once-pretty face. Feeling better, he slammed the door and headed for the woods. If she brought it up again, he'd shut Blanche's mouth good and proper—with his fist.

Walker hadn't been to church since his pa died. He was amazed at how the Bible reading and prayer and singing soothed his soul.

*God, it's not just because she has such a beautiful singing voice. I am reminded of Thanksgiving. I'm reminded that life is Yours to give and take away. It was Pa's time. No matter how wrong Priscilla was, and how foolish I was, You count the days we're granted.*

Walker prayed as Annette sang her songs of thanks. When the last note died, Walker, who'd listened with his head bowed, looked up. "Thank you. I'm glad you stayed home and suggested we worship here. I feel closer to God than I have in a long time."

"Since that woman hurt your father." Annette's eyes went soft.

Walker realized something. "You lost your pa, too. We have that in common."

"Yes, but I hadn't seen my father since I was a little girl. My loss is not nearly as painful as yours."

Something warm and sad unfolded inside Walker's chest, and he stood up and offered Annette his hand. She took it and he pulled her to her feet. "I think maybe yours is more painful. I had my pa all the time." Walker fumbled for the words to say that would comfort her. Comfort them both. "Why do you call him *father*? You grew up out here, at least in your early years. Folks call their father *pa* out here."

Shrugging, Annette looked down at her hands, still held by him. "It's what the girls back in St. Louis called their fathers, I guess. I got in the habit. I suppose if he was here and I could actually speak his name, I might remember the old ways. But because h–he'd mostly abandoned me, I don't feel the affection that went with the name *pa*."

Walker tugged her hands a bit and she looked up into his eyes. "Your pa was an old curmudgeon, no doubt about it. But I think he

loved you, Annette." Walker wasn't a bit sure of that. Old Man Talbot didn't seem to like anyone or anything. But maybe that was because he'd lost everything that was most important to him.

"I'll never know, will I?"

"There was a loneliness to him that doesn't go with a married man with a daughter. Maybe losing your ma was too much for him. Maybe caring for a little girl-child was overwhelming. How could he ride the range after his cattle? How could he hunt for food? Maybe he had to bury his heart to live with losing you and your ma."

Annette's eyes warmed even more. And then they filled with tears. She blinked her eyes rapidly, and Walker could see from her expression that she remembered he hated tears.

He felt that old reflex to jump in and comfort. To do *anything* to stop the water from flowing. Then he remembered a tear or two he'd shed when his pa died. He'd covered them up with anger, for the most part, or walked off to be alone. But if a person couldn't cry over losing a pa, then there was no reason for God to have even invented tears. And He had. So Walker decided to let the little woman cry.

"I'm sorry." She wiggled loose from one of his hands, pulled a handkerchief free that was tucked in the wrist of her dress, and turned away.

He pulled her into his arms. Not for any reason that was disrespectful, just to hold a woman as she cried.

"No, let me go. I'll go to my room and pull myself together. I'm sorry."

Walker held her tighter. "Settle down. It's okay to shed a few tears over your pa. I'm not going to fuss at you."

She lifted her chin, and her eyes, drenched and shining, spilled over. Then she got her other hand loose and threw her arms around his waist, buried her face against his chest, and cried.

Tears surprised Walker by welling up in his eyes. For her loss, for Ma's, for his. Since he was holding her so close, she couldn't see his breaking down like a little baby. They stood like that for a long time, and pain seemed to flow out of Walker on those tears, easing the tightness that had held him in a vise for a year now. Washed away, just as Christ promised to wash away all sins.

The tears passed and left him feeling lighter, cleaner, forgiven. He leaned closer to Annette and whispered in her ear, "One of my favorite Psalms says something about God washing away all my sin. I feel like that's happened to me today. I feel like God has finally forgiven me."

Annette looked up, studied his eyes, and had to see his tears. But she said nothing, thank goodness. "Oh, Elijah, God always forgives. You didn't have to worry that He wouldn't."

"No, you're right. I said that wrong. I've been carrying this burden all this time, but it was my own burden. God didn't set it on me. I set it on myself. Forgiving myself. . .has been impossible."

"But no more?" Annette's clouded eyes lightened.

"No more. I think I can finally let God make the decisions about life and death. I can lay down that load of guilt."

Joy lit up Annette's eyes. Joy for him, he thought. Annette Talbot was a good woman. She wasn't a liar. She wasn't driven by greed like Priscilla.

At this moment, if it had been Priscilla in his arms, she'd have kissed him. She'd have thrown herself at him as if only his strong arms could ease her suffering.

Annette instead pulled free, beaming with joy but also holding herself to high standards of behavior. "I'm so glad. And thank you for giving me a safe place to cry. I'll try not to do that again."

"I'd appreciate it."

She looked up, hurt.

Walker laughed.

She swatted him on the arm and laughed along. "Thank you for worshipping with me." Dabbing her eyes, Annette turned to the kitchen. "Your ma was planning to fry chicken for dinner. I need to get a baking of bread rising then go fetch a couple of the young roosters from the coop."

Liking that Annette felt enough at home to get to work in the kitchen, Walker headed for his coat and Stetson. "I'll wrangle the chickens and get 'em plucked while you work on the bread. I think there are a couple more squash in the cellar, too. They'll be going soft soon. I have a hankerin' for squash again."

"Sounds wonderful." She looked over her shoulder and smiled, then turned back to the kitchen, rolling up her sleeves.

As she walked away, Walker's heart pounded in a way it never had before. Hard, unsteady, almost painful.

She fit in here. She loved Ma and Ma loved her. Walker had never been able to see Priscilla living here with him and his folks. But Annette could manage just fine.

And that was the dead-last time he was ever going to compare sweet, good-hearted, God-fearing Annette with that rattlesnake, Priscilla.

Walker went to do his part to feed his womenfolk, thinking, this time, maybe he had his mind on a family that God would approve of.

# Twenty-Two

"Can you fetch the eggs, Annie?"

Annie had just emerged from her bedroom in the dark of the morning. She'd yet to beat Ruby out of bed. The woman could work circles around her. "I'd be glad to, Ma."

"Eli's already gone. He and the men have a long ride today to check some cattle in a high valley. He'll push all day to get there and back. I told him you and I would do the barnyard chores this morning. So, we've got a cow to milk, eggs to fetch, livestock to water. I thought maybe you'd welcome a chance to get outdoors." Ruby began pulling on her coat.

"I'd love to help." Annie reached for her coat. As she pulled it on, Ruby handed her warm gloves, a wool scarf, and a heavy bonnet that would cover her ears.

"We'll put in an hour or so then come in for breakfast. I'll make ham and eggs and biscuits."

"That sounds wonderful." Annie had never felt this cared for. Mentally, she apologized to her mother, but it was true. Father had standoffish ways even before Mother died. And Mother had stepped carefully around him to avoid his uncertain temper. She was affectionate and took good care of Annie, but she'd been a nervous woman.

Ruby opened the door and led the way into the bitter December

morning. The biting edge of cold moved Annie along smartly.

She headed for the chicken coop, and Ruby went to the barn carrying the milk pail. They finished with those chores in short time and turned to the corral.

Elijah and the cowhands had left riding, and most of the other horses in the Walker remuda had been turned out to a pasture that gave them access to the river. But several horses remained in the yard.

Annie and Ruby began leading horses to the river to drink. Annie held the lead rope for her horse as they walked a narrow trail leading down to the Medicine Bow. One part of the path was perilous, rocks rearing up high on one side while dropping away on the other.

The horses drank the icy water.

Annie looked at the fast-moving current and shuddered to think she'd come flying down this river. She closed her eyes and praised God for her survival. She counted it as a pure miracle.

"What do you say we make a really special meal for Eli tonight?" Ruby asked as they stood side by side on the river's edge.

Annie's eyes popped open.

Ruby frowned with concern. "Are you thinking about how you almost drowned?"

"I'm not upset about being swept down the river." Annie smiled. "Don't ever think that. I'm singing a song of joy that God wrapped me in His arms and protected me. 'A Mighty Fortress Is Our God.'"

Nodding, Ruby's furrowed brow eased. "One of my favorites." The horses finished and the two walked back together, singing in union about their shared faith.

They worked well together all day, managing a beef roast and dipping into Ruby's precious store of sugar to make a cake.

When the cake was finally cooling on the kitchen table, Ruby washed her hands and surprised Annie by producing a length of pipe from her sleeve.

"Your weapon?" Annie smiled. "You got a new one."

"I noticed you don't have yours anymore. What happened to it?"

Annie wrinkled her brow. "I left it at Father's house. I dropped it and never picked it back up."

"Well, I've always got spares." Ruby produced another pipe that she'd obviously found for just this purpose. "Let me show you how to make a harness to keep from dropping it."

Ruby had leather handy, and they spent the rest of the afternoon with Ruby giving Annie good advice and considerable scolding about being defenseless.

The sun set early, the dinner preparations were done, and Annie was securely armed when Ruby whispered as if they were conspiring, "I'm sure Eli will scold us, but let's do the evening chores for him so he can come on in and warm up. He and the men will be half frozen from their long day in the mountains."

"That will be a nice surprise for him. Uh, them, I mean." Annie had to admit she didn't really give much thought to the other men. Well, she had to admit it to herself. She wasn't about to admit it to Ruby. She saw Ruby smile and turn quickly away. So maybe Annie hadn't corrected her verbal slip quickly enough.

They milked and checked for a spare egg or two, fed the chickens and pigs, and then set out for the river again, leading a horse apiece. The drop-off fell away too far for Annie to estimate the distance. They got past that gap, and then the mountains again rose wild and rugged and steep on both sides. At its most precarious, the trail was narrow enough Annie and Ruby had to walk single file, leading the horses.

On their way back, they reached the dangerous section of the path. Annie saw movement in the rocks across the gap. "Did you see that?" she called ahead to Ruby. "I think Elijah is back."

Ruby chuckled. "We're in for it now. He'll scold us something fierce for doing the evening chores."

"Your cake will cheer him up, I'll bet." Annie looked again and gasped. That wasn't Elijah, it was—

A gunshot rang through the air.

*"Ma!"* Annie screamed. "Get down!"

Ruby cried out with pain and stumbled to her knees. The horse, startled by the loud gunshot, jumped over Ruby's collapsing form and ran for home.

Dropping her reins, Annie rushed for Ruby. Her own horse caught her in the shoulder as it scrambled past her, heading for the barn, and knocked Ruby forward.

Ruby landed facedown on the slippery trail, then toppled sideways over the edge of the cliff.

Annie grabbed a handful of Ruby's skirt and stopped the fall. Annie saw the elderly lady's hands claw at the edge of the cliff. A thin cry of terror ripped from Ruby's throat.

Annie scrambled forward, clinging to fabric that slipped through her fingers, desperate to get a better grip. She flung herself flat on her belly and managed to grab Ruby by the arm.

Ruby's eyes met Annie's. They were full of life and determination. The elderly lady found a handhold with her right hand as Annie clung to her left. Once Ruby took some of the weight off Annie's arm, she could shift and sit up. Most of Ruby's weight still pulled on Annie.

"Let me get my feet braced." Annie groaned from the wrenching pain in her shoulders.

"Okay, I–I've got a handhold. Slick. I can't hang on for more than a few seconds." The exertion in Ruby's voice seemed wrong, laced with pain.

Bright color drew Annie's gaze. Shocked, she saw blood soaking their joined hands. It undermined their grip.

Ruby's face twisted with pain but she didn't speak a word of complaint. "Are you set, Annie? I don't want to pull you over with me."

"Yes, I'm good." Annie grappled for a handhold on the too-smooth ground to keep from being pulled over the edge herself. "I'm ready." She was as ready as she'd ever be.

*Please, God, let it be enough. Give me the strength to hold on.*

"Let's get you up." Annie dispensed more pain to her elderly friend as she tried to pull Ruby back to solid ground.

"We're fine. We'll do it."

Relieved by Ruby's strong voice, Annie quit reacting instinctively and managed to think. . .and see. She looked across that gap, straight into the eyes of a masked man.

It was Claude Leveque.

She couldn't swear to it, but she knew. Even with a neckerchief pulled up to his eyes, she saw the corners of his eyes crinkle and knew he smiled through the curling smoke of his gun. She opened her mouth to scream.

Claude aimed his gun square at Ruby's back while touching his index finger to his lips.

Annie got the message. He'd shoot Ruby if she yelled.

Claude gave a little tip of his hat then ducked behind the rock, but Annie saw the protruding tip of his gun and an aim that held true. She remembered the beating he'd given her. Elva's battered face. He was capable of pulling that trigger. Annie had no doubt.

He might have deliberately winged Ruby the first time, but now he was letting Annie know clearly that she was at his mercy. And more importantly, so was Ruby.

Ruby drew Annie's attention as she groaned with the exertion necessary to pull herself higher. Annie felt her grasp slithering on Ruby's blood-soaked hand.

"No, Ruby, I—I'm losing you." She let go of her tenuous purchase so she could grab Ruby with both hands. Annie's voice rose. "My hand is slipping."

Annie inched toward the cliff. The rock bracing her foot crumbled. And Annie fell backward with a *thud*.

Ruby rose up as if she were flying.

From flat on her back, Annie looked up and saw. . .

Elijah.

Ruby was firmly in his grasp as he lifted his mother to solid ground.

With a gasp of relief, Annie sat up, her eyes darting back to the masked man.

He lifted one finger to his concealed lips, smiled again, and aimed that shushing finger at Ruby as if he were aiming his gun. His message was clear. He'd hurt Ruby even worse if Annie said she'd seen him. Claude dropped from sight.

Trembling, Annie knew she didn't dare keep this to herself. But once she spoke Claude's name, she'd be expected to explain the trouble she'd brought along with her. Heart sinking, Annie knew she could well be set out on the trail this very hour.

It didn't matter. The Walkers had to know the danger so they could protect themselves. Ruby had to stay inside. All the cowhands had to be on alert.

Elijah had to stay safe.

Two hired hands were right beside Elijah.

"See to Annie. She's bleeding, too, Walker." Frank, who'd been hurt on his ride to the Talbot ranch trying to protect Annie, now lifted Ruby, who'd been hurt because she was standing beside Annie. Frank swung up on horseback with Ruby in his arms.

Elijah dropped to his knees beside Annie, grabbing at her blood-soaked hand.

"No, I'm not hurt."

"Of course you're not." All the plans for honesty at whatever cost fled from Annie's mind at the sound of Elijah's voice. He sounded furious. "I can see plain that it's my ma's blood on your hands."

Trying to shake off the words that battered her, Annie excused sweet Elijah. His mother had nearly died. It was his way to yell when he was upset. Annie remembered that from her own father. Most likely all men behaved that way.

There was no time to calm him down. Claude might still be close at hand. They had to get off this trail.

Ruby and Frank crested the hill ahead and were swallowed up by the trail that now lifted high on both sides. They were safe from Claude's viciousness. That left only Elijah vulnerable. Annie might be in danger from Claude's fists, but he didn't intend to shoot her. He wanted her back in his clutches.

Lurching to her feet, Annie slipped free of the grip Elijah had on her hands and darted behind his horse, which stood quietly on the trail. As she knew he would, Elijah followed, the better to shout at her. They were both concealed from another gunshot. She caught the horse's reins and moved forward until they were undercover.

She could relax now and let Elijah yell out all his fear and worry.

"What were you trying to do? Make it look good before you *accidentally* let her go?"

That surprised her. Annie quit moving and turned to Elijah. This wasn't about his fear for his mother, hidden in anger. This was about—

"I came along just in time to pull her up. I could hear it in your voice you were getting ready to *slip* and let her go."

Her gasp sounded like an inverted scream. "You think I pushed your mother off that cliff?"

His eyes narrowed. His glare inflicted stab wounds on her heart. "I heard you. 'I can't hang on.' That was all for show, wasn't it? Acting like you were trying to save her. The only thing I can't understand is why you bothered to pretend. Or maybe you knew I was coming. Maybe you heard me yell. Tell me this, Annette, did you shoot her, too, or do you have a man friend around here who did the dirty work for you? You were looking around a bit too much for a woman trying to save someone's life."

Annie just shook her head, speechless in the face of Elijah's fury.

"No defense? No pretty lies? No suggestion we sell the Walker ranch and move back to the city where you'd be more comfortable?"

And that's when she finally got it. "Priscilla did all this? You said she killed your father."

"Leave my father and that murderous woman out of this. I've heard the talk about you in town. I didn't believe any of it. But I refuse to deny the truth when I see it with my own eyes."

The news that there had been gossip should have shocked her, but she well remembered Claude's way with a quiet whisper. He'd speak so

discreetly that later no one would know where the scandal had originated. But they'd certainly know who the scandal was about. The town of Ranger Bluff was closed to her then. But that didn't matter either.

Annie knew what she had to do. Leave.

And she would. She'd get out. She wouldn't sleep another night in Elijah's house. Maybe Ruby would protest, but if her husband had died in a way similar to her accident, then Ruby would have doubts, too. And it didn't matter even if Ruby defended her. This was Elijah's home. He was the head. He decided who stayed and who went.

She'd leave tonight. And on foot. She'd head down that secret trail for her own ranch with no ride borrowed from Elijah Walker's stable. If she froze or starved, could that hurt any more than Elijah's accusations? If that put her into Claude's hands, at least none of the Walkers would be in danger anymore. And yes, she might face terror, but God would be with her. Her chance to be truly brave had arrived.

She dropped her chin to her chest. She'd return to her father's house and wait. With the shortcut, she had a chance of getting there without freezing. There was food there. She knew a bit about hunting and fishing. If God wanted her to live, she'd live. If not, she'd die. . .or worse if Claude had his way.

Annie's legs shook but she forced herself to remain upright. Quietly she said, "I did not push your mother over that cliff."

"Don't bother—"

Annie cut him off by lifting her hand and nearly shoving the flat of her blood-soaked palm into his face. "If you choose to believe such a thing about me then there's nothing I can do. Furthermore, I don't want to be a charity case for someone who would think me capable of such a dreadful thing. I'll leave, Elijah. We've shared a few softer moments between us. . ."

Annie looked into his eyes and saw them shift, remembering those softer times. They'd been sweet and she'd believed they meant he had feelings for her. But he could never accuse her of such a thing if that were true.

She lowered her hand and slipped her coat off her shoulders. "But for the most part, you've wanted me to leave from the moment I got here." She handed it to him.

"Keep it."

"You'll notice I've kept the dress your mother gave me. Handing that over on the trail might be a bit much."

"Where do you think you're going?"

Annie nearly laughed, the irony was so rich. "Don't pretend you care. Or are you worried I'll hide in the hills, bide my time, waylay Ruby on the path, then once I've finished her off, I'll come back and hope you neither notice nor mind that your mother has been dispatched so I can wiggle my way into your life again? All the better to get my hands on your perfect ranch."

Annie didn't wait for an answer. Since he didn't take the coat, she dropped it on the ground and turned. The dusk already closed in around her as she headed away. Even with her father's trail, she'd walk in the bitter cold for hours. It didn't matter.

Elijah didn't speak. Not a word came from him.

The only One there to hold her hand was her heavenly Father, but she trusted Him implicitly and she held on tight.

# TWENTY-THREE

Walker didn't think his ma was still allowed to wash his mouth out with soap.

When he turned twenty-seven close to a year ago, he figured he oughta be able to make his own choices about cussing. But he didn't want to test the theory.

And because of his raisin', he'd pretty much gotten in the habit of watching his mouth.

He also had too much respect for God to let his mouth take over and his brain shut down.

He was tempted though, mighty tempted as he watched the little pill walk away in the freezing cold with no coat.

He tossed her coat over his shoulder, swung up on horseback, and rode after that fool woman. He grabbed Annette by the back of her already-cold dress.

She squeaked with surprise as he dragged her up onto his black stallion and turned her, belly down, over his saddle. "You let me go, Elijah Walker!" She took a backward swing at his head and caught his arm. The blow had surprising force until Walker realized the crazy woman had a length of lead pipe stuffed up her sleeve.

*Good work, Ma. Did you ever think your little student might beat me with your homemade weapon?*

With her backside right there, giving her a swat was more tempting than lapsing into mouth-soaping language. He controlled that urge, too, and threw her coat over her like a blanket. Mad as he was, he ignored her yelling, her thrashing feet and hands, and rode toward home.

"I'm not letting you out of my sight until we settle this." That was good. It sounded like a threat. It sounded like he was planning to dispense justice. The plain bald truth was he couldn't let the little half-wit walk off in the freezing cold.

Toss her off the cliff maybe, but not walk off into the mountains in the dead of winter.

Ma would have his hide.

God probably wouldn't approve.

He didn't want to do it either.

But oh, a swat on the backside. Yeah, he was tempted.

"Stay still!" he yelled, and that felt good. Dragging his bleeding gunshot mother off the edge of a cliff left him with a raging temper and nowhere to vent it.

And here was Annette, right at hand. Another conniving female. Walker scooted back behind the cantle of his saddle so he could nudge Annette off the saddle horn, although knowing she had a saddle horn poking her in the belly didn't bother him all that much.

Walker realized he had achieved new heights in stupidity. He was, without a doubt, the worst judge of women who had ever walked the face of the earth.

"Let me go!" Annette tried to roll onto her side, most likely so she could take a swing at him again. But she was mainly scaring his horse.

"If you upset this horse badly enough that we take a spill, I swear I will drag you all the way home by your hair!"

Annette lifted her head and twisted enough to glare at him.

He saw the blood on her hands. It might as well be on his. He'd brought destruction to his family for the second time. Although this time he hadn't really brought her here. Dragging her out of the river didn't count. But it made him hurt deep in his heart to think how badly

he'd wanted to keep her.

Annette drooped forward, suddenly limp. She stopped shrieking, just dangling there like a rag doll. And then she sniffled.

"Tears, of course." He hoped his sarcasm wasn't lost on her with her hanging upside down like she was. "The sunrise should be as dependable as a woman crying."

Annette glared up again. "Put me down. I will not stay one more night under your roof. I did *not* push Ruby over that cliff. And I will *not* stand by and be accused of such a thing."

Walker watched her close when she said that. It sure sounded true. "Then what did happen? There's a bullet wound in my ma's arm. What happened out there?"

Annette looked away.

It cut like a tomahawk. She was lying. She might not have done the shooting or the shoving, but Miss Talbot knew what happened.

"You know something. . ." It ate at Walker to delay getting back to Ma, but he pulled his horse to a stop and grabbed his little liar of a guest by the waist and flipped her right side up. He plunked her none too gently on his horse so she faced him, sitting sidesaddle. Walker scooted back farther to put some space between them.

To think he'd held her in his arms.

To think he'd kissed her.

To think he'd decided she should just stay and join the Walker family by marrying him.

Walker was tempted to toss himself off a cliff. But that wouldn't do much good now, would it? "Tell me what happened. Right now. I'm not letting you freeze to death, but I am sorely tempted to ride back down to the Medicine Bow." Walker caught her by both shoulders and lifted her off the saddle.

Her eyes widened in fear.

Good. The way he was feeling she oughta be scared.

"And dunk your head under the icy water."

"I was trying to help her."

Walker suspected that was true. So what *was* Annette lying about?

His grip tightened. "And hold your head under, *until you tell me the truth!*" He roared straight into her face and shook her as if he could rattle the truth loose.

"I can't tell you." Her head dropped forward. Her voice died on a sob.

"No!" He lurched back to keep her head from touching him. "I'm not letting tears get in the way of this. You're going to talk to me."

Walker wasn't sure, but he might have spit on her by accident. Heaven knew he was raving like a madman. Slobbering probably went along with that.

Still, raving, spitting, shaking notwithstanding, he wasn't going to let up.

"He'll kill you."

He dropped her back onto the saddle. Frozen in shock, he leaned closer. "What? What did you say?"

"There was a man. He shot Ruby. He looked at me and smiled and aimed the gun again—right dead center at the middle of her back while she was hanging there helpless. That's what I was looking at. He put his finger to his lips. He was telling me clear as day he'd shoot her while she dangled there if. . ."

"If what?" The raging hot blood that coursed through his veins turned as cold as the mountains soaring around them.

Annette shook her head. Refusing him.

Well, Walker would see about that.

"Just let me go. Let me get away from you before I bring more harm to your family." She lifted her head. Tears coursed down.

He saw grief, as if Ma had died out there. Fear was written on her face so clearly Walker could barely suppress the urge to pull her into his arms and protect her from anyone who would harm her.

"I never should have come here. Why did I believe my father would care?"

"Tell me what's going on."

"No. They're like snakes, slithering around, striking when you don't expect them. They'll hurt you and Ruby. This isn't your problem. I'll go home to my father's ranch. If I live or die it will only be me. No one else." Swiping one hand across her face, which did no good to stem the flow of tears, she lifted her chin and glared. "No one else is going to be hurt because of me. And if you keep me at your house, you'd better plan on locking me up, because I'm leaving the first chance I get."

The bedroom door slammed shut in her face.

"You're staying till I get the truth!"

She pounded on the door. "You let me out of here."

Elijah opened the door and glared at her. "I told you what I want. You're going to stop letting lies drip out of your mouth."

He swung the door shut again.

Annie jammed her foot in so it wouldn't close. She glared at him out of the three-inch-wide opening in the door. "Just let me go. If—if I tell you the truth, you'll—you'll—" Her voice broke and she hated herself for resorting to tears. Although she wasn't really resorting to them. More like she was just plain heartbroken.

"I'll what?" Elijah's eyes could have burned her to a cinder through that opening if she hadn't already gone up in flames of guilt from bringing disaster to the Walker family.

"You'll hate me."

"I already hate you, pretty, courageous, fine-Christian-woman Annette Talbot. So don't hold back on account of that. Whatever is following you has brought trouble to my home and near death to my mother."

Annie nodded silently. "All right. Yes, I have to tell. If you'd let me leave, the trouble that's following me will come after me. You'll be safe. I just—I just didn't want to leave with y–your contempt ringing in my ears. But yes, I'll tell you everything."

Elijah's eyes snapped with temper. . .and satisfaction. He swung the door open about a foot before a shout sounded from upstairs.

"Walker, get up here and help me with your ma."

Elijah jerked around as if he'd been lassoed and a horse had skidded to pull him in the other direction. He glanced back for a second. "No time for your confession now. And if my ma dies, there's no excuse you can give me that'll stop me from having you locked up right next to Priscilla in the territorial prison." The door slammed.

The snick of a key turning told Annie he'd locked her in. Hammering began outside her window. One of Elijah's cowhands must be nailing the shutters closed to keep her in.

*"If my ma dies"?*

Elijah's stomping shook the house as he sprinted upstairs.

It had been Ruby's arm. She couldn't be dying from that. But there'd been so much blood. People bled to death, didn't they?

Annie staggered away from the door and sank onto the bed. She was stuck in here, and all the danger she brought with her was going to land slap on top of the Walkers. She had to tell him. But not while he was seeing to Ruby.

Annie longed to help but she didn't even bother to offer. Elijah would never hear of it.

It was pure dark outside. Claude would have gone back to his comfortable bed. The foul man wasn't one to suffer personal discomfort.

The Walkers were inside and they'd be safe until morning. Then she'd tell Elijah the truth. It was the only honorable thing to do, so they could protect themselves.

But if they'd just let her leave instead, she wouldn't have to live with that sneering contempt she sometimes got when the mission group had traveled the land. She hadn't known what it meant at first, but she'd gotten a cold shoulder from townsfolk. The night Claude had laughed as his fists landed, he'd told her how he'd soiled her reputation. Claude and, even more so, Blanche were talented liars. Elijah would believe it all.

Even so, because of the attack on Ruby, if she told the truth, Elijah would go storming into town, and that snake, Claude, with his sidewinder

wife, Blanche, would slither into hiding, wait until it was safe, and then strike.

The thought of Elijah dying made Annie collapse onto her back on the bed as she admitted something terrifying to herself.

She was in love with Elijah Walker.

Moreover, she loved Ruby Walker like a mother.

And she'd brought danger to rain down on their heads.

Whatever happened, Annie would still be cast out of this house. Only once Claude had his say, she'd be scorned and condemned. Why couldn't Elijah have just let her go?

She rested her aching head on the pillow, only distantly noting that Ruby's blood still coated her hands. As that registered fully, Annie found a burst of strength and stood to check the pitcher on the nearby chest of drawers. There was water in it.

The water turned pink with Ruby's blood. Annie's tears began flowing again. Tears—such a waste of time and energy. She stared down at the bloody water dripping off her fingers then washed again. She continued washing long after every bit of Ruby's blood was gone from her skin.

The piece of lead pipe up her sleeve kept getting in the way, and she pulled it out and wished Claude was within her reach. Clutching the weapon, she realized the futility of rage. When she'd needed to defend herself, the pipe had been useless.

She set the heavy length of metal aside and looked at her sparkling clean hands, admitting that what she really wanted was to wash away her guilt and to wipe out the memory of Ruby bleeding and hanging on for dear life. No amount of soap and water would ever do that.

Annie gave up and slowly dried her hands. Stumbling sightlessly through tears, she went back to the bed and lay down, too wrung out to even undress, thinking that she'd never truly be able to wash away the blood she'd spilled from sweet Ruby.

God could forgive her. Maybe even Ruby could. But Elijah never would, and even worse, she'd never forgive herself. She'd be cast out tomorrow after she confessed everything. Then she'd live or die on her own in these bitter, cold mountains.

A quiet voice from a dark place in her mind whispered to her, *"You deserve this for being such a coward."*

## TWENTY-FOUR

Unlock that door right this instant, Elijah Walker."

Ruby's voice jerked Annie awake. Her eyes hurt, burning from the salt of tears. Her head ached. Her throat was raw from crying. Ruby's voice dragged her out of a haunted sleep broken by nightmares of death and bleeding and the horrors promised if Claude and Blanche got their hands on her. Being awakened was a mercy.

"I raised you better'n that, young man!"

Annie sat upright just as the door opened.

Elijah glared at her and jerked his head in the direction of Ruby's voice. "Ma wants to see you."

Annie looked past Elijah and saw Ruby sitting at the breakfast table, her arm in a sling. She walked toward Ruby, wanting to run to her, to beg forgiveness, to care for her.

Elijah didn't move. He blocked Annie's exit from the bedroom as if he were a human shield protecting his mother. . .from Annie.

To think Elijah would consider her a danger to Ruby almost set her off crying again. She stopped out of arm's reach and stared up at him.

His fury seemed to shoot bullets at her, just like Claude. Only Elijah's hurt more and the bleeding was all inside.

A twist of resentment that Annie didn't deserve to feel made her whisper in anger, "I would *never* hurt your mother."

"I think last night proved just the opposite." Elijah crossed his arms, as stubborn as a pile of rocks avalanched onto the trail. No one could pass.

"No!" Annie tried to keep her voice down, hoping Elijah would at least believe this. "I love her. She is the sweetest, kindest woman who ever lived."

"Eli, if you make me come over there and shove you out of the way, I will bring a switch with me and warm your backside."

"Sweet, huh?" Elijah's eyes widened and a smile quirked his lips for a second before he got his scowl back in place.

"Now you step aside and let that girl out of there."

His gaze threatened dismemberment, but Elijah gave way an inch or two.

Annie had to brush against him to get through the narrow opening he left.

*I deserve this.*

Annie thought the words over and over as she went toward Ruby, studying the tough old lady.

Ruby was pale.

Yes, Annie resented Elijah's treatment and she was cut to the heart by his anger, but she needed to accept her part in this travesty. She hadn't hurt Ruby, but her cowardice resulted in her injuries.

*I deserve every bit of this.*

Annie dropped to her knees in front of Ruby. She caught Ruby's hand, the one *not* in the sling and held it to her lips. "I'm so sorry you were hurt," Annie whispered, wanting the apology between her and Ruby, not Elijah. Crying, begging, all of it might earn her forgiveness she didn't deserve from Elijah. Best he go on hating her anyway; it would make it easier when he threw her out into the snow. "This is my fault, Ruby. I never dreamed that what I ran away from in my past would bring danger to you."

The stupid tears. Annie fought against them.

"Of course I forgive you, child."

She felt Ruby's hand on her head, as if she were giving a blessing. And Ruby's touch, given with her wounded arm, had to hurt with every movement, because Annie clung to her uninjured hand. Annie was causing this sweet lady even more pain.

She freed Ruby's hand and rose to her feet. Squaring her shoulders, Annie said, "I'll tell you what brought that gunfire down on us."

Ruby looked into her eyes, and Annie felt the connection as deeply as her soul. "Yes, sit up here and tell me. Tell us."

Annie felt Elijah standing over her.

He took her arm and firmly set her in a chair. He moved to the side of the table straight across from Annie. She couldn't hide from him at all. "Tell us." There was none of the kindness in Elijah's voice Annie had heard in Ruby's. Well, it was no surprise that Elijah was a tougher nut to crack than Ruby.

Where to start? The beginning went all the way back to her father sending her away. But the Walkers knew that part of the story already.

"I was part of a traveling mission group. We were mainly around St. Louis. The elderly couple who led our group took me in when I graduated from high school and there was no money from my father to come home. After a year or so with the group, the elderly couple retired, and a younger couple who had recently joined the group took over—Claude and Blanche Leveque. I didn't realize at first because they put on a good show of piousness, but the Leveques weren't believers. They used the mission troupe as a front."

"A front for what?" Ruby asked.

"They'd have me singing out front, and behind closed doors they'd run a gambling hall. They were playing poker and selling whiskey in the back room while I—" Annie's voice faltered.

Ruby rested a steadying hand on Annie's wrist.

Elijah's eyes followed the movement and his eyes narrowed in anger.

"Anyway, I walked through the wrong door one night and found out about it and confronted Claude and Blanche." Annie couldn't go on.

The silence stretched.

"And what happened?" Elijah's voice startled her out of her dark memories.

Steadying herself, she said, "He knocked me down."

Elijah surged to his feet and walked away from the table with his fists clenched.

Ruby's hand tightened on Annie's until the pain made her go on.

"We were in a logging camp, very remote. He dragged me into this little cabin. Claude said he'd—he'd hurt me until I'd do anything he asked. He told me there are worse things than a fist. Worse even than death. He promised to do all of them if I didn't go on that night, sing the awful songs he wanted me to sing, wear his indecent costume. He locked me in and left.

"Later, Elva, the lady who played the piano for me while I sang, came and let me out. She'd been with the show for a long time and was like a mother to me. When she came to my cabin, she was battered, far worse then I had been.

"Claude had done the same to Elva that he'd done to me. Somehow Elva had gotten away from him. When she came to me, she was staggering, barely able to stay on her feet. She shoved a reticule with money into my hands and told me to run. Then she clutched her chest and fell to the floor. Her last words begged me to run as far as possible from the ugliness Claude had planned for me. So I did."

"And how did that lead to Ma getting shot?"

"I saw Claude and Blanche out at Pa's cabin. I fell into the river while I was running from them—again—always running. I'm nothing but a coward."

Ruby made a sound of protest and patted her hands.

"Claude must have shot me when I fell. I woke up here, and at first I couldn't remember what happened. Then I saw Claude in town when we went in to see Frank, and it all came back to me."

"In town? In Ranger Bluff?" Elijah asked. "He's still hanging around?"

"Yes, and I saw him last night. He was on the high ground across

that gap. He wore a mask, so I can't swear it was him, but I know it was. He's the one who shot you, Ruby. I looked up and he aimed his gun right at you. Then he put his finger to his lips. He still wants me. My singing voice really draws in the crowd. Claude will hurt anyone who tries to protect me. He wants me to keep singing, but he wants other things from me, too. I told him I'd die first, but he obviously has no intention of killing me. Elva died, and now, Ruby, and you, Elijah, could. He has no conscience that will stop him from killing."

"Why didn't you say something?" Elijah snapped. "When you saw him in town, we could have arrested him on the spot for chasing you off that cliff."

"There's more." Annie looked up and saw Elijah's lips thin and his jaw go rigid.

"Let's hear it."

"Claude's like a snake. He won't come after you openly. He'll slither around and strike when you're not expecting it. You and the sheriff will fight fair. Claude will not."

"Anything else?" Elijah sounded cold, his eyes were narrow, and finally Annie knew that the rumors had reached Elijah's ears.

"Yes."

Elijah sat back down. "I thought there might be. How deeply involved were you with the gambling, Annette?"

Annie jerked her chin up and glared at Elijah. "I didn't even know about it until the day I ran away."

"That's not what I've heard."

Her heart sank. Annie knew what came next. Claude had done his work, blackened her name. She'd known when she first saw him in town, obviously not afraid of what Annie would say. He'd arranged it so no one would believe her.

"Claude is a master at spreading rumors. What have you heard?" Annie knew she shouldn't ask. She couldn't stop herself from adding quickly, "This is why I didn't attend church last week. And why I wanted to slip away last night. I knew Claude would be busy fueling gossip. He did it in every town we went to, though I didn't know that until the end either. It kept people away from me so I'd have no protection if I decided to leave the show."

Annie looked up and saw Elijah's suspicions. "Claude will no doubt say I stole money from him. The money Elva gave me. But Elva would never have broken a commandment. God was the center of her life. She didn't just talk about her faith, she lived it every day. I know she died that night because she refused to submit herself to Claude's will when it opposed God's. I should have done the same. Instead of running, I should have stood my ground even if it cost me my life."

Ruby patted her hand. "If Elva was a good friend and wise, then you were right to do as she said. She died so you could get away. To stay would have meant her sacrifice was for nothing."

Elijah's voice broke into Ruby's kind reassurance. "I've heard the rumors. They cast you in a very dim light, Annette. Very dim."

*I deserve this.*

What's more, it didn't matter. The truth or not, Annie was still a danger to the Walker family and she had to leave.

*I deserve this.*

Annie admitted with a broken heart that through her own actions, Elijah would never believe her.

## TWENTY-FIVE

Walker was falling for her lies. Admitting it made him sick, but he was.

He'd believed all of Priscilla's lies, too. He was dumber than the longhorns he was supposed to be in charge of. And yet he believed Annette.

Worse yet, she was takin' his ma in. Did that mean she was that much a better liar than Priscilla, or was she really telling the truth? Trying to decide made Walker want to hit his head against something hard.

Frank had brought in several more dark rumors about Annette since the first one. Not because he believed in gossip—Frank didn't play in that filth—but because he felt that Walker needed to know what was being said.

It made sense that Leveque was starting them, but it wasn't a natural assumption. True, the rumors about Annette had started when Leveque came to town, but Leveque had come to town at the same time as Annette, so Walker had just put it down to Annette being known by someone, or maybe she'd said the wrong thing and someone had put a twist on it. Gossips could make a quiet little story nasty if a person had some spare time and the inclination.

Walker studied Annette, who was busy holding hands with his ma.

If it made him a fool or not, he believed her.

Then Ma turned to him. "We've got to button this ranch up tight. We need lookouts, sentries posted on all the trails and high ground so no one can get in position to take another shot at us. When we first came out here, there was no law and we always saw to our own protection. We'll go back to that. We should stay out of town for a while. The trail in is too risky. And somehow we've got to alert the sheriff. If this Leveque is spreading rumors, the sheriff ought to be able to get to the bottom of it."

Walker nodded. His only plan had been to stay away from Annette until he could be sure of the truth, despite his temptation to believe her. What he wanted to do was ignore Annette's description of the sneaky Leveques and ride into Ranger Bluff and run Claude out of town.

As usual his ma's head was working clearly. Even with a bullet wound in her arm, near death on a cliff, and little or no sleep, the woman was smarter than he'd ever be.

Walker figured he was going to get his ear chewed off by his ma, but that didn't mean he was going to let Annette run loose around this ranch, drawing danger onto herself and everyone else. Nor did he plan to give her a chance to slip away. "Annette's going to spend her nights locked in that bedroom, Ma."

Annette gasped and clenched her fists on the table.

"Elijah Walker," his ma started in on him, "don't you even—"

"She'll run off, Ma. Sure as you're born, she'll take to the hills the second we take our eyes off of her." Elijah wasn't used to trying to be boss over his ma, and he didn't have a whole lot of hope that she'd start minding him now.

But his ma's eyes got real serious and she looked away from Walker to Annette. "You will, won't you, Annie? You'd risk your life to protect us."

"Ruby, I can't stay and—"

"I agree, Eli. We'll lock her in at night." Ruby cut her off. "I'll watch her during the day, and we won't even venture outside unless you say the sentries are in place."

"Lock me in?" Annette gasped. "You can't."

"Give me your word you won't run off." Ruby held her gaze steady on Annette.

Walker waited for false promises and more lies.

Dead silence stretched in the room.

Annette looked at Ruby then glanced at Walker.

Swallowing visibly, Walker saw the color rise in Annette's cheeks and a stubborn look of defiance flash in her eyes. "I—I will. . .st—st. . ." Her voice faded. Her eyes dropped to the tabletop.

"You can't lie, can you, Annie?" Ruby laid one hand over Annette's.

"She's been lying since she came here, Ma. Don't fool yourself."

Ruby shook her head. "She's been leaving things out, things she should have told me right away." Ruby tightened her grip on Annie's hands. "She thought her silence protected all of us."

"No, I don't deserve that much credit, Ruby."

"We agreed you'd call me Ma."

Walker was swallowing at that exact instant and he started to choke.

Annette's eyes flew open wide. "I can't. I will not. I don't deserve—"

"Nonsense. I told you people call me Ma Walker. I prefer it. Except skip the Walker part."

Walker had put up with this when he'd thought Annie was honest. He'd never heard anyone call Ruby Walker Ma but himself. But he probably counted as "some" people, so now his ma was "not exactly lying" just like Annette. No wonder these two got along.

Disgusted, especially by the strange, warm lump he felt in his chest at the thought of Annette calling his mother Ma, Walker got up from the table so abruptly he knocked his chair over backward. "Just keep your eye on her. She doesn't have the sense God gave to a fencepost."

He turned his eyes on Annette and did his best to bore a hole in her head to see if she had a lick of sense in there. "And if you don't stay inside, you'll find yourself locked in that room all day every day. You won't so much as go to the *outhouse* without an armed guard." Walker jammed his hat on his head and grabbed his coat.

His ma said, "What happened to that lead pipe I gave you?"

Slamming the door, he realized he'd never had breakfast. He'd missed supper, too. He'd been up with Ma most of the night. He was starving and cold and mad and exhausted and scared to the bone to think of that madman pointing his gun at his ma and Annette.

He headed for the bunkhouse. He had some sentry duty to assign.

"I'm not going to call you Ma anymore." Annie twined her fingers in her lap and stared at them. She'd be sinking to a low she'd never dreamed of to use that affectionate name on the sweet lady she'd nearly gotten killed. "If you don't like Ruby, I'll call you Mrs. Walker, but I don't deserve to call you—"

Ruby slapped her hand on the table.

Annie jumped and looked up to find Ruby's eyes burning right into her own.

"I am sick to death of that word: *deserve*. You've said it until I want to lose the food in my belly. None of us *deserves* a thing, Annie. *None* of us deserves love or forgiveness or food or a warm house. We're all born unto trouble, as the sparks fly upward. We are living on the sole mercy of God. Now, I don't give a *hoot* if you think you deserve to call me Ma *or* live in this house *or* eat our food.

"I"—Ruby jabbed her index finger at her own chest—"don't deserve to live with the knowledge that I was so worried about myself last night I'd have let a young woman wander out into the cold night and die."

"You'd been shot!"

Ruby talked right over her. "That's what you're trying to hang around my neck, isn't it? Eli told me he had to drag you in here."

"No, I wanted to protect you from my own mistakes. I wanted to draw those evil people away from you."

"Well, you might think that's brave, honey." Ruby's jabbing finger nearly poked Annie in the nose and Annie straightened away from

Ruby's fury. "You might even think that's honorable. You may even think you *deserve* to die because—why? I can't quite remember where your twisted thinking took you. You deserve to die because you didn't catch on to the Leveques sooner?"

Annie shook her head frantically. "No! I deserve—"

Ruby cut her off, her eyes flashing fire. "Or because you didn't stand in that cabin and let yourself be killed rather than run?"

"I didn't say—" She might as well not have spoken.

"Or was it because you left your friend behind? She *died* trying to set you free, but you think it was cowardly to take that chance she *died* to give you." Ruby stood without a single grimace. She was tougher with her arm in a sling than Annie was at full strength. "I can't quite follow that hopping rabbit trail in your head that leads to 'I deserve to die.'"

Annie's mouth gaped open, but even if she could clear up Ruby's twisted thinking, she was a little afraid to. Elijah had said his ma was tough. Well, he hadn't told her the half of it. Ruby Walker mad was a formidable, scary woman.

"Now, get up and let's get breakfast on. Eli will bring in the eggs and milk and, knowing him, he plans to hide all day. We'll have to move fast or he'll go without breakfast. I see you slept in your dress. Good, saves time. Get to cracking what's left of yesterday's eggs. While you scramble them, I'll slice some ham and put some biscuits on to bake."

Her eyes wide with fear, Annie nodded frantically. "Yes, ma'am."

Ruby jammed her one good hand on her hip. "What did I tell you to call me?"

With a quick flash of memory, Annie recalled a switch her mother had bandied about. She hadn't used it often, but Annie knew well enough she would if Annie didn't mind and right quick. Her ma had taken much the same tone as Ruby just before she'd gone for that switch. "M-M-Ma?"

"That's better. I don't want to hear another name for me come out of your mouth."

"Yes, M–M–Ma." Annie hurried to follow Ma's orders.

Gabriel Michaels slipped into a chair at one of the scarred tables in the makeshift theater.

He studied the woman singing. Blanche Leveque. He knew the name well. Fingering the papers in his shirt pocket, he didn't pull them out. He had them all memorized, not the least of which was a WANTED poster with Annette Talbot's name on it.

Blanche hit a sour note and Gabriel flinched. Glancing around, he saw Claude sitting at another table, talking quietly with a man dressed like a cowpoke. Another man joined their table, then another. The foursome seemed oblivious to the singing onstage, which was odd. Why come in except for the singing? There wasn't much else.

Gabriel looked away. He had a feeling Claude didn't miss much going on around him and Gabe didn't want to be caught staring.

Touching the papers again, Gabe decided it was time for another visit with the closely guarded Miss Talbot. Those Walkers had her next thing to under lock and key. Gabe needed time with her, a lot of time. Gabe had a lot of anger to work off, and he'd start with Annette Talbot.

Blanche screeched again, and only fury and determination kept Gabe in that chair. He'd start with Annette, and what he learned there would lead him somewhere else.

Unless Annette was the end of the line.

She might well give him a final resting place for his rage.

One of Claude's tablemates stood and walked out the front door. A second followed within five minutes. During another awful song, the last friend of Claude's left, and finally, Claude made his move. He stood so casually none of the other dozen or so people in the theater even glanced his way. Then Claude went toward his singing partner and slipped past her into some back room.

The littlest *squeak* of a back door soon told Gabe that Claude had opened it, letting in his new suckers. Gabe didn't have to hear a thing to

know chairs were being scooted up to a table and cards were being shuffled and money was being lost by men who could ill afford to lose it.

Poker wasn't Gabe's game. But he had one of his own. It was time to deal himself in. Round one started with another visit to pretty Annette Talbot. He'd met the Walkers' requirements by buying a stretch of land he might even stay to run when this was over. He'd attended church and persuaded the parson he was a decent man. The parson had written him a letter of introduction and would speak up for him if the Walkers asked.

With all that, he knew the Walkers would just find some other way to run him off. He'd seen the look in Elijah Walker's eyes. The man had his own interest in Annie. But Gabe wasn't a man to be run off. So, he'd find a way past the watchdogs and get his hands on Miss Talbot.

Checking his Colt revolver to make sure it slid easily in and out of his holster, he felt his anger focus and spread. He sat through two more songs out of pure stubbornness then headed to the boardinghouse to savor finally that he was done waiting.

Revenge was within his grasp.

# TWENTY-SIX

*Plague* was a good way to describe women.

Walker did his best to avoid the ones infecting his house before he caught something.

Like a wife.

Normally Walker exempted his mother from his dim view of womankind, but not on the topic of Annette Talbot. When it came to Annette, his ma had some kind of fever burning up her brain, and if Walker wasn't afraid of back shooters, he'd have taken both women to town and dumped 'em off on the doc. As it was, Walker avoided the house because he couldn't stand listening to Annette call his very own mother Ma.

And Ma only made it worse. Walker was onto her. The feisty old lady had set her sights on matchmaking between Walker and Annette, and she wasn't being subtle.

Ma, who had never taken it easy on herself in her life, was being purely a baby about that measly bullet scratch. Her arm still wasn't out of the sling, and she was using that as an excuse to duck chores after mealtime and rest, leaving Walker alone far too often with that pretty little probably-not-a-liar Annette. Walker was now washing the dishes for breakfast, dinner, and supper. He'd even taken to helping cook. And all because Ma would press the back of her hand to her forehead and

claim she needed to rest.

Annette kept trying to shoo Walker out. No, the little woman hadn't cast her eyes in his direction. But they were both at the mercy of Walker's ma, and they couldn't be hard on her when she fussed that Annette had too much to do and she, herself, was a failure and a burden and couldn't Walker just please, please help out a bit.

His beloved mother used guilt like she was pulling a Colt revolver. And the woman had become the fastest draw in Wyoming.

Walker was trapped. He saw clear that Annette was, too. They could deny Ma nothing, and the cagey old biddy used that ruthlessly. Maybe it was because the womenfolk had been almost completely shut up in the house for days, not even allowed out for church—Ma had sure kicked up a fuss about that. The plain, bald truth was his mother had too much spare time and energy and she'd taken to scheming.

When Ma made her way up the stairs after the noon meal, looking like she could barely keep her knees from wobbling long enough to get upstairs and lie down, Annette looked after the woman with worried eyes. As soon as Ma's door shut, Annette turned to Walker. "I am worried about Ma, Elijah."

"Don't call her that!" Walker tied on his apron, feeling like a fool. The pink-flowered gingham was humiliating. If he was going to permanently do women's work, he ought to at least get an apron in a manly color. With no flowers or ruffles. Maybe a nice soft buckskin.

Annie arched both her brows nearly to her hairline. "I have to. You can't believe how she acts when I don't." Annie sounded scared.

"Yeah, I can." Walker knew exactly how scary Ma could be.

"It's been a week since the accident." Annie wrung her hands together, fretting. "She should be feeling stronger by now. I think the sling should have come off after a couple of days, but she says it hurts too badly. I think you should send for the doctor, even if it is dangerous to go to town."

"You know she's just fine." Walker felt like the world's most heartless, low-down polecat, but he had to tell Annette the hard facts. "You've seen her yourself, spry as a ten-year-old, working around the house all the time except when I'm—"

*She knows.*

Walker wasn't going to say it. Annette knew and she approved. Despite her confused, innocent expression, Walker couldn't believe Annette wasn't plotting and planning with Ma behind his back.

"Except what?"

*Maybe she doesn't know.*

Walker scrubbed on an already-clean plate while he tried to figure out how to say it.

He looked at her. Words failed.

He slid the tin plate out onto the edge of the sink where it'd drain until Annette got around to wiping it dry. Then he squared his shoulders. He'd faced down cantankerous longhorns bent on stomping him to death then carrying him around on their horns like a trophy. Surely he could talk honestly with one little woman. One pretty little woman. One pretty little woman with the pinkest lips and eyes so light blue Walker forgot he was on the ground and imagined himself floating around in the clouds every time he looked at them. Which is why he did his best to never look.

Except he was looking now.

Whipping his head around to his rapidly cooling soapy water, he said, "My ma has—has—" In sudden annoyance, Walker slapped the dishcloth down into the water and splattered himself and his ridiculous pink apron with soap suds. He turned on Annette and looked right in those eyes. "You don't expect me to believe you don't know."

Shaking her head, her pretty eyes wide in fear, she said, "I don't know what? Ma has. . .what?"

"Ma has—" He was going to have to say it. He swallowed and wiped his hands on his flouncy apron, taking a second to straighten the ruffles and bat away a few foaming balls of soap. "She has decided we—we suit."

Annette leaned a bit closer. "She wants me to. . .sew you a suit?"

Walker's patience snapped. He caught Annette by her upper arms. "No. She's decided we *suit*. Each other. She wants to keep you. For me. For herself. She's not having you call her Ma because it's a nickname. *She really wants to be your ma.* She's matchmaking. She's playing sick so we get left alone. She's hoping we'll. . .I'll. . ."

Walker didn't even mean to kiss the confounded woman. He was absolutely clear on that as his lips touched hers. His hands slid around her waist even while he was denying this was what he wanted.

She was so soft, so gentle as her arms came around his neck. He tilted his head and deepened the kiss, wondering how such lying lips could taste so sweet. How such shining, honest blue eyes could hide the soul of a deceiver.

*God, what am I doing? Who is Annette Talbot? When will I start to use my head and keep my heart from drawing me into trouble with women?*

He pulled her closer and she came along quietly. In fact, he lifted her up onto her toes and ran one hand up to bury in her beautiful hair. He'd do it. There was no way to trust himself after the mistakes he'd made, but he'd trust Ma. And that meant he could do what he wanted and trust Annette. He'd tell her he thought they'd suit, too, just as soon as he finished kissing the daylights out of her.

A fist slammed against the front door and began pounding so loudly Walker wondered if the knocker had been at it for a long time.

He wrenched his lips away from hers, set her back onto her feet, and unwound her arms from his neck, scared by the wide-eyed, dazed look in her beautiful eyes, fastened right on him.

Well, honestly, he wasn't a man to tell a lie—not even to himself—and *scared* wasn't the right word at all. He wished like crazy he was scared instead of being more certain of how he felt than he'd ever been before in his life.

Her knees gave out. He caught her and dragged her to the nearest chair. Plunking her down in it, he went to the rattling door before whoever was pounding snapped the hinges.

As his head cleared, Walker wondered why the man always had to keep his head when there was kissing going on. Why wasn't that at least partly a woman's job?

And why was there any kissing going on in the first place?

What tomfool notion had taken hold? And why was Ma doing this?

She and Pa had made a production out of never leaving Walker alone with Prissy, not even for a split second. It wasn't proper to leave him alone with Annette, and he was going to tell his ma. He was done with Ma's foolishness, and he was done being alone with Annette. It was time Ma figured out that he had absolutely no interest whatsoever, not a speck in the whole wide world, in the pretty little filly who had invaded his home.

He swung the door open on Gabe Michaels, the sidewinder who was trying to steal his woman.

&#x269C;

Gabe wondered if he was going to have to fight his way past Walker. . . and his pink apron.

He felt an itch between his shoulder blades that made him want to use his fists to wipe the scowl off Walker's face, but he didn't. No sense doing that until it was necessary. He didn't discount it as a fallback position.

He'd talk to Annette today or know the reason why. If he couldn't get her alone, overprotective Elijah Walker might have to witness something he'd rather not.

Walker glowered and Gabe braced himself. Finally, Walker glanced behind him at Annette, who looked flustered.

Then Gabe took a better look.

Annette looked more than flustered. She looked dazed and her eyes kept going to Walker with a longing that told Gabe he had serious competition in courting Annette, even if he was only courting her for his own reasons.

If he was readin' signs right, Annette's lips were a little swollen and

Walker's hair had a look about it like maybe a pretty woman had just run her fingers through it.

If Walker was sparking Annette, then she might well agree to talk to Gabe alone rather than have a man she was sweet on hear of the trouble swirling around. After all, if she was willing to kiss the man while he wore that stupid apron, she must be more than a little interested.

Gabe pulled his Stetson off his head, ran a gloved hand through his overly long hair to keep it out of his eyes, and did his best to live up to his ma's high standards of good raisin'.

"Howdy, Walker. I've come to call on Miss Talbot, as I said I would. I'm settled and have something to offer a young lady now." Walker's manners goaded Gabe into forgetting he'd prefer the man's goodwill. And what difference did it make? Walker wasn't going to be nice about Gabe talking with Annie, so Gabe might as well be nasty right back. "By the way, pink's a good color on you."

The temperature in the house was dropping by about ten degrees a second. Still, Walker didn't step aside and let Gabe in. He crossed his arms as if he were proud he was wearing gingham and ruffles.

Gabe had to fight to keep a smile off his face. This wasn't a man who was very confident of his woman. Jealous and confused and even irritated. Gabe had come before it was too late.

Finally, looking as bothered as a man could, Walker stepped back and swung the door wide so Gabe could step inside.

"Put your coat and hat on that hook." Walker jabbed a finger at some elk antlers by the front door then turned away from Gabe and shouted up the stairs, "Ma, that cowboy's here again, the one sparkin' Annette. Get down here."

Annette snapped, "Elijah, your mother's resting." Turning to Gabe, really looking at him for the first time, Annette added, "We had an. . . incident out here a few days back. Ma was wounded and she's still very fragile and ailing. She needs peace and quiet."

Ruby Walker came charging out of some room upstairs. A door slammed hard and her feet thudded on the floor. She came down the stairs with the delicate finesse of a stampeding herd of longhorns and skidded to a halt right beside Annette.

Guard dog number two had arrived. And not looking wounded at all.

"Ma, where's your sling?" Annette went to Ruby's side.

"Ma?" Gabe hung up his hat and shrugged off his duster to put it on the elk antlers alongside a row of coats and hats. He turned back to the Walker clan, wondering when they'd started counting Annette as part of the family. "So you've adopted Miss Talbot then? She's your sister now?"

Walker's eyes narrowed. Annette flushed. Ruby's chin came up.

"Of course not." Annette seemed to gather her manners first.

Not a great accomplishment considering the rude treatment Gabe always got at this house. And, truth be told, he'd have deserved it if they knew what he was here for.

"Everyone around these parts calls her Ma."

Gabe had never heard such a thing in town, and he'd listened close for mention of the Walkers and Annette.

"Ma, can I invite Mr. Michaels in to sit and share a cup of coffee with us?"

Ruby made a snorting sound that was pure rude.

Walker crossed his arms and glared at Annette as if she'd invited a rabid she-wolf in for tea and cookies. "Sure, fine, get him a cup." Walker jerked his head at that same stupid rocking chair.

Gabe had to think fast or he'd find himself out on the front steps as fast as last time.

"I am now the owner of a parcel of land just southeast of town. There were a lot of silver mines there at one time, but they've played out and the claims have been abandoned. I own about a thousand acres with good grass and water. And I've bought cull cows from a couple of herds. I know it's not a big setup like the Walker ranch, not established at all, but I believe I've put down enough roots that it would be acceptable for me to ask Miss Talbot to come for a ride to town for lunch. I rented a buggy—"

"No!" Annette dropped the tin coffee cup.

"Buggy rides are out!" Walker's refusal came on top of Annette's.

"She can't go. It's out of the question." Ruby came up with two whole sentences.

"I see it's unanimous." Gabe smiled. He could tell they'd heard the gossip, too, so maybe Annette was embarrassed or maybe she was hiding. One made her innocent, the other, a cold-blooded killer.

Gabe tested them. "Any reason she can't come to Ranger Bluff with me? You could ride along. . . ." Gabe let a few seconds lapse before he looked at Ruby and added, "Ma."

Walker's whole body clenched like a drawn-back fist.

Gabe wanted to laugh in his face. If any of them thought they were being subtle, they weren't. Gabe decided he wouldn't be either. He strode right up to Walker's face. "I need to talk to Annette alone. You don't look inclined to allow that. So you ask her."

"Ask her what?" Walker glared.

Gabe turned and gave Annette an assessing look. "Ask her if there's anything she'd rather not have aired in front of one and all."

Annette gasped and clutched that stupid cup that she had retrieved from the floor to her chest like it was a shield. Not a very good one considering some of the slings and arrows flying around her.

"She's not going anywhere with you." Walker caught Gabe's arm. "What's going on?"

Gabe turned back to have this out. "You gonna use that fist, Walker?"

Walker looked down at his clenched fist.

" 'Cuz if you are, take the apron off first. I'll feel like a fool, punching a man wearing ruffles." Gabe didn't want this to descend to a brawl, especially since Walker might be all Gabe could handle.

Gabe thought he could take him, but Gabe didn't discount Ruby. That woman could do some damage while Gabe was occupied shoving Walker's bad attitude down his throat.

Walker let go of Gabe and jerked at apron strings, his eyes flashing so much fire, no amount of pink ruffles could soften his potential for danger.

"Ask her." Gabe jerked his head at Annette without taking his eyes off of Walker. "It's that simple. Ask her if there's anything I could say she'd rather not have you hear. Annette and I could step outside for a few minutes. Out of earshot but in clear sight of you and Ma."

"I told you to call her Miss Talbot. And my mother's name is Mrs. Walker to you." Walker was about an inch taller than Gabe, and like all ranchers, he probably had muscles forged in the iron of hard work.

But Gabe had lived a long time on the brutal trails blazed by the cavalry. He could hold his own with any man. But that wasn't the way Gabe wanted it. "Annie, in or out?" Gabe had given more than his share of orders in his day. "Public or private? Decide right now."

Walker finally stopped trying to burn Gabe to a cinder with his eyes and turned to look at the wide-eyed woman.

Gabe wondered what all things were rushing around in her head. Did the woman have so many secrets she couldn't sift through them all to decide what might be going to come out?

"I know there's talk about me in Ranger Bluff. It's not true, but it—it frightens me to think of what awful thing might come out of your mouth, Mr. Michaels." Annie squared her shoulders and set the cup on the counter beside the sink with a sharp *click* of tin on wood. "But I choose to hear it in front of Elijah and Ma. In public. Say whatever vile thing you've heard repeated about me for all of us to hear."

"It's not gossip that brings me here, Annie."

Annie's expression eased from fear to confusion. "Then what?"

"I've come to find out if you killed my ma."

"What?" Annie gasped; her hand flew to her throat.

Gabe saw the shock and horror of the accusations. But he refused to back down. He'd waited too long as it was. "And if you did, I'm here to see you hanged."

# TWENTY-SEVEN

Killed someone?" Annie staggered backward and nearly fell over the table. A chair tripped her and she managed to sit down hard. "Hanged?"

Ruby was at her side in an instant, kneeling, dabbing Annie's brow with a kerchief. "He's talking nonsense, Annie honey. We'll get to the bottom of it."

Annie's eyes flew to Elijah's and her stomach swooped. Yet another accusation against her. This one about putting someone else's mother in danger. She was sorely afraid Elijah was inclined to believe the worst.

She did her best to gather her nerve and shore up her backbone. Then she turned to Gabe Michaels and didn't even try to keep the anger out of her voice. It was a far better choice than terror. "What are you talking about, Mr. Michaels? In the past, whatever the horrible lies spread about me, I've never been accused of *harming* anyone. . .or have I? I thought Claude and Blanche's rumors usually circled around my sins of the flesh, although I've been accused of being a thief of late."

As she spoke, the fear leached away and she was left exhausted. She really was a coward. Rather than face people with the lies and defend herself and try to win their trust, she'd chosen to hide, to run, to move on and leave behind the distrust of many. Of course she hadn't known about it at first. But she knew about it now, and here she was, hiding while the good people of Ranger Bluff believed the worst. With a sickening twist of her stomach, she realized that by letting Claude's gossip stand, she'd undone any good her singing might have brought to a thirsty soul.

*Lord God, I really do deserve this.*

"Who is it I'm supposed to have killed? Your mother? Who is that?"

Gabe got down on one knee less than a foot in front of Annie, almost as if he were preparing to ask for her hand in marriage, but his eyes were ice cold. He clearly got down to eye level because he wanted to see every expression that crossed her face when he made his accusation.

Annie looked in his eyes, aware that Elijah had moved in close behind the kneeling man. Ma stayed at her side, holding her hands.

"Elva Lasley."

Annie gasped, then reached out her hands and clasped hold of Gabe's shoulders. "You're Elva's son? Gabriel Michaels?"

"Gabriel Michael Lasley." He nodded.

She didn't even consider any other action. She threw her arms around his neck and hugged him tight.

"She talked about you all the time."

Gabriel jumped a bit, rising to his feet. He put his hands on her waist, and for a second, Annie expected to be shoved away.

She couldn't bear it so she talked fast. "You and—how many was it—seven brothers, right? Her beloved sons." The first tears caught her by surprise. She was so delighted to meet this man Elva was so proud of. "She had your picture, one picture with all of you in it." Pulling back, Annie studied his face. "You were all of fourteen years old."

Gabe's face had faded from its icy anger. Now she saw confusion and the deep lines of sadness rooted in the love he had for his mother. "It's the only picture the family ever had taken. Pa died three years later."

"That mustache." Annie traced it with one finger then dropped her

hand back to his shoulder. "Your mother would have scolded you for it and for letting your hair get so long."

"Stop!" Gabe swung his hands between Annie and himself. "I'm not going to listen to you talk about my mother. You left her. There was talk in the camp that you'd stolen her life savings. That you killed her and left her or maybe saw her dying and took her money and left her. They said you—" Gabe's voice broke and he turned his back on her.

Annie's heart broke along with Gabe's voice, to think that kind of filth had been left in the wake of her escape. She was such a coward. She deserved Gabe's hate. She deserved the ugly gossip because she hadn't stood up against it. She'd hoped to leave behind faith and worship and joy.

"I heard you were with her when she died," he went on unsteadily.

"I was." Annie nodded. "It was terrible. She had a heart attack, or at least—"

"And you just ran away?" The anger crept back into Gabe's voice. "Abandoned her? Did you even try to get her to a doctor?"

He grabbed her arms and dragged her to her feet. "When I got to that logging camp, she'd been dead two months. She was buried in an unmarked grave. No one there was even sure where it was."

"Oh, Gabe, no." Annie couldn't hold back the tears. Precious Elva.

"So there she lies alone, so far away from all of us. I couldn't even put flowers on her grave. And all because you wanted her few dollars."

Suddenly Walker pulled her back, planting himself firmly between Annie and Gabe.

Annie stood on her tiptoes so she could still see Elva's beloved youngest son. "I'll tell you everything, Gabe. I loved your mother. She *did* die of a heart attack, but she'd been hurt." Annie dodged around Elijah and put a gentle hand on Gabe's shoulder, guiding him to the nearest chair. She took the rocking chair next to him and settled in. "The man who led the mission group was a fine man, but his health was failing and he turned the ministry over to a couple who were newcomers—Claude and Blanche Leveque."

"I know the Leveques were involved. I've been watching them, too." Gabe's jaw firmed until it was a hard, grim line.

"Claude asked me to perform songs other than my usual hymns. It was patriotic music and other fun, harmless songs. Nothing inappropriate, but I refused. And he tried to get me to change my dress to something fancier. Again, not sinful, but brighter colors, silky fabrics. I felt like it wasn't fit for me to stand in front of a crowd dressed that way and sing to them purely for their entertainment. Claude went along with my refusal, but he pressed me repeatedly to change my mind. I saw glimpses of his temper when I'd refuse."

Once or twice, more than glimpses. How could she not have known?

"And he was—was. . .well, his behavior wasn't exactly improper, but he made me uncomfortable. He touched me too often. Just on the arm or resting his hand on my back." Annie looked down at her hands twisted together. "I didn't like him but I didn't speak up. I told myself I was overreacting. I told myself he was my moral leader and God calls us to submit ourselves to our leaders. I treated him with respect, sang and dressed as I chose, and did my best to never be alone with him. I felt convicted of the sin of disobedience and believed that to share my dislike of Claude was a sin. I made certain my part of the mission was pure and didn't ask questions or stir up trouble. Claude was very careful to never do anything clearly inappropriate, but somehow I knew, even though he was married, his touches were. . .overtures. He hoped I'd return those overtures."

"You didn't tell my ma even?" Gabe asked.

"No." Annie raised her eyes, determined to be honest. "You might as well know it, Gabe. I had a hint of Claude's true nature, but it was easier to ignore my discomfort rather than confront him. Because I hesitated, Claude was able to pick his moment."

"Pick his moment for what?"

"His moment to attack." Annie's hands came up to her neck as she remembered the terror in that remote cabin. "He came to me in that mining camp and told me I'd sing his songs and wear the costumes he

selected. Only now the dress he chose was scandalous and the songs were bawdy. I refused, even when he used his fists on me. He told me he'd spread rumors about me and no one would take my side. Instead, they'd line up and pay money to see me prance about in that dress. Claude had spread the word that I'd be willing to do that—had in fact done it many times."

A dark noise pulled her attention away from Gabe to Elijah. His teeth were gritted and his brows slammed down over his eyes. She wished so desperately he'd been there with her that dark night. He'd have protected her and Elva. She should have given others a chance. Why had she been such a coward?

"When I still refused to do his bidding, he told me he'd hurt Elva if I didn't. Then he charged out. Later, your mother came and let me out. She was bleeding, clutching her chest. She gave me money and told me to run. I refused to leave her, and she begged me to save myself. She told me she was going home to her heavenly Father and I was to go home to Wyoming. Her dying wish was for me to save myself. So I did. She died in my arms and I abandoned her there." Her voice broke. "I should have stayed. Claude couldn't have used Elva as a threat anymore. I should have stayed and defied him and died for my faith if it was asked of me."

"No!" Ruby came to her side and wrapped her arms around Annie. "No, I know a mother's heart, Annie. Elva was wise and she knew what needed to be done. You were right to escape from that mining camp."

Annie shook her head silently.

"So, Claude Leveque and his wife are behind her death?"

Annie steadied her voice. "But I can't prove it."

Gabe stood from the chair so fast it skidded across the floor. "I don't need any more proof."

Annie stood and touched Gabe's arm. "They didn't kill her. I'm sure she died of a heart attack."

"But he put his hands on her. He hurt her until her heart failed."

"You have nobody to testify to that except me, a witness to her condition and her dying words. And my word isn't worth a cent." Annie firmed her jaw, knowing she spoke the brutal truth. "Claude has seen to it that I will at the very least be doubted. In fact, he's arranged for me to be blamed. Just like you blamed me. You're willing to believe me now?"

"I half believed you already." Gabe's kind words helped calm her. "Ma sent letters to all of us." Gabe touched his pocket in an absent way and Annie heard paper *crackle*.

"She sent one letter a week to her oldest son." Annie smiled. "With instructions that he read it and mail it on to the next brother in line."

"She loved you like the daughter she never had." He reached up and rested one hand on the back of her fingers resting on his upper arm.

"Your mother loved everybody. She had the most beautiful soul."

"Yes, she did." Gabe nodded. "But you were special. She always wanted a daughter."

His eyes warmed and suddenly Annie could see the resemblance to Elva. "Your eyes are the same dark shade as hers. And you've got her coloring. It's hard with the mustache, but I can see Elva in you."

"I'm flattered." Gabe stroked his mustache. "When I was a kid I hated it. The rest of my brothers take after Pa, but lookin' like Ma, well, they tormented me something fierce."

"She talked about her sons. They kept her hopping, but she adored you all."

The shine from his dark eyes faded as Gabe's expression grew more solemn. "I always thought there'd be time to get the wanderlust out of my system and live closer to her, let her stay with me in her declining years. But I waited too long."

"Elva was a strong woman." Annie turned her hand so she held on to Gabe's. She could see the same kind, decent soul as Elva's. "She'd have swatted you for the phrase 'declining years.' And she'd have never left her ministry to settle into some comfortable cottage and sit in a rocker for the last years of her life. She was the bravest soldier for the Lord I've ever known. I prayed every day to have half her courage."

"You're right about her being brave. She had the heart of a lion. And she'd been known to swat one of us from time to time, too." Gabe smiled. "I remember one time—"

"Sorry to break up the big reunion." Elijah managed to insert himself between Annie and Gabe. "But maybe you can reminisce later. For now, how about we quit jabbering about the old days and figure out how to make Leveque pay for his crimes?"

Annie had forgotten Elijah was there. Remembering the good about Elva healed some of the grief in her heart, and she sensed it did the same for Gabe. But Elijah was right, now wasn't the time. She looked to Elijah then back to Gabe. "We can talk more later."

"Hurting Elva isn't the only crime he committed," Elijah reminded her. "He chased you off a cliff."

"I fell. True, I was trying to get away from him, but he never touched me."

"He shot you."

"I have a gunshot wound, mostly healed. And I didn't see where it came from."

"He shot Frank."

"I'm certain he was behind that, but who could testify?"

"He hurt my ma, too," Elijah said.

"Again, I'm the only witness, and I can't swear it was him. He wore a mask."

"He must have a taste for hurting those who are helpless." Ma rubbed her chin.

"I know what drives him," Annie said.

"What's that?" Gabe asked.

"He wants me in his show. He wants me to sing for him because I draw in a crowd. Then he can run his gambling den in the back room. I suppose if I was willing, he'd move the gambling and whiskey out front. He sees himself running a saloon with me as the entertainment. The dress he planned to force me to wear—" Annie had to exert her will to go on. "It wasn't the costume of a decent woman. I believe he had plans for me that went beyond singing, beyond decency."

"What good does it do to know what drives him?" Walker stayed smack in between Annie and Gabe. Gabe stood and moved to one side and Ruby to the other. They all three watched her closely, eager to hear of any ideas to deal with that low-down Claude Leveque.

Annie shuddered at the direction of her thoughts. "I've always been a coward." Saying the words out loud set off a deep trembling in her bones.

"You're not a coward, sweet girl," Ma said softly.

Annie took a moment to realize that Elva wasn't the only beautiful, courageous soul she'd been lucky enough to have in her life. Ruby was just as brave and just as faithful.

"I am." It was a confession. She'd confessed to God many times but that wasn't enough. The Bible called for a sinner to ask forgiveness of those who'd been sinned against, and Annie's sins had brought Claude here, hurt Ruby, threatened all of them. "I spent my growing-up years calling it obedient, and maybe back then it was all right, in school. A student is supposed to behave, right? And having no other home to go to, I wasn't inclined to do something that might get me expelled. Then in the traveling mission group it was simple, surrounded by people of faith, to be good and take orders. No one asked anything of me I wasn't glad to do. But I knew in my heart I'd never made a stand for my faith, and I always wondered, if the moment came, would I do it? Would I face danger, even death, rather than deny God?"

The room was silent. She looked from Ruby's stout kindness to Gabe's grief and anger to Walker's fiery eyes and suspicion and rough affection.

"Now's my chance. I've asked God to give me crosses to bear, and every time He's answered, I've failed. Maybe now it's time to face my darkest fear. Claude will come for me. If he hears I'm alone at my father's ranch, he'll—"

"No!" Elijah took a step forward.

Annie stepped back at the fire in his eyes.

He kept coming. "Your plan is to lay yourself out like bait to lure in a hungry wolf?"

"It will work." Annie kept backing.

"It's out of the question." Ruby came up beside her cranky son, looking every bit as stubborn.

"So, I hide here and Claude—yes, just like a hungry wolf—waits and maybe hurts others until he can catch me alone like he did in that mining camp? Better to plan it. Better to do it when we control the outcome."

"I'm going to see to it you're never alone." Elijah leaned down, trying to glare her into submission.

She tried to step back again and found her back was pressed against the stones that made up the edges of their fireplace. Well, since she could no longer retreat, she'd finally act with courage. "Then I'm all safe and cozy while he guns down your mother again."

Elijah caught her by her upper arms and lifted her to her toes. "I'm capable of protecting what's mine. Ma won't go out alone either."

She jerked against his hold but couldn't budge him. "Fine, then he can't get to us so he gives up and leaves to find some other young woman to prey on. He never pays for harming Elva or your mother. You know he attacked Frank, too. He's a dangerous man. Are you content to let him roam around free, Elijah? While I stay safe under lock and key?"

"I'll find a way to make him pay for hurting my ma without putting you in danger," Gabe interjected. They'd left him behind while Elijah had stalked her across the room. But now he came up beside them, looking as adamant as Elijah.

She turned to Ruby, hoping someone here had a lick of sense. "And what about you? Are you content to let him shoot you and not pay any price? Does that fit with your sense of justice? He's a dangerous man."

"That's exactly right." Ruby crossed her arms and added herself to the row of mules. "He's a dangerous man. You're not going anywhere near him."

"I'm listening for someone else to come up with a plan." Annie looked from one face to the next. Finally she stopped on Elijah. He had the strongest will of all, not that the other two were slouches. In fact, there was no doubt that she possessed the weakest will of the group. And hadn't that just been the plain truth her whole cowardly life?

But not this time. This time she'd stand boldly for what she believed to be right. She'd stand boldly for God. She thought of a verse that she'd always loved and clung to.

*"What doth the Lord require of thee, but to do justly, and to love mercy, and to walk humbly with thy God?"*

Well, she'd always tried to be just and merciful, and she'd certainly walked humbly with her God. But maybe she'd walked a bit too humbly with her fellow man. And while she was thinking of that verse, she decided there wasn't a lick of humility in this group facing her. They were ordering her around like they were generals and she was a lowly foot soldier. And she was sick of it. She intended to take this stand.

Convincing Elijah would be hardest, so she might as well focus on him. She opened her mouth, but before she could speak, his hands softened, though he still held her.

"I want you to be safe." That tone was amazingly good at making her forget every thought in her head. He glanced at Ruby then at Gabe. "Let me talk to her alone, please."

Ruby was gone in a trice, heading for something vital in the back room, which was a cold little pantry and nowhere anyone wanted to stay, not even for a minute. "Gabe, I could use a hand, please."

"I want to hear what's decided." Gabe didn't move. "I've got just as big a stake in this as any of you. Whatever—" His head jerked sideways. "Ouch!"

Ruby had him by the ear. "You get out here and help me carry these—" Ruby's voice faltered. "Just you come on now." She stopped to grab two coats, hers and Gabe's, obviously intending to stay in that cold, ridiculous little room as long as it took for Elijah to enforce his marching orders. Then Ruby yanked, and Gabe went, in order to keep his ear attached to his head.

As they stepped out the back door, Annie heard Gabe say with

240

considerable affection. . .under the circumstances, "My ma used to grab my ear just like this." The door to the pantry slammed shut.

"Nothing's more important than keeping you safe." Elijah drew her attention back to him and only him.

"Yes, some things *are* more important than safety. Justice, courage, honor. It is our duty to stop Claude. If not for those he already hurt then for those he'll hurt on down the road."

Elijah ran his thumbs in little circles on her arms. He was no longer restraining her, so she could have gotten away if she wanted.

Although getting away seemed foolish when his hands felt so nice. "Please, Elijah."

"No. We've got a couple of quiet minutes without that yammering Gabe mixing everything up."

"He's a nice man—"

Elijah's kiss cut off her defense of Gabe. "Hush, we're not wasting time talking about him. Now, I think you're right about Claude wanting you, but you know we can't possibly risk your safety to catch him."

"You could make it safe."

Elijah shook his head. "The trouble with putting yourself in a trap as bait is sometimes the predator snatches the bait away without getting caught. It's never gonna happen."

"Elijah, please, we can talk to the sheriff."

"The sheriff's not about to use some innocent woman to snare a villain."

"I'm willing to risk that." Annie jerked against his hold and got loose.

He put his arms around her waist and pulled her close, then continued as if she hadn't spoken. "He'll go question Leveque. That's how a sheriff gets to the bottom of things."

"Well, if the sheriff won't help trap him, then we'll get extra men from among your cowhands to stand guard."

"Annie?" His voice was so soft it sneaked in between her protesting and her newfound courage and her determination to never, never, never back down.

"Yes?" Finally he'd either admit hers was the only way or tell her a better idea.

His lips settled on hers.

The man wasn't helping her come up with a better plan at all.

And she intended to tell him that, just as soon as she got her arms free from where they were wrapped around his neck, and regained sole possession of her mouth.

# TWENTY-EIGHT

This isn't getting us anywhere." Gabe Michaels—or whatever his name was today—was back.

Walker snarled when that pest interrupted the...conversation...he was having with Annette.

Annette squeaked and jumped back. She almost dragged him into the fireplace, and unwinding her arms kept them both busy for a few minutes.

"I said I just needed a minute alone." Walker glared at the man who'd interrupted him.

"We gave you a lot longer than that." Ma shook his shoulder.

When had she come in?

Walker's vision cleared and he glanced around. The sun looked way past high noon. Hadn't this all started when Gabe showed up right after the midday meal?

He looked down at Annette's flushed cheeks and wondered just how long he'd been kissing her. He should have checked his pocket watch before he started.

Maybe next time.

"I thought you wanted to talk some sense into her."

Walker glanced at "her." No sense to be found there at all. None in himself either, if he cared to be honest. "We were sorta getting there."

243

Ma broke in before he got anywhere else. "Annie's right that we need to have Claude—"

"And Blanche," Annette interjected.

"Arrested," Ma finished. "Both of them."

Annette rubbed her mouth like she was wiping away the taste of him.

Walker couldn't quite stop letting that bother him.

She stopped wiping. "For what? What's his crime? No jury will find him guilty on the word of a woman with my sullied reputation. I'm more likely to end up in prison than he is."

"That new lawyer who was on the stage is spending too much time in the new theater." Gabe crossed his arms and glared at Walker. "I've been keeping my eyes open, and they're sneaky about it, but I think they knew each other before they came to Ranger Bluff."

"Okay," Walker said, willing to arrest anyone who caused Annette or his ma one speck of trouble. "We'll get him, too. But not by putting Annette at risk. We'll find another way."

"There is no other way." Annette's shoulders squared. "I will clear my name somehow. Then maybe I'll be a suitable witness against Claude and Blanche."

Gabe moved up on Elijah's left. "Or else you end up with your good name in shambles."

"I don't have a good name," Annie reminded him.

"You do, so quit saying that." Walker was good and sick of hearing it.

"Besides you, the Leveques were the only ones nearby when my ma died." Gabe shrugged off his coat. "And they're skillful liars, Annie. No man spreads rumors as skillfully as Leveque without being a good hand with a quiet, well-placed falsehood. You could end up being accused of my ma's murder."

Annette looked from Elijah to Gabe to Ruby, who stood at Elijah's right side.

"You're not talkin' to the sheriff." Walker needed to talk some sense

into the little fluff head. He'd really like just a little more time alone with her to do it. But he didn't think he'd get his ma to budge. "I'll talk to him. We'll explain what's going on. Gabe can speak up for you, maybe even show the sheriff those letters from his ma that will speak to your character."

"That's a good idea, son." Ruby smiled at him. Walker knew good and well his ma had deliberately dragged Gabe out of the room to give Walker a chance to coax Annette into another kiss. Same as she'd faked being so tired she couldn't help with the dishes.

He'd thank her later. "None of us gives on this. You'd do well to accept our protection."

"While I hide safely without taking one bit of action to end this nightmare?" Annette jerked her fists straight down at her side in exasperation. "That makes me an even bigger coward. I'm going to find a way to lure Claude out in the open."

"No, you are not!" Walker fumed.

Then the little woman, who never stopped claiming she was a coward, surprised him by stepping right up into his face. "I am, too. Just watch me."

"I'll watch you all right." He jabbed her right in the second button of her pretty blue dress. "You're not going to make a move I don't know about."

"Well, you can't watch me all day and night."

"I can and I will." Walker leaned down until his nose nearly touched hers.

"I'm going to get Claude." Annette shoved him back.

He didn't budge an inch and Walker decided her soft little shove was even more proof she couldn't face Leveque. "You are not."

He grabbed her shoving hands and held her still. "I won't allow it."

"Isn't this exactly where we were before?" Gabe's arms flew straight out in disgust. "We might as well have never left you two alone."

"Shut up, Michaels," Walker growled, but he let Annette go. He'd liked being left alone with Annette very much. Too much.

245

"It's Lasley, Gabe Lasley."

"Well, tell me when you're done changing your name and then I'll just have to learn it once."

"You don't allow or not allow anything. I'll do what I need to do." Annette tilted her nose in the air.

"You'll do as you're told."

Annette gasped, jammed her fists on her trim hips, and narrowed her eyes.

Walker almost smiled. She was so cute when she was trying to be bossy. Sweet and cute and completely wasting her time because she'd never change his mind. He remembered why he'd asked his ma and Gabe to leave him alone with her in the first place.

"I'm not going to back down on this." She returned the little jab he'd given her with interest.

It kind of tickled. "Oh yes, you are."

"We're doing this my way—" Her eyes flashed like blue lightning.

"You'd do best to learn to mind me, woman." She'd learn even if he had to spend the rest of his days teaching her. He'd dedicate his life to it.

"And you can't stop me."

The door slammed shut in her face and that blasted key clicked in the lock. Being brave was not working out for her at all.

"God, have You got any inspiration for me?" Her prayer was met with silence.

So she did what she wanted. She hammered her fist on the door. "Ruby, you let me out of here!" She couldn't believe Ruby was the one who'd run for the key. The traitor.

"Unlock this door this instant!" Orders—maybe the three of them would respond to direct orders.

Annie thought maybe she heard the sound of coffee being poured.

"I told you we should have just left her in there after you got shot, Ma. She doesn't have the sense to be allowed to run around loose."

"Your motives were wrong then, son. We aren't locking her up because she was involved in that shooting. We're locking her up for her own protection."

"You let me out of here." Annie hammered away. Chairs scraped. The boots in the outer room seemed to be settling under the table.

"Thanks kindly for the coffee, ma'am."

That polecat son of Elva's sounded like he'd taken her place at the table.

"Call me Ma, Gabe."

Annie gasped so hard it hurt her throat. Ruby was *her* ma. Well, no she wasn't. . .not really. She thought of Elijah's kiss. *Not yet, she's not my ma, but she might be if Elijah meant anything with those kisses.* And she sure as certain wasn't Gabe's.

"Be careful. It's blazing hot."

They didn't even offer her a cup.

"I've got pie left from dinner." The sound of a knife clicking against a tin pie plate followed that statement.

Feeling sorry for herself, Annie stormed over to the bed and sat down in a huff. Fine, let them figure out a better way. And in the meantime she'd make some plans. . .all depending on her getting out of here of course. . .which was pretty hard to manage.

"Apple pie's my favorite, Ma." Gabe was no doubt finishing up her slice of pie.

Ruby was now serving Annie's dessert to Elva's low-down stubborn son.

The three of them had teamed up against her.

Well fine, she'd find a way to do this on her own.

*God, You know I have to.*

*Before someone else dies.*

⁕

"Why'd you bother to shoot if you were going to miss? You had a chance to thin out that herd of folks watching over our girl."

"Shut up!" Claude had taken just about all he could. Blanche had been nagging him ever since that shooting nearly a week ago. She was about one wrong word from tasting his fist.

"Don't you talk to me that way. If you could still deal a crooked hand of cards, we wouldn't need that little girl."

Claude slammed his fist onto the table and launched himself to his feet. "You shut your mouth or I'll shut it for you."

Blanche must have believed him because she turned away and went grumbling into the back room of the theater.

Why hadn't he just shot the old woman out at the Walker ranch? He should have. It'd have set that watchdog of a son of hers off, running after whoever shot his ma, and in the confusion, Claude could have grabbed his songbird and gotten away.

Lately, the bitter cold temperature was convincing him to head south. But not back toward St. Louis. He'd left some enemies behind in Missouri. And there'd been bits of thieving along the way on the trail here so he couldn't go back that way. California sounded better. Anywhere but in these filthy mountains. His bones ached in this ugly weather.

He had some money now. He'd had a few lucky nights. He could go. He'd been considering just taking off. Leaving the songbird and Blanche. His money would stretch further alone, unless he ran into a card game. Lately it seemed like he needed to risk everything on a hand of poker. There was a thrill to it that he craved. Playing cards wasn't just about making money anymore. Without the threat of going under big, he didn't feel fully alive. Anyhow, betting big was the only way to score big. And that big score tantalized him. It had been out of his reach all his life. When he'd first heard the songbird, it had hit him that this was it. She was it. She was his big score.

The fact that he'd let her slip away wasn't his fault any more than other failures had been his fault. Something always stopped him— either Blanche's stupidity or the songbird got inside his head or some fool would sharp him. There'd been a day when no one could deal off

the bottom of the deck more smoothly.

So if he took off, left without any woman to help him make more money, he'd end up stranded somewhere. And being stranded in the West with no way to live terrified him.

No, he'd stay. A couple more weeks to hover, skim money off the townsfolk and try to grab hold of his little songbird. And in the meantime he needed to keep his old crow happy. "Blanche, get back here."

She came in, looking sullen. It deepened the lines on her face, making her ugly. He had to get rid of her.

He pulled her into his arms. "I'm sorry. You know I've never hit you." He had a few times, but that didn't count. It wasn't a regular thing, and Blanche had told him enough about her violent upbringing in the back room of the house her ma worked out of that he knew she didn't count a few impatient slaps and shoves as being beaten.

Her pout eased, but there were still lines around her eyes. It made him sick to see how washed up she was. Sick and scared. But he kept all of that off his face.

"I should have probably just killed that old woman, Blanche, but I've never killed before." He had, but no one who didn't have it coming. He didn't count Elva. He'd left her unconscious but alive. If he'd have killed her outright, she'd have never been able to set the songbird free. And the man he'd shot on the trail out to the Talbot ranch hadn't died, not that Claude hadn't thought he'd fired a killing shot.

Once he had Annette back in his hands, he'd make sure she never again had a chance to befriend anyone again. "And from the talk around town, it sounds like Walker is one tough *hombre*. I didn't want him coming after me, killin' mad. I decided to just wing the old woman and hope to scare the songbird into flight. But it didn't work. Next time I get a chance at that girl, I'll take her no matter how many people I have to clear out of the way."

Blanche smiled. For a second Claude could almost see the young girl he'd found. He and Blanche had been together for over ten years now. They'd done okay as a team until her voice started to go. Right about the same time his hands had started to shake.

Claude leaned down and kissed his wife. He'd used a lot of women in his life, but Blanche was the only one he'd ever married. They were a pair. He'd miss her when he took off with the songbird.

He lifted his head and smiled. Her own smile was a match for his: satisfaction, scheming, a lot of greed. As he pulled her tighter into his arms, he realized that she wasn't really his match.

If she was, she'd know what he was thinking and she'd never let him touch her.

# TWENTY-NINE

I'm watching every move you make." Walker swung the door open. "C'mon out and eat supper, but don't think you're gonna set a single foot outside this cabin."

Annette about burned him to a cinder with her eyes. With a sniff of that pert little nose, she swept past him. "I'm hungry so I'll eat. You've kept me in here all day."

"We only locked the door about an hour ago. Women always exaggerate." Walker snorted at the cute little spitfire. "I had to go see to some chores. I decided you were too wily so I took the key in case you softened Ma up and talked her into letting you loose. I'm only gonna let you out when I'm in the house. I throw a lasso a lot better'n Ma."

"Lasso!" Annette whirled on him, her fists clenched.

Laughing at her would be wrong, wrong, wrong. Then he wished he'd have laughed, because fighting to keep a straight face led his mind in the direction of kissing her. She was so sweet. So alive. So vulnerable and brave and decent and pretty.

He dropped his voice to a whisper, although his ma had ears that'd hear through stone so he doubted she missed much. "Don't you know I just want you safe? Haven't you figured out from one or two of the kisses we've swapped that you matter to me? I *cannot stand* the thought of you being at risk, and you are as long as that dry-gulching

Claude Leveque is around."

"Have you come up with a better plan, then?" Her words were spoken with the sharp, swift cutting power of a Shoshoni tomahawk. Such a little woman to hold such a hot temper. Couldn't she see he just wanted to take care of her?

"No, but Gabe headed back to town to talk with the sheriff."

"So I can expect to be arrested soon, then?" She shrugged as if she didn't care, but Walker saw the small tremor of fear she couldn't control. "Fine. I'll be locked in jail. No different than here."

"Annette, the sheriff won't come after you. Gabe plans to show him the letters from Elva and tell the whole story. The sheriff might be able to send out some telegrams and track down information about Claude and Blanche. A pair like that have trouble on their back trail. Maybe he'll find a WANTED poster or two on 'em and be able to lock 'em right up."

"I hope you're right, Elijah."

He'd told her about a dozen times to call him Walker. This was the first he'd noticed how much he liked her calling him Elijah. Calling her Annette suited him, too.

"I'll let you handle this. I'll give the sheriff a chance." She gave him an innocent, obedient smile.

He didn't buy it for a minute. "Nice try." Leaning down, he said, "But I'm still locking you up every time I leave the house."

"Oh, you—"

Walker caught her fist. She probably wouldn't have slugged him—he glanced at the fist caught tight in his hand—hard. But just to be on the safe side, he held on and dragged her to the kitchen table, where Ma was setting a big ham.

Sliding her chair in to force her to sit down at her place between the table and the wall, Walker rounded to his own seat at the head.

"I should have helped you, Ma." Annette sounded sincere.

Walker realized it was clear as day the difference when she was telling the truth or trying to mislead him. The woman was a poor liar, and that usually meant she had a lack of practice. That perked him right up.

As he passed the mashed potatoes, he realized this was the happiest he'd been since Pa died. No, long before that, because despite his stubborn defense of everything that Priscilla did, he realized now that he'd never been happy with her. Worried, entranced, stressed, passionate, overly polite, torn between his folks and her. . .looking back, it seemed as if Priscilla was a witch and she'd put him under a spell. A wicked witch.

Now, despite the fact that his ma had been shot, despite the fact that ugly rumors swirled around the woman he'd decided to claim, despite the fact that his foolishness had a hand in his pa's death, he was calm, even cheerful.

Somehow, since she'd come here, Annette had given him his life back, his faith back, his common sense back, his clear thinking completely, finally, totally back.

$\mathcal{C} \quad \mathcal{D}$

Annie was going out of her mind. Pretending to be relaxed and content was killing her.

It was nearing Christmas. Ruby was letting Annie use scraps of yarn to knit a warm scarf for Elijah. She needed something to occupy her time.

She'd lately started jumping at noises, like the wind blowing. Not on her life was she going to let Elijah handle the Leveque problem. But as long as he kept her locked up, she didn't have much choice. The fact that going for a walk in the winter wind might kill her was also a stumbling block.

She sat in her comfortable chair before the fire and looked at the little pine tree Elijah had dragged in today. He'd set it up, and tonight the three of them were stringing popcorn on thread and decorating it.

Elijah wheedled until Annie sang a few beloved Christmas hymns.

The words to "Silent Night" had accompanied the soft *creak* of her rocking chair while she pulled a needle through the fluffy corn. The hearth crackled with warmth and joined with the spirit of the season and the beloved words to her music. Her heart softened until even her bones seemed to ease and relax. She was safe and warm and comfortable.

As she realized just how comfortable, the sight of Elva, bleeding and dying, hit so hard the popcorn kernel she held snapped in two. And Ruby, bleeding and hanging on to the edge of a cliff. Frank with the ugly scar on his head. The bullet wound that had healed but left behind a mark that would stay with her forever. Her mind rebelled at this comfort when Claude could be, right this instant, plotting against the Walkers or choosing a new victim.

Her hands shook. The popcorn string was long enough. She snipped the thread with her teeth and tied it off.

Ruby smiled and took it from her to further adorn the tree. "Your voice is beautiful, Annie." Ruby brushed Annie's hair so gently, tears burned in Annie's eyes. "Having you here is a blessing."

Having her here was a curse. She needed to get back to her father's house and somehow let Claude and Blanche know she was there. And since Elijah wouldn't cooperate, then she needed to figure out a way to let him know, too, but not right away. Just in the nick of time to save her.

Complicated? Yes. But she had a plan.

Unlike Elijah.

First, it meant no more kissing.

Elijah rose from his rocking chair, extended his arm to her, and escorted her to her door. With just the barest inches to take them out of Ma's sight, he leaned close. "I'm not locking you in your room anymore. You're safe as long as you stay in the house. I've got enough sentries posted it's safe enough you can go back to gathering eggs and doing other chores outside. You've got to be getting sick of staying in the house."

"Good, it's about time." Her heart softened a bit. He'd been letting her loose in the house during the day, but she hadn't stepped outside in nearly a week. Neither had Ma.

"I just want you to be safe, Annette." Elijah stopped at the door and swung it open.

She turned to go through, but he stopped her with a restraining hand on her arm. Not kissing Elijah was proving to be a very difficult part of her plan. And, since she'd yet to enact any other part of her plan, she was clearly failing, or at least she hoped she'd be failing soon.

She turned back. "I know you do."

Somehow he'd gotten much closer. "And I said I'd let you menfolk handle the Leveques."

"Yeah, you said it." His hand slid up from her wrist to her elbow to her shoulder. "But only after you'd been locked up for three days. I can't help doubting your sincerity."

"A nice way of calling me a liar." Annie decided not to pursue that anymore. Since she was kind of lying in the sense that she was planning on disobeying Elijah with all her might as soon as she figured out a way to escape from him, she didn't pursue the subject.

*God, forgive me. I just want to protect the people I love.*

She was motivated by the same things Elijah was.

"I want to be nice to you, sweetheart."

"I'm not your sweetheart."

"You are. Maybe you don't know it yet, but you're the last to figure it out." His lips brushed hers.

She did know it. But her plan. . . She couldn't kiss him. Absolutely not.

And she did stop. . .less than two minutes later. . .when Ruby came around the corner and slapped Elijah on the arm.

"Break it up, you two." She had a strict, starchy, chaperone-ish tone to her voice, but her eyes beamed.

Annie backed quickly away from Elijah, which was impossible since her back was pressed against the door.

The plan she'd concocted was not going as expected at all. She shook her head to try and clear the fog away. The man had done one tiny sweet thing, granting her *permission* to step outside, for heaven's sake, and she'd melted. She was ashamed of herself. But she did need to tell him she was grateful.

With words.

"Thank you so much, Elijah. I hated being behind that locked door. What if there'd been a fire? I appreciate your trust."

Elijah stepped back and made a gesture for her to go into her room. When she walked past, she saw him drag that blasted key out of his pocket.

"I thought you said you weren't going to lock me in."

"I'm not—" Elijah smiled at her as if he'd offered her a fist full of posies.

Annie frowned at the key and waited.

"Except at night."

Annie gave a tiny scream of outrage and whirled away from the devious man.

"Shame on you, son, for teasing her."

Annie turned back, hopeful. Maybe, finally, Ma would side with her.

"Are you saying I shouldn't lock her up? When she's got that harebrained scheme of putting herself in danger to trap Leveque?"

Full of hope and just a bit smug to have Ma on her side instead of Elijah's, Annie smiled at Ruby.

"No, I agree about the lock."

Annie's smile drooped at both ends.

"I just don't think you should tease."

The door swung shut as the Walkers bickered. The key turned with a distinctive *click* that Annie was now hearing in her dreams. Dreams that always began with her trying to throttle Elijah. Instead she'd end up kissing him.

Well, if teasing rat Elijah had told the truth, at least now she could roam outside a bit during the day.

The next day, she tested it and was allowed to milk the cow and gather eggs. But come nightfall, Elijah rounded her up like she was a maverick calf, herded her into her room, and bolted the door. She probably should have been thanking her Father in heaven that the confounded man didn't take a notion to slap a brand on her.

After the night of teasing, Annie refused the man any more kissing, at least outside her dreams. Since she was furious, it wasn't hard to refuse him.

Well, honesty forced her to admit it was still a little hard. The crazy man acted like escorting her to her door after an evening rocking in front of the fire was the end of a date and he ought to be able to kiss her good night.

Tempting, she couldn't deny it. But she'd held firm and refused Elijah's offer of a good-night kiss.

She was more inclined to slap his face, but she did neither. No kiss. No slap.

Elijah felt bad about locking her in, she could tell. But he still did it faithfully and she faithfully snarled at him. The man needed to think she was angry with him because she was defeated. She hoped that convinced him she had no plans, no ideas, no way out.

Which led her to part two of her plan.

Frank.

True, he was probably the one who'd nailed her windows shut, so he'd never defy Elijah, but Frank was young and sweet and, best of all, gullible.

Annie felt bad taking advantage of that, but she was not letting the Leveques walk away from their crimes.

A few more days of snarling and she could pick a moment and slip away. That secret trail would hide her well. Frank would carry the message that informed the Leveques, and then he'd tell Elijah, who would come to save her in the nick of time. But only after Claude had attacked her again. which would give her plenty of evidence to convict Claude and Blanche.

She knew the sheriff hadn't come up with anything to incriminate Claude. In fairness to the lawman, he hadn't shown up to arrest her either, so that was something to be grateful for. With no action on the part of the sheriff, another week crept by, and it looked more and more like it was going to fall to Annette to catch the Leveques.

# THIRTY

The day before Christmas Eve, Annie woke up to hear not a breath of wind.

It was the day Frank usually ran to Ranger Bluff, and Annie had heard talk of some special needs for Christmas Day, so she knew Frank was going. This was the day. One way or another, she had the weather she needed.

She prayed, searching her heart for confirmation that her actions were done with an honorable spirit. She asked the Lord for His protection and clung to the knowledge that she was finally going to have her chance to truly pick up a cross and bravely follow Jesus.

Feeling at peace with her plans, she wrote a note for Frank to carry with him and dressed quickly. She slipped the note into her dress pocket and was ready to start the day when she heard that key turn in her lock. She wrenched open the door and glared at Elijah.

He had the nerve to smile. His smug bossiness made it all the easier to disregard his wishes.

She ate breakfast, the note in her pocket crinkling occasionally. She held her breath every time it made a sound, afraid Elijah or Ma would hear it.

Wound so tight she could barely breathe for fear she'd give herself away, she helped clear the table and wash the breakfast dishes.

Although Annie knew Elijah always kept a sharp eye on her, this morning he seemed especially focused. Was it her imagination? Could he read her mind? Or was there some expression on her face that made him suspicious?

She did her very best to continue being snippy when she wanted to throw her arms around his neck and beg him to care for her. She was sorely afraid that after today he might wash his hands of Annie once and for all.

"I'll milk the cow and fetch the eggs." Annie went to her own personal antler and lifted her coat and bonnet loaned to her by Ma Walker. Everything she had was due to their generosity. Today she'd pay them back by dealing with that woman-beating, back-shooting Claude once and for all. She grabbed the milk pail and headed for the barn.

Frank was hitching up the buckboard for his run to Ranger Bluff.

She set the bucket aside and approached him. *Stay calm. Act like this isn't life and death.* "Frank, can you take a letter to town for me today?"

"Why, sure, Miss Annie." Frank stepped away from the docile team he was bridling. "You need it mailed?"

"No, not mailed. The new lawyer in town offered to help me with some business, and I need to ask him a question. If you could just give this letter to Carlyle Sikes, I'd appreciate it."

"Sure, glad to do it. I can wait for him to send an answer, too, if you'd like."

A spike of nerves nearly stripped the bland expression from her face. Sikes's only answer was going to be to take this letter directly to the Leveques. "Oh, no. No need for that. It will take him a—awhile to look into this."

Frank took the letter and tucked it in his pocket.

Annie thanked him and went to get her bucket. But she didn't get a drop of milk.

The second Frank pulled out with the *creak* of wagon wheels, Annie stepped away from the cow and headed for the henhouse, which stood directly in front of a straggly stand of scrub pine. She looked around quickly, then ducked behind the chicken coop and strode toward the trail. If she pushed hard, she could be at her father's house well before noon.

Sikes would tell Claude about the note within the hour. She knew faithful Frank would drop off the letter first. Then Claude, as predictable as he was evil, would come as fast as he could ride. Hopefully Claude would arrive only a little while before Elijah, who would notice her missing at some point. She knew Claude well enough to know he might hurt her, but he wouldn't kill her. Taking her alive was always part of Claude's plan. And if he laid his hands on her, then he'd be arrested.

Annie crossed her arms to preserve the warmth and realized in her nervous state this morning she'd forgotten to bring the pipe. Her only weapon. She didn't dare go back because she wouldn't be given a second chance to slip away. Thinking of how Elijah would react when he got his hands on her made her walk faster and faster, despite the perilous trail. In fact, while it was true she was rushing to face Claude, a case could be made that she was also running away from home.

Elijah would be furious, but he'd protect her—once he got to her. And until he did, God would have to provide. This was the danger she'd face with God at her side. This was the cross she'd willingly bear. Once this reckless day was over, Ruby and all the other potential victims of Claude's evil would be safe.

Even Blanche, though she was a full partner in Claude's treachery, had been dragged down by Claude. Perhaps even that cruel woman could be set free to live a decent life.

As Annie raced along the increasingly steep, narrow shortcut trail, she forced herself to include Blanche in her prayers. Maybe there was something left inside Blanche's hardened heart that could be reached once Claude was no longer controlling her.

❧

Sheltered by the heavy stand of trees, Annette made good time.

It was hard climbing up to the lookout her father had used. The

ground was frozen and icy in spots. She occasionally found a spot so steep she needed to pull herself up with scant handholds and footholds.

Though she and her father—her pa—had stood at the top of this trail many times, looking down on the Walkers, they'd never climbed down. Her pa had pointed the way and said he'd done it a time or two, but he'd never taken her.

She reached the top and hesitated before she plunged down the far side that led home. Turning back, she looked at the home she'd just run from.

Home.

Where she was headed couldn't qualify as that anymore.

"God, please put it in Elijah's heart to forgive me." Her voice lifted as a prayer. "Protect me as I bear this cross. Give me the courage to live boldly for You. And let Your will be done today."

The wind whispered in the trees that surrounded her. Annie listened but no still, small voice spoke in the biting cold to tell her if this was the right thing to do. Only her need to protect Elijah and Ma and everyone else goaded her into this rash action.

Waiting silently, she hoped for some message to come that would give her full knowledge of the rightness of her actions. Nothing came. Nothing stopped her.

She did her best to soak in the memory of the pretty Walker spread, with the smoke curling out of the cabin and the bunkhouse, the placid horses grazing on winter grass in the corrals, the chickens scratching around for yesterday's corn because Annie hadn't thrown any out for them today. Her behavior today might forever bar her from that place she'd come to think of as home.

And if things went really wrong, she might go home to meet her Maker yet this day. But she'd do it courageously.

*God, please let me live my life boldly for You.*

At last, though the cold wasn't killing, it was enough to force her onward. She turned to the trail to the J Bar T. The way down was smooth and easy and fast.

She'd been on the trail no more than two hours when she caught sight of her father's house, as cold and forbidding as her father's heart. Her throat swelled and she thought, with self-contempt, that she was going to cry again. Tears seemed to be her response to everything these days.

She rushed along faster, trying to keep herself so winded she didn't have the breath to cry. It didn't take her long to get to the cabin and go inside. Once there, looking around, she was reminded again that her father was gone.

Her shoulders slumped as she did a turn around the cold little room. Its condition was much improved because of her efforts at cleaning the day she'd come here, but it was still a miserable wreck of a house, so different than Ruby and Elijah's warm, welcoming home.

She stiffened her spine. "All right, no sniveling." Speaking aloud helped her buck up her spirits. "Frank will be slow going to town in the buckboard. It will take him at least an hour. So he should have been to town for an hour by now."

The note would come first, thanks to Frank's conscientiousness. So Sikes would have it and he'd move quickly to show it to Claude and Blanche. "Claude and Blanche won't tarry. They'll come straight out here with the thought of taking me away. That's nearly a two-hour ride on a fast horse." So, they'd be coming fast toward her right now. She could expect them in less than one hour's time.

"If all went as planned, Elijah and Ruby noticed me missing within a few minutes of my disappearance, and Elijah and maybe a posse of his men, who don't know about the shortcut, will come rushing to save me." They'd take far less time to follow the same trail on horseback than Frank had in the ponderous wagon. In fact, the weak part of Annie's plan was that Elijah might catch up with Frank before he could hand the note off. If that happened, Elijah would know just what she had planned, stop Frank from delivering the note, and get to the ranch to drag her home.

"Claude has to get here first." She shouted that to the rickety walls of her cabin. Even if Claude was far ahead, the only way out of the

Talbot ranch was straight back toward Ranger Bluff.

"We'll meet Elijah on the trail. No matter how late Elijah is, he'll be in time to catch Claude before he can get me out of the area." She hoped Claude didn't get here first by much. She had no illusions about his cruelty. But he'd be in a hurry to get her away, which would mean any severe beating would wait until later.

And before later came, long before later came she prayed, Elijah would rescue her.

"Look at this, Claude." Sikes wiped the drool off his mouth.

Claude controlled the desire to shudder as he watched. The man was so excited it was sickening. Of course, Claude had woken up ill from too much whiskey.

"Look at what? You shouldn't be talking to me." Claude shifted, waiting in the alley across from the stage depot. There was no wind today for a change, but it was still bitter cold. So here he stood, suffering, waiting for the stage because he expected at least two of his old partners to come in today. He wanted to get them settled without them making contact with anyone in town.

His friends knew to be cautious. They'd have their eyes open and respond to a single jerk of Claude's head. But if he wasn't here, they'd either stand around drawing attention to themselves or they'd mention Claude's name to find him. Neither suited Claude.

Sikes's hand trembled as he extended a piece of paper. Claude knew Sikes had overindulged on the rotgut whiskey last night. Claude knew because he'd matched Sikes drink for drink while they'd played cards with a few cowpokes. And in the process, Claude had lost most of the stake he'd been building up for when he left town. He owed a couple of men money, too, plus his landlord had come by asking for rent money this morning. The gullible fool had mentioned Claude's bloodshot eyes and the stench of whiskey and wasn't quite so gullible anymore.

His need for the songbird had just gotten desperate.

"One of the hands from the Walker outfit just gave me a note from Annette Talbot," Sikes whispered.

Claude looked up, his discomfort and impatience forgotten. He snatched the scrap of paper. "Why'd she write you?"

Not waiting for an answer, Claude unfolded the note.

*Dear Mr. Sikes,*

*You offered your assistance should I need it, and I find I need an attorney's advice. It is no longer possible for me to remain at the Walker home. I am returning alone to my father's house immediately this morning, and I wonder what the laws are concerning my rights in Father's absence?*

*I'm getting settled today, and of course tomorrow will be Christmas Eve, so I won't bother you on that day. But as soon as I can get to Ranger Bluff, I'd like to call on you to learn your legal opinion on this matter.*

*Regards,*
*Annette Talbot*

Claude jerked his head up and realized his own lips were wet. Swiping them with his hand, he said, "Stay here. Richie and Lloyd will be on today's stage and someone needs to meet 'em. I'm going to ride out and drag her back to town. Then we'll get some horses"—Claude meant steal but Sikes knew that—"and get out of this town."

"Without the Walker bunch backing her, she'll be simple to grab." Sikes pulled his collar up around his ears.

Knowing how close to the edge he was skating made Claude's hands tremble as badly as the aftereffects of his rotgut whiskey.

Blanche had taken a few dollars in last night. Then she'd had her share of the whiskey, too. The old woman was still asleep.

He'd relieve her of enough coins to rent a horse and maybe, just maybe, he wouldn't even stop by in Ranger Bluff. Maybe he'd bypass the town and head for California without telling any of his men the plan.

Sikes pulled a bottle of home brew out of his coat and uncorked it. Claude grabbed it.

"Hey!" Sikes tried to retrieve it.

Dodging Sikes, Claude took a few quick swallows to stop the headache and the shakes. "If she's broken ties with the Walkers we'll be in the clear. No one else in town knows her, or if they do, what they know isn't good. The Walkers were the only ones willing to protect her."

He handed Sikes back his precious bottle. After today, Claude would be able to afford the best liquor sold. A laugh, colder than the weather, slipped past Claude's lips as he gave a few seconds of thought to the way he'd make Annette submit to him. That warmed his blood more than the firewater.

Clapping Sikes on the back, he said, "We're on our way. Finally." Claude strode into their building and didn't even bother to creep around.

Blanche lay motionless on the bed, not nearly done sleeping off the night's excesses.

He found her hideout money and took it all. Then he hurried toward the livery and rented a couple of horses. He'd grab Annette and knock her cold, then toss her over the saddle. Then he'd avoid Ranger Bluff and ride hard for Salt Lake City. From there they'd take the train to California. He'd be halfway to San Francisco before Blanche realized he wasn't coming back.

A quick change of his name and appearance and the West would swallow him and Annette up for good. He'd live out his days in California with his songbird earning enough that he didn't need to worry about a few bad nights with the cards, and he'd buy whiskey that went down smooth.

He laughed as he rode hard toward the Talbot ranch, his fingers itching to make Annette pay for the cold and hunger that had befallen him since she'd run away.

"Tell Annette to quit pouting and come out here." Walker couldn't believe the little pill was still mad at him for trying to save her life. He

265

could see clear as day why God had set it down in the Bible for a man to be head of the house. Annette didn't seem to have a single lick of sense. It was all up to him to keep his womenfolk safe, and some days the job was a trial.

Why, she should have been grateful. She should have thanked him, and she sure shouldn't be denying him a good-night kiss. Walker thought he might be pouting a little himself.

"She's not in her room." Ma looked up sharply. "I thought she was working outside. I thought you were with her."

Walker dropped his coat without making it to the antlers and raced for Annette's room. He slammed the door open. Nothing. And she wasn't outside. He'd been working around the place all morning. Striding for the door, he snagged his coat. "She's run off."

And he knew exactly where she'd gone. Her stupid plan to trap Claude Leveque.

Walker was shouting like a madman, and his hands ran for their horses without waiting to see exactly what the problem was. They were on the trail, thundering for Ranger Bluff and the Talbot ranch within minutes of Annette turning up missing.

But how long had she been gone?

All morning. Hours and hours and hours. Slapping his bare hand on the flank of his horse, he leaned down over his stallion's neck and fought to get every possible drop of speed out of the lively black.

## THIRTY-ONE

W ell, there's no sense sitting here freezing."

Annie built a fire. Ruby had taught her how to do it well. A crackling blaze jumped from the logs within minutes, and Annie added her voice to the sound. She let herself get lost in the beauty of the music as she tidied the cabin, more for something to do, to keep busy, than for any real purpose. Whatever happened this day, Annie knew she'd never live in this house again. Today was the last of it.

It made her feel less alone to sing so she let her voice soar through "Joy to the World" and "O Come, All Ye Faithful" and "It Came Upon a Midnight Clear." She saw the bittersweet she'd brought with her and left draped on the mantel. . .bright orange berries shining in the dreary room. She summoned up good memories of her mother as she rearranged the bittersweet with loving care. Then she dusted and straightened, trying to recapture happier times with her father, who had occasionally found a smile and a kind word for the daughter who adored him.

Despite the courage she garnered from the fire and her words of worship in song, Annie was on edge enough that she heard the whinny of a horse while it was still at a distance. She rushed to the door and peeked out.

Claude was coming at a fast clip, leading a pack horse.

Annie had no doubt what it was he intended to pack. "Be with me, Lord. Help me to face it bravely. Help me to bear this cross without dropping it on someone else's head."

Then, because she knew it would taunt Claude, she began singing "A Mighty Fortress Is Our God" at the top of her voice. "A mighty fortress is our God, a bulwark never failing; our helper He amid the flood of mortal ills prevailing. For still our ancient foe doth seek to work us woe—His craft and pow'r are great, and, armed with cruel hate, on earth is not His equal."

Today these weren't just words to an old hymn. They were the absolute truth. Today God was her fortress and He would see to her life. However this day ended, she would expect it and accept it as God's will.

Unless God's will was for her to stay at the Walker ranch where she was safe.

Annette shook her head to clear it of that bit of negative thinking. She opened the door wide and stepped out on the porch to confront Claude. And hopefully hold him at bay until rescue arrived.

Claude pulled his horse to a stop only a few feet in front of her, his eyes gleaming with satisfaction. He swung down and tied his horse to what was left of the hitching post.

Annie remembered her horse tearing free of it and running off.

"Glad to see you're keeping your voice in good form, little Songbird. You'll need it once you go back to work for me."

An odd thought came to Annie at that moment. "You've listened to me sing, Claude. You've enjoyed it and realized I have a gift, haven't you?"

"Oh yes, you're very gifted." Claude took the two rickety front porch steps a bit slowly, as if his feet were heavy. Annie studied him and saw his hands trembling and an unnatural pallor on his face. Claude was getting old. In fact, he'd aged a lot since she ran away from him. He'd just about used up his energy coming all this way to catch her.

"I'm not gifted. I have a gift. Gifted sounds like something I am, but a gift is something I've been given. God gave me this gift of music."

A cackling laugh nearly shook Claude's whole body. "Preaching

to me, girl? You really think you have a chance of convincing me to become a holy man?"

"What I think is—"

Claude came so close she had to fight not to back away.

There'd be no running today. There'd be no desperate ride down the river with God's hand miraculously holding her head above water. She stiffened her spine. "What I think is *you* need a chance, Claude."

"Oh, I've got my chance. Once I've got you, I'll have my chance at last."

"I'm sure you believe that. For some reason you've decided I'm the answer to all your problems. But I'm not, and deep inside you know it. How can you have listened to me sing and listened to the couple who led the mission group without letting any of it into your heart?"

Claude grabbed her arm. "You can talk while we ride."

"Change your ways, Claude. You're an old man now. Lucifer has a hold on your soul and he's hungry to claim it. But there's time to change. Time to make your peace with God. It's as easy as saying yes. . .as easy as accepting a gift."

"Don't waste your pretty voice." Claude jerked her toward the horse.

Annie waited until he took his first step off the porch and kicked his leg out from under him.

He was unsteady enough that he fell to the ground.

She staggered forward, but Claude lost his grip on her as he fell, and she remained on her feet on the porch. She had her freedom but she didn't run. Her running days were over. "I was given the gift of song and I use it to worship the Lord."

Lurching to his feet, Claude turned and charged toward her. He'd scraped his forehead when he fell and it oozed a bit, threatening to bleed.

Annie noticed that the frozen ruts had scraped his hands and torn the knees out of his pants.

Furious, he clenched his fist. Then his eyes widened with surprise when she didn't run. He stopped when they were face to face again. "Seems you've been growing a backbone since you were with me, Songbird. You were one to cower and obey, then you turned and ran."

Nodding, Annie had to admit it was true. "But no more. You can't make me do anything against my beliefs. You can't make me get up on a stage and sing."

Claude shoved her backward and she stumbled into the wall. "I can make you do a lot." He laughed and stalked toward her.

"You could force any woman to degradation, but then why come after me? It's my voice you need and you can't force songs from my throat. And no matter how you hurt me, you can't touch my soul." She had little hope that she could reach past the blackened wreckage of Claude's evil, but she had to try. God asked her to say His name boldly, even if she were dragged into the darkest pit. She finally knew she'd taken up a cross that she would gladly bear, no matter the cost.

Claude knocked her to the floor.

She scraped the side of her face against the cabin wall and tasted blood. Still, the Lord blessed her heart with supernatural peace and miraculous courage. Even pounded to the floor, the cross remained securely on her shoulders and her mind continued to work clearly. She landed on something hard and cold, and it reminded her of some lessons she'd learned while living with the Walkers. Just because she'd never lose her faith didn't mean she had to take a beating now, did it? She sagged to the floor in a heap. Let him think the blow had knocked her senseless.

His cruel laugh chilled her more deeply than the cold, but she kept thinking and preparing to fight back. She was ready and he grabbed her by the hair and jerked her to her feet. With two quick strides, he had her over his pack horse's saddle.

Annie lifted her head to see that Elijah had just rounded the corner, coming from town with a good-sized group of men riding at his side.

About time.

She didn't have time to gloat.

Claude saw them and shouted with rage. He dragged her off the saddle and back up onto the decrepit porch, holding her in front of him like a shield. His ugly pistol appeared from out of nowhere. She could just see it held, pointing straight up, only inches from her right eye.

"Stay back, Walker!" Claude's voice sounded across the valley and echoed off the mountains. Claude's arm went around Annie's throat, and the gun pivoted and pointed straight at her.

Elijah pulled his horse to a halt over a hundred feet from Annie. "Let her go, Leveque. There's no way out of here except through us, and we aren't about to let you take her."

"Then she'll die, Walker. I'll have her alive or leave her dead. You decide."

Annie looked into Elijah's eyes and was nearly burned to death by the pain she saw there. She'd done it again, brought pain to him. First she'd awakened his heart, which had been safely hidden away since Priscilla. Then she'd reminded him of the woman he'd loved so unwisely. And now, now that he had taken his own courageous steps to love again, to trust God with his soul and a woman with his heart, he might be hurt again terribly.

This was the sin of this day, this hurt she'd cause Elijah. This was a cross she failed to bear if Claude pulled that trigger and killed her. On the other hand, she wasn't dead yet. And she did have one small possible solution to this problem, thanks to Elijah's mother.

So the cross might yet be upheld.

"I'm sorry I've caused you such trouble, Elijah."

Claude growled in her ear like the mad dog he was.

"I know it hurts you to look at what this horrible man is doing to me. And I've got a bruise or two and my lip is bleeding from his mistreatment. But on the other hand, with you looking on and Claude publicly threatening to kill me, there are a lot of people now who can testify to this crime."

Annie knew Elijah was furious, but once this was over, he'd have to calm down and admit that she'd done the smart, sensible thing.

She was a stubborn little idiot.

Her face was bleeding. Claude's hands on her made him want to tear the man apart. And under it all, Walker was fighting a raging desire to—once he was sure she was safe—grab Annette and turn her over his knee. When he had her free and safe in his arms, he might well arrange for her to have to sit on a pillow for a month.

Walker focused on Claude, looking for an opening. He swung down off his horse.

The man's weasel eyes shifted from Walker to the men backing him up to Annette.

"Elijah," Annette cried, "stay back. Don't—"

Claude tightened his arm around her neck and cut off her voice.

Walker couldn't bear to look at Annette again. The fear she must be feeling would tear his guts out. And for right now, he needed his guts firmly in place. He needed to think, be rational, be ready for when this rat tried to slink out of the trap.

This low-down varmint shot Ma. He beat Gabe Michaels's mother, causing her death. Now he had his filthy hands on Annette and was manhandling her. . .and hiding behind her skirts.

"Get back on that horse and ride away, Walker. This little girl doesn't leave here alive if you don't back off."

Claude must be stupid to think he could somehow get out of this trap—a trap Annette had baited with her own life.

Walker's head had to keep working. Acting on feelings right now might lead to Annette's death.

"I told you to get back on that horse." Claude's voice turned shrill, panicky. He jerked on Annette's neck again and she squeaked.

Against his will, Walker glanced at her, sick to think of how scared she must be.

Fury flashed from her eyes. She wasn't afraid. She was enraged.

And she was thinking. And he must be imagining it, but she looked

satisfied and even a little smug.

Walker saw all that in an instant and it helped him get a better grip on his own nerves. He looked back at Claude and smiled.

Claude must have relaxed his grip a bit because Annette spoke again. "Well, you do have enough, right?"

Claude jerked her back, lifting her off her feet.

Walker nodded at her, hoping she realized he was answering the question. They definitely had enough. This was Wyoming Territory. A woman was a rare and glorious thing, and as a rule, she was treated gently by even the lowest scum.

That was one of the reasons he'd had so much trouble getting Priscilla locked up. A man's instinct was to protect a woman, and Priscilla had been a master at awakening protective instincts. No Western man mistreated a woman like this and walked away.

Claude was proving himself to be below the lowest of the low scum, and that didn't surprise Walker at all.

"Shut up, will you? This is man's business." Walker thought if Annette didn't have the sense to be quiet maybe he could make her so angry she wouldn't be able to talk. Plus, he wanted Claude to think Walker was listening, that there was a chance of getting out of here.

Annette crossed her arms, giving him a relaxed look when that couldn't have been a more ridiculous reaction to this mess.

A movement caused Walker to look at her again, just in time to see her drag a lead pipe out of the right sleeve of her dress and use her left hand to ram it straight backward into Claude's stomach. In the same instant, she caught his gun hand and shoved straight up.

The revolver went off into the ceiling of the ramshackle porch. The porch roof snapped.

Walker moved the same second Annette attacked. He was at Annette's side instantly, scooping her into his arms.

He dragged her out from under the collapsing roof then relieved her of the gun before it went off again and the pipe before she took her temper out on him.

Then the porch roof landed on Claude Leveque's head.

Walker dropped his arm from around her legs, and she swung down to stand on her own two feet. "Are you out of your mind?" Everything Walker had been holding inside exploded. "You could have been—"

Annette flung herself at him so hard it knocked him back a step. Her arms went around his neck, choking off his scolding. Her face buried in Elijah's neck, she whispered, "Thank God you came, Elijah. Thank God. Thank God. Thank God."

He dropped the pipe and the gun, caught her around the waist, and held her tight, lifting her toes off the ground. This suited him just fine. He could yell right in her face.

Then his little spitfire sobbed. How was he supposed to rant and rave at her when she thanked God for him and hugged him and cried?

Deciding he needed to be alone with her to think clearly, he looked up at his crew. "We'll be right back." He scooped her legs back up so he held her against his chest and carried her around the edge of the cabin to let her cry her eyes out in peace. For the first time in memory, tears didn't make him mad. He only wanted to comfort her.

He did a fair amount of comforting, and finally the tears had eased. And while he kissed the daylights out of her, he decided he'd stop by the parson's house and marry her on his way home. Why not? Ma was going to adopt her to get her into the family if Walker didn't act fast. Then he'd be up against having to marry his sister and that didn't set right.

Leaving off kissing her through her salty tears, he said, "Let's go home, Annette."

"Home?" Her eyes blinked slowly, as if her lids were too heavy to hold open. When she finally looked up at him, he saw her eyes watering, her cheeks soaked, her lips swollen, her nose red and running. And she was still the prettiest thing he'd ever seen.

He lowered her feet to the ground and fetched a kerchief out of his pocket for her to dry her soggy face. "Yes, home. Your plan worked. We got Claude and managed to keep you from getting hurt." Except it was

a reckless, ridiculous plan. He'd forgotten how badly he needed to tell her that.

She gasped. "I did, too, get hurt. I had to get hurt for the plan to work."

Walker went back to thinking about giving her a whoopin'. Then he noticed a tinge of blood on the corner of her mouth and gave the tender spot a kiss to make it all better.

"Will you ever be able to forgive me, Elijah?" she whispered against his doctoring lips.

"Now honey, if you can't reason out that my dragging you back here and kissing you isn't a sign of forgiveness then you're not using the good sense the Lord gave you." He kissed her again just to remind her.

Nodding, she said, "Yes, I'd like very much to go. . ." Her voice broke, but she squared her shoulders and pulled herself together.

Walker was relieved. He needed to have another serious talk about all this crying. He'd put if off for now if she could pull herself together.

Her eyes met his, and he saw love and trust and a woman of God. He saw that God had cared for him and brought him to this place in His own time.

"I'd like to go home." She nodded.

A shout from the front of the cabin turned them both around in time to see Claude rushing up the hill toward the trail. "Stop him!" Frank came around the building.

Walker let go of Annette and ran after Claude. "Don't let him get away!" Walker was a few paces behind Frank and J.R.

He pulled his gun, hating to use it, but he would to keep Claude from running loose. Then he realized where Claude was running.

"Ease back, boys." Walker sprinted to catch up to his cowpokes. Then he shouted at Claude, "There's nowhere to go in that direction, Leveque. Just give up and come along quietly."

Walker caught up to his men just as Claude reached the cliff that towered high above the Medicine Bow. Winter wind buffeted Leveque's tattered suit.

Annette was right beside them. The little woman just would *not* let herself be protected. Walker had a whole 'nother lecture he needed to give her.

"There's a high trail." She hissed it right in his ear and made him shiver even more than the cold. "That's how I walked here so fast. I don't know if he knows about it, but we need to keep him from going that way or he can get lost up in those mountains. Maybe even get to Ma."

Walker glanced down at her, and she very discreetly pointed at an outcropping of rock that seemed to corral off the high peaks. Walker eased that way, catching Annette's arm to keep her tucked behind him.

Claude glanced back and let himself be cut off from the chance of taking the high trail. He reached the edge of the cliff, turned around, and laughed.

"I'm never going to jail. Never."

"Come away from the edge, Leveque. You won't survive that fall."

"She did." Claude's eyes went to Annette with such fierce anger that Walker tucked her more firmly behind him.

"It was a miracle I lived, Claude." Annette stood on her tiptoes to talk over Walker's shoulder.

"I don't think you're in line for a miracle." Walker did his best to keep Annette under control, but she was a fiery little thing.

With a snort of disdain, Claude said, "I'm a hard man, Songbird. If you can survive a dip in a cold river then I can." Claude backed up again.

"No, Leveque, stop. She's right. There's a stretch of rapids and a waterfall between here and my place, and the riverbanks are so high no one can climb out of them. Sometimes the river is even frozen over in spots. No one had heard tell of someone surviving a fall into the river except for Annette. It *was* a miracle. You know how special she is."

"Oh, I know. I've known from the first she was my chance at a fortune." Leveque took another step and another. The smile on his face wasn't purely sane. A fanatic light gleamed in his eyes as he inched toward the edge.

It twisted Walker's stomach to think of Annette falling into this rattlesnake's hands. "If anyone might be given a miracle it's Annette. You know that because you've tried to crush that beautiful spirit of hers since you first got your hands on her. Don't risk your life when your heart isn't right with God. If you make your peace, then maybe you'd have a right to ask for holy protection."

An icy gust of wind buffeted Leveque and his coat flew wide, almost as if the hand of God was trying to hold him away from the edge.

"We'll just see who's stronger, that little songbird or me." A shaky laugh escaped Claude's throat as he swiped his sleeve against his mouth. "And be on the lookout, all of you." Leveque's finger swept past each of them, pointing, threatening them one and all. "Because I'm coming back for what's mine."

"No!" Annette screamed.

Claude whirled to face the cliff.

"Stop!" Walker sprinted to close the distance between himself and Leveque.

Leveque dived out into open space—and screamed.

"Maybe he'll make it," Walker yelled at his men. "Ride for the ranch. If he survives the rapids, he'll need—" Walker reached the edge and fell silent as he looked down at Claude's lifeless body sprawled face down on the frozen surface of the Medicine Bow.

Annette came up behind him.

When he felt her softness pressing past, he turned and caught her and moved her back. "Don't look. It's ugly."

She looked into his eyes, and Walker knew she felt some of the ugliness, or rather the sickness over having to see a man—much like his father was—lying broken and bleeding at the bottom of a cliff.

Her arms wrapped around his neck. "I'm sorry."

Walker didn't even tell her to stop apologizing. This once he knew it meant she was sorry for something besides her actions. Sorry for the sadness Walker carried with him. Sorry for the burden of it. He held her tight and let her ease some of his struggle, let himself believe happiness was possible, let himself picture a future full of Annette and a passel of young'uns.

With Annette's arms around him, finally Walker let his heart open fully to God for the first time in far too long.

He slung his arm around her and led her to their horse, planning to get her settled on his lap, then do his best to convince her to marry him before they rode home tonight.

It would be his best Christmas present ever.

Walker grinned and practiced just how he'd ask her.

## THIRTY-TWO

There was no wedding.

"I need to ask you some questions about this feller," Sheriff MacBride said. Cameron MacBride was as tough as the mountains surrounding Ranger Bluff and he could be just as cold if he got pushed. "You've got a dead man and I need to know what happened."

"We all saw it, Cam." Walker could barely control his impatience. He'd decided to get married, but his men had ridden too close all the way to town for him to ask.

Now the sheriff seemed bent on asking them questions until after the New Year. If Walker hadn't been so sure of his heart, he'd have wondered if God was trying to stop him from marrying Annette.

"Fine, I'll need to talk to you all separately."

"All of us?" Ten men had ridden with Walker. He ground his teeth together, trying to cooperate. "Separately?" Forget the New Year; they'd be here until spring. Then he'd have to finish roundup before he could propose.

"Yes, separately. I'm hearing tales of bad blood between Miss Talbot and this man, and there's been talk about you, Miss Talbot."

"I know about the talk." Annette stood primly behind one of two wooden chairs facing the sheriff's desk. Patient. No sign she was thinking about a wedding.

Of course Walker hadn't asked her, but he'd hoped her mind was riding along the same trail as his, at least to the point where she'd be itchy to spend a few minutes alone with him.

"It was Claude's way to start rumors quietly," Annette said. "It kept local people from approaching me. It was part of keeping me under his thumb."

Through narrow, searching eyes, the sheriff studied her.

Walker could well imagine the mean gossip that had been spread about Annette. He'd heard plenty, but he suspected it had kept growing.

"Bad blood," MacBride repeated. "And I never connected the talk to Leveque."

"Claude had a rare knack for sneaking a word in quietly."

"I've only got your word on that, miss, and I apologize for saying it, but your word ain't all that good in these parts."

Walker bristled. "Cam, I'm warning you, watch how you talk to Annette."

The sheriff slid assessing eyes between Walker and Annette and probably judged the situation just about right. "Now Leveque is dead. And the one woman in town who admits she's got a grudge against him was there. And the man backing her story is sweet on her."

Walker glanced at Annette and saw her looking back.

"I'm not just going to pat you folks on the back and say you can go." Cam's eyes turned on Walker. "I remember Priscilla just like the rest of this town does. You've done poorly choosing a woman before, Walker."

Walker considered Cam MacBride a friend, and he was a good man to have at a man's back. He wished for no trouble. Walker held on to that tight to keep from planting a fist in the sheriff's face.

"Ask your questions then and make it quick." Walker shed his buckskin gloves and his shearling coat. With a *clink* of spurs, he took two long strides to hang his things on a nail by the jail's front door. He assisted Annette with her wraps.

"Thank you, Elijah." Annette shrugged out of her coat.

Then the two of them sat down to face Cam across his battered wooden desk.

"Before we start—" The sheriff strode to the door, opened it, and hollered, "Sid, get Blanche Leveque in here. She lives in that building at the end of the street."

Someone shouted back an okay. Walker thought it was the deputy, Sid Reed.

Cam closed the door and came back. "We'll hear her side of things next. She needs to be told her husband is dead."

Annette told her side of the story, with Walker throwing in details of what he'd seen. He could tell Cam was inclined to believe Annette. She was so sweet and sincere, even with a fat lip and a bruise rising on her cheek, who could resist?

Then Blanche came in sobbing. The woman was next thing to dressed in rags, and though she buried her face in her hands, she looked up to see where she was going. Walker saw a pretty woman, careworn with a few wrinkles carved into her face by life. Well, life with Claude had probably done that for her. "What will become of me without my husband?" Her voice, however, put an end to any sympathy he had for her. Which wasn't much.

Annette surged to her feet and stepped between Walker and the sheriff, backing away from Blanche. Walker saw Annette's expression and knew she feared Blanche every bit as much as Claude. And that ended Walker's last bit of sympathy. Obviously Annette knew her best and was afraid. That was good enough for Walker.

"Mrs. Leveque, uh. . .have a chair." The sheriff looked at the chair Annette had abandoned. Annette jerked her chin and gestured at the chair as if to say it was fine with her to give it to Blanche. Annette clearly wanted someone standing between her and Blanche.

"Miss Talbot has made some serious accusations against your husband, ma'am." The sheriff's voice was drowned out by the caterwauling woman.

"Claude—my poor, poor Claude only wanted his money back. She stole from us."

"No, that's a lie!"

"Then she ran off." Blanche's voice broke, her shoulders trembled, and she couldn't go on.

"I ran for my life."

Blanche raised her eyes, flashing with what looked like righteous indignation. "You ran with our money, you mean. Claude only wanted it back." Blanche looked away from Annette to turn beseeching eyes on the sheriff. "He thought she owed him and he followed after her. He would have forgotten the thieving if she'd agreed to rejoin our mission group."

"He threatened her with a gun, Mrs. Leveque. He said terrible things, ugly things."

"I don't know what he said, but he was furious. I'm sure he let his temper get away from him and he said things he shouldn't have. But she's a thief. Claude believed himself to be in the right."

Walker had heard much this same business in some of the gossip going around. Even Gabe Michaels—Lasley—had suspected Annette was guilty of a few things.

Annette's hands fisted at her sides but she stayed well away from Blanche. "I did not steal any money."

"Now he's dead." Blanche talked over Annette's denial. "Yes, he was angry. Yes he might have gone too far. But *she's* the criminal."

Blanche jabbed an accusing finger straight at Annette. "My husband tried to get his money back and ended up dead. And now I'm alone and I don't know what I'll do. I'll starve. I'll end up in the cold, freezing."

"That's not so. None of what she says is the truth." Annette's complexion had paled, but Walker saw her spine stiffen. She'd stand here and defend herself for as long as it took.

Walker was proud of her. And he saw only truth in her expression. No more running for Annette soon-to-be-Walker. She'd proved it when she'd gone to face Leveque alone.

Blanche went back to sobbing.

"Sheriff, you have to arrest her." Annette turned to the lawman.

"She was part of this all the way. She stood by gloating when Claude assaulted me that first day at the cabin, when I fell in the river."

"He wanted his money. That was all. And if he had to make you work it off by singing, that's only fair. We had nothing! You took it all!" The woman was screeching like a chicken with its tail feathers in a crack.

In the end, more to stop the noise than anything, the sheriff said, "We're looking for WANTED posters, Mrs. Leveque. If we find any, I'll be over to arrest you. For now you can go. But if you run, I'll be after you with a posse."

"I'm not going anywhere until this woman is arrested." Blanche sniffed through her tears. "I'll stay to see justice done for my Claude if it takes me the rest of my life." She stood and whirled out of the building, slamming the door with a flourish that looked like an actress auditioning for a play.

"That was quite a scene she just acted out." Annette stayed on Walker's right side, as if afraid the door would open and Blanche would return.

"So, was she in on it or not, Miss Talbot?" The sheriff stared at the closed door thoughtfully.

"Oh, she was right there at Claude's side, but I can't believe a woman would be as evil as Claude." Annette shook her head.

"I've seen some plumb evil women, so I'm inclined to disagree."

Annette stepped closer to Walker and rested a hand on his shoulder.

"Blanche without Claude doesn't seem too dangerous, though." He and Annette looked at each other and finally she shrugged and nodded. He wondered if it was almost time for him to drag Annette off to a private spot and propose.

"I'd almost let her go just so I didn't have to listen to her squawking anymore." The sheriff rubbed the back of his neck with one hand as if Blanche had given him a headache.

The jailhouse door banged open and Gabe Lasley strode in. "Why is that woman walking away from here? I want her locked up!" Lasley ranted while Walker chafed over having his plans to coax Annette into a wedding further delayed.

Lasley's tantrum ended up with the sheriff hauling in that weasel lawyer, Sikes.

All in all, the commotion wrecked the rest of the day.

Before it could all be settled, word had reached the ranch and Ma had convinced the hands out at Walker's place that with Claude dead it was safe to come to town. She immediately took charge. "Some of the hands will escort Annie and me out to the ranch, Eli. Come on home when you can. Annie shouldn't be exposed to this kind of talk."

The woman was obviously trying to protect Annette's delicate ears.

Delicate? Walker snorted. He had a good mind to tell his ma about Annette's delicate application of that lead pipe to Claude's belly.

Ma was gonna be so proud.

Ma wouldn't be stopped, and short of shouting at the bossy old hen—in front of everyone—that he wanted to keep Annette in town to marry her, Walker didn't have much choice but to let the womenfolk leave.

Tomorrow was Christmas Eve. Walker decided as he and a few of his cowhands rode home in the dusk that he'd join in on the Christmas Eve church service and turn it into a wedding.

He had to ask Annette if she was agreeable, of course, but she'd let him kiss her in such a way that Walker believed his chances were good.

As they neared the ranch, Walker decided it was just as well to wait.

He'd had his woman run away from home.

He'd watched her get punched and pawed by that slime Leveque.

He'd jumped in too late to stop her from attacking Claude and collapsing a house on him—that pinched Walker's manly pride a bit.

He'd witnessed an unnecessary death.

Then he'd been questioned by the sheriff for nearly three hours.

All in all it had been a hard, cold, trying day.

Adding a wedding would just be too much. After a day like this, he might have trouble even remembering he'd gotten married. Really, the day ought to be set aside from death and terror and weeping widows if possible.

By the time he finished the chores he'd neglected to chase down Annette and watch her save herself while he stood by like an incompetent oaf, the moon was high in the sky, the cabin was dark, he was starving, asleep on his feet, and he smelled none too good.

And still he caught himself grinning like a fool.

He ate his supper of ham and cold mashed potatoes alone, taking frequent glances at Annette's closed door. He was sorely tempted to go knock. He'd ask her to come on out. They'd have their talk and get things settled for tomorrow.

But what if she was a woman who woke up cranky? What if she objected to a man covered with dirt and grime proposing to her? What if she took exception to the familiarity of interrupting her sleep?

Walker wasn't used to being nervous, and he didn't like it. He decided to leave the whole thing until morning. Maybe he could sweet talk his ma into gathering the eggs, giving him a chance to steal a moment alone with Annette when she was rested and he was a mite cleaner.

Ma would play along. She was definitely on Walker's side.

Happy with his new plan, he finished his supper with some gusto and headed for bed.

ᘓ

Shouts woke Annie up in the full dark of night. She rushed to her door and swung it open in time to see Elijah dash outside, jerking his coat on as he ran. "Ma, where's Elijah going?"

"It's a stampede, girl. Can't you hear the thunderin' hooves?"

Annie had definitely been in the East too long. "And now they're out in the pitch dark trying to stop the stampede?" Annie's stomach clenched. Elijah could be hurt, even killed.

285

"He'll be fine."

Annie hadn't said a word, and the light was cast by the single lantern Ruby held in her hand. But still the woman had read her mind. Annie wondered if that was a skill a person could acquire.

"He and the men will be up all night rounding them up. It'll make for a mighty long day. And Christmas Eve, too." Ruby sighed and headed for the cookstove to build up a fire. "Get dressed, Annie. We'll have some food cooking for the men whenever they get back."

Annie was back in the kitchen in minutes and she noticed the sky lightening a bit. Winter made for short days so the stampede hadn't happened in the dead of night. If Claude had still been on the loose, Annie would have been afraid. Instead, she worried, but only about a possible accident.

Ma scooped a bit of butter with her knife and, with a sharp *click* of the knife against the cast-iron skillet, greased the heavy pan. The hot sizzle of the fat wafted up and filled the room with the savory smell. Next Ruby broke eggs into her frying pan so deftly Annie envied the woman's skill.

Annie sighed as Ruby whipped the eggs. If only there'd been a few minutes alone with Elijah today. Not for any special reason. It was just that yesterday had been such a trying day. And he'd kissed her so sweetly and looked into her eyes a few times in a way that made her think he wanted to spend more time with her. It might have been her wishful thinking, but there'd been no chance to see if she'd imagined it or not.

"I think things have cleared up in town enough that we can chance going to church. There'll be a Christmas Eve service tonight."

"Is Elijah planning to go?" Annie sliced the loaf of yeasty, freshly baked bread perched on the kitchen table. There were only two plates set out, forks and knifes in place, butter and sparkling red jam, and glasses of milk. Ruby was obviously only cooking for two.

"If he gets back in time, he said he'd go."

Annie looked up from her work to meet Ma's shining eyes. "Really?"

"Yes." Ma smiled and nodded. "I think he's finally really forgiven himself."

The two of them shared a harmonious moment as they waited for Elijah.

# THIRTY-THREE

Elijah never came back.

As the day stretched on, a few of the hands rode in, gathered up food, updated Annie and Ma on the progress of rounding up the cattle, and left again.

Annie kept busy helping Ma with Christmas baking. There were some hands around so the homeplace wasn't deserted.

As the afternoon wore down, Ruby asked, "Will you accompany me to church, Annie?"

Annie felt her stomach twist, but she was a new woman. And she wanted to go to church, so she would.

She and Ruby both dragged their heels, hoping Elijah would show up, but at last time ran out and they had no choice but to leave for the evening service. The available cowhands surrounded them so they were safe.

When they dismounted and walked into church, Annie nodded her greeting to everyone. She thought the church members were a bit cool to her, but not openly unkind, and having Ruby at her side eased her way. She kept a quiet running prayer for courage and for a communion with God worthy of this sacred day.

Annie and Ruby found seats near the back of the crowded building. Already men stood, lining the room and filling the aisle as they gave their seats up for the ladies.

In the crowded church in the bitter winter cold, the parson stood and raised his hand high, and a hush fell over the room. "Join me in singing "O Come, All Ye Faithful" —a wonderful hymn to call worshippers together.

Annie started singing. She knew her voice would carry. She tried to sing quietly, but the words were so beautiful she couldn't help letting them lift her heart and her voice.

The crowd around her slowly fell silent as they gave her their attention.

Tonight, she didn't want to take over the singing and make it a solo, as often happened when she sang in a group, so she tried with all her soul to worship the Lord fully without doing it loudly.

They next sang "Hark! the Herald Angels Sing." It was one of her favorites, so hard to not sing out, trying to let God know that if she'd been there on that holy night, Annie would have added her words of alleluia, along with the angels.

The parson then took over, and a reverent quiet surrounded all the believers. He spoke simply of the true meaning of Christmas. As he finished his message, he looked out at Annie. "You're here with Ruby Walker tonight?" he asked right in front of everyone.

Annie felt her cheeks warm as she nodded.

"You have a tremendous gift, young lady. You bless us with your singing."

She could barely push the words out. "Thank you, Parson." She didn't sing to glorify herself. It was for God. But to state that aloud would only draw more attention. She prayed the parson would know her heart was right.

"We'll sing another song or two." He looked around at his flock. "Please join in. We worship together tonight. It was a heavenly host of angels, not one lone voice." Then his gentle, kind eyes went back to Annie. "But perhaps you'll favor us with a solo another day."

"Yes." Annie's fears receded. "I'd be honored to do that. Thank you." She'd guarded herself too well since she'd heard of Claude's rumors. She should have attended church. She should have stood and proclaimed her faith boldly to these people. She knew if it were ever asked of her again, to stand against evil, she'd do it. Her days of being a coward were finally, truly over.

"Let's all sing 'O Holy Night.'" The parson raised his hands to beckon them all to join him.

This time the music surrounding Annie remained strong. Ruby had a lovely voice and lifted it high to sing the beautiful song. Feeling more a part of something than she had in years, Annie let the music bless her.

And when it ended, the parson asked for one more: "Silent Night."

Her favorite. To her thinking, it was the loveliest of the many powerful hymns to celebrate Jesus' birth.

As the music at last faded, a moment of silence hung over the crowd. It was a holy moment, as if God hovered there, amid them, above them, inside them. God had come down to earth on that silent night—long ago—in the form of a child. And just as then, His Spirit was here now, in this congregation and in each and every heart that believed.

The parson strode down the center aisle, squeezing between his many parishioners. Then the rest of them began to file out. Voices rose in happy greetings and cheerful wishes for the New Year. It was nearly deafening, but so joyful, Annie loved it.

As Annie inched down the aisle, pressed among the happy folks of Ranger Bluff, she was given many kind touches and compliments. Everyone had a kind word of welcome for her and a warm hug for Ruby. Many of the older women even pulled Annie into their arms.

Annie hadn't belonged to anything this wonderful in years, maybe never. The parson stood at the door, defying the cold, to shake each and every hand.

As she neared the door, chatting away with everyone who drew near, she saw snow sifting gently down from the black sky.

The parson shook hands with each worshipper and wished a "Merry Christmas." His greeting to Annie was as warm as if the sun were high in the sky.

As she passed onto the steps, she saw a full moon glow dimly through the overhead clouds. Once in a while a star would peek out. The wind had died and it would be a perfect ride home.

Then she saw Elijah coming up the pathway to the church. He led a half a dozen more hands. His eyes met hers instantly and he smiled.

She quickly descended the three front steps to close the distance between them.

He moved toward her at a near run, and as they met, his hands reached out and caught hers. "I tried to get here sooner."

"I'm glad you came."

"I heard you singing. It was beautiful. Everyone singing together was beautiful, like being carried along on a current of music, sweeping me toward the church and God and you."

Barely able to whisper, Annie said, "That's a lovely thing to say."

The crowd pressed her forward, down the stairs, and she was crushed against Elijah.

Completely surrounded and yet somehow alone with him in the midst of the throng, Elijah leaned to her ear and whispered, "Annette, I—"

"She's a thief!"

The shrill, cruel voice cut through the multitude of cheerful folks.

Annie knew that voice and wheeled to face Blanche Leveque.

"My husband is dead and all he wanted was for her to return the money she stole."

Suddenly all Annie could see was Elijah's back. He'd moved so he was between Blanche and Annie, and he'd done it so swiftly Annie had no time to register the motion. Protecting her was as instinctive as breathing. To have such strength on her side was glorious.

Over his shoulder, Annie saw Blanche's pretty, if tired, face, bright red with rage. The woman's eyes flashed fit to set fire to anyone they landed on. "I will not be denied. I have proof that she stole from us. She needs to work that money off with our show or go to jail."

A murmur from around Annie was indistinguishable. She heard disapproval but dared to hope the focus was Blanche and not her.

"You know how she sings," Blanche raved, her cheeks red with fury, her hands clenched and raised to the sky. "You can all see why we'd have hired her and trusted her."

The churchgoers continued whispering. Annie thought she heard someone remark on her voice.

Annie's recently discovered backbone wavered. When Blanche had thrown these accusations at her in front of only the sheriff, Annie had thought it was unbearable, but that was nothing compared to the public disgrace of this moment. Even with Elijah there to shield her, she recognized that urge to run, to placate, to make peace.

Ignoring the cowardly reflex, Annie stayed safely tucked behind Elijah's broad shoulders.

"Mrs. Leveque, this is Christmas Eve." Elijah's voice was strong but also kind. "We've already settled that your husband tried to harm Annie, and when we stopped him, he ran. If his accusations were true and fair why did he run? Why did he try and climb down that path to the river rather than come with us back to the sheriff? His own actions brought him to a bad end."

If Annie's heart wasn't already mush when it came to the man, it would have melted away just from listening to him try to be compassionate to a woman with the charm of a rabid skunk.

"He was desperate. We're ruined by her actions. Yes, he may have grabbed her; then when you came at him with guns he did something foolish, but my Claude was a good man."

Annie had worked with Blanche on the stage enough to know Blanche was good with a crowd. She was a talented actress. Even Annie was swayed by the sincerity in her voice.

Annie had always considered Blanche a victim of Claude's criminal behavior. Annie stepped just a bit from behind Elijah. Facing Blanche was her burden, her cross to bear. Elijah couldn't do it for her. "I know you loved Claude."

"Don't you speak his name!" Blanche's eyes brimmed over with tears. Was she acting or was her heart really broken? Annie couldn't be

sure. "He was a good man until you betrayed him."

Elijah blocked Annie's forward movement. "We're sorry for your loss, ma'am, but what happened wasn't Annie's fault."

"It *was* her fault. She's a thief and a liar. And she has all of you convinced she's such a fine woman because of that singing voice. She's always manipulated people with her singing. I've heard rumors about her ever since she came to town."

Blanche made it sound like she'd been in Ranger Bluff a long time and Annie was the newcomer.

The murmuring shifted a bit and Annie knew all these folks had heard rumors.

"Lies spread by your husband." Elijah pushed Annie a bit so he was more fully in front of her. Ruby came up beside Annie and took hold of her arm, lending support.

"No, not lies. The truth!" Blanche reached into a pocket of her dress and produced a piece of paper, unfolding it to reveal a WANTED poster with Annie's picture on it.

Gasps spread through the crowd.

"Have your sheriff telegraph for the truth. He'll find out she's a wanted woman."

"I stole nothing!" Annie was suddenly nearly as furious as Blanche. She took a step toward the woman, determined to shake the truth out of her.

Elijah held her in place and Ruby helped.

"I demand she be arrested. This is a charge against her and the law must act!"

The sheriff came into Annie's view then, from out of the crowd of worshippers. Sheriff MacBride walked past everyone to take the poster from Blanche's hand. "I'll not believe a poster like this. These are easily created."

A voice rang out of the crowd from behind Annie, "I saw that same poster somewhere. It's not a forgery."

Annie gasped and whirled around but she couldn't find who'd spoken.

Someone else called out, "That very poster is well known back East because a woman being wanted is so unusual and she's rarely beautiful. Send a wire to St. Louis. She's a known woman in those parts."

Annie, with her back now to Elijah, searched the crowd for the second man.

"Claude Leveque isn't the first man she's destroyed," a third voice rang out with similar accusations. "You have to arrest her. You're bound by law."

The voice had a faint accent, but Annie suspected it was the same man who'd yelled before, trying to make the crowd seem to be turning on her, when in fact all these fine people had been so kind.

"No!" Blanche cried out. "She owes me. You have to force her to come and work off her debt to me. Now, without a husband and no money, I'll starve because of her actions."

Annie looked again at the crowd and saw doubt. Blanche was convincing. The poster looked real. Had she really been accused of crimes? Had Claude seen to that, too?

The sheriff took the poster. "It's Miss Talbot all right."

Annie turned to face him. "I have done nothing wrong."

The sheriff looked dubious as he raised his gaze from the picture to look at Annie. "I can't ignore this. You'll have to come with me."

"No, she's coming out to our place." Elijah tugged the brim of his hat low. "You have my word she won't go anywhere, Cam."

"She ran away just yesterday, Walker. You can't make promises for someone else."

"It's her word against this woman, a cohort of Claude's."

"Well, it would be two against one if Leveque wasn't dead, virtually at Annie's hand."

"That wasn't how it happened and you know it."

Sheriff MacBride gave Elijah a sad look then turned his eyes on Annie. She knew it was coming. "You're under arrest, Miss Talbot."

The crowd seemed farther away as if suddenly she had a bad smell. Annie could hardly blame them.

"Send her along with me, Sheriff." Blanche's perfect act slipped and Annie could see the hunger in Blanche's eyes—for money. This woman wasn't grieving her husband. She was driven by greed, maybe even more than Claude had been. But could the rest of the crowd see it? "She owes me," Blanche squawked. "Locking her up only cheats me a second time."

The sheriff looked at Annie. "The accusations on this poster could be cleared up if you'd work off your debt to Mrs. Leveque. Would you be willing to do that?"

In this, Annette could be very brave. She'd gladly face jail before Blanche. "No, I'll go along with you, Sheriff MacBride."

Ruby practically threw herself in front of the sheriff. "For heaven's sake, Cam, this poor, innocent girl isn't going to spend Christmas Eve locked up. Let her come home with us. Let her have her Christmas Day. I give you my word Eli and I will watch her. . .as if that's necessary. She's a good girl and you know it."

The sheriff had Annie's arm and was dragging her along.

Annie's eyes went to Ruby's and Elijah's. Both blocked the way for the sheriff. But the rest of the town didn't step forward. Was there no one else?

Annie looked around and saw Gabe standing in the crowd. His gaze locked on her, doubt there for all to see. Was it possible? Did he believe Blanche's lies? His mother had died in the madness of Annie's escape. The voices that had called out were vaguely familiar. Had one of them been Gabe's? Could Annie even blame Gabe having doubts when faced with that poster?

She saw Gabe reach for the pocket of his white Sunday-go-to-meeting shirt and withdraw a piece of paper. With one flick of his wrist he unfolded a WANTED poster, the same one Blanche had. He'd already seen it. He carried a copy with him.

*I deserve this.*

Annie couldn't stop the mentally battering thought. If she'd have stayed, faced up to Claude instead of taking Elva's money and running, the accusations against her would have been settled back then. And in the end, she hadn't outrun anything. And she'd found Elijah and Ruby to protect her, but they couldn't protect her from the law.

She dropped her eyes to the ground. "Don't fight this, Elijah. I will face this trouble honestly. If the sheriff says I need to be locked up until it's settled, then I'll stay in his jail." She swerved around Elijah's still form. Her eyes lifted and for one split second as she passed him, she saw doubt. Did Elijah believe this, too?

Her heart broke as she looked away. She was too afraid to look closer and have all hope stripped away.

*I deserve all of this, God, for being a coward, but I will face it bravely. My cowardly days are over.*

The sheriff kept a firm grip on her arm as they strode quickly across the street. That suited Annie. What was the sense in lingering?

Ruby was right at the lawman's side, badgering him.

Annie didn't see Elijah, but perhaps he wasn't that sorry to see her behind bars.

The sheriff let her into the cold little building.

"This isn't justice." Blanche came in after Ruby. "She owes me money. You turn that worthless girl over to me to work off what she owes."

"If you lock her up, Cameron MacBride, you're going to have to lock me up, too." Ruby caught the sheriff's arm as it reached for the key hanging from the large metal ring.

"You're cheating me!" Blanche shoved her way in front of the sheriff, but the sheriff just kept moving.

The two women talked over top of each other. Ruby kept glaring at Blanche, and Annie hoped Ruby didn't do anything that resulted in getting herself tossed into jail, too—although Annie would enjoy the company.

"You can stay if you want, Ruby. But you'll be on the outside of the jail cell and she'll be on the inside." Moving swiftly, the sheriff pulled Annie through the single cell door and swung it shut with a loud *bang*.

"You let her out of there!" Blanche clenched her fists.

"You go on home. I'm not turning this girl over to you and I'm not letting you stay in this building." Cam MacBride glared. "She says she's innocent and I'm going to wait until the day after Christmas then start sending telegraphs. I'll get to the bottom of the charges, and if she's wanted like you say, we'll have a trial as soon as the circuit judge comes through. He comes around the first of the month if he's not delayed, so he'll be through here in about a week to sort this out."

He turned and scowled at Ruby. "And I'm taking the key home with me so you can't let her out."

Elijah appeared at the outside door. "I'll be staying, too. We don't aim to see Annette spend her Christmas Eve alone in jail."

"You just go on home, Cameron." Ruby sounded completely insincere. "Enjoy your quiet night alone."

The sheriff's gray mustache quivered as if he wanted to start yelling, but he kept ruthless control over himself. "I'll be back in the morning." He jabbed a beefy finger at Ruby. "My Christmas is ruined because of this, too."

"You don't have anything to do for Christmas anyway. You live alone." Ruby took a step forward as if she wasn't one speck afraid of the growling lawman.

"The parson invited me to share his Christmas dinner. His wife's a fine cook."

"Humph!" Ruby smirked. "She is indeed. Hope you can swallow it around that lump of guilt over locking up a sweet girl like Annie."

The sheriff rolled his eyes and stormed out of the building.

Frank came to the door, holding two bedrolls. "Half the hands are going home. The rest of us'll bunk down in the livery. Gibby said it's okay. He had the forge going today so it's warm in there."

Frank looked past the Walkers, straight at Annie. "I know what those Leveques are made out of, Miss Annie. We don't put any stock in that woman's lies." Frank left the blankets behind as he headed for his own hard floor for Christmas Eve.

After the door was shut and Walker had stoked the potbellied stove,

Annie said, "I suppose I don't have it as bad as Mary and Joseph did. I need to remember that."

Hard to remember with the bars right there. She did have a bed. If she'd been thinking, she'd have asked Sheriff MacBride to take it out of the cell so Ma could have it.

Annie said quietly, "You know I didn't do this, don't you?" She looked at Ruby, but she wanted desperately to hear it from Elijah.

Ruby came up and laid her callused hands, full of the strength it took to wrest a living out of the rugged Rockies, on top of Annie's hands, which clutched the bars. "Of course we know it. Don't we, Elijah?"

Elijah was too slow about it for Annie's taste. But he didn't come over to the cell, and he quietly said to his mother, "Can I talk to her for just a few minutes?"

"Why sure, son. I'll step outside."

"No, that's not necessary. I don't want you out in the cold, and I don't mind you hearing me. I just need to rig things so I can get ahold of her hands instead of you."

Annie looked at her feet, sure Elijah would now express all his doubts, explain to her why she wasn't fit to be in his household, tell her yes, he'd look out for her and help her get out of jail, but then it was time to leave, go back East. Her heart breaking, Annie raised her head, determined to take Elijah's words bravely.

She deserved this.

She'd brought too much shame to the Walkers with her cowardice. It was time to go away. Annie would begin again, and wherever she ended up, she'd live bravely for the Lord, and she'd remember these two people who'd been wounded so badly that it wasn't in them to trust a woman with a shadow hanging over her.

As her eyes lifted, she saw the two Walkers grinning at each other like a pair of lunatics.

She forgot all her noble self-sacrifice. "What about any of this is the slightest bit funny?"

Ruby walked to the stove and began fussing with her bedroll, humming softly.

"I think this is probably my best chance to corner you." He settled his hands gently but firmly right where Ma's had been.

"What?" Annie's temper ignited though she tried to control it. Where had her soft, accommodating spirit gone? She'd wanted to be brave for the Lord, but suddenly she wanted to strangle Elijah for his insensitivity, and she didn't think God would consider that part of being brave. Though Annie suspected God would understand that she'd been through a trying day, and Elijah wasn't helping.

"It seems like I spend most of my time either hunting for you or rescuing you or—"

"Or yelling at me." Annie was tempted to grab the confounded man right through the bars.

He leaned closer. "Or kissing you." He spoke so low it was possible his ma couldn't hear but not probable, because the woman could hear a hummingbird sucking on a flower a mile away; but Elijah did speak very quietly.

Annie's face got hot so fast she knew she was turning a brilliant shade of red. "Elijah Walker, I will not discuss such a thing with you while I am locked behind bars." Annie did her best to keep her voice down, but it was ridiculous to have this conversation now.

"Sure you will. What are you going to do, walk out on me? Move back to your pa's house?" Elijah turned to his mother. "You know, bars aren't a bad idea. Maybe we should get a set for our bedroom at the house. Gibby could maybe rig something up."

*Our bedroom?* "Elijah!" Annie's embarrassment was pushed aside by anger.

Ruby snickered as she spread out her blanket close to the stove.

Elijah turned back. "We're going to fix this, Annette honey."

*Honey?* "Fix this?"

"Sure. Cam's just being stubborn because he swore an oath to uphold the law and all, but he'll let you go. He'll send his telegrams and find out you're as sweet and innocent as we all know you are, and he'll let you loose." Elijah leaned closer and his grip on her hands tightened. "And if he doesn't do it right quick, I think we should just have the parson come on over and marry us right here in the jail. Then maybe Cam'd let me move in there with you."

"M–Marry me?"

Elijah just smiled.

"M–Move in?" Her voice squeaked, mouselike. She couldn't make it behave. But why should she behave when Elijah certainly wasn't?

"I think a husband and his wife oughta live together, don't you?"

"H–Husband and wi—" Annie had lost track of her common sense—and her hearing apparently— because she couldn't understand a thing Elijah was saying.

"Eli Walker, you quit teasing that girl."

Walker laughed. He released her hands and kissed her right through the bars.

She wrenched her head sideways. "You cannot even consider marrying me. The whole town will always believe you've found another low-down woman. They'll think you're *hunting* for one. Why, it will ruin your reputation."

"Ma, she's givin' me trouble."

"You should have never teased, boy. Not the time or place."

Elijah still held her close, bars notwithstanding. "I suppose these bars make a woman think even more ridiculous thoughts than usual." Elijah's head jerked and knocked into the bars.

Annie looked past him to see that Ma had come up behind him and swatted him in the back of the head. "Behave yourself, Eli."

Elijah looked back at Annie. "I love you, sweetheart. I've been wanting to ask you to marry me ever since you saved yourself from Claude, but things got hectic."

"You saved me from Claude, Elijah."

He shook his head. "I probably distracted him some, but I think you'd have knocked him out with that pipe in a few seconds, with or

without me. So no, you saved yourself."

"You used the pipe on Claude?" Ma actually sounded sort of envious.

Annie wondered if she'd ever had occasion to bash someone.

"She sure did." Elijah glanced at his mother, grinning, then turned back to Annie. "You wanted to live bravely for God, and I believe jamming Claude in the stomach with a pipe is proof you've found the knack."

Annie shook her head. "I'll ruin you. I'll drag your whole family down. I need to move on, start over, get to know people before they've heard such awful rumors. With Claude dead, I have a chance."

"I saw a few people doubting you tonight, sweetheart. That's only human nature to be presented with facts—"

"They weren't facts. They were Blanche's lies."

"And believe them. But I didn't let that influence me. And considering some of what I've been through, I think if I can overlook a WANTED poster, the other folks in town oughta be able to."

"I can't marry you, Elijah. Just go on home. Forget about me."

"You're marrying me. And I might just tell Cam to keep you locked up in there until you come to your senses, even though he's gonna probably find out those charges are a pack of lies in about two days' time and be able to let you go."

Annie glared at him.

Elijah smiled back.

"How can you trust me?"

"Because I know you. I know your words and your deeds and your heart. You're as pure as the driven snow in body and soul."

Elijah's words were like balm. Even with the locked door, Annie felt freer than she ever had. . .from her fears and her loneliness. . .from her hurt at her father's neglect and the Leveques' cruelty.

"You really trust me." It wasn't a question. Annie could see that trust shining out of his eyes.

"So, will you marry me?"

The jailhouse door slammed open. Sheriff MacBride came in muttering. "I caught this whole pack in that theater they opened, plotting against Miss Talbot."

A group followed MacBride in. Blanche, dragged along whining by Gabe Lasley. Sikes in the fist grip of J.R. Two more men, held by Frank and Gibby. Annie recognized them instantly from the old troupe. They'd joined shortly after the Leveques had taken over and were obviously in cahoots with them. Annie now realized theirs were the voices she'd heard shouting accusations in front of the church. The Leveques had brought them in to work the gambling tables, and they'd been handy to add to the suspicions surrounding her.

All of the group were prodded along by cowhands from the Walker ranch and followed by several more townspeople and the parson.

"I knew you were innocent, miss," the sheriff said. "This saves me some time proving it." He produced his key, opened the cell door, and shooed Annie out, shoving the rest of his prisoners in.

"Since most of the people we'd invite are here, why don't we have the parson speak our vows right now, Annette?" Elijah caught her wrist and dragged her over in front of the man of God.

Annie wanted to shout at Elijah. This wasn't the way a girl dreamed of getting married. This wasn't the sentimental memory she wanted to carry with her for a lifetime.

"Can we step over to the church?" Ruby asked. "It's Christmas Eve— the night before Jesus' birthday. It's a perfect day for a new marriage to be born."

"Annette? What do you say?" Elijah jiggled her arm to get her attention as if she could forget him for a single heartbeat.

"Are you sure, Elijah? Will you have doubts and regrets tomorrow?"

"No, never. And no unkind rumors will survive in this town either." Elijah looked around. "Will they, folks?"

The whole crowd cheered.

Annie jerked around to really look and saw nearly everyone who'd been at church. They hadn't just gone on home thinking the worst of her.

They'd listened and believed. In her.

Elijah caught her shoulders and pulled her around to face him. "Will you marry me, Annette?" Elijah's hands slid down her arms until their fingers entwined. "Please? I love you and trust you and want you to be with me forever."

"Yes, Elijah." She threw her arms around his neck. "Because I love you and trust you and want to be with you forever."

The whole crowd broke out into a celebration.

Annie felt her toes lift off the ground as Elijah spun her around in a circle. Then he swept her out of the jail and toward the church.

The snow had stopped. Overhead the night sky gleamed, cloudless, with a million stars. None twinkled as brightly as that single star so long ago over the stable where the Christ Child was born.

Surrounded by friends, bright stars led Annette and Elijah to the church as surely as a long-ago star had led many to the baby Jesus. Together, they shared their sacred vows on that holy night.

# ABOUT THE AUTHOR

**MARY CONNEALY** is a Christie Award Finalist. She is the author of the Lassoed in Texas series which includes *Petticoat Ranch*, *Calico Canyon*, and *Gingham Mountain*. She has also written a romantic cozy mystery trilogy, *Nosy in Nebraska*, and her novel *Golden Days* is part of the *Alaska Brides* anthology. You can find out more about Mary's upcoming books at www.maryconnealy.com and www.mconnealy.blogspot.com.

Mary lives on a Nebraska ranch with her husband, Ivan, and has four grown daughters: Joslyn (married to Matt), Wendy, Shelly (married to Aaron), and Katy. And she is the grandmother of one beautiful granddaughter, Elle. And even though she *begged*, Barbour Publishing would *not* put Elle on the cover of *Montana Rose*.